THE BEST WE'VE GOT . . .

A voice in front of him, the eternal sergeant, a role that persisted though its portrayers came and went. "Men, we're in a bad hole. The enemy has fanned out upstairs, looking for us. We've got to hold this area until reinforcements get here. You're the best we've got, our only hope. Go on up there and keep them busy."

Harker moved with the group. He didn't even wonder who the "they" were that he was supposed to keep busy. It didn't matter. Perhaps it never had. He was alive again, and at war.

—*from* "But as a Soldier,
For His Country"
by Stephen Goldin

Space Infantry

From the best minds in military science fiction—writers like Joe W. Haldeman, David Drake, Michael Shaara, Jerry Pournelle and more . . .

SPACE INFANTRY

**EDITED BY
DAVID DRAKE**
WITH CHARLES G.
WAUGH AND MARTIN
HARRY GREENBERG

ACE BOOKS, NEW YORK

SPACE INFANTRY

An Ace Book / published by arrangement with
the editors

PRINTING HISTORY
Ace edition / November 1989

ISBN: 0-441-77747-3

Ace Books are published
by The Berkley Publishing Group,
200 Madison Avenue, New York, New York 10016.
The name "ACE" and the "A" logo are trademarks belonging to
Charter Communications, Inc.

PRINTED IN THE UNITED STATES OF AMERICA

10 9 8 7 6 5 4 3 2 1

CONTENTS

INTRODUCTION

HEROES

David Drake

Some years ago, Joe Haldeman served in Southeast Asia as a combat engineer attached to an infantry unit. Joe was co-editor of a previous Ace anthology about SF armored vehicles, *Supertanks*. He points out in his introduction to that volume that he had very little to do with tanks and that was just how he liked it.

A few years after Joe had been there, I became an interrogator attached to an armored regiment in the same general neck of the woods. I knew some people who were technically infantry (they qualified for the Combat Infantry Badge as soon as they came under fire, which was very soon for most of them), but in my unit they almost invariably fought from armored vehicles.

As for me personally, little as I wanted to be in Nam, I wanted even less to be there with an outfit which didn't have cal fifties and 90 mm cannon with which to respond when trouble started.

I'm planning to suggest two further anthologies to Ace. For Joe to edit, there'll be *Space Interrogators*. And for me . . .

I read "The Rocketeers Have Shaggy Ears" when I was thirteen. Though I didn't have any personal contact with the military, much less with war, I was absolutely convinced that the writer knew what he was talking about.

I'm thirty years older now than when I first read the story. My opinion of it hasn't changed.

"Rocketeers" first appeared in *Planet Stories*, whose letter column (*The Vizigraph*) was known for permitting unbridled discussion. "Rocketeers" was universally praised, even by letter writers who began "Your Spring issue was terrible. Out of the whole magazine, there were only seven stories that were any good at all. . . ."

Perhaps the most glowing (as well as the most intelligent) discussion of "Rocketeers" was by Marion Zimmer Bradley. Among her comments were: " 'The Rocketeers' may not be science—but it is fiction, and oh, what wonderful fiction! . . . What I have been saying in this long and roundabout fashion, is that you, dear Payne, [Paul L. Payne, the editor of PS at the time of the story's publication] have at one blow wiped out your past record of a literary Payne-in-the-neck, with the publication of this one darn-near-perfect story. Frankly, you've only published one other which can anywhere touch it—Bradbury's 'Asleep in Armageddon'. . . ."

Ms. Bradley was almost the only reader to comment on the story without wondering what the silly title was about. Maybe she knew. *I* sure didn't when I first read "Rocketeers."

The men of the story are singing a song that begins, "The Rocketeers have shaggy ears. They're dirty—". It breaks off there, because "The rest of the lyrics wouldn't look well in print."

The question of just what the rest of the lyrics *were* has fascinated a lot of people. When Ballantine reprinted "Rocketeers" in 1975, Judy-Lynn del Rey ran a contest for the best completion of them. I don't know what the result was, but I suspect most of the entries were in line with a 1950 offering to *The Vizigraph*:

> Mars was met and conquered,
> Venus also fell—
> But it's still ever onward,
> Into the gates of Hell.
>
> The Rocketeers have shaggy ears,
> They're dirty sons of Space
> They drink and smoke and fight and swear,
> They're the strongest of our race!

And so on. After all, the characters are heroes; so they'll be singing something heroic, right?

Wrong.

Some years ago, I asked my friend Manly Wade Wellman whether he knew the author of "The Rocketeers Have Shaggy Ears." Manly didn't know Keith Bennett; but to my amazement, he did know the song. (It had never struck me that the song might be real; and I suspect I had a lot of company in my ignorance.)

To be precise, Manly knew three verses (he said he'd forgotten a fourth) of a song called *The Mountaineers Have Hairy Ears*. A friend mentioned that information to his father, a civil engineer, who grinned and started humming *The Engineers Have Shaggy Ears*. And there's a book titled *The Cannoneers Have Hairy Ears* (the author was coy about the derivation of his title). From internal evidence in the story, I believe this third version is the one Keith Bennett himself sang.

In 1949, the lyrics really were unprintable in a newsstand magazine; that being the case, Bennett should probably have chosen another title. People weren't going to understand that men who were struggling heroically, under conditions that were going to kill most of them, might be singing something scurrilous and not heroic in the least.

But Bennett may have thought that there were a lot of things in his story that people weren't going to understand unless they'd been there. That's a comment you hear a lot when you're talking to veterans.

It's partly true, because nobody can live in another man's head . . . but saying that nobody can understand *all* of it, is very different from saying that they won't understand anything. Marion Zimmer Bradley and my adolescent self didn't have Bennett's background, but he spoke to us.

In Nam, the phrase was, "Don't mean nothin'." I heard a man use it when he realized he'd just lost his right eye. "The Rocketeers have shaggy ears," in context, is the same thing.

So for the Infantry, and for my late friend Manly—and with the warning that these *are* obscene verses—I give you the song that Manly sang to me:

> The mountaineers have hairy ears,
> They go without their britches,
> They pop their cocks with jagged rocks,
> They're hardy sons of bitches.
>
> They screw the whores right through their drawers,
> They do not care for trifles—
> They hang their balls upon the walls
> And shoot at them with rifles.

Much joy they reap by diddling sheep
In divers nooks and ditches.
Nor give they a damn if it be a ram—
They're hardy sons of bitches.

THE ROCKETEERS HAVE SHAGGY EARS

Keith Bennett

I

The Commander's voice went droning on, but Hague's fatigued brain registered it as mere sound with no words or meaning. He'd been dazed since the crash. Like a cracked phonograph, his brain kept playing back the ripping roar of jet chambers blowing out with a sickening lurch that had thrown every man in the control room to the floor. The lights had flickered out, and a sickening elevator glide began as Patrol Rocket One smashed down through the Venusian rainforest roof, and crashed in a clearing blasted by its own hurtling passage.

Hague blinked hard and tried to focus his brain on what hard-faced Commander Devlin was saying, something about the Base and Odysseus, the mother ship.

"We've five hundred miles before we'll be in their vicinity, and every yard of it we walk. Hunting parties will shoot food animals. All water is to be boiled and treated with ultra-violet by my section. The photographers will march with the science section, which will continue classifying and writing reports. No actual specimens will be taken. We can't afford the weight."

To Hague, the other five men seated around the little charting table appeared cool, confidently ready to march through five hundred, or a thousand miles of dark, unexplored, steaming Hell that is Venusian rainforest. Their faces tight-set, icily calm, they nodded in turn as the Commander looked at each one of them; but Hague wondered if his own face wasn't betraying the fear lurking within him. Suddenly Commander Devlin grinned, and pulled a brandy bottle from his pocket, uncorking it as he spoke: "Well, Rocketeers, a short life and a merry one. I never did give a damn for riding in these tin cans." The tension broke, they were all smiling, and saying they'd walk into the base camp with some kind of a Venusian female under each arm for the edification of Officers' Mess.

Leaden doubt of his own untried abilities and nerve lay icy in Hague's innards, and he left after one drink. The others streamed from the brightly lighted hatch a moment later. The Commander made a short speech to the entire party. Then Navigator Clark, a smiling, wiry little man, marched out of the clearing with his advance guard. Their voices muffled suddenly as they vanished down a forest corridor that lay gloomy between giant tree holes.

Commander Devlin slapped Hague cheerfully on the shoulder as he moved past; and the second section, spruce and trim in blue-black uniforms, with silver piping, followed him. Crewmen Didrickson and Davis followed with rifles and sagging bandoliers of explosive bullets crossing their chests, and then Arndt, the lean craggy geologist, his arm in a sling; and marching beside him was rotund, begoggled Gault, the botanist. The little whippet tank clattered by next with Technician Whittaker grinning down at Hague from the turret.

"It pains me somethin' awful to see you walkin' when I'm ridin'," Whittaker piped over the whippet's clanking growl.

Hague grinned back, then pinched his nose between two fingers in the ageless dumb show of disgust, pointed at the tank, and shook his head sadly. The two carts the whippet towed swayed by, and the rest of the column followed. First Bachmann, the doctor, and Sewell, his beefy crotchety assistant. The two photographers staggered past under high-piled equipment packs, and Hague wondered how long they would keep all of it. Lenkranz, Johnston, Harker, Szachek, Hirooka, Ellis—each carried a pack full of equipment. The rest filed by until finally Swenson, the big Swede technician, passed and the clearing was empty.

Hague turned to look over his own party. In his mind's eyes bobbed the neatly typed "Equipment, march order, light field artillery" lists he'd memorized along with what seemed a thousand other neatly typed lists at Gunnery School.

The list faded, and Hague watched his five-man gun-section lounge against their rifles, leaning slightly forward to ease the heavy webbing that supported their marching packs and the sectioned pneumatic gun.

"All right," Hague said brusquely. He dredged his brain desperately then for an encouraging speech, something that would show the crew he liked them, something the Commander might say, but he couldn't think of anything that sounded witty or rang with stirring words. He finally muttered a disgusted curse at his own blankheadedness, and said harshly, "All right, let's go."

The six men filed silently out of the clearing battered in the forest by Patrol Rocket One, and into damp gloom between gargantuan trunks that rose smoothly out of sight into darkness. Behind them a little rat-like animal scurried into the deserted slot of blasted trees, its beady black eyes studying curiously the silver ship that lay smashed and half-buried in the forest floor.

Base Commander Chapman shuffled hopelessly through the thick sheaf of onion-skin papers, and sank back sighing. Ammunition reports, supply reports, medical reports, strength reports, reconnaissance reports, radio logs, radar logs, sonar logs, bulging dossiers of reports, files full of them, were there; and elsewhere in the ship efficient clerks were rapping out fresh, crisp battalions of new reports, neatly typed in triplicate on onion-skin paper.

He stared across his crowded desk at the quiet executive officer.

"Yes, Blake, it's a good picture of local conditions, but it isn't exploration. Until the Patrol Rocket gets in, we can send only this local stuff, and it just isn't enough."

Blake shrugged.

"It's all we've got. We can send parties out on foot from the base here, even if we do lose men, but the dope they'd get would still be on a localized area."

The Commander left his desk, and stared through a viewport at the plateau, and beyond that at the jungled belt fringing an endless expanse of rainforest lying sullenly quiet under the roof of racing grey clouds.

"The point is we've got to have more extensive material than this when we fire our robot-courier back to earth. This wonderful mountain of papers—what do they do, what do they tell? They describe beautifully the physical condition of this Base and its complement. They describe very well a ten mile area around the Base—but beyond that area they tell nothing. It's wonderful as far as it goes, but it only goes ten miles, and that isn't enough."

Blake eyed the snowy pile of papers abstractedly. Then he jumped up nervously as another bundle shot into a receiving tray from the pneumatic message tube. He began pacing the floor.

"Well, what can we do? Suppose we send the stuff we have here, get it microfilmed and get it off—what then?"

The Commander swore bitterly, and turned to face his executive.

"What then?" he demanded savagely. "Are we going into that again? Why, the minute every other branch of the services realize that we haven't got any kind of thorough preliminary report on this section of Venus, they'll start pounding the war drums. The battleship admirals and the bayonet generals will get to work and stir up enough public opinion to have the United States Rocket Service absorbed by other branches—the old, old game of military politics."

Blake nodded jerkily. "Yes, I know. We'd get the leftovers after the battleships had been built, or new infantry regiments activated, or something else. Anyway we wouldn't get enough money to carry on rocket research for space explorations."

"Exactly," the Commander cut in harshly. "These rockets would be grounded on earth. The generals or admirals would swear that the international situation demanded that they be kept there as weapons of defense and that would be the end of our work.

"We've got to send back a good, thorough report, something to prove that the Rocket Service can do the job, and that it is worth the doing. And, until the patrol rocket gets back, we can't do it."

"Okay, Commander," Blake called as he went through the steel passage opening onto the mother ship's upper corridor, "I'll be holding the Courier Rocket until we get word."

Seven hours later it lightened a little, and day had come. Hague and the Sergeant had pulled the early morning guard shift, and began rolling the other four from their tiny individual tents.

Bormann staggered erect, yawned lustily, and swore that this was worse than spring maneuvers in Carolina.

"Shake it," Brian snarled savagely. "That whistle will blow in a minute."

When it did sound, they buckled each other into pack harness and swung off smartly, but groaning and muttering as the mud dragged at their heavy boots.

At midday, four hours later, there was no halt, and they marched steadily forward through steaming veils of oppressive heat, eating compressed rations as they walked. They splashed through a tiny creek that was solidly slimed, and hurried ahead when crawling things wriggled in the green mass. Perspiration ran in streams from each face filing past on the trail, soaked through

4

pack harness and packs; and wiry Hurd began to complain that his pack straps had cut through his shoulders as far as his navel. They stopped for a five minute break at 1400, when Hurd stopped fussing with his back straps and signalled for silence, though the other five had been too wrapped in their own discomfort to be talking.

"Listen! Do you hear it, Lieutenant? Like a horn?" Hurd's wizened rat face knotted in concentration. "Way off, like."

Hague listened blankly a moment, attempted an expression he fondly hoped was at once intelligent and reassuring, then said, "I don't hear anything. You may have taken too much fever dope, and it's causing a ringing in your ears."

"Naw," with heavy disgust. "Listen! There it goes again!"

"I heard it." That was Sergeant Brian's voice, hard and incisive, and Hague wished he sounded like that or that he would have heard the sound before his second in command. All of the six were hunched forward, listening raptly, when the Lieutenant stood up.

"Yes, Hurd. Now I hear it."

The whistle blew then, and they moved forward. Hague noticed the Sergeant had taken a post at the rear of the little file, and watched their back trail warily as the marched.

"What do you think it was, sir?" Bucci inquired in the piping voice that sounded strange coming from his deep chest.

"The Lord knows," Hague answered, and wondered how many times he'd be using that phrase in the days to come. "Might have been some animal. They hadn't found any traces of intelligent life when we left the Base Camp."

But in the days that followed there was a new air of expectancy in the marchers, as if their suspicions had solidified into a waiting for attack. They'd been moving forward for several days.

Hague saw the pack before any of his men did, and thanked his guiding star that for once he had been a little more alert than his gun-section members.

The canvas carrier had been set neatly against one of the buttressing roots of a giant tree bole, and, from the collecting bottles strapped in efficient rows outside, Hague deduced that it belonged to Bernstein, the entomologist. The gunnery officer halted and peered back into the gloom off the trail, called Bernstein's name, and when there was no reply moved cautiously into the hushed shadows with his carbine ready. He sensed that Sergeant Brian was catfooting behind him.

Then he saw the ghostly white bundle suspended six feet above the forest floor, and moved closer, calling Bernstein's name softly.

The dim bundle vibrated gently, and Hague saw that it hung from a giant white lattice radiating wheel-like from the green gloom above. He raised his hand to touch the cocoon thing, noted it was shaped like a man well-wrapped in some woolly material, and on a sudden hunch pulled his belt knife and cut the fibers from what would be the head.

It was Bernstein suspended there, his snug, silken shroud bobbing gently in the dimness. His dark face was pallid in the gloom, sunken and flaccid of feature, as though the juices had been sucked from his corpse, leaving it a limp mummy.

The lattice's sticky white strands vibrated—something moved across it overhead, and Hague flashed his lightpak up into the darkness. Crouched twenty feet above him, two giant legs delicately testing the strands of its lattice-like web, Hague saw the spider, its bulbous furred body fully four feet across, the monster's myriad eyes glittering fire-like in the glow of Hague's lightpak, as it gathered the great legs slightly in the manner of a tarantula ready to leap.

Brian's sharp yell broke Hague from his frozen trance. He threw himself down as Brian's rifle crashed, and the giant arachnid was bathed in a blue-white flash of explosive light, its body tumbling down across the web onto Hague where he lay in the mud. The officer's hoarse yells rang insanely while he pulled himself clear of the dead spider-beast, but he forced himself to quiet at the sound of the Sergeant's cool voice.

"All clear, Lieutenant. It's dead."

"Okay, Brian. I'll be all right now." Hague's voice shook, and he cursed the weakness of his fear, forcing himself to walk calmly without a glance over his shoulder until they were back on the trail. He led the other four gunners back to the spider and Bernstein's body, and as a grim object lesson, warned them to leave the trail only in pairs. They returned their weary footslogging pace down the muddy creek marked by Clark's crew. When miles had sweated by at the same steady pace, Hague could still feel in the men's stiff silence their horror of the thing Brian had killed.

Hours, and then days, rolled past, drudging nightmares through which they plowed in mud and steamy heat, with punctually once every sixteen hours a breathtaking, pounding torrent of rain. Giant drops turned the air into an aqueous mixture that was almost unbreathable, and smashed against their faces until the skin was numb. When the rain stopped abruptly the heat came back and water vapor rose steaming from the mud they walked through; but always they walked, shoving one aching foot ahead of the other

6

through sucking black glue. Sometimes Bormann's harmonica would wheedle reedy airs, and they would sing and talk for a time, but mostly they swung forward in silence, faces drawn with fatigue and pale in the forest half light. Hague looked down at his hands, swollen, bloody with insect bites, and painfully stiff; and wondered if he'd be able to bend them round his ration pan at the evening halt.

Hague was somnambulating at the rear of his little column, listening to an ardent account from Bormann of what his girl might expect when he saw her again. Bucci, slowing occasionally to ease the pneumatic gun's barrel assembly across his shoulder, chimed in with an ecstatic description of his little Wilma. The two had been married just before the Expedition blasted Venusward out of an Arizona desert. Crosse was at the front end, and his voice came back nasally.

"Hey, Lieutenant, there's somebody sitting beside the trail."

"Okay. Halt." The Lieutenant swore tiredly and trotted up to Crosse's side. "Where?"

"There. Against the big root."

Hague moved forward, carbine at ready, and knew without looking that Sergeant Brian was at his shoulder, cool and self-sufficient as always.

"Who's there?" the officer croaked.

"It's me, Bachmann."

Hague motioned his party forward, and they gathered in a small circle about the Doctor, seated calmly beside the trail, with his back against a root flange.

"What's the matter, Doc? Did you want to see us?"

"No. Sewell seems to think you're all healthy. Too bad the main party isn't as well off. Quite a bit of trouble with fever. And, Bernstein gone, of course."

Hague nodded, and remembered he'd reported before.

"How's the Commander?" he inquired.

The Doctor's cherubic face darkened. "Not good. He's not a young man, and this heat and walking are wrecking his heart. And he won't ride the tank."

"Well, let's go, Doc." It was Brian's voice, cutting like a knife into Hague's consciousness. The Doctor looked tired and drawn.

"Go ahead, lads. I'm just going to sit here for a while." He looked up and smiled weakly at the astonished faces, but his eyes were bleakly determined.

"This is as far as I go. Snake bite. We've no antivenom that seems to work. All they can do is to amputate, and we can't afford another sick man." He pulled a nylon wrapper from one leg that

7

sprawled at an awkward angle beneath him. The bared flesh was black, swollen, and had a gangrenous smell. Young Crosse turned away, and Hague heard his retching.

"What did the Commander say?"

"He agreed this was best. I am going to die anyway."

"Will—will you be all right here? Don't you want us to wait with you?"

The Doctor's smile was weaker, and he mopped at the rivulets of perspiration streaking his mudspattered face.

"No. I have an X-lethal dosage and a hypodermic. I'll be fine here. Sewell knows what to do." His round face contorted. "Now, for God's sake, get on, and let me take that tablet. The pain is driving me crazy."

Hague gave a curt order, and they got under way. A little further on the trail, he turned to wave at Doctor Bachmann, but the little man was already invisible in forest shadows.

The tenth day after the crash of Patrol Rocket One, unofficially known as the Ration Can, glimpses of skylight opened over the trail Clark's crew were marking; and Hague and his men found themselves suddenly in an opening where low, thick vines and luxuriant, thick-leaved shrubs struggled viciously for life. Balistierri, the zoologist, slight wisp of a dark man always and almost a shadow now, stood wearily beside the trail waiting as they drew up. Their shade-blinded eyes picked out details in the open ground dimly. Hague groaned inwardly when he saw that this was a mere slit in the forest, and the great trees loomed again a hundred yards ahead. Balistierri seized Hague by the shoulder and pointed into the thick mat of green, smiling.

"Watch, all of you."

He blew a shrill blast on his whistle and waited, while Hague's gunners wondered and watched. There was a wild, silvery call, a threshing of wings, and two huge birds rose into the gold-tinted air. They flapped up, locked their wings, and glided, soared, and wheeled over the earth-stained knot of men—two great white birds, with crests of fire-gold, plumage snowy save where it was dusted with rosy overtones. Their call was bell-like as they floated across the clearing in a golden haze of sunlight filtered through clouds.

"They're—they're like angels." It was Bormann, the tough young sentimentalist.

"You've named them, soldier," Balistierri grinned. "I've been trying for a name; and that's the best I've heard. Bormann's angels they'll be. In Latin, of course."

8

Unfolding vistas of eternal zoological glory left Bormann speechless and red-faced. Sergeant Brian broke in.

"I guess they would have made those horn sounds. Right, Lieutenant?" His voice, dry and a little patronizing, suggested that this was a poor waste of valuable marching time.

"I wouldn't know, Sergeant," Hague answered, trying to keep dislike out of his voice, but the momentary thrill was broken and, with Balistierri beside him, Gunnery Officer Hague struck out on the trail that had been blasted and hacked through the clearing's wanton extravagance of greedy plant life.

As they crossed the clearing, Bucci tripped and sprawled full length in the mud. When he tried to get up, the vine over which he'd stumbled clutched with a woody tendril that wound snakelike tightly about his ankle; and, white faced, the rest of the men chopped him free of the serpentine thing with belt knives, bandaged the thorn wounds in his leg, and went on.

The clearing had one more secret to divulge, however. A movement in the forest edge caught Brian's eye and he motioned to Hague, who followed him questioningly as the Sergeant led him off trail. Brian pointed silently and Hague saw Didrickson, Sergeant in charge of Supplies, seated in the lemon-colored sunlight at the forest edge, an open food pack between his knees, from which he snatched things and swallowed them voraciously, feeding like a wild dog.

"Didrickson! Sergeant Didrickson!" the Lieutenant yelled. "What are you doing?"

The supply man stared back, and Hague knew from the man's face what had happened. He crouched warily, eyes wild with panic and jaw hanging foolishly slack. This was Didrickson, the steady, efficient man who'd sat at the chart table the night they began this march. He had been the only man Devlin thought competent and nerveless enough to handle the food. This was the same Didrickson, and madder now than a March hare, Hague concluded grimly. The enlisted man snatched up the food pack, staring at them in wild fear, and began to run back down the trail, back the way they'd come.

"Come back, Didrickson. We've got to have that food, you fool!"

The madman laughed crazily at the sound of the officer's voice, glanced back for a moment, then spun and ran.

Sergeant Brian, as always, was ready. His rifle cracked, and the explosive missile blew the running man nearly in half. Sergeant Brian silently retrieved the food pack and brought it back to Hague.

"Do you want it here, Lieutenant, or shall I take it up to the main party?"

"We'll keep it here, Sergeant. Sewell can take it back tonight after our medical check." Hague's voice shook, and he wished savagely that he could have had the nerve to pass that swift death sentence. Didrickson's crime was dangerous to every member of the party, and the Sergeant had been right to shoot. But when the time came—when perhaps the Sergeant wasn't with him—would he, Hague, react swiftly and coolly as an officer should? He wondered despairingly.

"All right, lads, let's pull," he said, and the tight-lipped gun crew filed again into the hushed, somber forest corridors.

II

Communications Technician Harker took a deep pull at his mug of steaming coffee, blinked his eyes hard at the swimming dials before him, and lit a cigarette. Odysseus warning center was never quiet, even now in the graveyard watch when all other lights were turned low through the great ship's hull. Here in the neat grey room, murmuring, softly clicking signal equipment was banked against every wall in a gleaming array of dials and meters, heavy power leads, black panels, and intricate sheafs of colored wire. The sonar kept up a sleepy drone, and radar scoped glowed fitfully with interference patterns, and the warning buzzer beeped softly as the radar echoed back to its receivers the rumor of strange planetary forces that radar hadn't been built to filter through. What made the interference, base technicians couldn't tell, but it practically paralyzed radio communication on all bands, and blanketed out even radar warnings.

The cigarette burned his fingertips, and Harker jerked awake and tried to concentrate on the letter he was writing home. It would be microfilmed, and go on the next courier rocket. A movement at the Warnings Room door brought Harker's head up, and he saw Commander Chapman, lean and grey, standing there.

"Good evening, sir. Come on in. I've got coffee on." The Communications Technician took a pot from the glow heater at his elbow, and set out another cup.

The Commander smiled tiredly, pulled out a stubby metal stool, and sat across the low table from Harker, sipping the scalding coffee cautiously. He looked up after a moment.

"What's the good word, Harker? Picked up anything?"

Harker ran his fingers through his mop of black hair and grimaced.

"Not a squeak, sir. No radio, no radar. Of course, the interference may be blanketing those. Creates a lot of false signals, too, on the radar screens. But we can't even pick 'em up with long-range sonar. That should get through. We're pretty sure they crashed, all right."

"How about our signals, Harker? Do you think we're getting through to them?"

Harker leaned back expansively, happy to expound his specialty.

"Well, we've been sending radio signals every hour on the hour, and radio voice messages every hour on the half-hour. We're sending a continuous sonar beam for their direction-finder. That's about all we can do. As for their picking it up, assuming the rocket has crashed and been totally knocked out, they still have a radio in the whippet tank. It's a transreceiver. And they have a portable sonar set, one of those little twenty-pound armored detection units. They'll use it as a direction finder."

Chapman swirled the coffee around in the bottom of his cup and stared thoughtfully into it.

"If they can get sonar, why can't we send them messages down the sonar beam? You know, flick it on and off in Morse code?"

"It won't work with a small detector like they have, sir. With our big set here, we could send them a message, but that outfit they have might burn out. It has a limited sealed motor supply that must break down an initial current resistance on the grids before the rectifiers can convert it to audible sound. With the set operating continuously, power drainage is small, but begin changing your signal beam and the power has to break down the grid resistance several hundred times for every short signal sent. It would burn out their set in a matter of hours.

"It works like a slide trombone, sort of. Run your slide way out, and you get a slowly vibrating column of air, and that is heard as a low note, only on sonar it would be a short note. Run your slide way up, and the vibrations are progressively faster and higher in pitch. The sonar set, at peak, is vibrating so rapidly that it's almost static, and the power flow is actually continuous. But, starting and stopping the set continuously, the vibrators never have a chance to reach a normal peak, and the power flow is broken at each vibrating in the receiver—and a few hours later your sonar receptor is a hunk of junk."

"All right, Harker. Your discussion is vague, but I get the general idea that my suggestion wasn't too hot. Well, have who-

11

ever is on duty call me if any signals come through." The Commander set down his cup, said good night, and moved off down the hushed corridor. Harker returned to his letter and a chewed stub of pencil, while he scowled in a fevered agony of composition. It was a letter to his girl, and it had to be good.

Night had begun to fall over the forest roof, and stole thickening down the muddy cathedral aisles of great trees, and Hague listened hopefully for the halt signal from the whippet tank, which should come soon. He was worried about Bucci, who was laughing and talking volubly; the officer decided he must have a touch of fever. The dark, muscular gunner kept talking about his young wife in what was almost a babble. Once he staggered and nearly fell, until Hurd took the pneumatic gun-barrel assembly and carried it on his own shoulders. They were all listening expectantly for the tank's klaxon, when a brassy scream ripped the evening to echoing shreds and a flurry of shots broke out ahead.

The scream came again, metallic and shrill as a locomotive gone amok; yells, explosive-bullet reports, and the sound of hammering blows drifted back.

"Take over, Brian," Hague snapped. "Crosse, Hurd—let's go!"

The three men ran at a stagger through the dragging mud around a turn in the trail, and dropped the pneumatic gun swiftly into place—Hurd at firing position, Crosse on the charger, and Hague prone in the slime snapping an ammunition belt into the loader.

Two emergency flares someone had thrown lit the trail ahead in a garish photographic fantasy of bright, white light and ink-black shadow, a scene out of Inferno. A cart lay on its side, men were running clear, the whippet tank lay squirming on its side, and above it towered the screaming thing. A lizard, or dinosaur, rearing up thirty feet, scaly grey, a man clutched in its two hand-like claws, while its armored tail smashed and smashed at the tank with pile-driver blows. Explosive bullets cracked around the thing's chest in blue-white flares of light, but it continued to rip at the man twisting pygmy-like in its claws—white teeth glinting like sabers as its blindly malevolent screams went on.

"On target," Hurd's voice came strained and low.

"Charge on," from Crosse.

"Let her go!" Hague yelled, and fed APX cartridges as the gun coughed a burst of armor-piercing, explosive shells into the rearing beast. Hague saw the tank turret swing up as Whittaker tried to get his gun in action, but a slashing slap of the monster's tail spun it back brokenly. The cluster of pneumatic shells hit then and burst within that body, and the great grey-skinned trunk was

12

hurled off the trail, the head slapping against a tree trunk on the other side as the reptile was halved.

"Good shooting, Crosse," Hague grunted. "Get back with Brian. Keep the gun ready. That thing might have a mate." He ran toward the main party, and into the glare of the two flares.

"Where's Devlin?"

Clark, the navigation officer, was standing with a small huddle of men near the smashed supply cart.

"Here, Hague," he called. His eyes were sunken, his face older in the days since Hague had last seen him. "Devlin's dead, smashed between the cart and a tree trunk. We've lost two men, Commander Devlin and Ellis, the soils man. He's the one it was eating." He grimaced.

"That leaves twenty-three of us?" Hague inquired, and tried to sound casual.

"That's right. You'll continue to cover the rear. Those horn sounds you reported had Devlin worried about an attack from your direction. I'll be with the tank."

Sergeant Brian was stoically heating ration stew over the cook unit when Hague returned, while the crew sat in a close circle, alternately eyeing nervously the forest at their backs, and the savory steam that rose from Brian's mixture. There wasn't much for each of them, but it was hot and highly nutritious, and after a cigarette and coffee they would feel comfort for a while.

Crosse, seated on the grey metal charger tube he'd carried all day, fingered the helmet in his lap, and looked inquiringly at the Lieutenant.

"Well, sir, anybody hurt? Was the tank smashed?"

Hague squatted in the circle, sniffed the stew with loud enthusiasm, and looked about the circle.

"Commander Devlin's dead, and Ellis. One supply cart smashed, but the tank'll be all right. The lizard charged the tank. Balistierri thinks it was the lizard's mating season, and he figured the tank was another male and he tried to fight it. Then he stayed–to–lunch and we got him. Lieutenant Clark is in command now."

The orange glow of Brian's cook unit painted queer shadows on the stained faces around him, and Hague tried to brighten them up.

"Will you favor us with one of your inimitable harmonica arrangements, Maestro Bormann?"

"I can't right now. I'm bandaging Helen's wing." He held out something in the palm of his hand, and the heater's glow glittered on liquid black eyes. "She's like a little bird, but without her feathers. See?" He placed the warm lump in Hague's hand. "For

13

wings, she's just got skin, like a bat, except she's built like a bird."

"You ought to show this to Balistierri, and maybe he'll name this for you, too."

Bormann's homely face creased into a grin. "I did, sir. At the noon halt when I found it. It's named after my girl. 'Bormann's Helen', only in Latin. Helen's got a broken wing."

As they ate, they heard the horn note again. Bucci's black eyes were feverishly bright, his skin hot and dry, and the vine scratches on his leg badly inflamed; and when the rest began to sing he was quiet. The reedy song of Bormann's harmonica piped down the quiet forest passages, and echoed back from the great trees; and somewhere, as Hague dozed off in his little tent, he heard the horn note again, sandwiched into mouth organ melody.

Two days of slogging through the slimy green mud, and at noon halt Sewell brought back word to be careful, that a man had failed to report at roll call that morning. The gun crew divided Bucci's equipment between them, and he limped in the middle of the file on crutches, fashioned from ration cart wreckage. Crosse, who'd been glancing off continually, like a wizened, curious rat, flung up his arm in a silent signal to halt, and Hague moved in to investigate, the everpresent Brian moving carefully and with jungle beast's silent poise just behind him. Crumpled like a sack of damp laundry, in the murk of two root buttresses, lay Romano, one of the two photographers. His Hasselbladt camera lay beneath his body crushing a small plant he must have been photographing.

From the back of Romano's neck protruded a gleaming nine-inch arrow shaft, a lovely thing of gleaming bronze-like metal, delicately thin of shaft and with fragile hammered bronze vanes. Brian moved up behind Hague, bent over the body and cut the arrow free.

They examined the thing, and when Brian spoke Hague was surprised that this time even the rock-steady Sergeant spoke in a hushed voice, the kind boys use when they walk by a graveyard at night and don't wish to attract unwelcome attention.

"Looks like it came from a blowgun, Lieutenant. See the plug at the back. It must be poisoned; it's not big enough to kill him otherwise."

Hague grunted assent, and the two moved back trailward.

"Brian, take over. Crosse, come on. We'll report this to Clark. Remember, from now on wear your body armor and go in pairs when you leave the trail. Get Bucci's plates onto him."

Bormann and Hurd set down their loads, and were buckling the

14

weakly protesting Bucci into his chest and back plates, as Hague left them.

Commander Chapman stared at the circle of faces. His section commanders lounged about his tiny square office. "Well, then, what are their chances?"

Bjornson, executive for the technical section, stared at Chapman levelly.

"I can vouch for Devlin. He's not precisely a rulebook officer, but that's why I recommended him for this expedition. He's at his best in an unusual situation, one where he has to depend on his own wits. He'll bring them through."

Artilleryman Branch spoke in turn. "I don't know about Hague. He's young, untried. Seemed a little unsure. He might grow panicky and be useless. I sent him because there was no one else, unless I went myself."

The Commander cleared his throat brusquely. "I know you wanted to go, Branch, but we can't send out our executive officers. Not yet, anyway. What about Clark? Could he take over Devlin's job?"

"Clark can handle it," Captain Rindell of the Science Section, was saying. "He likes to follow the rule book, but he's sturdy stuff. He'll bring them through if something happens to Devlin."

"Hmmmm—that leaves Hague as the one questionable link in their chain of command. Young man, untried. Of course, he's only the junior officer. There's no use stewing over this; but I'll tell you frankly, that if those men can't get their records through to us before we send the next courier rocket to earth, I think the U.S. Rocket Service is finished. This attempt will be chalked up as a failure. The project will be abandoned entirely, and we'll be ordered back to earth to serve as a fighter arm there."

Bjornson peered from the space-port window and looked out over the cinder-packed parade a hundred feet below. "What makes you so sure the Rocket Service is in immediate danger of being scrapped?"

"The last courier rocket contained a confidential memo from Secretary Dougherty. There is considerable war talk, and the other Service Arms are plunging for larger armaments. They want their appropriations of money and stock pile materials expanded at our expense. We've got to show that we are doing a good job, show the Government a concrete return in the form of adequate reports on the surface of Venus, and its soils and raw materials."

"What about the 'copters?" Rindell inquired. "They brought in some good stuff for the reports."

15

"Yes, but with a crew of only four men, they can't do enough."

Branch cut in dryly. "About all I can see is to look hopeful. The Rocket would have exhausted its fuel long ago. It's been over ten weeks since they left Base."

"Assuming they're marching overland, God forbid, they'll have only sonar and radio, right?" Bjornson was saying. "Why not keep our klaxon going? It's a pretty faint hope, but we'll have to try everything. My section is keeping the listeners manned continually, we've got a sonar beam out, radio messages every thirty minutes, and with the klaxon we're doing all we can. I doubt if anything living could approach within a twenty-five mile range without hearing that klaxon, or without us hearing them with the listeners."

"All right." Commander Chapman stared hopelessly at a fresh batch of reports burdening his desk. "Send out ground parties within the ten-mile limit, but remember we can't afford to lose men. When the 'copters are back in, send them both West." West meant merely in a direction west from Meridian O, as the mother rocket's landing place had been designated. "They can't do much searching over that rainforest, but it's worth a try. They might pick up a radio message."

Chapman returned grumpily to his reports, and the others filed out.

III

At night, on guard, Hague saw a thousand horrors peopling the Stygian forest murk; but when he flashed his lightpak into darkness there was nothing. He wondered how long he could stand the waiting, when he would crack as Supply Sergeant Didrickson had, and his comrades would blast him down with explosive bullets. He should be like Brian, hard and sure, and always doing the right thing, he decided. He'd come out of OCS Gunnery School, trained briefly in the newly-formed U.S. Rocket Service. Then the expedition to Venus—it was a fifty-fifty chance they said, and out of all the volunteers he'd been picked. And when the first expedition was ready to blast off from the Base Camp on Venus, he'd been picked again. Why? he cursed despairingly. Sure, he wanted to come, but how could his commanders have had faith in him, when he didn't know himself if he could continue to hold out.

Sounds on the trail sent his carbine automatically to ready, and he called a strained, "Halt."

"Okay, Hague. It's Clark and Arndt."

The wiry little navigation officer, and lean, scraggy Geologist Arndt, the latter's arm still in a sling, came into the glow of Hague's lightpak.

"Any more horns or arrows?" Clark's voice sounded tight, and repressed; Hague reflected that perhaps the strain was getting him too.

"No, but Bucci is getting worse. Can't you carry him on the cart?"

"Hague, I've told you twenty times. That cart is full and breaking down now. Get it through your head that it's no longer individual men we can think of now, but the entire party. If they can't march, they must be left, or all of us may die!" His voice was savage, and when he tried to light a cigarette his hand shook. "All right. It's murder, and I don't like it any better than you do."

"How are we doing? What's the over-all picture?" Both of the officers tried to smile a little at the memory of that pompous little phrase, favorite of a windbag they'd served under.

"Not good. Twenty-two of us now."

"Hirooka thinks we may be within radio range of Base soon," he continued more hopefully. "With this interference, we can't tell, though."

They talked a little longer, Arndt gave the gunnery officer a food-and-medical supply packet, and Hague's visitors became two bobbing glows of light that vanished down the trail.

A soul-crushing weight of days passed while they strained forward through mud and green gloom, like men walking on a forest sea-bottom. Then it was a cool dawn, and a tugging at his boot awoke the Lieutenant. Hurd, his face a strained mask, was peering into the officer's small shelter tent and jerking at his leg.

"Get awake, Lieutenant. I think they're here."

Hague struggled hard to blink off the exhausted sleep he'd been in.

"Listen, Lieutenant, one of them horns has been blowing. It's right here. Between us and the main party."

"Okay." Hague rolled swiftly from the tent as Hurd awoke the men. Hague moved swiftly to each.

"Brian, you handle the gun. Bucci, loader. Crosse, charger. Bormann, cover our right; Hurd the left. I'll watch the trail ahead."

Brian and Crosse worked swiftly and quietly with the lethal efficiency that had made them crack gunners at Fort Fisher, North Carolina. Bucci lay motionless at the ammunition box, but his eyes were bright, and he didn't seem to mind his feverish, swollen leg. The Sergeant and Crosse slewed the pneumatic gun to cover their back trail, and fell into position beside the gleaming grey tube. Hague, Bormann and Hurd moved quickly at striking tents and rolling packs, their rifles ready at hand.

Hague had forgotten his fears and the self-doubt, the feeling that he had no business ordering men like Sergeant Brian, and Hurd and Bormann. They were swallowed in intense expectancy as he lay watching the dawn fog that obscured like thick smoke the trail that led to Clark's party and the whippet tank.

He peered back over his shoulder for a moment. Brian, Bucci, and Crosse, mud-stained backs toward him, were checking the gun and murmuring soft comments. Bormann looked at the officer, grinned tightly, and pointed at Helen perched on his shoulder. His lips carefully framed the words, "Be a pushover, Helen brings luck."

The little bird peered up into Bormann's old-young face, and Hague, trying to grin back, hoped he looked confident. Hurd lay on the other side of the trail, his back to Bormann, peering over his rifle barrel, bearded jaws rhythmically working a cud of tobacco he'd salvaged somewhere, and Hague suddenly thought he must have been saving it for the finish.

Hague looked back into the green light beginning to penetrate the trail fog, changing it into a glowing mass—then thought he saw a movement. Up the trail, the whippet tank's motor caught with a roar, and he heard Whittaker traversing the battered tank's turret. The turret gun boomed flatly, and a shell burst somewhere in the forest darkness to Hague's right.

Then there was a gobbling yell and grey man-like figures poured out onto the trail. Hague set his sights on them, the black sight-blade silhouetting sharply in the glowing fog. He set them on a running figure and squeezed his trigger, then again, and again, as new targets came. Sharp reports ran crackling among the great trees. Sharp screams came, and a whistling sound overhead that he knew were blowgun arrows. The pneumatic gun sputtered behind him, and Bormann's and Hurd's rifles thudded in the growing roar.

Blue flashes and explosive bullets made fantastic flares back in the forest shadows; and suddenly a knot of man-shapes were running toward him through the fog. Hague picked out one in the glowing mist, fired, another, fired. Gobbling yells were around him, and he shot toward them through the fog at point-blank range. A thing rose up beside him, and Hague yelled with murderous fury, and drove his belt-knife up into grey leather skin. Something burned his shoulder as he rolled aside and fired at the dark form standing over him with a poised, barbed spear. The blue-white flash was blinding, and he cursed and leaped up.

There was nothing more. Scattered shots, and the forest lay quiet again. After that shot at point-blank range, Hague's vision had blacked out.

"Any one else need first-aid?" he called, and tried to keep his voice firm. When there was silence, he said, "Hurd, lead me to the tank."

He heard the rat-faced man choke, "My God, he's blind."

"Just flash blindness, Hurd. Only temporary." Hague kept his face stiff, and hoped frantically that he was right, that it was just temporary blindness, temporary optic shock.

Sergeant Brian's icy voice cut in. "Gun's all right, Lieutenant. Nobody hurt. We fired twenty-eight rounds of H.E. No A.P.X. Get going with him, Hurd."

He felt Hurd's tug at his elbow, and they made their way up the trail.

"What do they look like, Hurd?"

"These men-things? They're grey, about my size, skin looks like leather, and their heads are flattish. Eyes on the side of their heads, like a lizard. Not a stitch of clothes. Just a belt with a knife and arrow holder. And they got webbed claws for feet. They're ugly-looking things, sir. Here's the tank."

Clark's voice came, hard and clear. "That you, Hague?" Silence for a moment. "What's wrong? You're not blinded?"

Sewell had dropped his irascibility, and his voice was steady and kindly.

"Just flash blindness, isn't it, sir? This salve will fix you up. You've got a cut on your shoulder. I'll take care of that too."

"How are your men, Hague?" Clark sounded as though he were standing beside Hague.

"Not a scratch. We're ready to march."

"Five hurt here, three with the advance party, and two at the tank. We got 'em good, though. They hit the trail between our units and got fire from both sides. Must be twenty of them dead."

Hague grimaced at the sting of something Sewell had squeezed into his eyes. "Who was hurt?"

"Arndt, the geologist; his buddy, Galut, the botanist; lab technician Harker, Crewman Harker, and Szachek the meteorologist man. How's your pneumatic ammunition?"

"We fired twenty-eight rounds of H.E."

Cartographer Hirooka's voice burst in excitedly.

"That gun crew of yours! Your gun crew got twenty-one of

19

these—these lizard men. A bunch came up our back trail, and the pneumatic cut them to pieces."

"Good going, Hague. We'll leave you extended back there. I'm putting in the advance party, and there'll be just two groups. We'll be at point, and you continue at afterguard." Clark was silent for a moment, then his voice came bitterly, "We're down to seventeen men, you know."

He cursed, and Hague heard the wiry little navigator slosh away through the mud and begin shouting orders. He and Hurd started back with Whittaker and Sergeant Sample yelling wild instructions from the tank as to what the rear guard might do with the next batch of lizard-men who came sneaking up.

Hague's vision was clearing, and he saw Balistierri and the photographer Whitcomb through a milky haze, measuring, photographing, and even dissecting several of the lizard-men. The back trail, swept by pneumatic gunfire was a wreck of wood splinters and smashed trees, smashed bodies, and cratered earth.

They broke down the gun, harnessed the equipment, and swung off at the sound of Clark's whistle. Bucci had to be supported between two of the others, and they took turnabout at the job, sloshing through the water and mud, with Bucci's one swollen leg dragging uselessly between them. It was punishing work as the heat veils shimmered and thickened, but no one seemed to consider leaving him behind, Hague noticed; and he determined to say nothing about Clark's orders that the sick must be abandoned.

Days and nights flashed by in a dreary monotony of mud, heat, insects and thinning rations. Then one morning the giant trees began to thin, and they passed from rainforest into jungle.

The change was too late for Bucci. They carved a neat marker beside the trail, and set the dead youth's helmet atop it. Lieutenant Hague carried ahead a smudged letter in his shirt, with instructions to forward it to Wilma, the gunner's young wife.

Hague and his four gunners followed the rattling whippet tank's trail higher, the jungle fell behind, and their protesting legs carried them over the rim of a high, cloudswept plateau, that swept on to the limit of vision on both sides and ahead.

The city's black walls squatted secretively: foursquare, black, glassy walls with a blocky tower set sturdily at each of the four corners, enclosing what appeared to be a square mile of low buildings. Grey fog whipped coldly across the flat bleakness and rustled through dark grass.

Balistierri, plodding beside Hague at the rear, stared at it warily, muttering, "And Childe Roland to the dark tower came."

Sampler's tank ground along the base of the twelve-foot wall, turned at a sharp right angle, and the party filed through a square cut opening that once had been a gate. The black city looked tenantless. There was dark-hued grass growing in the misted streets and squares, and across the lintels of cube-shaped, neatly aligned dwellings, fashioned of thick, black blocks. Hague could hear nothing but whipping wind, the tank's clatter, and the quiet clink of equipment as men shuffled ahead through the knee-high grass, peering watchfully into dark doorways.

Clark's whistle shrilled, the tank motor died, and they waited.

"Hague, come ahead."

The gunnery officer nodded at Sergeant Brian, and walked swiftly to Clark, who was leaning against the tank's mud-caked side.

"Sampler says we've got to make repairs on the tank. We'll shelter here. Set your gun on a roof top commanding the street—or, better yet, set it on the wall. I'll want two of your gunners to go hunting food animals."

"What do you think this place is, Bob?"

"Beats me," and the navigator's wind-burned face twisted in a perplexed expression. "Lenkranz knows more about metals, but he thinks this stone is volcanic, like obsidian. Those lizard-men couldn't have built it."

"We passed some kind of bas-relief or mural inside the gate."

"Whitcomb is going to photograph them. Blake, Lenkranz, Johnston, and Hirooka are going to explore the place. Your two gunners, and Crewman Swenson and Balistierri will form the two hunting parties."

For five days, Hague and Crosse walked over the sullen plateau beneath scudding, leaden clouds, hunting little lizards that resembled dinosaurs and ran in coveys like grey chickens. The meat was good, and Sewell dropped his role of medical technician to achieve glowing accolades as an expert cook. Balistierri was in a zoologist's paradise, and he hunted over the windy plain with Swenson, the big white-haired Swede, for ten and twelve hours at a stretch. Balistierri would sit in the cook's unit glow at night, his thin face ecstatic as he described the weird life forms he and Swenson had tracked down during the day; or alternately he'd bemoan the necessity of eating what were to him priceless zoological specimens.

Whittaker and Sampler hammered in the recalcitrant tank's bowels and shouted ribald remarks to any one nearby, until they emerged the third day, grease-stained and perspiring, to announce that "She's ready to roll her g—d—cleats off."

Whittaker had been nursing the tank's radio transreceiver beside the forward hatch this grey afternoon, when his wild yell brought Hague erect. The officer carefully handed Bormann's skin bird back to the gunner, swung down from the city wall's edge, and ran to Whittaker's side. Clark was already there when Hague reached the tank.

"Listen! I've got 'em!" Whittaker yelped and extended the crackling earphones to Clark.

A tinny voice penetrated the interference.

"Base . . . Peter One . . . Do you hear . . . to George Easy Peter One . . . hear me . . . out."

Whittaker snapped on his throat microphone.

"George Easy Peter One To Base. George Easy Peter One To Base. We hear you. We hear you. Rocket crashed. Rocket crashed. Returning overland. Returning overland. Present strength sixteen men. Can you drop us supplies? Can you drop us supplies?"

The earphones sputtered, but no more voices came through. Clark's excited face fell into tired lines.

"We've lost them. Keep trying, Whittaker. Hague, we'll march-order tomorrow at dawn. You'll take the rear again."

Grey, windy dawnlight brought them out to the sound of Clark's call. Strapping on equipment and plates, they assembled around the tank. They were rested, and full fed.

"Walk, you poor devils," Whittaker was yelling from his tank turret. "And, if you get tired, run awhile," he snorted, grinning heartlessly, as he leaned back in pretended luxury against the gunner's seat, a thinly padded metal strip.

Balistierri and the blond Swenson shouldered their rifles and shuffled out. They would move well in advance as scouts.

"I wouldn't ride in that armored alarm-clock if it had a built-in harem," Hurd was screaming at Whittaker, and hurled a well-placed mudball at the tankman's head as the tank motor caught and the metal vehicle lumbered ahead toward the gate, with Whittaker sneering but with most of his head safely below the turret rim. Beside it marched Clark, his ragged uniform carefully scraped clean of mud, and with him Lenkranz, the metals man. Both carried rifles and wore half-empty bandoliers of blast cartridges.

The supply cart jerked behind the tank, and behind it filed Whitcomb with his cameras; Johnston; cartographer Hirooka perusing absorbedly the clip board that held his strip map; Blake, the lean and spectacled bacteriologist, brought up the rear. Hague waited until they had disappeared through the gate cut sharply in the city's black wall, then he turned to his gun crew.

Sergeant Brian, saturnine as always, swung past carrying the pneumatic barrel assembly, Crosse with the charger a pace behind.

Next, Bormann, whispering to Helen, who rode his shoulder piping throaty calls. Last came Hurd, swaggering past with jaws grinding steadily at that mysterious cud. Hague cast a glance over his shoulder at the deserted street of black cubes, wondered at the dank loneness of the place, and followed Hurd.

The hours wore on as they swung across dark grass, through damp tendrils of cloud, and faced into whipping, cold wind, eyes narrowed against its sting. Helen, squawking unhappily, crawled inside Bormann's shirt and rode with just her brown bird-head protruding.

"Look at the big hole, Lieutenant," Hurd called above the wind.

Hurd had dropped behind, and Hague called a halt to investigate Hurd's find, but as he hiked rapidly back, the wiry little man yelled and pitched out of sight. Brian came running, and he and Hague peered over the edge of the funnel-shaped pit, from which Hurd was trying to crawl. Each time he'd get a third of the way up the eighteen-foot slope, gravelly soil would slide and he'd again be carried to the bottom.

"Throw me a line."

Brian pulled a hank of nylon line from his belt, shook out the snarls, and tossed an end into Hurd's clawing hands. Hague and the Sergeant anchored themselves to the upper end and were preparing to haul, when Hague saw something move in the gravel beneath Hurd's feet, at the funnel bottom, and saw a giant pincers emerging from loose, black gravel.

"Hurd look out!" he screamed.

The little man, white-faced, threw himself aside as a giant beetle head erupted through the funnel bottom. The great pincer jaws fastened around Hurd's waist as he struggled frantically up the pit's side. He began screaming when the beetle monster dragged him relentlessly down, his distorted face flung up at them appealingly. Hague snatched at his rifle and brought it up. When the gun cracked, the pincers tightened on Hurd's middle, and the little man was snipped in half. The blue-white flash and report of the explosive bullet blended with Hurd's choked yells, the beetle rolled over on its back, and the two bodies lay entangled at the pit bottom. Brian and Hague looked at each other in silent, blanched horror, then turned from the pit's edge and loped back to the others.

Bormann and Crosse peered fearfully across the wind-whipped grass and inquired in shouts what Hurd was doing.

"He's dead, gone," Hague yelled savagely over the wind's whine. "Keep moving. We can't do anything. Keep going."

IV

At 1630 hours Commander Technician Harker slipped on the earset, threw over a transmitting switch, and monotoned the routine verbal message.

"Base to George Easy Peter One . . . Base to George Easy Peter One . . . Do you hear me George Easy Peter One . . . Do you hear me George Easy Peter One . . . reply please . . . reply please." Nothing came from his earphones but bursts of crackling interference, until he tried the 'copters next, and "George Easy Peter Two" and "George Easy Peter Three" reported in. They were operating near the base.

He tried "One" again, just in case.

"Base to George Easy Peter One . . . Base to George Easy Peter One . . . Do you hear me . . . Do you hear me . . . out."

A scratching whisper resolved over the interference. Harker's face wore a stunned look, but he quickly flung over a second switch and the scratching voice blared over the mother ship's entire address system. Men dropped their work throughout the great hull, and clustered around the speakers.

"George One . . . Base . . . hear you . . . rocket crashed . . . overland . . . present strength . . . supplies . . . drop supplies."

Interference surged back and drowned the whispering voice, while through Odysseus' hull a ragged cheer grew and gathered volume. Harker shut off the address system and strained over his crackling earphones, but nothing more came in response to his radio calls.

He glanced up and found the Warning Room jammed with technicians, science section members, officers, men in laboratory smocks, or greasy overalls, or spotless Rocket Service uniforms watching intently his own strained face as he tried to get through. Commander Chapman looked haggard, and Harker remembered that someone had once said that Chapman's young sister was the wife of the medical technician who'd gone out with Patrol Rocket One.

Harker finally pulled off the earphones reluctantly and set them on the table before him. "That's all. You heard everything they said over the P.A. system. Nothing more is coming through."

Night came, another day, night again, and they came finally to the plateau's end, and stood staring from a windy escarpment across an endless roof of rainforest far below, grey-green under the continuous roof of lead-colored clouds. Hague, standing back a little, watched them. A thin line of ragged men along the rim,

24

peering mournfully out across that endless expanse for a gleam that might be the distant hull of Odysseus, the mother ship. A damp wind fluttered their rags and plastered them against gaunt bodies.

Clark and Sampler were conferring in shouts.

"Will the tank make it down this grade?" Clark wanted to know.

For once, Sergeant Sampler's mobile, merry face was grim.

"I don't know, but we'll sure try. Be ready to cut that cart loose if the tank starts to slip."

Drag ropes were fastened to the cart, a man stationed at the tank hitch, and Sampler sent his tank lurching forward over the edge, and it slanted down at a sharp angle. Hague, holding a drag rope, set his heels and allowed the tank's weight to pull him forward over the rim; and the tank, cart, and muddy figures hanging to drag ropes began descending the steep gradient. Bormann, just ahead of the Lieutenant, strained back at the rope and turned a tight face over his shoulder.

"She's slipping faster!"

The tank was picking up speed, and Hague heard the clash of gears as Sampler tried to fight the downward pull of gravity. Gears ground, and Sampler forced the whippet straight again, but the downward slide was increasing. Hague was flattened under Bormann, heels digging, and behind him he could hear Sergeant Brian cursing, struggling to keep flat against the downward pull.

The tank careened sideways again, slipped, and Whittaker's white face popped from her turret.

"She's going," he screamed.

A drag rope parted. Clark sprang like a madman between tank and cart, and cut the hitch. The tank, with no longer sufficient restraining weight, tipped with slow majesty outward, then rolled out and down, bouncing, smashing as if in a slow motion film, shedding parts at each crushing contact. It looked like a toy below them, still rolling and gathering speed, when Hague saw Whittaker's body fly free, a tiny rag doll at that distance, and the tank was lost to view when it bounced off a ledge and went floating down through space.

Clark signalled them forward, and they inched the supply cart downward on the drag ropes, legs trembling with strain, and their nerves twitching at the memory of Whittaker's chalky face peering from the falling turret. It was eight hours before they reached the bottom, reeling with exhaustion, set a guard, and tumbled into their shelter tents. Outside, Hague could hear Clark pacing restlessly, trying to assure himself that he'd been right to cut the tank free, that there'd been no chance to save Whittaker and Sampler when the tank began to slide.

Hague lay in his little tent listening to the footsteps splash past in muddy Venusian soil, and was thankful that he hadn't had to make the decision. He'd been saving three cigarettes in an oilskin packet, and he drew one carefully from the wrapping now, lit it, and inhaled deeply. Could he have done what Clark did—break that hitch? He still didn't know when he took a last lung-filling pull at the tiny stub of cigarette and crushed it out carefully.

As dawn filtered through the cloud layer, they were rolling shelter tents and buckling on equipment. Clark's face was a worn mask when he talked with Hague, and his fingers shook over his pack buckles.

"There are thirteen of us. Six men will pull the supply cart, and six guard, in four-hour shifts. You and I will alternate command at guard."

He was silent for a moment, then watched Hague's face intently as he spoke again.

"It'll be a first-grade miracle if any of us get through. Hague, you—you know I had to cut that tank free." His voice rose nervously. "You know that! You're an officer."

"Yeah, I guess you did." Hague couldn't say it any better, and he turned away and fussed busily with the bars holding the portable Sonar detection unit to the supply cart.

They moved off with Hague leaning into harness pulling the supply cart bumpily ahead. Clark stumbled jerkily at the head, with Blake, a lean, silent ghost beside him, rifle in hand. The cart came next with Hague, Bormann, Sergeant Brian, Crosse, Lenkranz and Sewell leaning in single file against its weight. At the rear marched photographer Whitcomb, Johnston, Hirooka with his maps, and Balistierri, each carrying a rifle. The big Swede Swenson was last in line, peering warily back into the rainforest shadows. The thirteen men wound Indian file from sight of the flatheaded reptilian thing, clutching a sheaf of bronze arrows, that watched them.

Hague had lost count of days again when he looked up into the shadowy forest roof, his feet finding their way unconsciously through the thin mud, his ears registering automatically the murmurs of talk behind him, the supply cart's tortured creaking, and the continuous Sonar drone. The air felt different, warmer than its usual steam-bath heat, close and charged with expectancy, and the forest seemed to crouch in waiting with the repressed silence of a hunting cat.

Crosse yelled thinly from the rear of the file, and they all halted to listen, the hauling crew dropping their harness thankfully. Hague turned back and saw Crosse's thin arm waving a rifle overhead, then pointing down the trail. The Lieutenant listened carefully until he caught the sound, a thin call, the sound of a horn mellowed by distance.

The men unthinkingly moved in close and threw wary looks into the forest ways around them.

"Move further ahead, Hague. Must be more lizard men." Clark swore, with tired despair. "All right, let's get moving and make it fast."

The cart creaked ahead again, moving faster this time, and the snicking of rifle bolts came to Hague. He moved swiftly ahead on the trail and glanced up again, saw breaks in the forest roof, and realized that the huge trees were pitching wildly far above.

"Look up," he yelled, "wind coming!"

The wind came suddenly, striking with stone-wall solidity. Hague sprinted to the cart, and the struggling body of men worked it off the trail, and into a buttress angle of two great tree roots, lashing it there with nylon ropes. The wind velocity increased, smashing torn branches overhead, and ripping at the men who lay with their heads well down in the mud. Tiny animals were blown hurtling past, and once a great spider came flailing in cartwheel fashion, then smashed brokenly against a tree.

The wind drone rose in volume, the air darkened, and Hague lost sight of the other men from behind his huddled shelter against a wall-like root. The great trees twisted with groaning protest, and thunderous crashes came downward through the forest, with sometimes the faint squeak of a dying or frightened animal. The wind halted for a breathless, hushed moment of utter stillness, broken only by the dropping of limbs and the scurry of small life forms—then came the screaming fury from the opposite direction.

For a moment, the gunnery officer thought he'd be torn from the root to which his clawing fingers clung. Its brutal force smashed breath from Hague's lungs and held him pinned in his corner until he struggled choking for air as a drowning man does. It seemed that he couldn't draw breath, that the air was a solid mass from which he could no longer get life. Then the wind stopped as suddenly as it had come, leaving dazed quiet. As he stumbled back to the cart, Hague saw crushed beneath a thigh-sized limb a feebly moving reptilian head; and the dying eyes of the lizard-man were still able to stare at him in cold malevolence.

The supply cart was still intact, roped between buttressing roots to belt knives driven into the tough wood. Hague and Clark freed it, called a hasty roll, and the march was resumed at a fast pace through cooled, cleaner air. They could no longer hear horn sounds; but the grim knowledge that lizard-men were near them lent strength, and Hague led as rapidly as he dared, listening carefully to the Sonar's drone behind him, altering his course when the sound faded, and straightening out when it grew in volume.

A day slipped by and another, and the cart rolled ahead through thin greasy mud on the forest floor, with the Sonar's drone mingled with murmuring men's voices talking of food. It was the universal topic, and they carefully worked out prolonged menus each would engorge when they reached home. They forgot heat, insect bites, the sapping humidity, and talked of food—steaming roasts, flanked by crystal goblets of iced wine, oily roasted nuts, and lush, crisp green salads.

V

Hague, again marching ahead with Balistierri, broke into the comparatively bright clearing, and was blinded for a moment by the sudden, cloud-strained light after days of forest darkness. As their eyes accommodated to the lemon-colored glare, he and Balistierri sighted the animals squatting beneath low bushes that grew thickly in the clearing. They were monkey-like primates with golden tawny coats, a cockatoo crest of white flaring above dog faces. The monkeys stared a moment, the great white crests rising doubtfully, ivory canine teeth fully three inches long bared.

They'd been feeding on fruit that dotted the shrub-filled clearing; but now one screamed a warning, and they sprang into vines that made a matted wall on every side. The two rifles cracked together again, and three fantastically colored bodies lay quiet, while the rest of the troop fled screaming into tree tops and disappeared. At the blast of sound, a fluttering kaleidoscope of color swept up about the startled Rocketeers, and they stood blinded, while mad whorls of color whirled around them in a miniature storm.

"Giant butterflies," Balistierri was screaming in ecstasy. "Look at them! Big as a dove!"

Hague watched the bright insects coalesce into one agitated mass of vermilion, azure, metallic green, and sulphur yellow twenty feet overhead. The pulsating mass of hues resolved itself into single insects, with wings large as dinner plates, and they streamed out of sight over the forest roof.

"What were they?" he grinned at Balistierri. "Going to name them after Bormann?"

The slight zoologist still watched the spot where they'd vanished.

"Does it matter much what I call them? Do you really believe any one will ever be able to read this logbook I'm making?" He eyed the gunnery officer bleakly, then added, "Well, come on. We'd better skin these monks. They're food anyway."

Hague followed Balistierri, and they stood looking down at the golden furred primates. The zoologist knelt, fingered a bedraggled white crest, and remarked, "These blast cartridges don't leave much meat, do they? Hardly enough for the whole party." He pulled a tiny metal block, with a hook and dial, from his pocket, loped the hook through a tendon in the monkey's leg and lifted the dead animal.

"Hmmm. Forty-seven pounds. Not bad." He weighed each in turn, made measurements, and entered these in his pocket notebook.

The circle around Sewell, who presided over the cook unit, was merry that night. The men's eyes were bright in the heater glow as they stuffed their shrunken stomachs with monkey meat and the fruits the monkeys had been eating when Hague and Balistierri surprised them. Swenson and Crosse and Whitcomb, the photographer, overate and were violently sick; but the others sat picking their teeth contentedly in a close circle. Bormann pulled his harmonica from his shirt pocket, and the hard, silvery torrent of music set them to singing softly. Hague and Blake, the bacteriologist, stood guard among the trees.

At dawn, they were marching again, stepping more briskly over tiny creeks, through green-tinted mud, and the wet heat. At noon, they heard the horn again, and Clark ordered silence and a faster pace. They swung swiftly, eating iron rations as they marched. Hague leaned into his cart harness and watched perspiration staining through Bormann's shirted back just ahead of him. Behind, Sergeant Brian tugged manfully and growled under his breath at buzzing insects, slapping occasionally with a low howl of muted anguish. Helen, the skin bird, rode on Bormann's shoulder, staring back into Hague's face with questioning chirps; and Hague was whistling softly between his teeth at her when Bormann stopped suddenly and Hague slammed into him. Helen took flight with a startled squawk, and Clark came loping back to demand quiet. Bormann stared at the two officers, his young-old face blank with surprise.

"I'm, I'm shot," he stuttered, and stared wonderingly at the thing thrusting from the side opening in his chest armor. It was one of the fragile bronze arrows, gleaming metallically in the forest gloom.

Hague cursed, and jerked free of the cart harness.

"Here, I'll get it free." He tugged at the shaft, and Bormann's face twisted. Hague stepped back. "Where's Sewell? This thing must be barbed."

"Back off the trail! Form a wide circle around the cart, but stay under cover! Fight 'em on their own ground!" Clark was yelling, and the men clustered about the cart faded into forest corridors.

Hague and Sewell, left alone, dragged Bormann's limp length beneath the metal cart. Hague leaped erect again, manhandled the pneumatic gun off the cart and onto the trail, spun the charger crank, and lay down in firing position. Behind him, Sewell grunted, "He's gone. Arrow poison must have paralyzed his diaphragm and chest muscles."

"Okay. Get up here and handle the ammunition." Hague's face was savage as the medical technician crawled into position beside him and opened an ammunition carrier.

"Watch the trail behind me," Hague continued, slamming up the top cover plate and jerking a belt through the pneumatic breech. "When I yell charge, spin the charger crank; and when I yell off a number, set the meter arrow at that number." He snapped the cover plate shut and locked it.

"The other way! They're coming the other way!" Sewell lumbered to his knees, and the two heaved the gun around. A blowgun arrow rattled off the cart body above them, and gobbling yells filtered among the trees with an answering crack of explosive cartridges. A screaming knot of grey figures came sprinting down on the cart. Hague squeezed the pneumatic's trigger, the gun coughed, and blue-fire-limned lizard men crumpled in the trail mud.

"Okay, give 'em a few the other way."

The two men horsed the gun around and sent a buzzing flock of explosive loads down the forest corridor opening ahead of the cart. They began firing carefully down other corridors opening off the trail, aiming delicately less their missiles explode too close and the concussion kill their own men; but they worked a blasting circle of destruction that smashed the great trees back in the forest and made openings in the forest roof. Blue fire flashed in the shadows and froze weird tableaus of screaming lizard-men and hurtling mud, branches, and great splinters of wood.

An exulting yell burst behind them. Hague saw Sewell stare over his shoulder, face contorted, then the big medical technician sprang to his feet. Hague rolled hard, pulling his belt knife, and saw Sewell and a grey man-shape locked in combat above him, saw leathery grey claws drive a bronze knife into the medic's unarmored throat; and then the gunnery officer was on his feet, knife slashing, and the lizard-man fell across the prone Sewell. An almost audible silence fell over the forest, and Hague saw Rocketeers filtering back onto the cart trail, rifles cautiously extended at ready.

"Where's Clark?" he asked Lenkranz. The grey-haired metals man gazed back dully.

"I haven't seen him since we left the trail. I was with Swenson."

The others moved in, and Hague listed the casualties. Sewell, Bormann, and Lieutenant Clark. Gunnery Officer Clarence Hague was now in command. That the Junior Lieutenant now commanded Ground Expeditionary Patrol Number One trickled into his still numb brain; and he wondered for a moment what the Base Commander would think of their chances if he knew. Then he took stock of his little command.

There was young Crosse, his face twitching nervously. There was Blake, the tall, quiet bacteriologist; Lenkranz, the metals man; Hirooka, the Nisei; Balistierri; Johnston; Whitcomb, the photographer, with a battered Hasselbladt still dangling by its neck cord against his armored chest. Swenson was still there, the big Swede crewman; and imperturbable Sergeant Brian, who was now calmly cleaning the pneumatic gun's loading mechanism. And Helen, Bormann's skin bird, fluttering over the ration cart, beneath which Bormann and Sewell lay in the mud.

"Crosse, Lenkranz, burial detail. Get going." It was Hague's first order as Commander. He thought the two looked most woebegone of the party, and figured digging might loosen their nerves.

Crosse stared at him, and then sat suddenly against a tree bole. "I'm not going to dig. I'm not going to march. This is crazy. We're going to get killed. I'll wait for it right here. Why do we keep walking and walking when we're going to die anyway?" His rising voice cracked, and he burst into hysterical laughter. Sergeant Brian rose quietly from his gun-cleaning, jerked Crosse to his feet, and slapped him into quiet. Then he turned to Hague.

"Shall I take charge of the burial detail, sir?"

Hague nodded; and suddenly his long dislike of the iron-hard Sergeant melted into warm liking and admiration. Brian was the man who'd get them all through.

The Sergeant knotted his dark brows truculently at Hague.

"And I don't believe Crosse meant what he said. He's a very brave man. We all get a little jumpy. But he's a good man, a good Rocketeer."

Three markers beside the trail, and a pile of dumped equipment marked the battleground when the cart swung forward again. Hague had dropped all the recording instruments, saving only Whitcomb's exposed films, the rations, rifle ammunition, and logbooks that had been kept by different members of the science section. At his command, Sergeant Brian reluctantly smashed the pneumatic gun's firing mechanism, and left the gun squatting on its tripod beside charger and shell belts. With the lightened load, Hague figured three men could handle the cart, and he took his place with Brian and Crosse in the harness. The others no longer walked in the trail, but filtered between great root-flanges and tree boles on either side, guiding themselves by the Sonar's hum.

They left no more trail markers, and Hague cautioned them against making any unnecessary noise.

"No trail markers behind us. This mud is watery enough to hide footprints in a few minutes. We're making no noise, and we'll drop no more refuse. All they can hear will be the Sonar, and that won't carry far."

On the seventy-first day of the march, Hague squatted, fell almost to the ground, and grunted, "Take ten."

He stared at the stained, ragged scarecrows hunkered about him in forest mud.

"Why do we do it?" he asked no one in particular. "Why do we keep going, and going, and going? Why don't we just lie down and die? That would be the easiest thing I could think of right now." He knew that Rocket Service officers didn't talk that way, but he didn't feel like an officer, just a tired, feverish, bone-weary man.

"Have we got a great glowing tradition to inspire us?" he snarled. "No, we're just the lousy Rocketeers that every other service arm plans to absorb. We haven't a Grant or a John Paul Jones to provide an example in a tough spot. The U.S. Rocket Service has nothing but the memory of some ships that went out and never came back; and you can't make a legend out of men who just plain vanish."

There was silence, and it looked as if the muddy figures were too exhausted to reply. Then Sergeant Brian spoke.

"The Rocketeers have a legend, sir."

"What legend, Brian?" Hague snorted.

"Here is the legend, sir. 'George Easy Peter One.'"

Hague laughed hollowly, but the Sergeant continued as if he hadn't heard.

"Ground Expeditionary Patrol One—the outfit a planet couldn't lick. Venus threw her grab bag at us, animals, swamps, poison plants, starvation, fever, and we kept right on coming. She just made us smarter, and tougher, and harder to beat. And we'll blast through these lizard-men and the jungle, and march into Base like the whole U.S. Armed Forces on review."

"Let's go," Hague called, and they staggered up again, ten gaunt bundles of sodden, muddy rags, capped in trim black steel helmets with cheek guards down. The others slipped off the trail, and Hague, Brian, and Crosse pulled on the cart harness and lurched forward. The cart wheel-hub jammed against a tree bole, and as they strained blindly ahead to free it, a horn note drifted from afar.

"Here they come again," Crosse groaned.

"They—won't be—up—with us—for days." Hague grunted, while he threw his weight in jerks against the tow line. The cart lurched free with a lunge, and all three shot forward and sprawled raging in the muddy trail.

They sat wiping mud from their faces, when Brian stopped suddenly, ripped off his helmet and threw it aside, then sat tensely forward in an attitude of strained listening. Hague had time to wonder dully if the man's brain had snapped, before he crawled to his feet.

"Shut up, and listen," Brian was snarling. "Hear it! Hear it! It's a klaxon! Way off, about every two seconds!"

Hague tugged off his heavy helmet, and strained every nerve to listen. Over the forest silence it came with pulse-like regularity, a tiny whisper of sound.

He and Brian stared bright-eyed at each other, not quite daring to say what they were thinking. Crosse got up and leaned like an empty sack against the cartwheel with an inane questioning look.

"What is it?" They stared at him without speaking, still listening intently. "It's the Base. That's it, it's the Base!"

Something choked Hague's throat, then he was yelling and firing his rifle. The rest came scuttling out of the forest shadow, faces breaking into wild grins, and they joined Hague, the forest rocking with gunfire. They moved forward, and Hirooka took up a thin chant:

> Ooooooh, the Rocketeers
> have shaggy ears.
> They're dirty—

The rest of their lyrics wouldn't look well in print; but where the Rocketeers have gone, on every frontier of space, the ribald song is sung. The little file moved down the trail toward the klaxon sound. Behind them, something moved in the gloom, resolved itself into a reptile-headed, man-like thing that reared a small wood trumpet to fit its mouth; a soft horn note floated clear; and other shapes became visible, sprinting forward, flitting through the gloom . . .

When a red light flashed over Chapman's desk, he flung down a sheaf of papers and hurried down steel-walled corridors to the number one shaft. A tiny elevator swept him to Odysseus' upper side, where a shallow pit had been set in the ship's scarred skin, and a pneumatic gun installed. Chapman hurried past the gun and crew to stand beside a listening device. The four huge cones loomed dark against the clouds, the operator in their center was a blob of shadow in the dawn-light, where he huddled listening to a chanting murmur that came from his headset. Blake came running onto the gundeck; Bjornson and the staff officers were all there.

"Cut it into the Address system," Chapman told the Listener operator excitedly; and the faint sounds were amplified through the whole ship. From humming Address amplifiers, the ribald words broke in a hoarse melody.

> The Rocketeers have shaggy ears,
> They're dirty—

The rest described in vivid detail the prowess of rocketeers in general.

"How far are they?" Chapman demanded.

The operator pointed at a dial, fingered a knob that altered his receiving cones split-seconds of angle. "They're about twenty-five miles, sir."

Chapman turned to the officers gathered in an exultant circle behind him.

"Branch, here's your chance for action. Take thirty men, our whippet tank, and go out to them. Bjornson, get the 'copters aloft for air cover."

Twenty minutes later, Chapman watched a column assemble beneath the Odysseus' gleaming side and march into the jungle, with the 'copters buzzing west a moment later, like vindictive dragon flies.

Breakfast was brought to the men clustered at Warnings equipment, and to Chapman at his post on the gundeck. The day

34

ticked away, the parade ground vanished in thickening clots of night; and a second dawn found the watchers still at their posts, listening to queer sounds that trickled from the speakers. The singing had stopped; but once they heard a note that a horn might make, and several times gobbling yells that didn't sound human. George One was fighting, they knew now. The listeners picked up crackling of rifle fire, and when that died there was silence.

The watchers heard a short cheer that died suddenly, as the relief column and George One met; and they waited and watched. Branch, who headed the relief column, communicated with the mother ship by the simple expedient of yelling, the sound being picked up by the listeners.

"They're coming in, Chapman. I'm coming behind to guard their rear. They've been attacked by some kind of lizard-men. I'm not saying a thing—see for yourself when they arrive."

Hours rolled past, while they speculated in low tones, the hush that held the ship growing taut and strained.

"Surely Branch would have told us if anything was wrong, or if the records were lost," Chapman barked angrily. "Why did he have to be so damned melodramatic?"

"Look, there—through the trees. A helmet glinted!" The laconic Bjornson had thrown dignity to the winds, and capered like a drunken goat, as Rindell described it later.

Chapman stared down at the jungle edging the parade ground and caught a movement.

A man with a rifle came through the fringe and stood eyeing the ship in silence, and then came walking forward across the long, cindered expanse. From this height, he looked to Chapman like a child's lead soldier, a ragged, muddy, midget scarecrow. Another stir in the trees, and one more man, skulking like an infantry flanker with rifle at ready. He, too, straightened and came walking quietly forward. A file of three men came next, leaning into the harness of a little metal cart that bumped drunkenly as they dragged it forward. An instant of waiting, and two more men stole from the jungle, more like attacking infantry than returning heroes. Chapman waited, and no more came. This was all.

"My God, no wonder Branch wouldn't tell us. There were thirty-two of them." Rindell's voice was choked.

"Yes, only seven." Chapman remembered his field glasses and focused them on the seven approaching men. "Lieutenant Hague is the only officer. And they're handing us the future of the U.S. Rocket Service on that little metal cart."

The quiet shattered and a yelling horde of men poured from Odysseus' hull and engulfed the tattered seven, sweeping around them, yelling, cheering, and carrying them toward the mother ship.

Chapman looked a little awed as he turned to the officers behind him. "Well, they did it. We forward these records, and we've proven that we can do the job." He broke into a grin. "What am I talking about? Of course we did the job. We'll always do the job. We're the Rocketeers, aren't we?"

HIS TRUTH
GOES MARCHING ON

Jerry Pournelle

"As He died to make men holy, let us die to make them free. . . ."

The song echoed through the ship, along gray corridors stained with the greasy handprints of the thousands who had traveled in her before; through the stench of the thousands aboard, and the remembered smells of previous shiploads of convicts. Those smells were etched into the steel despite strong disinfectants which had only added their acrimony to the odor of too much humanity with too little water.

The male voices carried past crew work parties, who ignored them, or made sarcastic remarks, and into a tiny stateroom no larger than the bunk bed now hoisted vertical to the bulkhead to make room for a desk and chair.

Peter Owensford looked up to blank gray and beyond it to visions within his own mind. The men weren't singing very well, but they sang from their hearts. There was a faint buzzing discord from a loose rivet vibrating to a strong base. Owensford nodded to himself. The singer was Allan Roach, one-time professional wrestler, and Peter had marked him for promotion to noncom once they reached Santiago.

The trip from Earth to Thurstone takes three months in a Bureau of Relocation transport ship, and it had been wasted time for all of them. It was obvious to Peter that the CoDominium authorities aboard the ship knew that they were volunteers for the war. Why else would ninety-seven men voluntarily ship out for Santiago? It didn't matter, though. Political Officer Stromand was afraid of a trap. Stromand was always suspecting traps, and was desperate to "maintain secrecy"; as if there were any secrets to keep.

In all the three months Peter Owensford had held only a dozen classes. He'd found an empty compartment near the garbage disposal and assembled the men there; but Stromand had caught them. There had been a scene, with Stromand insisting that Peter call him "Commissar" and the men address him as "Sir." Instead, Peter addressed him as "Mister" and the men made it come out like "Comics-star." Stromand had become speechless with anger; but he'd stopped the meetings.

And Peter had ninety-six men who knew nothing of war; most had never fired a weapon in their lives. They were educated men, intelligent for the most part, students, workers, idealists; but it might have been better if they'd been ninety-six freakouts with a long history of juvenile gangsterism.

He went back to his papers, jotting notes on what must be done when they reached dirtside. At least he'd have some time to train them before they got into combat.

He'd need it.

Thurstone is usually described as a hot, dry copy of Earth and Peter found no reason to dispute that. The CoDominium Island is legally part of Earth, but Thurstone is thirty parsecs away, and travelers go through customs to land. The ragged group packed away whatever military equipment they had bought privately, and dressed in the knee breeches and tunics popular with businessmen in New York. Peter found himself just behind Allan Roach in the line to debark.

Roach was laughing.

"What's the joke?" Peter asked.

Roach turned and waved expressively at the men behind him. All ninety-six were scattered through the first two hundred passengers leaving the BuRelock ship, and they were all dressed identically. "Humanity League decided to save some money," Roach said. "What you reckon the CD makes of our comic-opera army?"

Whatever the CoDominium inspectors thought, they did nothing, hardly glancing inside the baggage, and the volunteers were hustled out of the CD building to the docks. A small Russian in baggy pants sidled up to them.

"Freedom," he said. He had a thick accent.

"No passaran!" Commissar Stromand answered.

"I have tickets for you," the Russian said. "You will go on the boat." He pointed to an excursion ship with peeling paint and faded gilt handrails.

"Man, he looks like he's lettin' go his last credit," Allan Roach muttered to Owensford.

Peter nodded. "At that, I'd rather pay for the tickets than ride the boat. Must have been built when Thurstone was first settled."

Roach shrugged and lifted his bags. Then, as an afterthought, he lifted Peter's as well.

"You don't have to carry my goddam baggage," Peter protested.

"That's why I'm doing it, Lieutenant. I wouldn't carry Stromand's." They went aboard the boat, and lined the rails, looking out at Thurstone's bright skies. The volunteers were the only passengers, and the ship left the docks to lumber across shallow seas. It was less than fifty kilometers to the mainland, and before the men really believed they were out of space and onto a planet again, they were in Free Santiago.

They marched through the streets from the docks. People cheered, but a lot of volunteers had come through those streets and they didn't cheer very loud. Owensford's men were no good at marching, and they had no weapons; so Stromand ordered them to sing war songs.

They didn't know very many songs, so they always ended up singing the Battle Hymn of the Republic. It said all their feelings, anyway.

The ragged group straggled to the local parish church. Someone had broken the cross and spire off the building, and turned the altar into a lecture desk. It was becoming dark when Owensford's troops were bedded down in the pews.

"Lieutenant?"

Peter looked up from the dark reverie that had overtaken him. Allan Roach and another volunteer stood in front of him. "Yes?"

"Some of the men don't like bein' in here, Lieutenant. We got church members in the outfit."

"I see. What do you expect me to do about it?" Peter asked. "This is where we were sent." And why didn't someone meet us instead of having a kid hand me a note down at the docks? he wondered. But it wouldn't do to upset the men.

"We could bed down outside," Roach suggested.

"Nonsense. Superstitious garbage." The strident, bookish voice came from behind him, but Peter didn't need to look around to

39

know who was speaking. "Free men have no need of that kind of belief. Tell me who is disturbed."

Allan Roach set his lips tightly together.

"I insist," Stromand demanded. "Those men need education, and I will provide it. We cannot have superstition within our company."

"Superstition be damned," Peter protested. "It's dark and gloomy and uncomfortable in here, and if the men want to sleep outside, let them."

"No," Stromand said.

"I remind you that I am in command here," Peter said. His voice was rising slightly and he fought to control it. He was only twenty-three standard years old, while Stromand was forty; and Peter had no experience of command. Yet he knew that this was an important issue, and the men were all listening.

"I remind *you* that political education is totally up to me," Stromand said. "It is good indoctrination for the men to stay in here."

"Crap." Peter stood abruptly. "All right, everybody outside. Camp in the churchyard. Roach, set up a night guard around the camp."

"Yes, sir," Allan Roach grinned.

Commissar Stromand found his men melting away rapidly; after a few minutes he followed them outside.

They were awakened early by an officer in synthileather trousers and tunic. He wore no badges of rank, but it was obvious to Peter that the man was a professional soldier. Someday, Peter thought, someday I'll look like that. The thought was cheering for some reason.

"Who's in charge here?" the man demanded.

Stromand and Owensford answered simultaneously. The officer looked at both for a moment, then turned to Peter. "Name?"

"Lieutenant Peter Avensford."

"Lieutenant. And why might you be a lieutenant?"

"I'm a graduate of West Point, sir. And your rank?"

"Captain, sonny. Captain Anselm Barton, at your service, God help you. The lot of you have been posted to the Twelfth Brigade, second battalion, of which battalion I have the misfortune to be adjutant. Any more questions?" He glared at both Peter and the commissar, but before either could answer there was a roar and the wind whipped them with red dust; a fleet of trucks rounded the corner and stopped in front of the church.

"Okay," Barton shouted. "Into the trucks. You too, Mister Comics-Star. Lieutenant, you will ride in the cab with me . . .

come on, come on, we haven't all day. Can't you get them to hop it, Owensford?"

No two of the trucks were alike. One Cadillac stood out proudly from the lesser breeds, and Barton went to it. After a moment Stromand took the unoccupied seat in the cab of the second truck, an old Fiat. Despite the early hour, the sun was hot and bright, and it was good to get inside.

The Cadillac ran smoothly, but had to halt frequently while the drivers worked on the others of the convoy. The Fiat could only get two or three centimeters above the road. Peter noted in wonder that there were ruts in the dirt track, and remarked on them.

"Sure," Barton said. "We've got wheeled transport. Lots of it. Animal-drawn wagons too. Tracked railroads. How much do you know about this place?"

"Not very much," Peter admitted.

"Least you know that," Barton said. He gunned the engine to get the Cadillac over a deeply pitted section of the road, and the convoy climbed up onto a ridge. Peter could look back and see the tiny port town, with its almost empty streets, and the blowing red dust.

"See that ridge over there?" Barton asked. He pointed to a thin blue line beyond the far lip of the saucer on the other side of the ridge. The air was so clear that Peter could see for sixty kilometers or more, and he had never seen farther than twenty; it was hard to judge distances.

"Yes, sir."

"That's it. Dons' territory beyond that line."

"We're not going straight there, are we? The men need training."

"You might as well be going to the lines for all the training they'll get. They teach you anything at the Point?"

"I learned something, I think." Peter didn't know what to answer. The Point had been "humanized" and he knew he hadn't had the military instruction that graduates had once received. "What I was taught, and a lot from books."

"We'll see." Barton took a plastic toothpick out of one pocket and stuck it into his mouth. Later, Peter would learn that many men developed that habit. "No hay tobacco" was a common notice on stores in Santiago. The first time he saw it, Allan Roach said that if they made their tobacco out of hay he didn't want any. "Long out of the Point?" Barton asked.

"Class of '93."

"Just out. U. S. Army didn't want you?"

"That's pretty personal," Peter said. The toothpick danced

41

across smiling lips. Peter stared out at the rivers of dust blowing around them. "There's a new rule, now. You have to opt for CoDominium in your junior year. I did. But they didn't have any room for me in the CD services."

Barton grunted. "And the U. S. Army doesn't want any commie-coddling officers who'd take the CD over their own country."

"That's about it."

"Hadn't thought it was that bad yet. Sounds like things are coming apart back home."

Peter nodded to himself. "I think the U.S. will pull out of the CoDominium pretty soon."

The toothpick stopped its movement while Barton thought about that. "So meanwhile they're doing their best to gut the Fleet, eh? What do the damned fools think will happen to the colonies when there's no CD forces to keep order?"

Peter shrugged. They drove on in silence, with Barton humming something under his breath, a tune that Peter thought he would recognize if only Barton would make it loud enough to hear. Then he caught a murmured refrain. "Let's hope he brings our godson up, to don the Armay blue . . ."

Barton looked around at his passenger and grinned. "How many lights in Cullem Hall, Mister Dumbjohn?"

"Three hundred and forty lights, sir," Peter answered automatically. He looked for the ring, but Barton wore none. "What was your class, sir?"

"Seventy-two. Okay, the U.S. didn't want you, and the CD's disbanding regiments. There's other outfits. Falkenberg's recruiting . . ."

"I'm not a mercenary for hire." Peter's voice was stiffly formal.

"Oh, Lord. So you're here to help the downtrodden masses throw off the yoke of oppression. I might have known."

"But of course I'm here to fight slavery!" Peter protested. "Everyone knows about Santiago."

"Everybody knows about other places, too." The toothpick danced again. "Okay, you're a liberator of suffering humanity if that makes you feel better. God knows, anything makes a man feel better out here is okay. But to help *me* feel better, remember that you're a professional officer."

"I won't forget." They drove over another ridge. The valley beyond was no different from the one behind them, and there was another ridge at its end.

"What do you think those people out there want?" Barton said. He waved expressively.

"Freedom."

"Maybe to be left alone. Maybe they'd be happy if the lot of us went away."

"They'd be slaves. Somebody's got to help them—" Peter caught himself. There was no point to this, and he thought Barton was laughing at him.

Instead, the older man wore a curious expression. He kept the sardonic grin, but it was softened almost into a smile. "Nothing to be ashamed of, Pete. Most of us read those books about knighthood and all that. We wouldn't be in the services if we didn't have that streak in us. Just remember this, if you don't get over most of that, you won't last."

"Without something like that, I wouldn't want to last."

"Just don't let it break your heart when you find out different."

What is he talking about? Peter wondered. "If you feel that way about everything, why are you here? Why aren't you in one of the mercenary outfits?"

"Commissars ask that kind of question," Barton said. He gunned the motor viciously and the Cadillac screamed in protest.

It was late afternoon when they got to Tarazona. The town was an architectural melange, as if a dozen amateurs had designed it. The church, now a hospital, was Elizabeth III modern, the post office was American Gothic, and most of the houses were white stucco. The volunteers were unloaded at a plastisteel barracks that looked like a bad copy of the quad at West Point. It had sally ports, phony portcullis and all, and there were plastic medieval shields pressed into the cornices.

Inside there was trash in the corridors and blood on the floors. Peter set the men to cleaning up.

"About that blood," Captain Barton said. "Your men seem interested."

"First blood some of 'em have seen," Peter told him. Barton was still watching him closely. "All right. For me too."

Barton nodded. "Two stories about that blood. The Dons had a garrison here, made a stand when the Revolutionaries took the town. Some say the Dons slaughtered their prisoners here. Others say when the Republic took the barracks, our troops slaughtered the garrison."

Peter looked across the dusty courtyard and beyond to the hills where the fighting was. It seemed a long way off. There was no sound, and the afternoon sun seemed unbearably hot. "Which do you think is true?"

"Both." Barton turned away toward the town. Then he stopped for a moment. "I'll be in the bistro after dinner. Join me if you get

43

a chance." He walked on, his feet kicking up little clods of dust that blew across the road.

Peter stood a long time in the courtyard, staring across fields stretching fifty kilometers to the hills. The soil was red, and a hot wind blew dust into every crevice and hollow. The country seemed far too barren to be a focal point of the struggle for freedom in the known galaxy.

Thurstone was colonized early in the CoDominium period but it was too poor to attract wealthy corporations. The third Thurstone expedition was financed by the Carlist branch of the Spanish monarchy, and eventually Carlos XII brought a group of supporters to found Santiago. They were all of them malcontents.

This was hardly unusual. All of space is colonized with malcontents or convicts; no one else wants to leave Earth. The Santiago colonists were protesting the Bourbon restoration in Spain, or John XXVI's reunification of Christendom, or the cruel fates, or, perhaps, unhappy love affairs. They got the smallest and poorest of Thurstone's three continents, but they did well with what little they received.

For thirty years Santiago received no one who was not a voluntary immigrant from Spanish Catholic cultures. The Carlists were careful of those they let in, and there was plenty of good land for everyone. The Kingdom of St. James had little modern technology, and no one was very rich, but there were few who were very poor either.

Eventually the Population Control Commission designated Thurstone as a recipient planet, and the Bureau of Relocation began moving people there. All three governments on Thurstone protested, but unlike Xanadu or Danube, Thurstone had never developed a navy; a single frigate from the CoDominium Fleet convinced them they had no choice.

Two million involuntary colonists came in BuRelock ships to Thurstone. Convicts, welfare frauds, criminals, revolutionaries, rioters, street gangsters, men who'd offended a BuRelock clerk, men with the wrong color eyes, and those who were just plain unlucky: all of them bundled into unsanitary transport ships and hustled away from Earth. The other nations on Thurstone had friends in BuRelock and money to pay for favors; Santiago got the bulk of the new immigrants.

The Carlists tried. They provided transportation to unclaimed lands for all who wanted it and most who did not. The original Santiago settlers had fled from industry and had built very little; and now, suddenly, they were swamped with citydwellers of a different culture who had no thought of the land and less love for it. Suddenly, they had large cities.

In less than a decade the capital grew from a sleepy town to a sprawling heap of tenement shacks. The Carlists abolished part of the city; the shacks appeared on the other side of town. New cities grew from small towns. There was a desperate need for industry.

When the industries were built, the original settlers revolted. They had fled from industrialized life, and wanted no more of it. A king was deposed and an infant prince placed on his father's throne. Then Cortez took government into its own hands. They enslaved everyone who did not pay his own way.

It was not called slavery, but "indebtedness for welfare services"; but debts were inheritable and transferable. Debts could be bought and sold on speculation, and everyone had to work off his debts.

In a generation half the population was in debt. In another the slaves outnumbered the free men. Finally the slaves revolted, and Santiago became a cause overnight: at least to those who'd ever heard of the place.

In the CoDominium Grand Senate, the U.S., listening to the other governments on Thurstone and the corporations who bought agricultural products from Santiago, supported the Carlists, but not strongly. The Soviet senators supported the Republic, but not strongly. The CD Navy was ordered to quarantine the war area.

The fleet had few ships for such a task. The Navy grounded all military aircraft in Santiago, and prohibited importation of any kind of heavy weapon. Otherwise they left the place alone to undergo years of indecisive warfare.

It was never difficult for the Humanity League to send volunteers to Santiago as long as they brought no weapons. As the men were not experienced in war, the League also sought trained officers to send with them.

They rejected mercenaries, of course. Volunteers must have the proper spirit to fight for freedom in Santiago.

Peter Owensford sat in the pleasant cool of the evening at a scarred table that might have been oak, but wasn't. Captain Anselm "Ace" Barton sat across from him, and a pitcher of dark red wine stood on the table.

"I thought they'd put me in the technical corps," Peter said.

"Speak Mandarin?" When Peter looked up in surprise, Barton continued, "Republic hired Xanadu techs. They don't have much equipment, what with the quarantine. Plenty of techs for what they do have."

45

"I see. So I'm infantry?"

Barton shrugged. "You fight, Pete. Just like me. They'll give you a company. The ones you brought, and maybe another hundred recruits. All yours. I guess you'll get that Stromand for political officer, too."

Peter grimaced. "What use is that?"

Barton looked around in an exaggerated manner. "Careful," he said. He wore a grin but his voice was serious. "Political officers are a lot more popular with the high command than we are. Don't forget that."

"From what I've seen the high command isn't very competent. . . ."

"Jesus," Barton said. "Look, Pete, they can have you shot for talking like that. This isn't any mercenary outfit with its own codes, you know. This is a patriotic war, and you'd better not forget it."

Peter stared at the packed clay floor of the patio, his lips set in a tight, thin line. He'd sat in this bistro, at this table, every night for a week now, and he was beginning to understand Barton's cynicism; but why was the man here at all? "There's not enough body armor for my men. The ones I've got. You say they'll give me more?"

"New group coming in tomorrow. No officer with them. Sure, they'll put 'em in with you. Where else? Troops have to be trained."

"Trained!" Peter snorted in disgust. "We have enough Nemourlon to make armor for about half the troops, only I'm the only one in the company who knows how to do it. We've got no weapons, no optics, no communications—"

"Yeah, things are tough all over." Barton poured another glass of wine. "What'd you expect in a nonindustrial society quarantined by the CD?"

Peter slumped back into the hard wooden chair. "Yeah, I know. But—I can't even train them with what I have. Whenever I get the men assembled, Stromand interrupts to make speeches."

Barton smiled. "Colonel Cermak, our esteemed International Brigade Commander, thinks the American troops have poor morale. Obviously, the way to deal with that is to make speeches."

"They've got poor morale because they don't know how to fight."

"Another of Cermak's solutions to poor morale is to shoot people for defeatism," Barton said softly. "I've warned you, kid. I won't again."

"The only damn thing my men have learned in the last week is how to sing and which red-light houses are safe."

"More'n some do. Have another drink."

Peter nodded in dejection. "That's not bad wine."

"Right. Pretty good, but not good enough to export," Barton said. "Whole goddam country's that way, you know. Pretty good, but not quite good enough."

The next day they gave Peter Owensford 107 new men fresh from the U.S. and Earth. There was talk of adding another political officer to the company, but there wasn't one Cermak trusted.

Each night Ace Barton sat at the table in the bistro, but he didn't see Owensford all week. Then, as he was having his third glass of wine, Peter came in and sat across from him. The proprietor brought a glass, and Barton poured from the pitcher. "You look like you need that. Thought you were ordered to stay on, nights, to train the troops."

Peter drank. "Same story, Ace. Speeches. More speeches. I walked out. It was obvious I wasn't going to have anything to do."

"Risky," Barton said. They sat in silence as the older man seemed to decide something. "Ever think you're not needed, Pete?"

"They act that way, but I'm still the only man with any military training at all in the company. . . ."

"So what? The Republic doesn't need your troops. Not the way you think, anyway. Main purpose of the volunteers is to see the right party stays in control here."

Peter sat stiffly silent. He'd promised himself that he wouldn't react quickly to anything Barton said. There was no one else Peter felt comfortable with, despite the cynicism that Peter detested. "I can't believe that," he said finally. "The volunteers come from everywhere. They're not fighting to help any political party, they're here to set people free."

Barton said nothing. A red toothpick danced across his face, twirling up and about, and a sly grin broke across the square features.

"See, you don't even believe it yourself," Peter said.

"Could be. Pete, you ever think how much money they raise back in the States? Money from people who feel guilty about not volunteerin'?"

"No. There's no money here. You've seen that."

"There's money, but it goes to the techs," Barton said. "That, at least, makes sense. Xanadu isn't sending their sharp boys for

47

nothing, and without them, what's the use of mudcrawlers like us?"

Peter leaned back in his chair. It made sense. "Then we've got pretty good technical support . . ."

"About as good as the Dons have. Which means neither side has a goddam thing. Either group gets a real edge that way, the war's over, right? But for the moment nobody's got a way past the CD quarantine, so the best way the Dons and the Republicans have to kill each other is with rifles and knives and grenades. Not very damn many of the latter, either."

"We don't even have the rifles."

"You'll get those. Meantime, relax. You've told Brigade your men aren't ready to fight. You've asked for weapons and more Nemourlon. You've complained about Stromand. You've done it all, now shut up before you get yourself shot as a defeatist. That's an order, Pete."

"Yes, sir."

"You'll get your war soon enough."

The trucks came back to Tarazona a week later. They carried coffin-shaped boxes full of rifles and bayonets from New Aberdeen, Thurstone's largest city. The rifles were covered with grease, and there wasn't any solvent to clean them with. Most were copies of Remington 2045 model automatic, but there were some Krupps and Skodas. Most of the men didn't know which ammunition fit their rifles.

"Not bad gear," Barton remarked. He turned one of the rifles over and over in his hands. "We've had worse."

"But I don't have much training in rifle tactics," Peter said.

Barton shrugged. "No power supplies, no maintenance ships, no base to support anything more complicated than chemical slug-throwers, Pete. Forget the rest of the crap you learned and remember that."

"Yes, sir."

Whistles blew, and someone shouted from the trucks. "Get your gear and get aboard!"

"But—" Owensford turned helplessly to Barton. "Get aboard for where?"

Barton shrugged. "I'd better get back to my area. Maybe they're moving the whole battalion up while we've got the trucks."

They were. The men who had armor put it on, and everyone dressed in combat synthileather. Most had helmets, ugly hemispheric models with a stiff spine over the most vulnerable areas.

A few men had lost theirs, and they boarded the trucks without them.

The convoy rolled across the plains and into a greener farm area; then it got dark, and the night air chilled fast under clear, cloudless skies. The drivers pushed on, too fast without lights, and Peter sat in the back of the lead truck, his knees clamped tightly together, his teeth unconsciously beating out a rhythm he'd learned years before. No one talked.

At dawn they were in another valley. Trampled crops lay all around them, drying dead plants with green stalks.

"Good land," Private Lunster said. He lifted a clod and crumbled it between his fingers. "Very good land."

Somehow that made Peter feel better. He formed the men into ranks and made sure each knew how to load his weapon. Then he had each fire at a crumbling adobe wall, choosing a large target so that they wouldn't fail to hit it. More trucks pulled in and unloaded heavy generators and antitank lasers. When Owensford's men tried to get close to the heavy weapons the gunners shouted them away. It seemed to Peter that the gunners were familiar with their gear, and that was encouraging.

Everyone spoke softly, and when anyone raised his voice it was like a shout. Stromand tried to get the men to sing, but they wouldn't.

"Not long now, eh?" Sergeant Roach asked.

"I expect you're right," Peter told him, but he didn't know, and went off to find the commissary truck. He wanted to be sure the men got a good meal that evening.

They moved them up during the night. A guide came to Peter and whispered to follow him, and they moved out across the unfamiliar land. Somewhere out there were the Dons with their army of peasant conscripts and mercenaries and family retainers. When they had gone fifty meters, they passed an old tree and someone whispered to them.

"Everything will be fine," Stromand's voice said from the shadows under the tree. "All of the enemy are politically immature. Their vacqueros will run away, and their peasant conscripts will throw away their weapons. They have no reason to be loyal."

"Why the hell has the war gone on three years?" someone whispered behind Peter.

He waited until they were long past the tree. "Roach, that wasn't smart. Stromand will have you shot for defeatism."

"He'll play hell doing it, Lieutenant. You, man, pick up your feet. Want to fall down that gully?"

"Quiet," the guide whispered urgently. They went on through the dark night, down a slope, then up another, past men dug into the hillside. They didn't speak to them.

Peter found himself walking along the remains of a railroad, with the ties partly gone and all the rails removed. Eventually the guide halted. "Dig in here," he whispered. "Long live freedom."

"No passaran!" Stromand answered.

"Please be quiet," the guide urged. "We are within earshot of the enemy."

"Ah," Stromand answered. The guide turned away and the political officer began to follow him.

"Where are you going?" Corporal Grant asked in a loud whisper.

"To report to Major Harris," Stromand answered. "The battalion commander ought to know where we are."

"So should we," a voice said.

"Who was that?" Stromand demanded. The only answer was a juicy raspberry.

"That bastard's got no right," a voice said close to Peter.

"Who's there?"

"Rotwasser, sir." Rotwasser was company runner. The job gave him the nominal rank of monitor but he had no maniple to command. Instead he carried complaints from the men to Owensford.

"I can spare the PO better than anyone else," Peter whispered. "I'll need you here, not back at battalion. Now start digging us in."

It was cold on the hillside, but digging kept the men warm enough. Dawn came slowly at first, a gradually brightening light without warmth. Peter took out his light-amplifying binoculars and cautiously looked out ahead. The binoculars were a present from his mother and the only good optical equipment in the company.

The countryside was cut into small, steep-sided ridges and valleys. Allan Roach lay beside Owensford and when it became light enough to see, the sergeant whistled softly. "We take that ridge in front of us, there's another just like it after that. And another. Nobody's goin' to win this war that way. . . ."

Owensford nodded silently. There were trees in the valley below, oranges and dates imported from Earth mixed in with native fruit trees as if a giant had spilled seeds across the ground. A whitewashed adobe peasant house stood gutted by fire, the roof gone.

Zing! Something that might have been a hornet but wasn't

50

buzzed angrily over Peter's head. There was a flat crack from across the valley, then more of the angry buzzes. Dust puffs sprouted from the earthworks they'd thrown up during the night.

"Down!" Peter ordered.

"What are they trying to do, kill us?" Allan Roach shouted. There was a chorus of laughs. "Sir, why didn't they use IR on us in the dark? We should have stood out in this cold—"

Peter shrugged. "Maybe they don't have any. We don't."

The men who'd skimped on their holes dug in deeper, throwing the dirt out onto the ramparts in front of them, laughing as they did. It was very poor technique, and Peter worried about artillery, but nothing happened. The enemy was about four hundred meters away, across the valley and stretched out along a ridge identical to the one Peter held. No infantry that ever lived could have taken a position by charging across that valley. Both sides were safe until something heavier was brought up.

One large-caliber gun was trained on their position. It fired on anything that moved. There was also a laser, with several mirrors that could be moved about between flashes. The laser itself was safe, and the mirrors probably were also because the monarchists never fired twice from the same position.

The men shot at the guns and at where they thought the mirror was anyway until Peter made them quit wasting ammunition. It wasn't good for morale to lie there and not fight back, though.

"I bet I can locate that goddam gun," Corporal Bassinger told Peter. "I got the best eyesight in the company."

Peter mentally called up Bassinger's records. Two ex-wives and an acknowledged child by each. Volunteered after being an insurance man in Brooklyn for years. "You can't spot that thing."

"Sure I can, Lieutenant. Loan me your glasses, I'll spot it sure."

"All right. Be careful, they're shooting at anything they can see."

"I'm careful."

"Let me see, man!" somebody shouted. Three men clustered in the trench around Bassinger. "Let us look!" "Don't be a hog, we want to see too." "Comrade, let us look—"

"Get away from here," Bassinger shouted. "You heard the lieutenant, it's dangerous to look over the ramparts."

"What about you?"

"I'm an observer. Besides, I'm careful." He crawled into position and looked out through a little slot he'd cut away in the dirt in front of him. "See, it's safe enough. I think I see—"

Bassinger was thrown back into the trench. The shattered

51

glasses fell on top of him, and he had already ceased breathing when they heard the shot that hit him in the eye.

By the next morning two men had toes shot off and had to be evacuated.

They lay on the hill for a week. Each night they lost a few more men to minor casualties that could not possibly have been inflicted by the enemy; then Stromand had two men with foot injuries shot by a squad of military police he brought up from staff headquarters.

The injuries ceased, and the men lay sullenly in the trenches until the company was relieved.

They had two days in a small town near the front, then the officers were called to a meeting. The briefing officer had a thick accent, but it was German, not Spanish. The briefing was for the Americans and it was held in English.

"Ve vill have a full assault, with all International volunteers to move out at once. Ve will use infiltration tactics."

"What does that mean?" Captain Barton demanded.

The staff officer looked pained. "Ven you break through their lines, go straight to their technical areas and disrupt them. Ven that is done, the var is over."

"Where are their technical corpsmen?"

"You vill be told after you have broken through their lines."

The rest of the briefing made no more sense to Peter. He walked out with Barton after they were dismissed. "Looked at your section of the line?" Barton asked.

"As much as I can," Peter answered. "Do you have a decent map?"

"No. Old CD orbital photographs, and some sketches. No better than what you have."

"What I did see looks bad," Peter said. "There's an olive grove, then a hollow I can't see into. Is there cover in there?"

"You better patrol and find out."

"You will ask the battalion commander for permission to conduct patrols," a stern voice said from behind them.

"You better watch that habit of walking up on people, Stromand," Barton said. "One of these days somebody's not going to realize it's you." He gave Peter a pained look. "Better ask."

Major Harris told Peter that Brigade had forbidden patrols. They might alert the enemy to the coming attack and surprise was needed.

As he walked back to his company area, Peter reflected that

Harris had been an attorney for the Liberation Party before he volunteered to go to Santiago. They were to move out the next morning.

The night was long. The men were very quiet, polishing weapons and talking in whispers, drawing meaningless diagrams in the mud of the dugouts. About halfway through the night forty new volunteers joined the company. They had no equipment beyond rifles, and they had left the port city only two days before. Most came from Churchill, but because they spoke English and the trucks were coming to this sector, they had been sent along.

Major Harris called the officers together at dawn. "The Xanadu techs have managed to assemble some rockets," he told them. "They'll drop them on the Dons before we move out. Owensford, you will move out last. You will shoot any man who hasn't gone before you do."

"That's my job," Stromand protested.

"You will be needed to lead the men," Harris said. "The bombardment will come at 0815 hours. Do you all have proper timepieces?"

"No, sir," Peter said. "I've only got a watch that counts Earth time. . . ."

"Hell," Harris muttered. "Okay, Thurstone's hours are 1.08 Earth hours long. You'll have to work it out from that. . . ." He looked confused.

"No problem," Peter assured him.

"Okay. Back to your areas."

Zero hour went past with no signals. Another hour passed. Then a Republican brigade to the north began firing, and a few moved out of their dugouts and across the valley floor.

A ripple of fire and flashing mirrors colored the ridge beyond as the enemy began firing. The Republican troops were cut down, and the few not hit scurried back into their shelters.

"Fire support!" Harris shouted. Owensford's squawk box made unintelligible sounds, effectively jammed as were all electronics Peter had seen on Santiago, but he heard the order passed down the line. His company fired at the enemy, and the monarchists returned it.

Within minutes it was clear that the enemy had total dominance in the area. A few large rockets rose from somewhere behind the enemy lines and crashed randomly into the Republican positions. There were more flashes across the sky as the Xanadu technicians backtracked the enemy rockets and returned counterfire. Eventually the shooting stopped for lack of targets.

It was 1100 by Peter's watch when a series of explosions lit the

53

lip of the monarchist ramparts. Another wave of rockets fell among the enemy, and the Republicans to the north began to charge forward.

"Ready to move out!" Peter shouted. He waited for orders.

There was nearly a minute of silence. No more rockets fell on the enemy. Then the ridge opposite rippled with fire again, and the Republicans began to go down or scramble back to their positions.

The alert tone sounded on Peter's squawk box and he lifted it to his ear. Amazingly, he could hear intelligible speech. Someone at headquarters was speaking to Major Harris.

"The Republicans have already advanced half a kilometer. They are being slaughtered because you have not moved your precious Americans in support."

"Bullshit!" Harris's voice had no tones in the tiny speaker. "The Republicans are already back in their dugouts. The attack has failed."

"It has not failed. You must show what high morale can do. Your men are all volunteers. Many Republicans are conscripts. Set an example for them."

"But I tell you the attack has failed."

"Major Harris, if your men have not moved out in five minutes I will send the military police to arrest you as a traitor."

The box went back to random squeals and growls; then the whistles blew and orders were passed down the line. "Move out."

Peter went from dugout to dugout. "Up and at them. Jarvis, if you don't get out of there I'll shoot you. You three, get going." He saw that Allan Roach was doing the same thing.

When they reached the end of the line, Roach grinned at Peter. "We're all that's left, now what?"

"Now we move out too." They crawled forward, past the lip of the hollow that had sheltered them. Ten meters beyond that they saw Major Harris lying very still.

"Captain Barton's in command of the battalion," Peter said.

"Wonder if he knows it? I'll take the left side, sir, and keep 'em going, shall I?"

"Yes." Now he was more alone than ever. He went on through the olive groves, finding men and keeping them moving ahead of him. There was very little fire from the enemy. They advanced fifty meters, a hundred, and reached the slope down into the hollow beyond. It was an old vineyard, and the stumps of the vines reached out of the ground like old women's hands.

They were well into the hollow when the Dons fired.

Four of the newcomers from Churchill were just ahead of Owensford. When the volley lashed their hollow they hit the dirt in perfect formation. Peter crawled forward to compliment them on how well they'd learned the training-book exercises. All four were dead.

He was thirty meters into the hollow. In front of him was a network of red stripes weaving through the air a meter above the ground. He'd seen it at the Point, an interlocking network of crossfire guided by laser beams. Theoretically the Xanadu technicians should be able to locate the mirrors, or even the power plants, but the network hung there, unmoving.

Some of the men didn't know what it was and charged into it. After a while there was a little wall of dead men and boys at its edge. No one could advance, and snipers began to pick off any of the still figures that tried to move. Peter lay there, wondering if any of the other companies were making progress. His men lay behind bodies for the tiny shelter a dead comrade might give. One by one his troops died as they lay there in the open, in the bright sunshine of a dying vineyard.

In late afternoon it began to rain, first a few drops, then harder, finally a storm that cut off all visibility. The men could crawl back to their dugouts and they did. There were no orders for a retreat.

Peter found small groups of men and sent them out for wounded. It was hard to get men to go back into the hollow, even in the driving rainstorm, and he had to go with them or they would melt away to vanish in the mud and gloom. Eventually there were no more wounded to find.

The scene in the trenches was a shambled hell of bloody mud. Men fell into the dugouts and lay where they fell, too tired and scared to move. Some were wounded and died there in the mud, and others fell on top of them, trampling the bodies down and out of sight because no one had energy to move them. Peter was the only officer in the battalion until late afternoon. The company was his now and the men were calling him "Captain."

Then Stromand came into the trenches carrying a bundle.

Incredibly, Allan Roach was unwounded. The huge wrestler stood in Stromand's path. "What is that?" he demanded.

"Leaflets. To boost morale," Stromand said nervously.

Roach stood immobile. "While we were out there you were off printing leaflets?"

"I had orders," Stromand said. He backed nervously away from the big sergeant. His hand rested on a pistol butt.

"Roach," Peter said calmly. "Help me with the wounded, please."

Roach stood in indecision. Finally he turned to Peter. "Yes, sir."

At dawn Peter had eighty effectives to hold the lines. The Dons could have walked through during the night if they'd tried, but they were strangely quiet. Peter went from dugout to dugout, trying to get a count on his men. Two hundred wounded sent to rear areas. He could count a hundred thirteen dead. That left ninety-four vanished. Died, deserted, ground into the mud; he didn't know.

There hadn't been any general attack. The International volunteer commander had thought that even though the general attack was called off, this would be a splendid opportunity to show what morale could do. It had done that, all right.

The Republican command was frantic. The war was stalemated; which meant the superior forces of the Dons were slowly grinding them down. The war for freedom would soon be lost.

In desperation they sent a large group to the south where the front was stable. The last attack had been planned to the last detail; this one was to depend entirely on surprise. Peter's remnants were reinforced with pieces of other outfits and fresh volunteers, and sent against the enemy. They were on their own.

The objective was an agricultural center called Zaragoza, a small town amid olive groves and vineyards. Peter's column moved through the groves to the edge of town. Surprise was complete.

The battle did not last long. A flurry of firing, quick advances, and the enemy retreated, leaving Peter's company with a clear victory. From the little communications he could arrange, his group had advanced further than any other. They were the spearhead of freedom in the south.

They marched in to cheering crowds. His army looked like scarecrows, but women held their children up to see their liberators. It made it all worthwhile: the stupidity of the generals, the heat and mud and cold and dirt and lice, all of it forgotten in triumph.

More troops came in behind them, but Peter's company camped at the edge of their town, their place of freedom. The next day the army would advance again; if the war could be made fluid, fought in quick battles of fast-moving men, it might yet be won. Certainly, Peter thought, certainly the people of Santiago were waiting for them. They'd have support from the population. How long could the Dons hold?

Just before dark they heard shots in the town.

He brought his duty squad on the run, dashing through the dusty streets, past the pockmarked adobe walls to the town square. The military police were there.

"Never saw such pretty soldiers," Allan Roach said.

Peter nodded.

"Captain, where do you think they got those shiny boots? And the new rifles? Seems we never have good equipment for the troops, but the police always have more than enough. . . ."

A small group of bodies lay like broken dolls at the foot of the churchyard wall. The priest, the mayor, and three young men. "Monarchists. Carlists," someone whispered. Some of the townspeople spat on the bodies.

An old man was crouched beside one of the dead. He held the youthful head cradled in his hands and blood poured through his fingers. He looked at Peter with dull eyes. "Why are you here?" he asked. "Are there not richer worlds for you to conquer?"

Peter turned away without answering. He could think of nothing to say.

"Captain!"

Peter woke to Allan Roach's urgent whisper.

"Cap'n, there's something moving down by the stream. Not the Dons. Mister Stromand's with 'em, about five men. Officers, I think, from headquarters."

Peter sat upright. He hadn't seen Stromand since the disastrous attack three hundred kilometers to the north. The man wouldn't have lasted five minutes in combat among his former comrades. "Anyone else know?"

"Albers, nobody else. He called me."

"Let's go find out what they want. Quietly, Allan." As they walked silently in the hot night, Peter frowned to himself. What were staff officers doing in his company area, near the vanguard of the advancing Republican forces? And why hadn't they called him?

They followed the small group down the nearly dry creekbed to the town wall. When their quarry halted, they stole closer until they could hear.

"About here," Stromand's bookish voice said. "This will be perfect."

"How long do ve have?" Peter recognized the German accent of the staff officer who'd briefed them. The next voice was even more of a shock.

"Two hours. Enough time, but we must go quickly." It was Cermak, second in command of the volunteer forces. "It is set?"

"Yes."

"Hold it." Peter stepped out from the shadows, his rifle held to cover the small group. Allan Roach moved quickly away from him so that he also threatened them. "Identify yourselves."

"You know who we are, Owensford," Stromand snapped.

"Yes. What are you doing here?"

"That is none of your business, Captain," Cermak answered. "I order you to return to your company area and say nothing about seeing us."

"In a minute. Major, if you continue moving your hand toward your pistol, Sergeant Roach will cut you in half. Allan, I'm going to have a look at what they were carrying. Cover me."

"Right."

"You can't!" The German staff officer moved toward Peter.

Owensford reacted automatically, the rifle swinging upward in an uppercut that caught the German under the chin. The man fell with a strangled cry and lay still in the dirt. Everyone stood frozen; it was obvious that Cermak and Stromand were more worried about being heard than Peter was.

"Interesting," Peter said. He squatted over the device they'd set by the wall. "A bomb of some kind, from the timers—Jesus!"

"What is it, Cap'n?"

"A fission bomb," Peter said slowly. "They were going to leave a fission bomb here. To detonate in two hours, did you say?" he asked conversationally. His thoughts whirled, but he could find no explanation; and he was very surprised at how calm he was acting. "Why?"

No one answered.

"Why blow up the only advancing force in the Republican army?" Peter asked wonderingly. "They can't be traitors. The Dons wouldn't have these on a platter—but—Stromand, is there a new CD warship in orbit here? New fleet forces to stop this war?"

More silence.

"What does it mean?" Allan Roach asked. His rifle was steady, and there was an edge to his voice. "Why use an atom bomb on their own men?"

"The ban," Peter said. "One thing the CD does enforce. No nukes." He was hardly aware that he spoke aloud. "The CD inspectors will see the spearhead of the Republican army destroyed by nukes, and think the Dons did it. They're the only ones who could benefit from it. So the CD cleans up on the Carlists, and these bastards end up in charge when the fleet pulls out. That's it, isn't it? Cermak? Stromand?"

"Of course," Stromand said. "You fool, come with us, then. Leave the weapon in place. We're sorry we didn't think we could trust you with the plan, but it was just too important . . . it means winning the war."

"At what price?"

"A low price. A few battalions of soldiers and one village. Far more are killed every week. A comparatively bloodless victory."

Allan Roach spat viciously. "If that's freedom, I don't want any. You ask any of them?" He waved toward the village.

Peter remembered the cheering crowds. He stooped down to the weapon and examined it closely. "Any secret to disarming this? If there is, you're standing as close to it as I am."

"Wait," Stromand shouted. "Don't touch it, leave it, come with us. You'll be promoted, you'll be a hero of the movement—"

"Disarm it or I'll have a try," Peter said. He retrieved his rifle and waited.

After a moment Stromand bent down to the bomb. It was no larger than a small suitcase. He took a key from his pocket and inserted it, then turned dials. "It is safe now."

"I'll have another look," Peter said. He bent over the weapon. Yes, a large iron bar had been moved through the center of the device, and the fissionables couldn't come together. As he examined it there was a flurry of activity.

"Hold it!" Roach commanded. He raised his rifle; but Political Officer Stromand had already vanished into the darkness. "I'll go after him, Cap'n." They could hear thrashing among the olive trees nearby.

"No. You'd never catch him. Not without making a big stir. And if this story gets out, the whole Republican cause is finished."

"You are growing more intelligent," Cermak said. "Why not let us carry out our plan now?"

"I'll be damned," Peter said. "Get out of here, Cermak. Take your staff carrion with you. And if you send the military police after me or Sergeant Roach, just be damned sure this story—and the bomb—will get to the CD inspectors. Don't think I can't arrange it."

Cermak shook his head. "You are making a mistake—"

"The mistake is lettin' you go," Roach said. "Why don't I shoot him? Or cut his throat?"

"There'd be no point in it," Peter said. "If Cermak doesn't stop him, Stromand will be back with the MP's. No, let them go."

They advanced thirty kilometers in the next three days, crossing the valley with its dry river of sand at the bottom, moving swiftly into the low brush on the other side, up to the top of the ridge: and they were halted. Artillery and rockets exploded all around them. There was no one to fight, only unseen enemies on the next ridge, and the fire poured into their positions for three days.

The enemy fire was holding them, while the glare and heat of Thurstone's sun punished them. Men became snowblind, and wherever they looked there was only one color, fiery yellow. When grass and trees caught fire they could hardly notice the difference.

When the water was gone they retreated. There was nothing else to do. Back across the valley, past the positions they'd won, halting to let other units get past while they held the road; and on the seventh day after they left it, they were back on the road where they'd jumped off into the valley.

There was no organization. Peter was the only officer among 172 men of a battalion that had neither command nor staff; just 172 men too tired to care.

"We've the night, anyway," Roach said. He sat next to Peter and took out a cigarette. "Last tobacco in the battalion, Cap'n. Share?"

"No, thanks. Keep it all."

"One night to rest," Roach said again. "Seems like forever, a whole night without anybody shooting at us."

Fifteen minutes later Peter's radio squawked. He listened, hearing the commands over static and jamming. "Call the men together," Peter ordered when he'd heard it out.

"It's this way," he told them. "We still hold Zaragoza. There's a narrow corridor into the town, and unless somebody gets down there to hold it open, we'll lose the village. If that goes, the whole position in the valley's lost."

"Cap'n, you can't ask it!" The men were incredulous. "Go back down into there? You can't make us do that!"

"No. I can't make you. But remember Zaragoza? Remember how the people cheered us when we marched in? It's our town. Nobody else set those people free. We did. And there's nobody else who can go help keep them free, either. No other reinforcements. Will we let them down?"

"We can't," Allan Roach said. "It needs doing. I'll come with you, Cap'n."

One by one the others got to their feet. The ragged column

marched down the side of the ridge, out of the cool heights where their water was assured, down into the valley of the river of sand.

They were half a kilometer from the town at dawn. Troops were streaming down the road toward them, others running through the olive groves on both sides.

"Tanks!" someone shouted. "Tanks are coming!"

It was too late. The enemy armor had passed around Zaragoza and was closing on them fast. Other troops followed behind. Peter felt a bitter taste and prepared to dig into the olive groves. It would be their last battle.

An hour later they were surrounded. Two hours passed as they fought to hold the useless olive groves. The tanks had long since passed their position and gone but the enemy was still all around them. The shooting stopped, and silence lay through the grove.

Peter crawled across the perimeter of his command: a hundred meters, no more. He had fewer than fifty men.

Allan Roach lay in a shallow hole at one edge. Ripe olives shaken from the trees fell into it with him, partially covering him, and when Peter came close, the sergeant laughed. "Makes you feel like a salad," he said, brushing away more olives. "What do we do, Cap'n? Why you think they quit shooting?"

"Wait and see."

It didn't take long. "Will you surrender?" a voice called.

"To whom?" Peter demanded.

"Captain Hans Ort, Second Friedland Armored Infantry."

"Mercenaries," Peter hissed. "How did they get here? The CD was supposed to have a quarantine. . . ."

"Your position is hopeless, and you are not helping your comrades by holding it," the voice shouted.

"We're keeping you from entering the town!" Peter answered.

"For a while. We can go in any time, from the other side. Will you surrender?"

Peter looked helplessly at Roach. He could hear the silence among the men. They didn't say anything, and Peter was proud of them. But, he thought, I don't have any choice. "Yes," he shouted.

The Friedlanders wore dark green uniforms, and looked very military compared to Peter's scarecrows. "Mercenaries?" Captain Ort asked.

Peter opened his mouth to answer defiance. A voice interrupted him. "Of course they're mercenaries." Ace Barton limped up to them.

Ort looked at them suspiciously. "Very well. You wish to speak with them, Captain Barton?"

"Sure. I'll get some of 'em out of your hair," Barton said. He waited until the Friedlander was gone. "Pete, you almost blew it. If you'd said you were volunteers, Ort would have turned you over to the Dons. This way, he keeps you. And believe me, you'd rather be with him."

"What are you doing here?" Peter demanded.

"Captured up north," Barton said. "By those guys. There's a recruiter for Falkenberg's outfit back in the rear area. I signed up, and they've got me out hunting good men for Falkenberg. You want to join, you can. We get off this planet next week; and of course you won't fight here."

"I told you, I'm not a mercenary—"

"What are you?" Barton asked. "Nothing you can go back to. Best you can look forward to is being interned. Here, come on to town. You don't have to make up your mind just yet." They walked through the olive groves toward the Zaragoza town wall. "You opted for CD service," Barton said.

"Yes. Not to be one of Falkenberg's—"

"You think everything's going to be peaceful out here when the CoDominium fleet pulls out?"

"No. But I like to choose my wars."

"You want a cause. So did I, once. Now I'll settle for what I've got. Two things to remember, Pete. In an outfit like Falkenberg's, you don't choose your enemies, but you'll never have to break your word. And just what will you do for a living now?"

He had no answer to that. They walked on in silence.

"Somebody's got to keep order out here," Barton said. "Think about it."

They had reached the town. The Friedland mercenaries hadn't entered it; now a column of monarchist soldiers approached. Their boots were dusty and their uniforms torn, so that they looked little different from the remnants of Peter's command.

As the monarchists reached the town gates, the village people ran out of their houses. They lined both sides of the streets, and as the Carlists entered the public square, there was a loud cheer.

BUT AS A SOLDIER, FOR HIS COUNTRY

Stephen Goldin

Harker awoke to dim lighting, to bells, to panic all around him. Fast, busy footsteps clacked down bunker corridors, scurrying to no visible result and no possible accomplishment. It was wartime. Naturally.

He was in the spacesuit he had worn last time, which meant that either this war was soon after that last one or else there had been no great improvements in spacesuits over the interval between. It fit him tightly, with an all-but-invisible bubble helmet close around his head. There was no need for oxygen tanks as there had been on the early models; somehow—the technology was beyond him—air was transmuted within the suit, allowing him to breathe.

There was a belt of diverse weapons around his waist. He knew instinctively how to use each of them.

A voice in front of him, the eternal sergeant, a role that persisted though its portrayers came and went. "Not much time for explanation, I'm afraid, men. We're in a bad hole. We're in a bunker, below some ruins. The enemy has fanned out upstairs, looking for us. We've got to hold this area for four more hours, until reinforcements get here. You're the best we've got, our only hope."

"Only hope" rang hollowly in Harker's ear. He wanted to laugh, but couldn't. There was no hope. Ever.

"At least with you now, we outnumber them about five to four.

Remember, just four hours is all we need. Go on up there and keep them busy."

A mass of bodies moved toward the door to the elevator that would take them to the surface. A quiet, resigned shuffling. Death in the hundreds of haggard faces around him, probably in his own as well.

Harker moved with the group. He didn't even wonder who the "they" were that he was supposed to keep busy. It didn't matter. Perhaps it never had. He was alive again, and at war.

"We're asking you, Harker, for several reasons." The captain is going slowly, trying to make sure there are no misunderstandings. "For one thing, of course, you're a good soldier. For another, you're completely unattached—no wife, girlfriends or close relatives. Nothing binding you to the here and now."

Harker stands silently, still not precisely sure how to answer.

After an awkward pause, the captain continues. "Of course, we can't *order* you to do something like this. But we would like you to volunteer. We can make it worth your while to do so."

"I'd still like more time to think it over, sir."

"Of course. Take your time. We've got all the time in the world, haven't we?"

Later with Gary, as they walk across the deserted parade field together. "You bet I volunteered," Gary says. "It's not every day you get offered a two-month leave and a bonus, is it?"

"But what happens after that?"

Gary waves that aside. He is a live-for-the-moment type. "That's two months from now. Besides, how bad can it be, after what we've already been through? You read the booklet, didn't you? They had one hundred percent success thawing the monkeys out the last four times. It won't be any harder for us."

"But the world will be changed when we wake up."

"Who cares? The Army'll still be the same. The Army's always the same, ever since the beginning of time. Come on, join me. I'll bet if we ask them nice, they'll keep us together as a team. Don't let me go in there alone."

Harker volunteers the next day and gets his two-month leave, plus the bonus paid to the experimental subjects. He and Gray leave the post together to spend their last two months of freedom.

The first month they are together almost constantly. It is a riot of clashing colors and flashing girls, of endless movies and shows and drinks. It is largely cheerless, but it occupies their time and keeps their minds on *today*. The days sweep by like a brash brass carousel, and only by keeping careful track can it be noticed that the carousel goes around in a circle.

With a month to go, Harker suddenly leaves his friend and goes off on his own. He lets desolation sink in until it has invaded the roots of his soul. He often walks alone at night, and several times is stopped by police. Even when someone is with him, generally a streetgirl, he is alone.

He looks at things, ordinary things, with new strangeness. The cars going by on the street are suddenly vehicles of great marvels. The skyscrapers that reach above him, their defaced walls and smog-dirtied windows, all become symbols of a world that will not exist for him much longer. He stares for an hour at a penny on the sidewalk, until someone notices what he is staring at and picks the coin up for himself.

He talks but little and even his thoughts are shallow. He disengages his brain and lives on a primal level. When he is hungry, he eats; when his bladder or bowels are full, he relieves them. He takes whores to his hotel room for couplings that are merely the release of excess semen. During the last week, he is totally impotent.

He returns to the post when his leave is up and, as promised, is assigned to a room with Gary. The latter still seems to be in good spirits, undaunted by the prospects of the immediate future. The presence of his friend should brighten Harker up, but for some reason it only makes him more depressed.

For a week, they run him and the other volunteers—three hundred in all—through a battery of medical tests that are the most thorough Harker has ever experienced. Then they lead him, naked, to a white room filled with coffins, some of which are occupied and some of which are still empty.

There they freeze him against the time when they will need a good soldier again.

It was dark up on the surface, not a night-dark but a dreary, rainy, cloud-dark. A constant drizzle came from the sky, only to steam upward again when it touched the smoldering ruins of what had recently been a city. Buildings were mostly demolished, but here and there a wall stood silhouetted against the dark sky, futilely defying the fearsomeness of war. The ground and wreckage were still boiling hot, but Harker's suit protected him from the temperature. The drizzle and steam combined to make the air misty, and to give objects a shadow quality that denied their reality.

Harker looked around on reflex, taking stock. All around him were his own people, who had also just emerged from the elevator. No sign yet of the mysterious "they" he was supposed to keep busy for four hours. "Spread out," somebody said, and ingrained instincts took over. Clustered together at the mouth of the elevator, they made too good a target. They scattered at random in groups of one, two or three.

Harker found himself with a woman—not a resurrectee, just another soldier. Neither of them spoke; they probably had little in common. One was rooted in time, the other drifted, anchorless and apart.

The clouds parted for a moment, revealing a green sun. I wonder what planet it is this time, Harker thought, and even before the idea was completely formed, apathy had erased the desire to know. It didn't matter. All that mattered was the fighting and killing. That was why he was here.

An unexpected movement off to the left. Harker whirled, gun at the ready. A wraithlike form was approaching out of the mists. Three meters tall, stick-man thin, it moved agonizingly, fighting what was, to it, impossibly heavy gravity. Memories flooded Harker's mind, memories of a planet with a red sun, gravity only a third of Earth's, of dust and sand and choking dryness. And tall thin forms like this one. The men at his side and an army advancing on him. The enemy. An enemy once more?

Harker fired. This gun fired pulses of blue that seemed to waft with dreamlike slowness to the alien being. They reached it with a crackling more felt than heard. Static electricity? The being crumpled lifeless on the ground.

The woman grabbed Harker's arm. "What'd you do that for?"

"It was a . . . a . . . ." What had they been called? "A Bjorgn."

"Yes," said the soldier. "But they're on our side now."

Resurrection is slow, the first time, and not a little painful.

Harker awakes to quiet and white. That is his first impression. Later, when he sorts it out, he knows there must have been heat too. A nurse in a crisp white blouse and shorts is standing beside him, welcoming him back to the land of the living. It's been seven years, she tells him, since he was frozen. There is a war in Africa now, and they need good fighting men like him. She tells him to rest, that nothing is expected of him just yet. He's been through an ordeal, and rest will be the best medicine. Accordingly, Harker sleeps.

The next day, there is a general briefing for all the resurrectees, piped in via TV to all their bedsides since they are still incapacitated. The briefing explains some of the background of the war, how the United States became involved, and which side they are fighting on. Then there is a review of the war to date and a quick, nondetailed discussion of strategy. The colonel in charge closes by thanking these men for volunteering for this most unusual and elite project, and by expressing confidence that they will be successful. Harker listens politely, then turns the set off and goes to sleep when the briefing is over.

Next day begins the calisthenics. Being in cold sleep for seven years has taken the tone out of the men's muscles, and they will have to get back into shape before going out onto the battlefield once again. In the exercise yard, Harker sees Gary and waves to him. They eat lunch together, congratulating one another on having survived the treatment. (Only five out of three hundred have not pulled through, and the project is considered a success.) Gary is as flamboyant as ever, and expresses optimism that this war will be over soon, and then they can return to civilian life.

They spend five days more in preparation, then go out into the field. War has not changed in seven years, Harker notices. The guns are a bit smaller and the artillery shoots a bit farther and with more accuracy, but the basic pattern is unchanged. The jungles of Africa are not greatly different from those of Asia where he learned his craft. The fears he had about being a stranger in the future when he awoke are proving pointless, and gradually his depression wears off. He fights with all the skill he learned in the last war, and learns a few new tricks besides.

The war continues for ten months, then finally breaks. Negotiations come through, the fighting ends. Celebrations are held all over the world at this latest outbreak of peace, but the joyousness is not completely echoed in the ranks of the soldiers. The resurrectees are used to war, and the thought of learning new peacetime skills makes them nervous. They know there is nothing out there in the world for them. They would be welcomed as veterans, but they would be strangers to this time. War is the only world they know.

Ninety-five percent of the surviving resurrectees, including Harker and Gary, sign up for another term of hibernation, to be awakened when needed to fight.

Harker took the other soldier down behind some rubble and talked with her. "On our side?"

The woman nodded. "Have been for the last, oh, hundred years or so. Where . . ." She cut off abruptly. She'd been about to ask, "Where have you been all that time?" then realized the answer.

"It doesn't matter too much, I suppose," she continued. *"They can always replay his tape if they need him."*

"How much else don't I know?" Harker demanded.

"This is a civil war. Humans and aliens on both sides. You can't tell what side a person's on just by his race."

Like Asia and Africa, *Harker thought.*

"About the only way you can tell is by the armtag." She pointed at her own, and at Harker's. *"We're green. They're red."*

"What's to keep a red soldier from putting on a green armtag?"

The woman shrugged. *"Nothing, I suppose. Except he'd likely get shot by his own side."*

"Unless they knew him by sight."

The soldier shook her head. *"No. They copied some of our tapes, which means they've been able to duplicate some of our personnel. Don't trust anyone just because you've seen them before. Look for the armtag."*

Bolts of energy went hurtling by their temporary shelter. *"Here comes the action,"* Harker said. *"Let's move."*

But before they could, the ground exploded in front of them.

The next resurrection is easier, the doctors having learned from experience. But it still is a shock.

Harker awakes to cold this time. He notices it even before the white of the hospital room. Not that the building isn't heated, but there is a chill in the atmosphere that pervades everything.

The nurse that stands beside him is older than the one he had last time. Her white blouse is not quite so crisp, and she wears a skirt that goes clear to the floor. It's a wonder she doesn't trip over it. The chill is part of her, too; she is not as friendly as that previous nurse. She tells him brusquely that he has been hibernating for fifteen years, and that the war is now in Antarctica.

He takes the news with quiet astonishment. Of all the places in the world where he'd thought war would never be, Antarctica headed the list. But here he is, and here he will fight. He learns that the United States is fighting China here over a section of disputed territory. So he is back to fighting Orientals, though on new terrain.

Gary is here also, and they renew their friendship. There is a week of calisthenics, as they get in shape once more. The atmosphere, Harker notices, is less relaxed than it was the first time, as though people are impatient to get the resurrectees out and fighting again.

Antarctica, needless to say, has different physical conditions than most of them are used to. They bundle up in heavy boots and thin, electrically warmed coats and gloves. They wear goggles to protect their eyes. Their weapons now fire laser beams instead of projectiles; the lack of recoil takes some getting used to. So does the climate. Cold instead of hot, snow instead of rain, bare plains and snow fields instead of jungles and farms. The terrain under dispute seems no different to Harker than any of the rest that is free for the taking, but his superiors tell him that *this* is what they must have and so this is what he fights for.

After three months of fighting, Harker is wounded. A laser beam grazes his arm, burning flesh down to the bone. He is taken to a hospital, where they heal the wound quite efficiently—but while they do so, the war comes to an end. The decision arises again whether to reenlist or leave the service. Many resurrectees opt out before becoming too estranged from the world. But the slang of the contemporary soldiers is already becoming unrecognizable, and the few pictures Harker has received of the rest of the "modern" world seems strange and out of phase. After talking it over with Gary, they both decide on one more try aboard the resurrection express.

There is a new slant to it this time, though. A *very* experimental program, top-secret, is being worked out whereby, instead of putting a man in hibernation, they can record his mind as an individual and reconstruct him later when needed. This will make the system much more maneuverable, since they won't have the problem of transporting frozen bodies to and from battlegrounds. This method is a bit riskier, since it hasn't been fully tested yet, but it offers more advantages in the long run.

Gary and Harker sign up and are duly recorded.

Harker was thrown clear by the explosion, but the other soldier had not been so lucky. The left side of her torso had been blown away and guts were spilling onto the steaming ground. Harker shook his head to clear it from the shock, and rolled quickly behind a barely standing section of wall.

It was not nearly so dark now. Energy weapons were being fired, lighting up the countryside with their multicolored glows. The drizzle continued steadily, and the mists still steamed up from the ground. Like ghosts, Harker thought. But he didn't have much time for thinking. He had a job to do.

There could be no strategy in this type of combat—it was strictly man-to-man, a series of individual battles where the only winners were those who remained alive. Move cautiously, ever alert, looking for someone with the other color armtag. When you see him, shoot immediately, before he can shoot you. If he's too far out of range, hurl a grenade. Reduce the number of the enemy to increase your own odds. Stay alive. That was the law here on this nameless world beneath a green sun.

Harker emerged from one doorway after killing seven of the enemy, onto a main "street"—or what had been one—of this city. It was now clogged with heaps of rubble from the fallen buildings; stone, cement, steel, plastiglas jumbled every which way. Among the wreckage were strewn the bodies of thousands of the original inhabitants. They were not human, but it was impossible for Harker to reconstruct what they had looked like. Many of the bodies were in pieces, with an unusually short leg lying here, an oddly shaped arm over there, a limbless, headless torso further on. Some bodies were pinned beneath pieces of debris; others had been hideously mutilated by the latest advances in war technology.

Harker's stomach felt no unease at what his eyes were viewing. He had seen scenes like this before, many times, in countless places throughout the universe. It took him barely a second to absorb the silent tragedy before him, then he started moving on.

A bolt of energy hit his right calf. He whirled and fired instinctively at his attacker, even as he felt himself falling.

This new type of resurrection is a sudden, frightening thing, a lightning bolt summoning his soul from the depths of limbo.

Harker awakes to sterility, to a place of abnormal quiet. The air smells funny, antiseptic, even more so than most of the hospitals he's been in. His body feels funny too, as though he were floating in some strangely buoyant liquid; yet he can feel a firm couch underneath his back. His heart bangs away inside his chest, much too fast, much too hard.

He is in a room with other men, other resurrectees, all of whom feel equally strange and perplexed. Their number has almost tripled now from the original three hundred, and they have been crowded closely together to fit into one large hall. Harker lifts his head, and after much looking, manages to spot Gary a dozen rows away. The presence of his friend allays some of the alienness he feels here.

"Welcome to the Moon, men," blares a voice from a loud-speaker. There is a reverberation of gasps throughout the room at this revelation of their location. The Moon! Only astronauts and scientists got to go there. Are there wars on the Moon now? What year is this and who—and how—are they expected to fight?

The loudspeaker goes on to give further information. For one thing, they are no longer a part of the U.S. Army. The United

States has been incorporated into the North American Union, which has inherited their tapes. The enemy is the South Americans, the Sammies, led largely by the Peruvian complex. The two powers are fighting for possession of the Mare Nectaris, which symbolizes the points of disagreement between them. Since the outlawing of war on Earth itself, aggressions have to be released here, on the Moon.

"The Moon!" Gary exclaims when they can finally talk together. "Can you believe it? I never thought I'd make it up here. Don't it knock you on your ass just thinking about it?"

Calisthenics are not necessary, since their bodies have been recreated in as good a shape as they were in when they were first recorded. But they do have to spend almost two weeks undergoing training to be able to deal with the lighter gravity of the Moon. There are also spacesuits they have to become accustomed to, and whole new instincts have to be drilled into the men to take care that nothing will rip their suits, the portable wombs they carry against Nature's hostility.

Projectile weapons are back, Harker notices, in use as antipersonnel armament. On the Moon, in spacesuits, a small sliver of shrapnel is just as deadly as a laser beam. Rifles that fire the lunar equivalent of buckshot are relied on heavily by the infantry in the field. Orbiting satellites cover their advances with wide-angle energy beams that Harker doesn't even begin to understand.

It is an entirely different style of fighting, he finds. Totally silent. There are radios in their spacesuits, but they are forbidden to use them because the enemy could triangulate their position. The soldiers make no noise, and on the airless surface of the Moon, the weapons make no noise. It is a battle in pantomime, with silent death ready to creep up at any time.

Gary is killed the third week out. It is during a battle at the open end of the crater Fracastorius, which proves to be the turning point of the war. Gary and Harker are part of a line advancing cautiously across the pockmarked plain, when suddenly Gary falls to the ground. Other men along the line fall too. Harker goes to the ground, feigning death so that the Sammie snipers will not waste any more ammunition on him. But Gary is not feigning it. Harker, otherwise motionless, can turn his head within the helmet and see the tiny tear in the right side of his friend's spacesuit. The wound would have been minuscule, but the explosive decompression had been fatal. Gary's eyes are bugged out, as though in horror at death, and blood is bubbling at his nostrils and mouth.

Harker cries for his friend. For the last time, he cries.

He lies there for three hours, motionless, until his air supply is almost exhausted. Then he is picked up by a Sammie sweep patrol and taken prisoner. He sits out the short remainder of the war in a Sammie camp where he is treated decently enough, suffering only a few indignities. When the war ends, he is exchanged back to the N.A.U., where, still numbed from Gary's death, he allows himself to be retaped and rerecorded for future use.

Harker fell and hit his head against a block of stone rubble. The helmet withstood the blow—unlike the primitive ones he had worn at first, which would have cracked open—but it started a ringing in his ears which momentarily drowned out the pain impulses coming from his leg. He lay there stunned, waiting for death, in the form of the enemy soldier, to claim him. But nothing happened. After a while his head cleared, which only meant that he could feel the searing agony in his leg more deeply. It was hardly an improvement.

If the soldier had not delivered the killing blow, it could mean that Harker's reflex shot had killed or wounded him. He had to find out quickly; his life might depend on it. He twisted around painfully, his leg pulsing with agony. There, about thirty meters down the street, a spacesuited body lay flat on the ground. It wasn't moving, but was it dead? He had to know.

Harker crawled over the field of death, over the remains of shattered bodies. The front of his spacesuit became caked with mud and some not-quite-dried blood that had an inhuman, oily consistency. The drizzle was becoming harder, turning to rain, but still steaming up from the radioactively heated ground. Clouds of vapor fogged his way, hiding the object of his search. Still Harker crawled, keeping to the direction he knew to be the true one.

His leg was on fire, and every centimeter of the crawl was hell, a surrealist's nightmare of the world gone mad. Once he thought he heard a scream, and he looked around, but there was no one nearby. It must have been a hullucination. He'd had them before on the battlefield, under pain.

He reached his goal after an eternity of crawling. He could detect faint twitches; the enemy was still alive then, though barely. Harker turned him over on his back to deliver the death blow, then looked into the man's face.

It was Gary.

All the resurrections now seem to run together in his memory. The next one, he thinks, is Venus, the place of hot, stinking swamps, of nearly killing atmospheric pressure and protective bubble-pockets of life. These are the first aliens he's ever killed, the tiny creatures no more than twenty-five centimeters high who can swarm all over a man and kill him with a million tiny stabs. At first it is easier to kill nonhumans, less wearing on the scruples. But eventually it doesn't matter. Killing is killing, no matter whom it is done to. It becomes a clinical, mechanical process, to be done as efficiently as possible, not to be thought over.

Then back on the Moon again—or is it Mars?—fighting other humans. The spacesuits are improved this time, tougher, but the fighting is just as silent, just as deadly.

Then a war back on Earth again. (Apparently that outlawing of war on the mother planet has not worked out as well as expected.) Some of the fighting is even done under the oceans, in and around large domes that house cities with populations of millions. There are trained dolphins and porpoises fighting in this one. It doesn't matter. Harker kills them no matter what they look like.

This war is the last time Harker ever sets foot upon his native planet.

Then comes the big jump to an interstellar war. He is resurrected on a planet under a triple sun—Alpha Centauri, someone says—and the enemy is two-foot-long chitinous caterpillars with sharp pincers. They fight valiantly despite a much more primitive technology. By this time Harker is no longer sure whom he is working for. His side is the one that resurrects him and gives him an enemy to fight. They give him shelter, food, clothing, weapons and, occasionally, relaxation. They no longer bother to tell him *why* he is fighting. It no longer seems to matter to him.

Wake up and fight until there is no more killing to do; then retreat into purgatory until the next war, the next battle. The killing machine named Harker has trod the surfaces of a hundred planets, leaving nothing but destruction and death in his wake.

Gary stared up into Harker's eyes. He was in pain, near death, but was there some recognition there? Harker could not speak to him, their communicators were on different frequencies, but there was something in Gary's eyes . . . a plea. A plea for help. A plea for a quick and merciful death.

Harker obliged.

His mind was numb, his leg was burning. He did not think of the paradox of Gary still being alive though he had seen him die on the Moon years (centuries? millennia?) ago. He knew only that his leg hurt and that he was in an exposed position. He crawled on his side, with his left elbow pulling him forward, for ten meters to a piece of wall. He lifted himself over it and tumbled to the ground.

73

If not completely safe, he was at least off the street, out of the open space.

He reached for the first-aid kit on his belt, to tend his leg. There was none there. The idea took a full minute to sink into his mind: THEY HADN'T GIVEN HIM A FIRST-AID KIT. He felt a moment of anger, but it subsided quickly. Why should they give him a kit? What was he to them? A pattern called out of the past, an anachronism—useful for fighting and, if necessary, dying. Nothing more. He was a ghost living far beyond his appointed hour, clinging to life in the midst of death. A carrion eater, feeding on death and destruction to survive, for he had no purpose except to kill. And when the killing was done, he was stored away until his time came round again.

He sat in the rubble with his back against the crumbling wall, and for the first time since Gary's death on the Moon, he cried.

Asia.
    Africa.
        Antarctica.
            Luna.
                Venus.
                    Pacifica.
                        Alpha Centauri 4.
                            The planet with the forests.
                              The world with oceans of ammonia.
                              Planets whose names he's never
                                even bothered to learn.

The ghosts of billions of war dead assault his conscience. And Harker cries with them, for them, about them, over them, to them.

There was a movement. A man in a red armtag. A strangely familiar figure. He hadn't seen Harker yet. Without thinking, Harker's hand raised the gun to fire.

His motion attracted the other's attention. The soldier, with reflexes as fast as his own, whirled to face him. It was himself.

"They copied some of our tapes," he had been told. Exactly. Then they could make themselves a Harker, just as this side could. He wanted to laugh, but the pain in his leg prevented it. It would have been his first laugh in uncounted incarnations. This was the ultimate irony—fighting himself.

The two Harkers' eyes joined and locked. For one joyless instant, each read the other's soul. Then each fired at the other.

74

SOLDIER BOY

Michael Shaara

In the northland, deep, and in a great cave, by an everburning fire the Warrior sleeps. For this is the resting time, the time of peace, and so shall it be for a thousand years. And yet we shall summon him again, my children, when we are sore in need, and out of the north he will come, and again and again, each time we call, out of the dark and the cold, with the fire in his hands, he will come.

—Scandinavian legend

Throughout the night thick clouds had been piling in the north; in the morning it was misty and cold. By eight o'clock a wet, heavy, snow-smelling breeze had begun to set in, and because the crops were all down and the winter planting done, the colonists brewed hot coffee and remained inside. The wind blew steadily, icily, from the north. It was well below freezing when, sometime after nine, an army ship landed in a field near the settlement.

There was still time. There were some last brief moments in which the colonists could act and feel as they had always done. They therefore grumbled in annoyance. They wanted no soldiers here. The few who had convenient windows stared out with distaste and a mild curiosity, but no one went out to greet them.

After a while a rather tall, frail-looking man came out of the

75

ship and stood upon the hard ground looking toward the village. He remained there, waiting stiffly, his face turned from the wind. It was a silly thing to do. He was obviously not coming in, either out of pride or just plain orneriness.

"Well, I never," a nice lady said.

"What's he just *standing* there for?" another lady said.

And all of them thought: Well, God knows what's in the mind of a soldier, and right away many people concluded that he must be drunk. The seed of peace was deeply planted in these people, in the children and the women, very, very deep. And because they had been taught, oh, so carefully, to hate war, they had also been taught, quite incidentally, to despise soldiers.

The lone man kept standing in the freezing wind.

Eventually, because even a soldier can look small and cold and pathetic, Bob Rossel had to get up out of a nice, warm bed and go out in that miserable cold to meet him.

The soldier saluted. Like most soldiers, he was not too neat and not too clean, and the salute was sloppy. Although he was bigger than Rossel he did not seem bigger. And, because of the cold, there were tears gathering in the ends of his eyes.

"Captain Dylan, sir." His voice was low and did not carry. "I have a message from Fleet Headquarters. Are you in charge here?"

Rossel, a small sober man, grunted. "Nobody's in charge here. If you want a spokesman I guess I'll do. What's up?"

The captain regarded him briefly out of pale-blue, expression-less eyes. Then he pulled an envelope from an inside pocket, handed it to Rossel. It was a thick, official-looking thing and Rossel hefted it idly. He was about to ask again what was it all about when the airlock of the hovering ship swung open creakily. A beefy, black-haired young man appeared unsteadily in the doorway, called to Dylan.

"C'n I go now, Jim?"

Dylan turned and nodded.

"Be back for you tonight," the young man called, and then, grinning, he yelled, "Catch," and tossed down a bottle. The captain caught it and put it unconcernedly into his pocket while Rossel stared in disgust. A moment later the airlock closed and the ship prepared to lift.

"Was he *drunk?*" Rossel began angrily. "Was that a bottle of *liquor?*"

The soldier was looking at him calmly, coldly. He indicated the envelope in Rossel's hand. "You'd better read that and get moving. We haven't much time."

He turned and walked toward the buildings and Rossel had to follow. As Rossel drew near the walls the watchers could see his lips moving but could not hear him. Just then the ship lifted and they turned to watch that and followed it upward, red spark-tailed, into the gray, spongy clouds and the cold.

After a while the ship went out of sight, and nobody ever saw it again.

The first contact man had ever had with an intelligent alien race occurred out on the perimeter in a small quiet place a long way from home. Late in the year 2360—the exact date remains unknown—an Alien force attacked and destroyed the colony at Lupus V. The wreckage and the dead were found by a mailship which flashed off screaming for the army.

When the army came it found this: Of the seventy registered colonists, thirty-one were dead. The rest, including some women and children, were missing. All technical equipment, all radios, guns, machines, even books, were also missing. The buildings had been burned; so had the bodies. Apparently the Aliens had a heat ray. What else they had, nobody knew. After a few days of walking around in the ash, one soldier finally stumbled on something.

For security reasons, there was a detonator in one of the main buildings. In case of enemy attack, Security had provided a bomb to be buried in the center of each colony, because it was important to blow a whole village to hell and gone rather than let a hostile Alien learn vital facts about human technology and body chemistry. There was a bomb at Lupus V too, and though it had been detonated it had not blown. The detonating wire had been cut.

In the heart of the camp, hidden from view under twelve inches of earth, the wire had been dug up and cut.

The army could not understand it and had no time to try. After five hundred years of peace and anti-war conditioning the army was small, weak, and without respect. Therefore the army did nothing but spread the news, and man began to fall back.

In a thickening, hastening stream he came back from the hard-won stars, blowing up his homes behind him, stunned and cursing. Most of the colonists got out in time. A few, the farthest and loneliest, died in fire before the army ships could reach them. And the men in those ships, drinkers and gamblers and veterans of nothing, the dregs of society that had grown beyond them, were for a long while the only defense earth had.

This was the message Captain Dylan had brought, come out from earth with a bottle on his hip.

77

An obscenely cheerful expression upon his gaunt, not too well shaven face, Captain Dylan perched himself upon the edge of a table and listened, one long booted leg swinging idly. One by one the colonists were beginning to understand. War is huge and comes with great suddenness and always without reason, and there is inevitably a wait between acts, between the news and the motion, the fear and the rage.

Dylan waited. These people were taking it well, much better than those in the cities had taken it. But then, these were pioneers. Dylan grinned. Pioneers. Before you settle a planet you boil it and bake it and purge it of all possible disease. Then you step down gingerly and inflate your plastic houses, which harden and become warm and impregnable; and send your machines out to plant and harvest; and set automatic factories to transmute dirt into coffee; and, without ever having lifted a finger, you have braved the wilderness, hewed a home out of the living rock, and become a pioneer. Dylan grinned again. But at least this was better than the wailing of the cities.

This Dylan thought, although he was himself no fighter, no man at all by any standards. This he thought because he was a soldier and an outcast; to every drunken man the fall of the sober is a happy thing. He stirred restlessly.

By this time the colonists had begun to realize that there wasn't much to say, and a tall, handsome woman was murmuring distractedly, "Lupus, Lupus—doesn't that mean wolves or something?"

Dylan began to wish they would get moving, these pioneers. It was very possible that the Aliens would be here soon, and there was no need for discussion. There was only one thing to do and that was to clear the hell out, quickly and without argument. They began to see it.

But when the fear had died down the resentment came. A number of women began to cluster around Dylan and complain, working up their anger. Dylan said nothing. Then the man Rossel pushed forward and confronted him, speaking with a vast annoyance.

"See here, soldier, this is our planet. I mean to say, this is our *home*. We demand some protection from the fleet. By God, we've been the freight for you boys all these years, and it's high time you earned your keep. We demand . . ."

It went on and on, while Dylan looked at the clock and waited. He hoped that he could end this quickly. A big gloomy man was in front of him now and giving him that name of ancient contempt, "soldier boy." The gloomy man wanted to know where the fleet was.

"There is no fleet. There are a few hundred half-shot old tubs that were obsolete before you were born. There are four or five new jobs for the brass and the government. That's all the fleet there is."

Dylan wanted to go on about that, to remind them that nobody had wanted the army, that the fleet had grown smaller and smaller . . . but this was not the time. It was ten-thirty already, and the damned aliens might be coming in right now for all he knew, and all they did was talk. He had realized a long time ago that no peace-loving nation in the history of earth had ever kept itself strong, and although peace was a noble dream, it was ended now and it was time to move.

"We'd better get going," he finally said, and there was quiet. "Lieutenant Bossio has gone on to your sister colony at Planet Three of this system. He'll return to pick me up by nightfall, and I'm instructed to have you gone by then."

For a long moment they waited, and then one man abruptly walked off and the rest followed quickly; in a moment they were all gone. One or two stopped long enough to complain about the fleet, and the big gloomy man said he wanted guns, that's all, and there wouldn't nobody get him off his planet. When he left, Dylan breathed with relief and went out to check the bomb, grateful for the action.

Most of it had to be done in the open. He found a metal bar in the radio shack and began chopping at the frozen ground, following the wire. It was the first thing he had done with his hands in weeks, and it felt fine.

Dylan had been called up out of a bar—he and Bossio—and told what had happened, and in three weeks now they had cleared four colonies. This would be the last, and the tension here was beginning to get to him. After thirty years of hanging around and playing like the town drunk, a man could not be expected to rush out and plug the breach, just like that. It would take time.

He rested, sweating, took a pull from the bottle on his hip.

Before they sent him out on this trip they had made him a captain. Well, that was nice. After thirty years he was a captain. For thirty years he had bummed all over the west end of space, had scraped his way along the outer edges of mankind, had waited and dozed and patrolled and got drunk, waiting always for something to happen. There were a lot of ways to pass the time while you waited for something to happen, and he had done them all.

Once he had even studied military tactics.

He could not help smiling at that, even now. Damn it, he'd been green. But he'd been only nineteen when his father died—of a hernia, of a crazy fool thing like a hernia that killed him just because he'd worked too long on a heavy planet—and in those days the anti-war conditioning out on the Rim was not very strong. They talked a lot about guardians of the frontier, and they got him and some other kids and a broken-down doctor. And . . . now he was a captain.

He bent his back savagely, digging at the ground. You wait and you wait and the edge goes off. This thing he had waited for all those damn days was upon him now, and there was nothing he could do but say the hell with it and go home. Somewhere along the line, in some dark corner of the bars or the jails, in one of the million soul-murdering insults which are reserved especially for peacetime soldiers, he had lost the core of himself, and it didn't particularly matter. That was the point: It made no particular difference if he never got it back. He owed nobody. He was tugging at the wire and trying to think of something pleasant from the old days when the wire came loose in his hands.

Although he had been, in his cynical way, expecting it, for a moment it threw him and he just stared. The end was clean and bright. The wire had just been cut.

Dylan sat for a long while by the radio shack, holding the ends in his hands. He reached almost automatically for the bottle on his hip, and then, for the first time he could remember, let it go. This was real; there was no time for that.

When Rossel came up, Dylan was still sitting. Rossel was so excited he did not notice the wire.

"Listen, soldier, how many people can your ship take?"

Dylan looked at him vaguely. "She sleeps two and won't take off with more'n ten. Why?"

His eyes bright and worried, Rossel leaned heavily against the shack. "We're overloaded. There are sixty of us, and our ship will only take forty. We came out in groups; we never thought . . ."

Dylan dropped his eyes, swearing silently. "You're sure? No baggage, no iron rations; you couldn't get ten more on?"

"Not a chance. She's only a little ship with one deck—she's all we could afford."

Dylan whistled. He had begun to feel lightheaded. "It 'pears that somebody's gonna find out firsthand what them aliens look like."

It was the wrong thing to say and he knew it. "All right," he said quickly, still staring at the clear-sliced wire, "we'll do what

80

we can. Maybe the colony on Three has room. I'll call Bossio and ask."

The colonist had begun to look quite pitifully at the buildings around him and the scurrying people.

"Aren't there any fleet ships within radio distance?"

Dylan shook his head. "The fleet's spread out kind of thin nowadays." Because the other was leaning on him he felt a great irritation, but he said as kindly as he could, "We'll get 'em all out. One way or another, we won't leave anybody."

It was then that Rossel saw the wire. Thickly, he asked what had happened.

Dylan showed him the two clean ends. "Somebody dug it up, cut it, then buried it again and packed it down real nice."

"The damn fool!" Rossel exploded.

"Who?"

"Why, one of . . . of us, of course. I know nobody ever liked sitting on a live bomb like this, but I never . . ."

"You think one of your people did it?"

Rossel stared at him. "Isn't that obvious?"

"Why?"

"Well, they probably thought it was too dangerous, and silly too, like most government rules. Or maybe one of the kids . . ."

It was then that Dylan told him about the wire on Lupus V. Rossel was silent. Involuntarily he glanced at the sky, then he said shakily, "Maybe an animal?"

Dylan shook his head. "No animal did that. Wouldn't have buried it, or found it in the first place. Heck of a coincidence, don't you think? The wire at Lupus was cut just before an alien attack, and now this one is cut too—newly cut."

The colonist put one hand to his mouth, his eyes wide and white.

"So something," said Dylan, "knew enough about this camp to know that a bomb was buried here and also to know why it was here. And that something didn't want the camp destroyed and so came right into the center of the camp, traced the wire, dug it up, and cut it. And then walked right out again."

"Listen," said Rossel, "I'd better go ask."

He started away but Dylan caught his arm.

"Tell them to arm," he said, "and try not to scare hell out of them. I'll be with you as soon as I've spliced this wire."

Rossel nodded and went off, running. Dylan knelt with the metal in his hands.

He began to feel that, by God, he was getting cold. He realized that he'd better go inside soon, but the wire had to be spliced. That was perhaps the most important thing he could do now, splice the wire.

All right, he asked himself for the thousandth time, who cut it? How? Telepathy? Could they somehow control one of us?

No. If they controlled one, then they could control all, and then there would be no need for an attack. But you don't know, you don't really know.

Were they small? Little animals?

Unlikely. Biology said that really intelligent life required a sizable brain, and you would have to expect an alien to be at least as large as a dog. And every form of life on this planet had been screened long before a colony had been allowed in. If any new animals had suddenly shown up, Rossel would certainly know about it.

He would ask Rossel. He would damn sure have to ask Rossel.

He finished splicing the wire and tucked it into the ground. Then he straightened up and, before he went into the radio shack, pulled out his pistol. He checked it, primed it, and tried to remember the last time he had fired it. He never had—he never had fired a gun.

The snow began falling near noon. There was nothing anybody could do but stand in the silence and watch it come down in a white rushing wall, and watch the trees and the hills drown in the whiteness, until there was nothing on the planet but the buildings and a few warm lights and the snow.

By one o'clock the visibility was down to zero and Dylan decided to try to contact Bossio again and tell him to hurry. But Bossio still didn't answer. Dylan stared long and thoughtfully out the window through the snow at the gray shrouded shapes of bushes and trees which were beginning to become horrifying. It must be that Bossio was still drunk—maybe sleeping it off before making planetfall on Three. Dylan held no grudge. Bossio was a kid and alone. It took a special kind of guts to take a ship out into space alone, when Things could be waiting. . . .

A young girl, pink and lovely in a thick fur jacket, came into the shack and told him breathlessly that her father, Mr. Rush, would like to know if he wanted sentries posted. Dylan hadn't thought about it but he said yes right away, beginning to feel both pleased and irritated at the same time, because now they were coming to him.

He pushed out into the cold and went to find Rossel. With the snow it was bad enough, but if they were still here when the sun

82

went down they wouldn't have a chance. Most of the men were out stripping down their ship, and that would take a while. He wondered why Rossel hadn't yet put a call through to Three, asking about room on the ship there. The only answer he could find was that Rossel knew that there was no room and wanted to put off the answer as long as possible. And, in a way, you could not blame him.

Rossel was in his cabin with the big, gloomy man—who turned out to be Rush, the one who had asked about sentries. Rush was methodically cleaning an old hunting rifle. Rossel was surprisingly full of hope.

"Listen, there's a mail ship due in, been due since yesterday. We might get the rest of the folks out on that."

Dylan shrugged. "Don't count on it."

"But they have a contract!"

The soldier grinned.

The big man, Rush, was paying no attention. Quite suddenly he said, "Who cut that wire, Cap?"

Dylan swung slowly to look at him. "As far as I can figure, an alien cut it."

Rush shook his head. "No. Ain't been no aliens near this camp, and no peculiar animals either. We got a planet-wide radar, and ain't no unidentified ships come near, not since we first landed more'n a year ago." He lifted the rifle and peered through the bore. "Uh-uh. One of us did it."

The man had been thinking. And he knew the planet.

"Telepathy?" asked Dylan.

"Might be."

"Can't see it. You people live too close; you'd notice right away if one of you wasn't . . . himself. And if they've got one, why not all?"

Rush calmly—at least outwardly calmly—lit his pipe. There was a strength in this man that Dylan had missed before.

"Don't know," he said gruffly. "But there are aliens, mister. And until I know different I'm keepin' an eye on my neighbor."

He gave Rossel a sour look and Rossel stared back, uncomprehending.

Then Rossel jumped. "My God!"

Dylan moved to quiet him. "Look, is there any animal at all that ever comes near here that's as large as a dog?"

After a pause Rush answered. "Yep, there's one. The viggle. It's like a reg'lar monkey but with four legs. Biology cleared 'em before we landed. We shoot one now and then when they get pesky." He rose slowly, the rifle held under his arm. "I b'lieve we might just as well go post them sentries."

Dylan wanted to go on with this, but there was nothing much else to say. Rossel went with them as far as the radio shack, with a strained expression on his face, to put through that call to Three.

When he was gone Rush asked Dylan, "Where you want them sentries? I got Walt Halloran and Web Eggers and six others lined up."

Dylan stopped and looked around grimly at the circling wall of snow. "You know the site better than I do. Post 'em in a ring, on rises, within calling distance. Have 'em check with each other every five minutes. I'll go help your people at the ship."

The gloomy man nodded and fluffed up his collar. "Nice day for huntin'," he said, and then he was gone, with the snow quickly covering his footprints.

The Alien lay wrapped in a thick electric cocoon, buried in a wide warm room beneath the base of a tree. The tree served him as antennae; curiously he gazed into a small view-screen and watched the humans come. He saw them fan out, eight of them, and sink down in the snow. He saw that they were armed.

He pulsed thoughtfully, extending a part of himself to absorb a spiced lizard. Since the morning, when the new ship had come, he had been watching steadily, and now it was apparent that the humans were aware of their danger. Undoubtedly they were preparing to leave.

That was unfortunate. The attack was not scheduled until late that night, and he could not, of course, press the assault by day. But *flexibility*, he reminded himself sternly, *is the first principle of absorption*, and therefore he moved to alter his plans. A projection reached out to dial several knobs on a large box before him, and the hour of assault was moved forward to dusk. A glance at the chronometer told him that it was already well into the night on Planet Three and that the attack there had probably begun.

The Alien felt the first tenuous pulsing of anticipation. He lay quietly, watching the small square lights of windows against the snow, thanking the Unexplainable that matters had been so devised that he would not have to venture out into that miserable cold.

Presently an alarming thought struck him. These humans moved with uncommon speed for intelligent creatures. Even without devices, it was distinctly possible that they could be gone before nightfall. He could take no chance, of course. He spun more dials and pressed a single button, and lay back again comfortably, warmly, to watch the disabling of the colonists' ship.

When Three did not answer, Rossel was nervously gazing at the snow, thinking of other things, and he called again. Several moments later the realization of what was happening struck him like a blow. Three had never once failed to answer. All they had to do when they heard the signal buzz was go into the radio shack and say hello. That was all they had to do. He called again and again, but nobody answered. There was no static and no interference and he didn't hear a thing. He checked frenziedly through his own apparatus and tried again, but the air was as dead as deep space. He raced out to tell Dylan.

Dylan accepted it. He had known none of the people on Three, and what he felt now was a much greater urgency to be out of here. He said hopeful things to Rossel and then went out to the ship and joined the men in lightening her. About the ship, at least, he knew something and he was able to tell them what partitions and frames could go and what would have to stay or the ship would never get off the planet. But even stripped down, it couldn't take them all. When he knew that, he realized that he himself would have to stay here, for it was only then that he thought of Bossio.

Three was dead. Bossio had gone down there some time ago, and if Three was dead and Bossio had not called, then the fact was that Bossio was gone too. For a long, long moment Dylan stood rooted in the snow. More than the fact that he would have to stay here was the unspoken, unalterable, heart-numbing knowledge that Bossio was dead—the one thing that Dylan could not accept. Bossio was the only friend he had. In all this dog-eared, aimless, ape-run universe Bossio was all his friendship and his trust.

He left the ship blindly and went back to the settlement. Now the people were quiet and really frightened, and some of the women were beginning to cry. He noticed now that they had begun to look at him with hope as he passed, and in his own grief, humanly, he swore.

Bossio—a big-grinning kid with no parents, no enemies, no grudges—Bossio was already dead because he had come out here and tried to help these people. People who had kicked or ignored him all the days of his life. And, in a short while, Dylan would also stay behind and die to save the life of somebody he never knew and who, twenty-four hours earlier, would have been ashamed to be found in his company. Now, when it was far, far too late, they were coming to the army for help.

But in the end, damn it, he could not hate these people. All they had ever wanted was peace, and even though they had never understood that the universe is unknowable and that you must always have big shoulders, still they had always sought only for peace. If peace leads to no conflict at all and then decay, well, that was something that had to be learned. So he could not hate these people.

But he could not help them either. He turned from their eyes and went into the radio shack. It had begun to dawn on the women that they might be leaving without their husbands or sons, and he did not want to see the fierce struggle that he was sure would take place. He sat alone and tried, for the last time, to call Bossio.

After a while an old woman found him and offered him coffee. It was a very decent thing to do, to think of him at a time like this, and he was so suddenly grateful he could only nod. The woman said that he must be cold in that thin army thing and that she had brought along a mackinaw for him. She poured the coffee and left him alone.

They were thinking of him now, he knew, because they were thinking of everyone who had to stay. Throw the dog a bone. Dammit, don't be like that, he told himself. He had not had anything to eat all day, and the coffee was warm and strong. He decided he might be of some help at the ship.

It was stripped down now, and they were loading. He was startled to see a great group of them standing in the snow, removing their clothes. Then he understood. The clothes of forty people would change the weight by enough to get a few more aboard. There was no fighting. Some of the women were almost hysterical and a few had refused to go and were still in their cabins, but the process was orderly. Children went automatically, as did the youngest husbands and all the women. The elders were shuffling around in the snow, waving their arms to keep themselves warm. Some of them were laughing to keep their spirits up.

In the end, the ship took forty-six people.

Rossel was one of the ones that would not be going. Dylan saw him standing by the airlock holding his wife in his arms, his face buried in her soft brown hair. A sense of great sympathy, totally unexpected, rose up in Dylan, and a little of the lostness of thirty years went slipping away. These were his people. It was a thing he had never understood before, because he had never once been among men in great trouble. He waited and watched, learning, trying to digest this while there was still time. Then the semi-naked colonists were inside and the airlock closed. But when the ship tried to lift, there was a sharp burning smell—she couldn't get off the ground.

Rush was sitting hunched over in the snow, his rifle across his knees. He was coated a thick white, and if he hadn't spoken Dylan would have stumbled over him. Dylan took out his pistol and sat down.

"What happened?" Rush asked.

"Lining burned out. She's being repaired."

"Coincidence?"

Dylan shook his head.

"How long'll it take to fix?"

"Four—five hours."

"It'll be night by then." Rush paused. "I wonder."

"Seems like they want to wait till dark."

"That's what I was figurin'. Could be they ain't got much of a force."

Dylan shrugged. "Also could mean they see better at night. Also could mean they move slow. Also could mean they want the least number of casualties."

Rush was quiet, and the snow fell softly on his face, on his eyebrows, where it had begun to gather. At length he said, "You got any idea how they got to the ship?"

Dylan shook his head again. "Nobody saw anything—but they were all pretty busy. Your theory about it maybe being one of us is beginning to look pretty good."

The colonist took off his gloves, lit a cigarette. The flame was strong and piercing and Dylan moved to check him but stopped. It didn't make much difference. The aliens knew where they were.

And this is right where we're gonna be, he thought.

"You know," he said suddenly, speaking mostly to himself, "I been in the army thirty years, and this is the first time I was ever in a fight. Once in a while we used to chase smugglers—never caught any, their ships were new—used to cut out after unlicensed ships, used to do all kinds of piddling things like that. But I never shot at anybody."

Rush was looking off into the woods. "Maybe the mail ship will come in."

Dylan nodded.

"They got a franchise, dammit. They got to deliver as long as they's a colony here."

When Dylan didn't answer, he said almost appealingly, "Some of those guys would walk barefoot through hell for a buck."

"Maybe," Dylan said. After all, why not let him hope? There were four long hours left.

Now he began to look down into himself, curiously, because he himself was utterly without hope and yet he was no longer really afraid. It was a surprising thing when you looked at it coldly, and he guessed that, after all, it was because of the thirty years. A part of him had waited for this. Some crazy part of him was ready—even after all this time—even excited about being in a fight. Well, what the hell, he marveled. And then he realized that the rest of him was awakening too, and he saw that this job was really his . . . that he had always been, in truth, a soldier.

Dylan sat, finding himself in the snow. Once long ago he had read about some fool who didn't want to die in bed, old and feeble. This character wanted to reach the height of his powers and then explode in a grand way—"in Technicolor," the man had said. Explode in Technicolor. It was meant to be funny, of course, but he had always remembered it, and he realized now that that was a small part of what he was feeling. The rest of it was that he was a soldier.

Barbarian, said a small voice, *primitive*. But he couldn't listen.

"Say, Cap," Rush was saying, "it's getting a mite chilly. I understand you got a bottle."

"Sure," he said cheerfully, "near forgot it." He pulled it out and gave it to Rush. The colonist drank appreciatively, saying to Dylan half seriously, half humorously, "One for the road."

Beneath them the planet revolved and the night came on. They waited, speaking briefly, while the unseen sun went down. And faintly, dimly, through the snow they heard at last the muffled beating of a ship. It passed overhead and they were sighting their guns before they recognized it. It was the mail ship.

They listened while she settled in a field by the camp, and Rush was pounding Dylan's arm. "She will take us all," Rush was shouting, "she'll take us all," and Dylan too was grinning, and then he saw a thing.

Small and shadowy, white-coated and almost invisible, the thing had come out of the woods and was moving toward them, bobbing and shuffling in the silent snow.

Dylan fired instinctively, because the thing had four arms and was coming right at him. He fired again. This time he hit it and the thing fell, but almost immediately it was up and lurching rapidly back into the trees. It was gone before Dylan could fire again.

They both lay flat in the snow, half buried. From the camp there were now no sounds at all.

"Did you get a good look?"

Rush grunted, relaxing. "Should've saved your fire, son. Looked like one o'them monkeys."

But there was something wrong. There was something that Dylan had heard in the quickness of the moment which he could not remember but which was very wrong.

"Listen," he said, suddenly placing it. "Dammit, that was no monkey."

"Easy—"

"I hit it. I hit it cold. It made a *noise*."

Rush was staring at him.

"Didn't you hear?" Dylan cried.

"No. Your gun was by my ear."

And then Dylan was up and running, hunched over, across the snow to where the thing had fallen. He had seen a piece of it break off when the bolt struck, and now in the snow he picked up a paw and brought it back to Rush. He saw right away there was no blood. The skin was real and furry, all right, but there was no blood. Because the bone was steel and the muscles were springs and the thing had been a robot.

The Alien rose up from his cot, whistling with annoyance. When that ship had come in his attention had been distracted from one of the robots, and of course the miserable thing had gone blundering right out into the humans. He thought for a while that the humans would overlook it—the seeing was poor and they undoubtedly would still think of it as animal, even with its firing ports open—but then he checked the robot and saw that a piece was missing and knew that the humans had found it. Well, he thought unhappily, flowing into his suit, no chance now to disable that other ship. The humans would never let another animal near.

And therefore—for he was, above all, a flexible being—he would proceed to another plan. The settlement would have to be detonated. And for that he would have to leave his own shelter and go out in that miserable cold and lie down in one of his bunkers which was much farther away. No need to risk blowing himself up with his own bombs; but still, that awful cold.

He dismissed his regrets and buckled his suit into place. It carried him up the stairs and bore him out into the snow. After one whiff of the cold he snapped his view-plate shut and immediately, as he had expected, it began to film with snow. Well, no matter, he would guide the unit by coordinates and it would find the bunker itself. No need for caution now. The plan was nearly ended.

In spite of his recent setback, the Alien lay back and allowed himself the satisfaction of a full tremble. The plan had worked very nearly to perfection, as of course it should, and he delighted in the contemplation of it.

When the humans were first detected, in the region of Bootes, much thought had gone into the proper method of learning their technology without being discovered themselves. There was little purpose in destroying the humans without first learning from them. Life was really a remarkable thing—one never knew what critical secrets a star borne race possessed. Hence the robots. And it was an extraordinary plan, an elegant plan. The Alien trembled again.

The humans were moving outward toward the rim; their base was apparently somewhere beyond Centaurus. Therefore a ring of defense was thrown up on most of the habitable worlds toward which the humans were coming—oh, a delightful plan—and the humans came down one by one and never realized that there was any defense at all.

With a cleverness which was almost excruciating, the Aliens had carefully selected a number of animals native to each world, and then constructed robot duplicates. So simple to place the robots down on a world with a single Director, then wait . . . for the humans to inhabit. Naturally the humans screened all the animals and scouted a planet pretty thoroughly before they set up a colony. Naturally their snares and their hunters caught no robots and never found the deep-buried Alien Director.

Then the humans relaxed and began to make homes, never realizing that in among the animals which gamboled playfully in the trees there was one which did not gambol, but watched. Never once noticing the monkeylike animals, or the small thing like a rabbit which was a camera eye, or the thing like a rat, which took chemical samples, or the thing like a lizard which cut wires.

The Alien rumbled on through the snow, trembling so much now with ecstasy and anticipation that the suit which bore him almost lost its balance. He very nearly fell over before he stopped trembling, and then he contained himself. In a little while, a very little while, there would be time enough for trembling.

"They could've been here till the sun went out," Rush said, "and we never would've known."

"I wonder how much they've found out," Dylan said.

Rush was holding the paw.

"Pretty near everything, I guess. This stuff don't stop at monkeys. Could be any size, any kind. . . . Look, let's get down into camp and tell 'em."

Dylan rose slowly to a kneeling position, peering dazedly out into the far white trees. His mind was turning over and over, around and around, like a roulette wheel. But at the center of his mind there was one thought, and it was rising up slowly now, through the waste and waiting of the years. He felt a vague surprise.

"Gettin' kind of dark," he said.

Rush swore. "Let's go. Let's get out of here." He tugged once at Dylan's arm and started off on his knees.

Dylan said, "Wait."

Rush stopped. Through the snow he tried to see Dylan's eyes. The soldier was still looking into the woods.

Dylan's voice was halting and almost inaudible. "They know everything about us. We don't know anything about them. They're probably sittin' out there right now, a swarm of 'em there behind those trees, waitin' for it to get real nice and dark."

He paused. "If I could get just one."

It was totally unexpected, to Dylan as well as Rush. The time for this sort of thing was past, the age was done, and for a long while neither of them fully understood.

"C'mon," Rush said with exasperation.

Dylan shook his head, marveling at himself. "I'll be with you in a little while."

Rush came near and looked questioningly into his face.

"Listen," Dylan said hurriedly, "we only need *one*. If we could just get one back to a lab we'd at least have some clue to what they are. This way we don't know anything. We can't just cut and run." He struggled with the unfamiliar, time-lost words. "We got to make a stand."

He turned from Rush and lay forward on his belly in the snow. He could feel his heart beating against the soft white cushion beneath him. There was no time to look at this calmly, and he was glad of that. He spent some time being very much afraid of the unknown things beyond the trees, but even then he realized that this was the one thing in his life he had to do.

It is not a matter of dying, he thought, but of *doing*. Sooner or later a man must do a thing which justifies his life, or the life is not worth living. The long, cold line of his existence had reached this point, here and now in the snow at this moment. He would go on from here as a man . . . or not at all.

Rush had sat down beside him, beginning to understand, watching without words. He was an old man. Like all earthmen, he had never fought with his hands. He had not fought the land or the tides or the weather or any of the million bitter sicknesses which man had grown up fighting, and he was beginning to realize that somewhere along the line he had been betrayed. Now, with a dead paw of the enemy in his hand, he did not feel like a man. And he was ready to fight now, but it was much too late and he saw with a vast leaden shame that he did not know how, could not even begin.

"Can I help?" he said.

Dylan shook his head. "Go back and let them know about the robots, and if the ship is ready to leave before I get back, well—then good luck."

He started to slither forward on his belly, but Rush reached out and grabbed him, holding with one hand to peace and gentleness and the soft days which were ending.

"Listen," he said, "you don't owe anybody."

Dylan stared at him with surprise. "I know," he said, and then he slipped up over the mound before him and headed for the trees.

Now what he needed was luck. Just good, plain old luck. He didn't know where they were or how many there were or what kinds there were, and the chances were good that one of them was watching him right now. Well, then, he needed some luck. He inched forward slowly, carefully, watching the oncoming line of trees. The snow was falling on him in big, leafy flakes and that was fine, because the blackness of his suit was much too distinct, and the more white he was, the better. Even so, it was becoming quite dark by now, and he thought he had a chance. He reached the first tree.

Silently he slipped off his heavy cap. The visor got in his way, and above all he must be able to see. He let the snow thicken on his hair before he raised himself on his elbows and looked outward.

There was nothing but the snow and the dead quiet and the stark white boles of the trees. He slid past the first trunk to the next, moving forward on his elbows with his pistol in his right hand. His elbow struck a rock and it hurt and his face was freezing. Once he rubbed snow from his eyebrows. Then he came through the trees and lay down before a slight rise, thinking.

Better to go around than over. But if anything is watching, it is most likely watching from above.

Therefore go around and come back up from behind. Yes.

His nose had begun to run. With great care he crawled among some large rocks, hoping against hope that he would not sneeze. Why had nothing seen him? Was something following him now? He turned to look behind him, but it was darker now and becoming difficult to see. But he would have to look behind him more often.

He was moving down a gorge. There were large trees above him and he needed their shelter, but he could not risk skipping down the sides of the gorge. And far off, weakly, out of the gray cold ahead, he heard a noise.

He lay down in the snow, listening. With a slow, thick shuffle, a thing was moving through the trees before him. In a moment he saw that it was not coming toward him. He lifted his head but saw nothing. Much more slowly, now, he crawled again. The thing was moving down the left side of the gorge ahead, coming away from the rise he had circled. It was moving without caution, and he worried that if he did not hurry he would lose it. But for the life of him he couldn't stand up.

The soldier went forward on his hands and knees. When his clothes hung down, the freezing cold entered his throat and shocked his body, which was sweating. He shifted his gun to his gloved hand and blew on the bare fingers of his right, still crawling. When he reached the other end of the gorge he stood upright against a rock wall and looked in the direction of the shuffling thing.

He saw it just as it turned. It was a great black lump on a platform. The platform had legs, and the thing was plodding methodically upon a path which would bring it past him. It had come down from the rise and was rounding the gorge when Dylan saw it. It did not see him.

If he had not ducked quickly and brought up his gun, the monkey would not have seen him either, but there was no time for regret. The monkey was several yards to the right of the lump on the platform when he heard it start running; he had to look up this time, and saw it leaping toward him over the snow.

All right, he said to himself. His first shot took the monkey in the head, where the eyes were. As the thing crashed over, there was a hiss and a stench and flame seared into his shoulder and the side of his face. He lurched to the side, trying to see, his gun at arm's length as the lump on the platform spun toward him. He fired four times. Three bolts went home in the lump; the fourth tore a leg off the platform and the whole thing fell over.

Dylan crawled painfully behind a rock, his left arm useless. The silence had come back again and he waited, but neither of the Alien things moved. Nothing else moved in the woods around him. He turned his face up to the falling snow and let it come soothingly upon the awful wound in his side.

After a while he looked out at the monkey. It had risen to a sitting position but was frozen in the motion of rising. It had ceased to function when he hit the lump. Out of the numbness and the pain he felt a great gladness rising.

The guide. He had killed the guide.

He would not be cautious any more. Maybe some of the other robots were self-directing and dangerous, but they could be handled. He went to the lump, stared at it without feeling. A black, doughy bulge was swelling out through one of the holes.

It was too big to carry, but he would have to take something back. He went over and took the monkey by a stiff jutting arm and began dragging it back toward the village.

Now he began to stumble. It was dark and he was very tired. But the steel he had been forging in his breast was complete, and the days which were coming would be days full of living. He would walk with big shoulders and he would not bother to question, because man was not born to live his days at home, by the fire.

It was a very big thing that Dylan had learned and he could not express it, but he knew it all the same, knew it beyond understanding. And so he went home to his people.

One by one, increasing, in the wee black corner of space which man had taken for his own, other men were learning. And the snow fell and the planets whirled; and when it was spring where Dylan had fought, men were already leaping back out to the stars.

CODE-NAME FEIREFITZ

David Drake

"Lord, we got one!" cried the trooper whose detector wand pointed toward the table that held the small altar. "That's a power-gun for sure, Captain, nothing else'd read so much iridium!"

The three other khaki-clad soldiers in the room with Captain Esa Mboya tensed and cleared guns they had not expected to need. The villagers of Ain Chelia knew that to be found with a weapon meant death. The ones who were willing to face that were in the Bordj, waiting with their households and their guns for the Slammers to rip them out. Waiting to die fighting.

The houses of Ain Chelia were decorated externally by screens and colored tiles; but the tiles were set in concrete walls and the screens themselves were cast concrete. Narrow cul-de-sacs lined by blank, gated courtyard walls tied the residential areas of the village into knots of strongpoints. The rebels had elected to make their stand in Ain Chelia proper only because the fortress they had cut into the walls of the open pit mine was an even tougher objective.

"Stand easy, troopers," said Mboya. The householder gave him a tight smile; he and Mboya were the only blacks in the room—or the village. "I'll handle this one," Captain Mboya continued. "The rest of you get on with the search under Sergeant Scratchard. Sergeant—" calling toward the outside door—"come in here for a moment."

Besides the householder and the troops, a narrow-faced civilian named Youssef ben Khedda stood in the room. On his face was dawning a sudden and terrible hope. He had been Assistant Superintendent of the ilmenite mine before Kabyles all over the planet rose against their Arabized central government in al-Madinah. The Superintendent was executed, but ben Khedda had joined the rebels to be spared. It was a common enough story to men who had sorted through the ruck of as many rebellions as the Slammers had. But now ben Khedda was a loyal citizen again. Openly he guided G Company from house to house, secretly he whispered to Captain Mboya the names of those who had carried their guns and families to the mine. "Father," said ben Khedda to the householder, lowering his eyes in a mockery of contrition, "I never dreamed that there would be contraband *here*, I swear it."

Juma al-Habashi smiled back at the small man who saw the chance to become undisputed leader of as much of Chelia as the Slammers left standing and alive. "I'm sure you didn't dream it, Youssef," he said more gently than he himself expected. "Why should you, when I'd forgotten the gun myself."

Sergeant Scratchard stepped inside with a last glance back at the courtyard and the other three men of Headquarters Squad waiting there as security. Within, the first sergeant's eyes touched the civilians and the tense enlisted men; but Captain Mboya was calm, so Scratchard kept his own voice calm as he said, "Sir?"

"Sergeant," Mboya said quietly, "you're in charge of the search. If you need me, I'll be in here."

"Sir," Scratchard agreed with a nod. "Well, get the lead out, daisies!" he snarled to the troopers, gesturing them to the street. "We got forty copping houses to run yet!"

As ben Khedda passed him, the captain saw the villager's control slip to uncover his glee. The sergeant was the last man out of the room; Mboya latched the street door after him. Only then did he meet the householder's eyes again. "Hello, Juma," he said in the Kabyle he had sleep-learned rather than the Kikuyu they had both probably forgotten by now. "Brothers shouldn't have to meet this way, should we?"

Juma smiled in mad irony rather than humor. Then his mouth slumped out of that bitter rictus and he said sadly, "No, we shouldn't, that's right." Looking at his altar and not the soldier, he added, "I knew there'd be a—a unit sent around, of course. But I didn't expect you'd be leading the one that came here, where I was."

"Look, I didn't volunteer for Operation Feirefitz," Esa blazed. "And Via, how was I supposed to know where you were anyway?

We didn't exactly part kissing each other's cheeks ten years ago, did we? And here you've gone and changed your name even— how was I supposed to keep from stumbling over you?"

Juma's face softened. He stepped to his brother, taking the other's wrists in his hands. "I'm sorry," he said. "Of course that was unfair. The—what's going to happen disturbs me." He managed a genuine smile. "I didn't really change my name, you know. 'Al-Habashi' just means 'the Black', and it's what everybody on this planet was going to call me whatever I wanted. We aren't very common on Dar al-B'heed, you know. Any more than we were in the Slammers."

"Well, there's one fewer black in the Slammers than before *you* opted out," Esa said bitterly; but he took the civilian's wrists in turn and squeezed them. As the men stood linked, the clerical collar that Juma wore beneath an ordinary jellaba caught the soldier's eye. Without the harshness of a moment before, Esa asked, "Do they all call you 'Father'?"

The civilian laughed and stepped away. "No, only the hypocrites like Youssef," he said. "Oh, Ain Chelia is just as Islamic as the capital, as al-Madinah, never doubt. I have a small congregation here . . . and I have the respect of the rest of the community, I think. I'm head of equipment maintenance at the mine, which doesn't mean assigning work to other people, not here." He spread his hands, palms down. The fingernails were short and the grit beneath their ends a true black and no mere skin tone. "But I think I'd want to do that anyway, even if I didn't need to eat to live. I've guided more folk to the Way by showing them how to balance a turbine than I do when I mumble about peace."

Captain Mboya walked to the table on top of which stood an altar triptych, now closed. Two drawers were set between the table legs. He opened the top one. In it were the altar vessels, chased brasswork of local manufacture. They were beautiful both in sum and in detail, but they had not tripped a detector set to locate tool steel and iridium.

The lower drawer held a powergun.

Juma watched without expression as his brother raised the weapon, checked the full magazine, and ran a fingertip over the manufacturer's stampings. "Heuvelmans of Friesland," Esa said conversationally. "Past couple contracts have been let on Terra, good products . . . but I always preferred the one I was issued when they assigned me to a tribarrel and I rated a sidearm." He drew his own pistol from its flap holster and compared it to the weapon from the drawer. "Right, consecutive serial numbers," the soldier said. He laid Juma's pistol back where it came from.

"Not the sort of souvenir we're supposed to take with us when we resign from the Slammers, of course."

Very carefully, and with his eyes on the wall as if searching for flaws in its thick, plastered concrete, Juma said, "I hadn't really . . . thought of it being here. I suppose that's grounds for carrying me back to a re-education Camp in al-Madinah, isn't it?"

His brother's fist slammed the table. The triptych jumped and the vessels in the upper drawer rang like Poe's brazen bells. "Re-education? It's grounds for being burned at the *stake* if I say so! Listen, the reporters are back in the capital, not here. My orders from the District Governor are to *pacify* this region, not coddle it!" Esa's face melted from anger to grief as suddenly as he had swung his fist a moment before. "Via, elder brother, why'd you have to leave? There wasn't a man in the Regiment could handle a tribarrel the way you could."

"That was a long time ago," said Juma, facing the soldier again.

"I remember at Sphakteria," continued Esa as if Juma had not spoken, "when they popped the ambush and killed your gunner the first shot. You cut'em apart like they weren't shooting at you too. And then you led the whole platoon clear, driving the jeep with the wick all the way up and working the gun yourself with your right hand. Nobody else could've done it."

"Do you remember," said Juma, his voice dropping into a dreamy caress as had his brother's by the time he finished speaking, "the night we left Nairobi? You led the Service of Farewell yourself, there in the starport, with everyone in the terminal joining in. The faith we'd been raised in was just words to me before then, but you made the Way as real as the tiles I was standing on. And I thought 'Why is he going off to be a soldier? If ever a man was born to lead other men to peace, it was Esa.' And in time, you did lead me to peace, little brother."

Esa shook himself, standing like a centipede in his body armor. "I got that out of my system," he said.

Juma walked over to the altar. "As I got the Slammers out of my system," he said, and he closed the drawer over the powergun within.

Neither man spoke for moments that seemed longer. At last Juma said, "Will you have a beer?"

"What?" said the soldier in surprise. "That's permitted on Dar al-B'heed?"

Juma chuckled as he walked into his kitchen. "Oh yes," he said as he opened a trapdoor in the floor, "though of course not

98

everyone drinks it." He raised two corked bottles from their cool recess and walked back to the central room. "There are some Arab notions that never sat very well with Kabyles, you know. Many of the notions about women, veils and the like. Youssef ben Khedda's wife wore a veil until the revolt . . . then she took it off and walked around the streets like the other women of Ain Chelia. I suspect that since your troops swept in, she has her veil on again."

"*That* one," said the captain with a snort that threatened to spray beer. "I can't imagine why nobody had the sense to throttle him—at least before they went off to their damned fortress."

Juma gestured his brother to one of the room's simple chairs and took another for himself. "Not everyone has seen as many traitors as we have, little brother," he said. "Besides, his own father was one of the martyrs whose death ignited the revolt. He was caught in al-Madinah with hypnocubes of Kabyle language instruction. The government called that treason and executed him."

Esa snorted again. "And didn't anybody here wonder who shopped the old man to the security police? Via! But I shouldn't complain—he makes my job easier." He swallowed the last of his beer, paused a moment, and then pointed the mouth of the bottle at Juma as if it would shoot. "What about you?" the soldier demanded harshly. "Where do you stand?"

"For peace," said Juma simply, "for the Way. As I always have since I left the Regiment. But . . . my closest friends in the village are dug into the sides of the mine pit now, waiting for you. Or they're dead already outside al-Madinah."

The soldier's hand tightened on the bottle, his fingers darker than the clear brown glass. With a conscious effort of will he set the container down on the terrazzo floor beside his chair. "They're dead either way," he said as he stood up. He put his hand on the door latch before he added, pausing but not turning around, "Listen, elder brother. I told you I didn't ask to be assigned to this mop-up operation; and if I'd known I'd find you here, I'd have taken leave or a transfer. But I'm here now, and I'll do my duty, do you hear?"

"As the Lord wills," said Juma from behind him.

The walls of Juma's house, like those of all the houses in Ain Chelia, were cast fifty centimeters thick to resist the heat of the sun. The front door was a scale with the wall, close-fitting and too massive to slam. To captain Mboya, it was the last frustration of the interview that he could elicit no more than a satisfied thump from the door as he stamped into the street.

• • •

The ballistic crack of the bullet was all the louder for the stillness of the plateau an instant before. Captain Mboya ducked beneath the lip of the headquarters dug-out. The report of the sniper's weapon was lost in the fire of the powerguns and mortars that answered it. "Via, Captain!" snarled Sergeant Scratchard from the parked commo jeep. "Trying to get yourself killed?"

"Via!" Esa wheezed. He had bruised his chin and was thankful for it, the way a child is thankful for any punishment less than the one imagined. He accepted Scratchard's silent offer of a fiber-optics periscope. Carefully, the Captain raised it to scan what had been the Chelia Mine and was not the Bordj—the Fortress—holding approximately one hundred and forty Kabyle rebels with enough supplies to last a year.

Satellite photographs showed the mine as a series of neatly-stepped terraces in the center of a plateau. From the plateau's surface, nothing of significance could be seen until a flash discovered the position of a sniper the moment before he dodged to fire again.

"It'd be easy," Sergeant Scratchard said, "if they'd just tried to use the pit as a big foxhole. . . . Have Central pop a couple anti-personnel rounds overhead and then we go in and count bodies. But they've got tunnels and spider holes—and command-detonated mines—laced out from the pit like a giant worm-farm. This one's going to cost, Esa."

"Blood and martyrs," the captain said under his breath. When he had received the Ain Chelia assignment, Mboya had first studied reconnaissance coverage of the village and the mine three kilometers away. It was now a month and a half since the rebel disaster at al-Madinah. The Slammers had raised the siege of the capital in a pitched battle that no one in the human universe was better equipped to fight. Surviving rebels had scattered to their homes to make what preparations they could against the white terror they knew would sweep in the wake of the government's victory. At Ain Chelia, the preparations had been damned effective. The recce showed clearly that several thousand cubic yards of rubble had been dumped into the central pit of the mine, the waste of burrowings from all around its five kilometer circumference.

"We can drop penetrators all year," Mboya said, aloud but more to himself than the non-com beside him. "Blow the budget for the whole operation, and even then I wouldn't bet they couldn't tunnel ahead of the shelling faster than we broke rock on top of them."

"If we storm the place," said Sergeant Scratchard, "and then go down the tunnels after the hold-outs, we'll have thirty per cent casualties if we lose a man."

A rifle flashed from the pit-edge. Almost simultaneously, one of the company's three-barreled automatic weapons slashed the edge of the rebel gunpit. The trooper must have sighted in his weapon earlier when a sniper had popped from the pit, knowing the site would be re-used eventually. Now the air shook as the powergun detonated a bandolier of grenades charged with industrial explosives. The sniper's rifle glittered as it spun into the air; her head was by contrast a ragged blur, its long hair uncoiling and snapping outward with the thrust of the explosion.

"Get that gunner's name," Mboya snapped to his first sergeant. "He's earned a week's leave as soon as we stand down. But to get all the rest of them . . ." and the officer's voice was the more stark for the fact it was so controlled, "we're going to need something better. I think we're going to have to talk them out."

"Via, Captain," said Scratchard in real surprise, "why would they want to come out? They saw at al-Madinah what happens when they faced us in the field. And nobody surrenders when they know all prisoners're going to be shot."

"Don't say nobody," said Esa Mboya in a voice as crisp as the gunfire bursting anew from the Bordj. "Because that's just what you're going to see this lot do."

The dead end of Juma's street had been blocked and turned into the company maintenance park between the time Esa left to observe the Bordj and his return to his brother's house. Skimmers, trucks, and a gun-jeep with an intermittent short in its front fan had been pulled into the cul-de-sac. They were walled on three sides by the courtyards of the houses beyond Juma's.

Sergeant Scratchard halted the jeep with the bulky commo equipment in the open street, but Mboya swung his own skimmer around the supply truck that formed a makeshift fourth wall for the park. A guard saluted. "Muller!" Esa shouted, even before the skirts of his one-man vehicle touched the pavement. "What in the name of heaven d'ye think you're about! I told you to set up in the main square!"

Bog Muller stood up beside a skimmer raised on edge. He was a bulky Technician with twenty years service in the Slammers. A good administrator, but his khakis were clean. Operation Feirefitz had required the company to move fast and long, and there was no way Muller's three half-trained subordinates could have coped with the consequent rash of equipment failures. "Ah, well,

101

Captain," Muller temporized, his eyes apparently focused on the row of wall spikes over Esa's head, "we ran into Juma and he said—"

"He *what*!" Mboya shouted.

"I said," said Juma, rising from behind the skimmer himself, "that security in the middle of the village would be more of a problem than anybody needed. We've got some hot-heads; I don't want any of them to get the notion of stealing a gun-jeep, for instance. The two households there—" he pointed to the entrances now blocked by vehicles, using the grease gun in his right hand for the gesture—"have both been evacuated to the Bordj." The half-smile he gave his brother could have been meant for either what he had just said or for the words he added, raising both the grease gun and the wire brush he held in his left hand: "Besides, what with the mine closed, I'd get rusty myself with no equipment to work on."

"After all," said Muller in what was more explanation than defense, "I know Juma back when."

Esa took in his brother's smile, took in as well the admiring glances of the three Tech I's who had been watching the civilian work. "All right," he said to Muller, "but the next time clear it with me. And you," he said, pointing to Juma, "come on inside for now. We need to talk."

"Yes, little brother," the civilian said with a bow as submissive as his tone.

In the surprising cool of his house, Juma stripped off the gritty jellaba he had worn while working. He began washing with a waterless cleaner, rubbing it on with smooth strokes of his palms. On a chain around his neck glittered a tiny silver crucifix, normally hidden by his clothing.

"You didn't do much of a job persuading your friends to your Way of Peace," Esa said with an anger he had not intended to display.

"No, I'm afraid I didn't," the civilian answered mildly. "They were polite enough, even the Kaid, Ali ben Cheriff. But they pointed out that the Arabizers in al-Madinah intended to stamp out all traces of Kabyle culture as soon as possible . . . which of course was true. And we did have our own martyr here in Ain Chelia, as you know. I couldn't—" Juma looked up at his brother, his dark skin glistening beneath the lather—"argue with their *military* estimate, after all, either. The Way doesn't require that its followers lie about reality in order to change it—but I don't have to tell you that."

"Go on," said the captain. His hand touched the catches of his body armor. He did not release them, however, even though the hard-suit was not at the moment protection against any physical threat.

"Well, the National Army was outnumbered ten to one by the troops we could field from the blacklands," Juma continued as he stepped into the shower. "That's without defections, too. And weapons aren't much of a problem. Out there, any jack-leg mechanic can turn out a truck piston in his back room. The tolerances aren't any closer on a machine gun. But what we didn't expect—" he raised his deep voice only enough to override the hiss of the shower—"was that all six of the other planets of the al-Ittihad al-Arabi—" for Arab Union Juma used the Arabic words, and they rasped in his throat like a file on bars—"would club together and help the sanctimonious butchers in al-Madinah hire the Slammers."

He stepped shining from the stall, no longer pretending detachment or that he and his brother were merely chatting. "I visited the siege lines then," Juma rumbled, wholly a preacher and wholly a man, "and I begged the men from Ain Chelia to come home while there was time. To make peace, or if they would not choose peace then at least to choose life—to lie low in the hills till the money ran out and the Slammers were off on somebody else's contract, killing somebody else's enemies. But my friends would stand with their brothers . . . and so they did, and they died with their brothers, too many of them, when the tanks came through their encirclement like knives through a goat-skin." His smile crooked and his voice dropped. "And the rest came home and told me they should have listened before."

"They'll listen to you now," said Esa, "if you tell them to come out of the Bordj without their weapons and surrender."

Juma began drying himself on a towel of coarse local cotton. "Will they?" he replied without looking up.

Squeezing his fingers against the bands of porcelain armor over his stomach, Esa said, "The Re-education Camps outside al-Madinah aren't a rest cure, but there's too many journalists in the city to let them be too bad. Even if the hold-outs are willing to die, they surely don't want their whole families wiped out. And if we have to clear the Bordj ourselves—well, there won't be any prisoners, you know that. . . . There wouldn't be even if we wanted them, not after we blast and gas the tunnels, one by one."

"Yes, I gather the Re-education Camps aren't too bad," the civilian agreed, walking past his brother to don a light jellaba of softer weave than his work garment. "I gather they're not very full, either. A—a cynic, say, might guess that most of the

103

trouble-makers don't make it to al-Madinah where journalists can see them. That they die in the desert after they've surrendered. Or they don't surrender, of course. I don't think Ali ben Cheriff and the others in the Bordj are going to surrender, for instance."

"Damn you!" the soldier shouted. "The choice is *certain* death, isn't it? *Any* chance is better than that!"

"Well you see," said Juma, watching the knuckles of his right hand twist against the palm of his left, "they know as well as I do that the only transport you arrived with was the minimum to haul your own supplies. There's no way you could carry over a hundred prisoners back to the capital. No way in . . . Hell."

Esa slammed the wall with his fist. Neither the concrete nor his raging expression showed any reaction to the loud impact. "I could be planning to put them in commandeered ore haulers, couldn't I?" he said. "Some of them must be operable?"

Juma stepped to the younger man and took him by the wrists as gently as a shepherd touching a newborn lamb. "Little brother," he said, "swear to me that you'll turn anyone who surrenders over to the authorities in al-Madinah, and I'll do whatever I can to get them to surrender."

The soldier snatched his hands away. He said, "Do you think I wouldn't lie to you because we're brothers? Then you're a fool!"

"What I think, what anyone thinks, is between him and the Lord," Juma said. He started to move toward his brother again but caught the motion and turned it into a swaying only. "If you will swear to me to deliver them unharmed, I'll carry your message into the Bordj."

Esa swung open the massive door. On the threshold he paused and turned to his brother. "Every one of my boys who doesn't make it," he said in a venomous whisper. "His blood's on your head."

Captain Mboya did not try to slam the door this time. He left it standing open as he strode through the courtyard. "Scratchard!" he roared to the sergeant with an anger not meant for the man on whom it fell. "Round up ben Khedda!" Mboya threw himself down on his skimmer and flicked the fans to life. Over their whine he added, "Get him up to me at the command dugout. Now!"

With the skill of long experience, the captain spun his one-man vehicle past the truck and the jeep parked behind it. Sergeant Scratchard gloomily watched his commander shriek up the street. The captain shouldn't have been going anywhere without the jeep, his commo link to Central, in tow. No point in worrying about that, though. The non-com sighed and lifted the jeep off the pavement. Ben Khedda would be at his house or in the cafe across the street from it. Scratchard hoped he had a vehicle of his own and wouldn't have to rise the jump seat of the jeep. He didn't like to sit that close to a slimy traitor.

But Jack Scratchard knew he'd done worse things than sit with a traitor during his years with the Slammers; and, needs must, he would again.

The mortar shell burst with a white flash. Seconds later came a distant *chunk*! as if a rock had been dropped into a trash can. Even after the report had died away, fragments continued ricocheting from rock with tiny gnat-songs. Ben Khedda flinched beneath the clear night sky.

"It's just our harassing fire," said Captain Mboya. "Your rag-heads don't have high-angle weapons, thank the Lord. Of course, all our shells do is keep them down in their tunnels."

The civilian swallowed. "Your sergeant," he said, "told me you needed me at once." Scratchard stirred in the darkness at the other end of the dugout, but he made no comment of his own.

"Yeah," said Mboya, "but when I cooled off I decided to take a turn around the perimeter. Took a while. It's a bloody long perimeter for one cursed infantry company to hold."

"Well, I," ben Khedda said, "I came at once, sir. I recognize the duty all good citizens owe to our liberators." Firing broke out, a burst from a projectile weapon answered promiscuously by powerguns. Ben Khedda winced again. Cyan bolts from across the pit snapped overhead, miniature lightning following miniature thunder.

Without looking up, Captain Mboya keyed his commo helmet and said, "Thrasher Four to Thrasher Four-Three. Anybody shoots beyond his sector again and it's ten days in the glass house when we're out of this cop." The main unit in Scratchard's jeep purred as it relayed the amplified signal. All the firing ceased.

"Will ben Cheriff and the others in the Bordj listen to you, do you think?" the captain continued.

For a moment, ben Khedda did not realize the officer was speaking to him. He swallowed again. "Well, I . . . I can't say," he blurted. He began to curl his upper lip as if to chew a moustache, though he was clean shaven. "They aren't friends of mine, of course, but if God wills and it would help you if I addressed them over a loudspeaker as to their true duties as citizens of Dar al-B'heed—"

"We hear you were second in command of the Chelia contingent at Madinah," Mboya said inflexibly. "Besides, there won't be a loudspeaker, you'll be going in in person."

Horror at past and future implications warred in ben Khedda's mind and froze his tongue. At last he stammered, "Oh no, C-captain, before G-god, they've lied to you! That accurst al-Habashi wishes to lie away my life! I did no more than any man would do to stay alive!"

Mboya waved the other to silence. The pale skin of his palm winked as another shell detonated above the Bordj. When the echoes died away, the captain went on in a voice as soft as a leopard's paw, "You will tell them that if they all surrender, their lives will be spared and they will not be turned over to the government until they are actually in al-Madinah. You will say that I swore that on my honor and on the soul of my house."

Ben Khedda raised a hand to interrupt, but the soldier's voice rolled on implacably. "They must deposit all their arms in the Bordj and come out to be shackled. The tunnels will be searched. If there are any hold-outs, three of those who surrendered will be shot for each hold-out. If there are any boobytraps, ten of those who surrendered will be shot for every man of mine who is injured."

Mboya drew a breath, long and deep as that of a power lifter. The civilian, tight as a house-jack, strangled his own words as he waited for the captain to conclude. "You will say that after they have done as I have said, all of them will be loaded on ore carriers with sun-screens. You will explain that there will be food and water brought from the village to support them. And you will tell them that if some of them are wounded or are infirm, they may ride within an ambulance which will be air-conditioned."

"Do you understand?"

For a moment, ben Khedda struggled with an inability to phrase his thoughts in neutral terms. He was unwilling to meet the captain's eyes, even with the darkness as a cushion. Finally he said, "Captain—I, I trust your word as I would trust that of no man since the Prophet, on whom be peace. When you say the lives of the traitors will be spared, there can be no doubt, may it please God."

"Trust has nothing to do with it," said Captain Mboya without expression. "I have told you what you will say, and you will say it."

"Captain, Captain," whimpered the civilian, "I understand. The trip is a long one and surely some of the most troublesome will die of heat stroke. They will know that themselves. But there will be no . . . general tragedy? I must live here in Ain Chelia with the friends of the, the traitors. You see my position?"

"Your position," Mboya repeated with scorn that drew a

chuckle from Scratchard across the dug-out. "Your position is that unless you talk your friends there out of the Bordj—" he gestured. Automatic weapons began to rave and chatter as if on cue. "Unless you go down there and come back with them, I'll have you shot on your doorstep for a traitor and your body left to the dogs. That's your position."

"Cheer up, citizen," Sergeant Scratchard said. "You're getting a great chance to pick one side and stick with it. The change'll do you good."

Ben Khedda gave a despairing cry and stood, his dun jellaba flapping as a lesser shadow. He stared over the rim of the dug-out into a night now brightened only by stars and a random powergun bolt, harrassment like that of the mortars. He turned and shouted at the motionless captain, "It's easy for you—you go where your colonel sends you, you kill who he tells you to kill. And then you come all high and moral over the rest of us, who have to make our own decisions! You despise me? At least I'm a man and not somebody's dog!"

Mboya laughed harshly. "You think Colonel Hammer told us how to clear the back country? Don't be a fool. My official orders are to co-operate with the District Governor, and to send all prisoners back to al-Madinah for internment. The colonel can honestly deny ordering anything else—and letting him do that is as much a part of my job as co-operating with a governor who knows that anybody really sent to a Re-education Camp will be back in his hair in a year."

There was a silence in the dug-out. At last the sergeant said, "He can't go out now, sir." The moan of a ricochet underscored the words.

"No, no, we'll have to wait till dawn," the captain agreed tiredly. As if ben Khedda were an unpleasant machine, he added, "Get him the hell out of my sight, though. Stick him in the bunker with the Headquarters Squad and tell them to hold him till called for. Via! but I wish this operation was over."

The guns spat at one another all through the night. It was not the fire that kept Esa Mboya awake, however, but rather the dreams that plagued him with gentle words whenever he did manage to nod off.

"Well," said Juma, scowling judiciously at the gun-jeep on the rack before him, "I'd say we pull the wiring harness first. Half the time that's the whole problem—grit gets into the conduits and when the fans vibrate, it saws through the insulation. Even if we're wrong, we haven't done anything that another few months of running on Dar al-B'heed wouldn't have required anyway."

"You should have seen him handle one a' these when I first knew him," said Bog Muller proudly to his subordinates. "Beat it to hell, he would, Via—bring her in with rock scrapes on both sides that he'd put on at the same time!"

The Kikuyu civilian touched a valve and lowered the rack. His hand caressed the sand-burnished skirt of the jeep as it sank past him. The joy-stick controls were in front of the left-hand seat. Finesse was a matter of touch and judgment, not sophisticated instrumentation. He waggled the stick gently, remembering. In front of the other seat was the powergun, its three iridium barrels poised to rotate and hose out destruction in a nearly-continuous stream.

"You won't believe it," continued the Technician, "but I saw with my own eyes—" that was a lie—"this boy here steering with one hand and working the gun with the other. Bloody miracle that was—even if he did give Maintenance more trouble than any three other troopers."

"You learn a lot about a machine when you push it, when you stress it," said Juma. His fingers reached for but did not quite touch the spade grips of the tribarrel. "About men, too," he added and lowered his hand. He looked Muller in the face and said, "What I learned about myself was that I didn't want to live in a universe that had no better use for me than to gun other people down. I won't claim to be saving souls . . . because that's in the Lord's hands and he uses what instruments he desires. But at least I'm not taking lives."

One of the younger Techs coughed. Muller nodded heavily and said, "I know what you mean, Juma. I've never regretted getting into Maintenance right off the way I did. Especially times like today. . . . But Via, if we stand here fanning our lips, we won't get a curst bit of work done, will we?"

The civilian chuckled without asking for an explanation of 'especially times like today.' "Sure, Bog," he said, latching open the left-side access ports one after another. "Somebody dig out a 239B harness and we'll see if I remember as much as I think I do about changing one of these beggars." He glanced up at the truncated mass of the plateau, wiping his face with a bandanna. "Things have quieted down since the sun came up," he remarked. "Even if I weren't—dedicated to the Way—I know too many people on both sides to like to hear the shooting at the mine."

None of the other men responded. At the time it did not occur

108

to Juma that there might be something about his words that embarrassed them.

"There's a flag," said Scratchard, his eyes pressed tight to the lenses of the periscope. "Blood and martyrs, Cap—there's a flag!"

"No shooting!" Mboya ordered over his commo as he moved. "Four to all Thrasher units, stand to but no shooting!"

All around the mine crater, men watched a white rag flapping on the end of a long wooden pole. Some looked through periscopes like those in the command dugout, others over the sights of their guns in hope that something would give them an excuse to fire. "Well, what are they waiting for?" the captain muttered.

"It's ben Khedda," guessed Scratchard without looking away from the flag. "He was scared green to go out there. Now he's just as scared to come back."

The flag staggered suddenly. Troopers tensed, but a moment later an unarmed man climbed full height from the Bordj. The high sun threw his shadow at his feet like a pit. Standing as erect as his age permitted him, Ali ben Cheriff took a step toward the Slammers' lines. Wind plucked at his jellaba and white beard; the rebel leader was a patriarch in appearance as well as in simple fact. On his head was the green turban that marked him as a pilgrim to al-Meccah on Terra. He was as devotedly Moslem as he was Kabyle, and he—like most of the villagers—saw no inconsistencies in the facts. To ben Cheriff it was no more necessary to become an Arab in order to accept Islam than it had seemed necessary to Saint Paul that converts to Christ first become Jews.

"We've won," the captain said as he watched the figure through the foreshortening lenses. "That's the Kaid, ben Cheriff. If he comes, they all do."

Up from the hidden tunnel clambered an old woman wearing the stark black of a matron. The Kaid paused and stretched back his hand, but the woman straightened without help. Together the old couple began to walk toward the waiting guns.

The flagstaff flapped erect again. Gripping it like a talisman, Youssef ben Khedda stepped from the tunnel mouth where the Kaid had shouldered aside his hesitation. He picked his way across the ground at increasing speed. When ben Khedda passed the Kaid and his wife, he skirted them widely as if he were afraid of being struck. More rebels were leaving the Bordj in single file. None of them carried visible weapons. Most, men and women alike, had their eyes cast down; but a red-haired girl leading a child barely old enough to walk glared around with the haughty rage of a lioness.

"Well, no rest for the wicked," grunted Sergeant Scratchard. Settling his sub-machinegun on its sling, he climbed out of the dugout. "Headquarters Squad to me," he ordered. Bent over against the possible shock of a fanatic's bullets, experienced enough to know the reality of his fear and brave enough to face it none the less, Scratchard began to walk to the open area between pit and siege lines where the prisoners would be immobilized. The seven men of HQ Squad followed; their corporal drove the jeep loaded with leg irons.

One of the troopers raised his powergun to bar ben Khedda. Scratchard waved and called an order; the trooper shrugged and let the Kabyle pass. The sergeant gazed after him for a moment, then spat in the dust and went on about the business of searching and securing the prisoners.

Youssef ben Khedda was panting with tension and effort as he approached the dugout, but there was a hard glint of triumph in his eyes as well. He knew he was despised, by those he led no less than by those who had driven him; but he had dug the rebels from their fortress when all the men and guns of the Slammers might have been unable to do so without him. Now he saw a way to ride the bloody crest to permanent power in Ain Chelia. He tried to set his flag in the ground. It scratched into the rocky soil, then fell with a clatter. "I have brought them to you," ben Khedda said in a haughty voice.

"Some of them, at least," said Mboya, his face neutral. Rebels continued to straggle from the Bordj, their faces sallow from more than the day they had spent in their tunnels. The Kaid had submitted to the shackles with a stony indifference. His wife was weeping beside him, not for herself but for her husband. Two of the nervous troopers were fanning the prisoners with detector wands set for steel and iridium. Anything the size of a razor blade would register. A lead bludgeon or a brass-barreled pistol would be ignored, but there were some chances you took in the service of practicality.

"As God wills, they are all coming, you know that," ben Khedda said, assertive with dreamed-of lordship. "If they were each in his separate den, many of them would fight till you blew them out or buried them. All are willing to die, but most would not willingly kill their fellows, their families." His face worked. "A fine joke, is it not?" If what had crossed ben Khedda's lips had been a smile, then it transmuted to a sneer. "They would have

110

been glad to kill me first, I think, but they were afraid that you would have been angry."

"More fools them," said the captain.

"Yes . . . ," said the civilian, drawing back his face like a rat confronting a terrier, "more fools them. And now you will pay me."

"Captain," said the helmet speaker in the first sergeant's voice, "this one says he's the last."

Mboya climbed the four steps to surface level. Scratchard waved and pointed to the Kabyle who was just joining the scores of his fellows. The number of those being shackled in a continuous chain at least approximated the one hundred and forty who were believed to have holed up in the Bordj. Through the clear air rang hammer strokes as a pair of troopers stapled the chain to the ground at intervals, locking the prisoners even more securely into the killing ground. The captain nodded. "We'll give it a minute to let anybody still inside have second thoughts," he said over the radio. "Then the search teams go in." He looked at ben Khedda. "All right," he said, "you've got your life and whatever you think you can do with it. Now, get out of here before I change my mind."

Mboya gazed again at the long line of prisoners. He was unable not to imagine them as they would look in an hour's time, after the Bordj had been searched and their existence was no longer a tool against potential hold-outs. He could not have broken with the Way of his childhood, however, had he not replaced it with a sense of duty as uncompromising. Esa Mboya, Captain, G Company, Hammer's Regiment, would do whatever was required to accomplish the task set him. They had been hired to pacify the district, not just to quiet it down for six months or a year.

Youssef ben Khedda had not left. He was still facing Mboya, as unexpected and unpleasant as a rat on the pantry shelf. He was saying, "No, there is one more thing you must do, as God wills, before you leave Ain Chelia. I do not compel it—" the soldier's face went blank with fury at the suggestion—"your duty that you talk of compels you. There is one more traitor in the village, a man who did not enter the Bordj because he thought his false god would preserve him."

"Little man," said the captain in shock and a genuine attempt to stop the words he knew were about to be said, "don't—"

"Add the traitor Juma al-Habashi to these," the civilian cried, pointing to the fluttering jellabas of the prisoners. "Put him there or his whines of justice and other worlds and his false god will

111

poison the village again like a dead rat stinking in a pool. Take him!"

The two men stood with their feet on a level. The soldier's helmet and armor increased his advantage in bulk, however, and his wrath lighted his face like a cleansing flame. "Shall I slay my brother for thee, lower-than-a-dog?" he snarled.

Ben Khedda's face jerked at the verbal slap, but with a wave of his arm he retorted, "Will you now claim to follow the Way yourself? There stand one hundred and thirty-four of your brothers. Make it one more, as your duty commands!"

The absurdity was so complete that the captain trembled between laughter and the feeling that he had gone insane. Carefully, his tone touched more wonder than with rage until the world should return to focus, the Kikuyu said, "Shall I, Esa Mboya, order the death of Juma Mboya? My brother, flesh of my father and of my mother . . . who held my hand when I toddled my first steps upright?"

Now at last ben Khedda's confidence squirted out like blood from a slashed carotid. "The name—" he said. "I didn't *know*!"

Mboya's world snapped into place again, its realities clear and neatly dove-tailed. "Get out, filth," he said harshly, "and wonder what I plan for you when I come down from this hill."

The civilian stumbled back toward his car as if his body and not his spirit had received the mortal wound. The soldier considered him dispassionately. If ben Khedda stayed in Ain Chelia, he wouldn't last long. The Slammers would be out among the stars, and the central government a thousand kilometers away in al-Madinah would be no better able to protect a traitor. Youssef ben Khedda would be a reminder of friends and relatives torn by blasts of cyan fire with every step he took on the streets of the village. Those steps would be few enough, one way or the other.

And if in the last fury of his well-earned fear ben Khedda tried to kill Juma—well, Juma had made his bed, his Way . . . he could tread it himself. Esa laughed. Not that the traitor would attempt murder personally. Even in the final corner, rats of ben Khedda's stripe tried to persuade other rats to bite for them.

"Captain," murmured Scratchard's voice over the command channel, "think we've waited about long enough?"

Instead of answering over the radio, Mboya nodded and began walking the hundred meters to where his sergeant stood near the prisoners. The rebels' eyes followed him, some with anger, most in only a dull appreciation of the fact that he was the nearest moving object on a static landscape. Troopers had climbed out of their gun pits all around the Bordj. Their dusty khaki blended with the soil, but the sun woke bright reflections from the barrels of their weapons.

"The search teams are ready to go in, sir," Scratchard said, speaking in Dutch but stepping a pace further from the shackled Kaid besides.

"Right," the captain agreed. "I'll lead the team from Third Platoon."

"Captain—"

"Where are the trucks, unbeliever?" demanded Ali ben Cheriff. His voice started on a quaver but lashed at the end.

"—there's plenty cursed things for you to do besides crawling down a hole with five pongoes. Leave it to the folks whose job it is."

"There's nothing left of this operation that Mendoza can't wrap up," Mboya said. "Believe me, he won't like doing it any less, either."

"Where are the trucks to carry away our children, dog and son of dogs?" cried the Kaid. Beneath the green turban, the rebel's face was as savage and unyielding as that of a trapped wolf.

"It's not for fun," Mboya went on. "There'll be times I'll have to send boys out to be killed while I stay back, safe as a staff officer, and run things. But if I lead from the front when I can, when it won't compromise the mission if I do stop a load—then they'll do what they're told a little sharper when it's me that says it the next time."

The Kaid spat. Lofted by his anger and the breeze, the gobbet slapped the side of Mboya's helmet and dribbled down onto his porcelain-sheathed shoulder.

Scratchard turned. Ignoring the automatic weapon slung ready to fire under his arm, he drew a long knife from his boot sheath instead. Three strides separated the non-com from the line of prisoners. He had taken two of them before Mboya caught his shoulder and stopped him. "Easy, Jack," the captain said.

Ben Cheriff's gaze was focused on the knife-point. Fear of death could not make the old man yield, but neither was he unmoved by the approach of its steel-winking eye. Scratchard's own face had no more expression than did the knife itself. The Kaid's wife lunged at the soldier to the limit of her chain, but the look Scratchard gave her husband dried her throat around the curses within it.

Mboya pulled his man back. "Easy," he repeated. "I think he's earned that, don't you?" He turned Scratchard gently. He did not point out, nor did he need to do so, the three gun-jeeps which had swung down to fifty meters in front of the line of captives. Their

113

crews were tense and still with the weight of their orders. They met Mboya's eyes, comprehending but without enthusiasm.

"Right," said Scratchard mildly. "Well, the quicker we get down that hole, the quicker we get the rest of the job done. Let's go."

The five tunnel rats from Third Platoon were already squatting at the entrance from which the rebels had surrendered. Captain Mboya began walking toward them. "You stay on top, Sergeant," he said. "You don't need to prove anything."

Scratchard cursed without heat. "I'll wait at the tunnel mouth unless something pops. You'll be out of radio contact and I'll be curst if I trust anybody else to carry you a message."

The tunnel rats were rising to their feet, silent men whose faces were in constant, tiny motion. They carried detector wands and sidearms; two had even taken off their body armor and stood in the open air looking paler than shelled shrimp. Mboya cast a glance back over his shoulder at the prisoners and the gun-jeeps beyond. "Do you believe in sin, Sergeant?" he asked.

Scratchard glanced sidelong at his superior. "Don't know, sir. Not really my field."

"My brother believes in it," said the captain, "but I guess he left the Slammers before you transferred out of combat cars. And he isn't here now, Jack, I am, so I guess we'll have to dispense with sin today."

"Team Three ready, sir," said the black-haired man who probably would have had sergeant's pips had he not been stripped to the waist.

"Right," said Mboya. Keying his helmet he went on, "Thrasher to Club One, Club Two. Let's see what they left us, boys." And as he stepped toward the tunnel mouth, without really thinking about the words until he spoke them, he added, "And the Lord be with us all."

The bed of the turbine driving Youssef ben Khedda's car was enough out of true that the vehicle announced its own approach unmistakably. Juma wondered in the back of his mind what brought the little man, but his main concentration was on the plug connector he was trying to reeve through a channel made for something a size smaller. At last the connector shifted the last two millimeters necessary for Juma to slip a button-hook deftly about it. The three subordinate Techs gave a collective sigh, and Bog Muller beamed in reflected glory.

"Father!" ben Khedda wheezed, oblivious to the guard frowning over his powergun a pace behind, "Father! You've got to . . . I've got to talk to you. You must!"

"All right, Youssef," the Kikuyu said. "In a moment." He tugged the connector gently through its channel and rotated it to mate with the gun leads.

Ben Khedda reached for Juma's arm in a fury of impatience. One of the watching Techs caught the Kabyle's wrist. "Touch him, rag-head," the trooper said, "and you better be able to grow a new hand." He thrust ben Khedda back with more force than the resistance demanded.

Juma straightened from the gun-jeep and put an arm about the shoulders of the angry trooper. "Worse job than replacing all the fans," he said in Dutch, "but it gives you a good feeling to finish it. Run the static test, if you would, and I'll be back in a few minutes." He squeezed the trooper, released him, and added in Kabyle to his fellow villager, "Come into my house, then, Youssef. What is it you need of me?"

Ben Khedda's haste and nervousness were obvious from the way his car lay parked with its skirt folded under the front from an over-hasty stop. Juma paused with a frown for more than the mechanical problem. He bent to lift the car and let the skirt spring away from the fans it was probably touching at the moment.

"Don't *worry* about that," ben Khedda cried, plucking at the bigger man's sleeve. "We've *got* to talk in private."

Juma had left his courtyard gate unlatched since he was working only a few meters away. Before ben Khedda had reached the door of the house, he was spilling the words that tormented him. "Before God, you have to talk to your brother or he'll kill me, Father, he'll kill *me*!"

"Youssef," said the Kikuyu as he swung his door open and gestured the other man toward the cool interior, "I pray—I have been praying—that at worst, none of our villagers save those in the Bordj are in danger." He smiled too sadly to be bitter. "You would know better than I, I think, who may have been marked out to Esa as an enemy of the government. But he's not a cruel man, my brother, only a very—determined one. He won't add you to whatever list he has out of mere dislike."

The Kabyle's lips worked silently. His face was tortured by the explanation that he needed to give but could not. "Father," he pleaded, "you *must* believe me, he'll have me killed. Before God, you must beg him for my life, you *must*!"

Ben Khedda was gripping the Kikuyu by both sleeves. Juma detached himself carefully and said, "Youssef, why would my

115

brother want you killed—of all the men in Ain Chelia? Did something happen?"

The smaller man jerked himself back with a dawning horror in his eyes. "You planned this with him, didn't you?" he cried. His arm thrust at the altar as if to sweep away the closed triptych. "This is all a lie, your prayers, your *Way*—you and your butcher brother trapped me to bleed like a sheep on Id al-Fitr! Traitor! Liar! Murderer!" He threw his hands over his face and flung himself down across a stool. The Kabyle's sobs held the torment of a man without hope.

Juma stared at the weeping man. There was something unclean about ben Khedda. His back rose and fell beneath the jellaba like the distended neck of a python bolting a young child. "Youssef," the Kikuyu said as gently as he could, "you may stay here or leave, as you please. I promise you that I will speak to Esa this evening, on your behalf as well as that of . . . others, all the others. Is there anything you need to tell me?"

Only the tears responded.

The dazzling sun could not sear away Juma's disquiet as he walked past the guard and the barricading truck. Something was wrong with the day, with the very silence. Though all things were with the Lord.

The jeep's inspection ports had been latched shut. The Techs had set a pair of skimmers up on their sides as the next project. The civilian smiled. "Think she'll float now?" he asked the trooper who had grabbed ben Khedda. "Let's see if I remember how to put one of these through her paces. You can't trust a fix, you see, till you've run her under full load."

There was a silence broken by the whine of ben Khedda's turbine firing. Juma managed a brief prayer that the Kabyle would find a Way open to him—knowing as he prayed that the impulse to do so was from his mind and not at all from his heart.

"Juma, ah," Bog Muller was trying to say. "Ah, look, this isn't—isn't our idea, it's the job, you know. But the captain—" none of the four Techs were looking anywhere near the civilian— "he ordered that you not go anywhere today until, until . . . it was clear."

The silence from the Bordj was a cloak that smothered Juma and squeezed all the blood from his face. "Not that you're a prisoner, but, ah, your brother thought it'd be better for both of you if you didn't see him or call him till—after."

"I see," said the civilian, listening to his own voice as if a third party were speaking. "Until after he's killed my friends, I suppose . . . yes." He began walking back to his house, his sandaled feet moving without being consciously directed. "Juma—" called Muller, but the Tech thought better of the words or found he had none to say.

Ben Khedda had left the door ajar. It was only by habit that Juma himself closed it behind him. The dim coolness within was no balm to the fire that skipped across the surface of his mind. Kneeling, the Kikuyu unlatched and opened wide the panels of his altar piece. It was his one conscious affectation, a copy of a triptych painted over a millenium before by the Master of Hell, Hieronymous Bosch. Atop a haywain rode a couple. Their innocence was beset by every form of temptation in the world, the World. Where would their Way take them? No doubt where it took all Mankind, saving the Lord's grace, to Hell and the grave—good intentions be damned, hope be damned, innocence be damned. . . . Obscurely glad of the harshness of the tiles on which he knelt, Juma prayed for his brother and for the souls of those who would shortly die in flames as like to those of Hell as man could create. He prayed for himself as well, for he was damned to endure what he had not changed. They were all travellers together on the Way.

After a time, Juma sighed and raised his head. A demon faced him on the triptych; it capered and piped through its own blue snout. Not for the first time, Juma thought of how pleasant it would be to personify his own weaknesses and urgings. Then he could pretend that they were somehow apart from the true Juma Mboya, who remained whole and incorruptible.

The lower of the two drawers beneath the altar was not fully closed.

Even as he drew it open, Juma knew from the lack of resistance that the drawer was empty. The heavy-barreled powergun had rested within when ben Khedda had accompanied the search team. It was there no longer.

Striding swiftly and with the dignity of a leopard, Mboya al-Habashi crossed the room and his courtyard. He appeared around the end of the truck barricade so suddenly that Bog Muller jumped. The Kikuyu pointed his index finger with the deliberation of a pistol barrel. "Bog," he said very clearly, "I need to call my brother at once or something terrible will happen."

"Via, man," said the Technician, looking away, "you know how I feel about it, but it's not my option. You don't leave here, and you don't call, Juma—or it's my ass."

"Lord blast you for a fool! the Kikuyu shouted, taking a step forward. All four Technicians backed away with their hands lifting. "Will you—" But though there was confusion on the faces watching him, there was nothing of assent, and there was no time to argue. As if he had planned it from the start, Juma slipped into the left saddle of the jeep he had just rewired and gunned the fans.

With an oath, Bog Muller grappled with the civilian. The muscles beneath Juma's loose jellaba had shifted driving fans beneath ore carriers in lieu of a hydraulic jack. He shrugged the Technician away with a motion as slight and as masterful as that of an earth tremor. Juma waggled the stick, using the vehicle's skirts to butt aside two of the younger men who belatedly tried to support their chief. Then he had the jeep clear of the repair rack and spinning on its own axis.

Muller scrambled to his feet again and waited for Juma to realize that there was not enough room between truck and wall for the jeep to pass. If the driver himself had any doubt, it was not evident in the way he dialed on throttle and leaned to bring the right-hand skirt up an instant before it scraped the courtyard wall. Using the wall as a running surface and the force of his turn to hold him there, Juma sent the gun-jeep howling sideways around the barricade and up the street.

"Hey!" shouted the startled guard, rising from the shady side of the truck. "Hey!" and he shouldered his weapon.

A Technician grabbed him, wrestling the muzzle of the gun skyward. It was the same lanky man who had caught ben Khedda when he would have plucked at Juma's sleeve. "Via!" cried the guard, watching the vehicle corner and disappear up the main road to the mine. "We weren't supposed to let him by."

"We're better off explaining that," said the Tech, "than we are telling the captain how we just killed his brother. Right?"

The street was empty again. All five troopers stared at it for some moments before any of them moved to the radio.

Despite his haste, Youssef ben Khedda stopped his car short of the waiting gun-jeeps and began walking toward the prisoners. His back crept with awareness of the guns and the hard-eyed men behind them; but, as God willed, he had chosen and there could be no returning now.

The captain—his treacherous soul was as black as his skin—was not visible. No doubt he had entered the Bordj as he had announced he would. Against expectation, and as further proof that God favored his cause, ben Khedda saw no sign of that damnable first sergeant either. If God willed it, might they both be blasted to atoms somewhere down in a tunnel!

The soldiers watching the prisoners from a few meters away were the ones whom ben Khedda had led on their search of the

118

village. The corporal frowned, but he knew ben Khedda for a confidant of his superiors. "Go with God, brother," said the civilian in Arabic, praying the other would have been taught that tongue or Kabyle. "Your captain wished me to talk once more with that dog—" he pointed to ben Cheriff. "There are documents of which he knows," he concluded vaguely.

The non-com's lip quirked nervously. "Look, can it wait—" he began, but even as he spoke he was glancing at the leveled tribarrels forty meters distant. "Blood," he muttered, a curse and a prophecy. "Well, go talk then. But watch it—the bastard's mean as a snake and his woman's worse."

The Kaid watched ben Khedda approach with the fascination of a mongoose awaiting a cobra. The traitor threw himself to the ground and tried to kiss the Kaid's feet. "Brother in God," the unshackled man whispered, "we have been betrayed by the unbelievers. Their dog of a captain will have you all murdered on his return, despite his oaths to me."

"Are we to believe, brother Youssef," the Kaid said with a sneer, "that you intend to die here with the patriots to cleanse your soul of the lies you carried?"

Others along the line of prisoners were peering at the scene to the extent their irons permitted, but the two men spoke in voices too low for any but the Kaid's wife to follow the words. "Brother," ben Khedda continued, "preservation is better than expiation. The captain has confessed his wicked plan to no one but me. If he dies, it dies with him—and our people live. Now, raise me by the hands."

"Shall I touch your bloody hands, then?" ben Cheriff said, but he spoke as much in question as in scorn.

"Raise me by the hands," ben Khedda repeated, "and take from my right sleeve what you find there to hide in yours. Then wait the time."

"As God wills," the Kaid said and raised up ben Khedda. Their bodies were momentarily so close that their jellabas flowed together.

"And what in the blaze of Hell is *this*, Corporal!" roared Sergeant Scratchard. "Blood and martyrs, who told you to let anybody in with the prisoners?"

"Via, Sarge," the corporal sputtered, "he said—I mean, it was the captain, he tells me."

Ben Khedda had begun to sidle away from the line of prisoners. "Where the hell do you think *you're* going?" Scratchard snapped in Arabic. "Corporal, get another set of leg irons and clamp him onto his buddy there. If he's so copping hot to be here, he can stay till the captain says otherwise."

The sergeant paused, looking around the circle of eyes focused nervously on him. More calmly he continued, "The Bordj is clear. The captain's up from the tunnel, but it'll be a while before he gets here—they came up somewhere in West Bumfuck and he's borrowing a skimmer from First Platoon to get back. We'll wait to see what he says." The first sergeant stared at Aliben Cheriff, impassive as the wailing traitor was shackled to his right leg. "We'll wait till then," the soldier repeated.

Mboya lifted the nose of his skimmer and grounded it behind the first of the waiting gun-jeeps. Sergeant Scratchard trotted toward him from the direction of the prisoners. The non-com was panting with the heat and his armor; he raised his hand when he reached the captain in order to gain a moment's breathing space.

"Well?" Mboya prompted.

"Sir, Maintenance called," said Scratchard jerkily. "Your brother, sir. They think he's coming to, to see you."

The captain swore. "All right," he said, "if Juma thinks he has to watch this, he can watch it. He's a cursed fool if he expects to do anything *but* watch."

Scratchard nodded deeply, finding he inhaled more easily with his torso cocked forward. "Right, sir, I just—didn't want to rebroadcast on the Command channel in case Central was monitoring. Right. And then there's that rag-head, ben Khedda—I caught him talking to green-hat over there and thought he maybe ought to stay. For good."

Captain Mboya glanced at the prisoners. The men of Headquarters Squad still sat a few meters away because nobody had told them to withdraw. "Get them clear," the captain said with a scowl. He began walking toward the line, the first sergeant's voice turning his direction into a tersely-radioed order. Somewhere down the plateau, an aircar was being revved with no concern for what pebbles would do to the fans. Juma, very likely. He was the man you wanted driving your car when it had all dropped in the pot and Devil took the hindmost.

"Jack," the captain said, "I understand how you feel about ben Khedda; but we're here to do a job, not to kill sons of bitches. If we were doing that, we'd have to start in al-Madinah; wouldn't we?"

Mboya and his sergeant were twenty meters from the prisoners. The Kaid watched their approach with his hands folded within the sleeves of his jellaba and his eyes as still as iron. Youssef ben

Khedda was crouched beside him, a study in terror. He retained only enough composure that he did not try to run—and that because the pressure of the leg iron binding him to ben Cheriff was just sharp enough to penetrate the fear.

A gun-jeep howled up onto the top of the plateau so fast that it bounced and dragged its skirts, still under full throttle. Scratchard turned with muttered surprise. Captain Mboya did not look around. He reached into the thigh pocket of his coveralls where he kept a magnetic key that would release ben Khedda's shackles. "We can't just kill—" he repeated.

"Now, God, *now*!" ben Khedda shrieked. "He's going to *kill* me!"

The Kaid's hands appeared, the right one extending a pistol. Its muzzle was a gray circle no more placable than the eye that aimed it.

Mboya dropped the key. His hand clawed for his own weapon, but he was no gunman, no quick-draw expert. He was a company commander carrying ten extra kilos, with his pistol in a flap holster that would keep his hand out at least as well as it did the wind-blown sand. Esa's very armor slowed him, though it would not save his face or his femoral arteries when the shots came.

Behind the captain, on a jeep still skidding on the edge of control, his brother triggered a one-handed burst as accurate as if parallax were a myth. The tribarrel was locked on its column; Juma let the vehicle's own side-slip saw the five rounds toward the man with the gun. A single two-centimeter bolt missed everything. Beyond, at the lip of the Bordj, a white flower bloomed from a cyan center as ionic calcium recombined with the oxygen from which it had been freed a moment before. Closer, everything was hidden by an instant glare. The pistol detonated in the Kaid's hand under the impact of a round from the tribarrel. That was chance—or something else, for only the Lord could be so precise with certainty. The last shot of the burst hurled the Kaid back with a hole in his chest and his jellaba aflame. Ali ben Cheriff's eyes were free of fear when they closed them before burying him, and his mouth still wore a tight smile. Ben Khedda's face would have been less of a study in virtue and manhood, no doubt, but the two bolts that flicked across it took the traitor's head into oblivion with his memory. Juma had walked his burst on target, like any good man with an automatic weapon; and if there was something standing where the bolts walked—so much the worse for it.

There were shouts, but they were sucked lifeless by the wind. No one else had fired, for a wonder. Troops all around the Bordj were rolling back into dug-outs they had thought it safe to leave.

Juma brought the jeep to a halt a few meters from his brother. He doubled over the joy-stick as if he had been shot himself. Dust and sand puffed from beneath the skirts while the fans wound down; then the plume settled back on the breeze. Esa touched his brother's shoulder, feeling the dry sobs that wracked the jellaba. Very quietly the soldier said in the Kikuyu he had not, after all, forgotten, "I bring you a souvenir, elder brother. To replace the one you have lost." From his holster, now unsnapped, he drew his pistol and laid it carefully down on the empty gunner's seat of the jeep.

Juma looked up at his brother with a terrible dignity. "To remind me of the day I slew two men in the Lord's despite?" he asked formally. "Oh, no, my brother; I need no trinket to remind me of that forever."

"If you do not wish to remember the ones you killed," said Esa, "then perhaps it will remind you of the hundred and thirty-three whose lives you saved this day. And my life, of course."

Juma stared at his brother with a fixity by which alone he admitted his hope. He tugged the silver crucifix out of his jellaba and lifted it over his head. "Here," he said, "little brother. I offer you this in return for your gift. To remind you that wherever you go, the Way runs there as well."

Esa took the chain. With clumsy fingers he slipped it over his helmet. "All right, Thrasher, everybody stand easy," the captain roared into his commo link. "Two-six, I want food for a hundred and thirty-three people for three days. You've got my authority to take what you need from the village. Three-six, you're responsible for the transport. I want six ore carriers up here and I want them fast. If the first truck isn't here loading in twenty, that's two-zero mikes, I'll burn somebody a new asshole. Four-six, there's drinking water in drums down in those tunnels. Get it up here. Now, *move!*"

Juma stepped out of the gun-jeep, his left hand gripping Esa's right. Skimmers were already lifting from positions all around the Bordj. G Company was surprised, but no one had forgotten that Captain Mboya meant his orders to be obeyed.

"Oh, one other thing," Esa said, then tripped his commo and added, "Thrasher Four to all Thrasher units—you get any argument from villagers while you're shopping, boys . . . just refer them to my brother."

It was past midday now. The sun had enough westering to wink from the crucifix against the soldier's armor—and from the pistol in the civilian's right hand.

THE
FOXHOLES OF MARS

Fritz Leiber

Ever inward from the jagged horizon, the machines of death crept, edged, scurried, rocketed and tunneled towards him. It seemed as if all this purple-sunned creation had conspired to isolate and smash him. To the west—for all planets share a west, if nothing else—the nuclear bombs bloomed, meaningless giant fungi. While invisibly overhead the space ships roared as they dipped into the atmosphere—distant as gods, yet shaking the yellow sky. Even the soil was treacherous, nauseated by artificial earth-quakes—nobody's mother, least of all an Earthman's.

"Why don't you cheer up?" the others said to him. "It's a mad planet." But he would not cheer up, for he knew what they said was literally true.

He ducked and compressed himself as objects many times shattered, spurted up and cascaded. Soon they would fall back and the enemy would retake the mangled thing they called an objective. Was it the sixth time? The seventh? And did the soldiers on the other side have six legs, or eight? The enemy was a pretty haphazard as to what troops he used in this sector.

Worst was the noise. Meaningless, mechanical screeches tore at his skull, until thoughts rattled around in it like dry seeds in a dry pod. How could anyone ever love the various shock-transmitting mixtures of gases humorously called air? Even the vacuum of space was less hateful—it was silent and clean. He started to lift his hands to his ears, then checked the gesture, convulsed in soundless laughter and tearless weeping. There had been a galactic society—a galactic empire—once. He had played an unnoticed part on one of its nice quiet planets. But now? Galactic empire? Galactic horse-dung! Perhaps he had always hated his fellow men as much. But in the prewar days his hatred had been closely bound and meticulously repressed. It was still bound, tighter than ever, but it was no longer repressed from his thoughts.

The deadly engine he tended, silent for a moment, began again to chatter to those of the enemy, although its voice was mostly drowned by their booming ones, like a spiteful child in a crush of complacent adults.

It turned out they had been covering a withdrawal of Martian sappers and must now escape as best they might. The officer running beside him fell. He hesitated. The officer cursed a new, useless joint that had appeared in his leg. All the others—including the black-shelled Martians—were ahead. He glanced around fearfully and tormentedly, as if he were about to commit a hideous crime. Then he lifted the officer and staggered on, reeling like a top at the end of its spin. He was still grinning in a spasmic way when they reached the security of lesser danger; and even when the officer thanked him with curt sincerity he couldn't stop. Nevertheless, they gave him the Order of Planetary Merit for that.

He stared at the watery soup and meat shreds in his mess tin. The cellar was cool, and its seats—though built for creatures with four legs and two arms—were comfortable. The purple daylight was pleasantly muted. The noise had gone a little way off, playing cat and mouse. He was alone.

Of course life had never had any meaning, except for the chillingly sardonic one perceptible to the demons in the nuclear bombs and the silver giants in space who pushed the buttons; and he had no stomach to aspire to that. They'd had ten thousand years to fix things, those giants, and still all they could tell you was go dig yourself a hole.

It was just that in the old days the possibility of relaxation and petty self-indulgence, against the magnificent sham background of galactic empire, had permitted him to pretend life had a meaning. Yet at a time like this, when such an illusion was needful, it ran out on you, jeered at you along with the lesser lies it had nurtured.

A three-legged creature skipped out of the shadows, halted at a distance, and subtly intimated it would like food. At first he thought it must be some Rigelian tripedal, but then he saw it was an Earth cat lacking a leg. Its movements were grotesque, but efficient, and not without a certain gracefulness. How it could have got to this planet, he found it hard to imagine.

"But you don't worry about that—or even about other cats, Three-legs," he thought bitterly. "You hunt alone. You mate with your own kind, when you can, but then only because it is most agreeable. You don't set up your own species as a corporate divinity and worship it, and yearn over the light-centuries of its empire, and eat out your heart because of it, and humbly spill your blood at its cosmic altar.

"Nor are you hoodwinked when the dogs bark about the greatness of humanity under a thousand different moons, or when the dumb cattle sigh from surfeit and gratefully chew their cuds under red, green and purple suns. You accept us as something sometimes helpful. You walk into our space ships as you walked up to our fires. You use us. But when we're gone, you won't pine on our graves or starve in the pen. You'll manage, or try to."

The cat mewed and he tossed it a bit of meat which it caught in its teeth, shifting about cleverly on the two good hind legs. But as he watched it daintily nibble (though scrawny with famine), he suddenly saw Kenneth's face, just as he had last seen it on Alpha Centauri Duo. It seemed very real, projected against the maroon darkness towards the other end of the cellar. The full, tolerant lips lined at the corners, the veiledly appraising eyes, the space-sallow skin were all exactly as they had been when they roomed together at the Sign of the Burnt-Out Jet. But there was a richness and a zest about the face that he had missed before. He did not try to move toward the illusion, though he wanted to. Only looked. Then there came the sound of boots on the floor above, and the cat bounded away, humping its hind quarters quite like a tripedal, and the vision quickly faded. For a long time he sat staring at the spot where it had been, feeling a strangely poignant unhappiness, as if the only worthwhile being in the world had died. Then he started to eat his food with the vague curiosity of a two-year-old, sometimes pausing with the spoon halfway to his mouth.

It was night and there was a ground mist through which the wine-colored moons showed like two sick eyes, and anything might have been moving in the shadows. He squinted and peered, but it was hard to make out the nature of any object, the landscape was so torn and distorted. Three men came out of the place of underground concealment to the left, joking together in hushed, hollow voices. One whom he knew well (a stocky soldier with big eyes and smirking lips and reddish stubble on his chin) greeted him with a friendly gibe about easy jobs. Then they wormed their way up and started to crawl toward where enemy scouts (six legs or eight?) were supposed to lie. He lost sight of them very quickly. He held his weapon ready, watching for the sight of the enemy.

Why did he hate the soldiers of the enemy so little? No more than a Martian hunting sand-dragons hates sand-dragons. His relationship with them was limited, almost abstract. How could he hate something so different from himself in form? He could only marvel that it too had intelligence. No, the enemy were merely, unfortunately, dangerous targets. Once he had seen one of them escape death, and it had made him feel happy, and he wanted to wave in a friendly way; even if it could only wriggle a tentacle in return. But as for the men who fought side by side with him, he hated them bitterly, loathed their faces, voices and physical mannerisms. The way this one chewed and that one spat. Their unchanging curses, clichés and jokes. All unendurably magnified, as if his nose were being rubbed in offal. For they were part of the same miserable, lying, self-worshipping galactic swarm as himself.

He wondered if he had hated the men at the office on Altair Una in the same way. Almost certainly. He recalled the long smoldering irritations over trifles that had seemed tremendous in the hours between the violin-moans of the time clock. But then there had been the safety valves and shock absorbers that make life tolerable, and also the illusion of purpose.

But now there was nothing, and everybody knew it.

They had no right to joke about it and continue the pretense.

He was shaking with anger. To kill indiscriminately would at least demonstrate his feelings. To focus death on the backs of men charging with inane hysteria. To toss a nuclear fizz-bomb into a dugout where men sought secret escape in dreams and repeated like prayers their rationalizations about galactic empires. Dying at his hand, they might for a moment understand their own vicious hypocrisy.

From out ahead, one of death's little mechanisms spoke concisely, rapidly. It seemed like a bugle call only he could hear.

Ruby moonlight slid suddenly across the grotesquely tortured ground. He raised his weapon and took aim. Its sound pleased him because it was like a soft groan of agony. Then he realized he had fired at the abruptly revealed shadow because it was that of the stocky soldier who had gibed and crawled away.

The moonlight blacked out as if a curtain had been drawn. His heart pounded. He ground his teeth and grinned. His feelings were fierce, but not yet determinate. He became aware of the smells of the ground and of the chemicals and metals: strong, sharp, interesting smells.

Then he found himself staring at a whitish patch that never got more than eight inches off the ground. Slowly it approached out of the darkness, like the inquisitive head of a huge ghost worm. It became a face with big eyes and smirking lips, fretted with red stubble. Mechanically he reached out a hand and helped the man down.

"Were you the one that winged him? That lousy spider would have gotten me for sure. I didn't see him until he fell on me. I'm all mucked up with his blue slime."

This then was the end. Hereafter he would give in to a mob, run with the hounds, die purposelessly like a lemming when the time came. He might even learn to nurse ideals, like dead dolls; dream in chaos. Never again would he aspire to the darker, icy insight that gave life a real, though horrible, meaning. He was a ridiculous little communal animal in a lemming horde racing across the galaxy and he would live like one.

He saw the small black object falling swiftly through the mist. The stocky soldier did not. There was a deafening blast that slapped the skin. Looking up he saw the stocky soldier still standing there. Without a head. As the body stumbled blindly forward, tripped and fell, he began to laugh in little hissing gusts through his teeth. His lips were drawn back, so that his jaw muscles twitched and pained him.

He felt contemptuous amusement at the blond soldier. The blond soldier had been to a third-rate nuclear technics school and believed it had been a serious mistake to put him in the infantry. Nevertheless the blond soldier was ambitious and took an unusual interest in the war.

They stood alone at the crest of a ridge thick with violet and yellow-spotted vines. In the valleys on either side, their units were pushing forward. Trails of dust and tracks of mashed vines extended as far as the eye could see. Various huge engines trompled forward, carrying men, and men ran fussily about, freeing engines that had met with some stop or hindrance, as if the two were inextricably united in an unimaginable symbiosis. Small machines bearing messengers went swiftly to and fro like centaurs, a superior type of individual. Other machines spied watchfully overhead. It was like some vast, clumsy monster feeling its way, cautiously putting out pseudopods, or horns like a snail's; withdrawing them puzzledly when they touched anything hurtful or strange; but always gathering itself for a new effort. It did not flow, but humped and hedged. Or scuttled. Like an army of Rigelian roaches. Or driver ants of Earth that were so like miniature Martians, with their black-weaponed soldiers, foragers, scouts, butchers, pack carriers.

And they were truly neither more nor less than ants. He was no more than an epidermal cell in a monster that was dueling with another monster, very careful of its inner organs but careless about its epidermis. There was something comfortingly abstract and impersonal about the idea of being united in such a way with many other men, not because of any shared purpose, but merely because they belonged to the same monster, a monster so large that it could readily do duty for fate and necessity. The fellowship of protoplasm.

The blond soldier murmured two or three words and for a moment he thought the whole army had spoken to him. Then he understood and made the necessary adjustment in the instrument they were setting up.

But those two or three words had plunged him with breathtaking abruptness into the worst sort of inner misery. What was abstract had become personal, and that was bad. To conceive a monster made of men was one thing; to feel the insensate, inescapable prod of a neighboring cell and realize the stifling, close-packed pressure of the whole was another. He lifted his hand to his collar. The very air seemed to convey to his skin the shoving and jostling of distant, invisible individuals. The nudge of the galactic horde.

They were at the end of the crest now, atop a little hillock, and he stared ahead to where the air was clearer. He felt as if he were suffocating. His new mood had come as utterly without warning as most of his moods now came, gushing up explosively from some wild, alien, ever expanding dimension within him.

Then, in the broad expanse of fantastically clouded sky ahead of him, he saw his friends' faces again, orderly and side by side but gigantic, like a pantheon of demigods. Just as he had in the cellar and several times since, only now altogether. The only faces that meant anything in the cosmos. Black George, with the wide grin that looked, but was not, stupid. Hollow-cheeked Loren, peering up with shy canniness, about to argue. Dark Helen, with her proud, subtle lips. Sallow Kenneth again, with his veiledly appraising eyes. And Albert, and Maurice, and Kate. And others whose features were blurred, heartbreakingly suggesting friends forgot. All transfigured and glowing with warmth and light. As meaningful as symbols, yet holding each within itself the quintessence of individuality.

He stood stock-still, beginning to tremble, feeling great guilt. How had he neglected and deserted them? His friends, the only ones deserving his loyalty, the only island for him in the cosmos-choking sea of humanity, the only ones with worth and meaning; compared to which race and creed and humanity were without significance. It was as self-evident and undeniable as a premise in mathematics. Heretofore he had seen only the masks of reality, the reflections, the countershadows. Now, at a bound, he stood beside the gods in darkness who pulled the wires.

The vision faded, became part of his mind. He turned, and it was as if he saw the blond soldier for the first time. How had he ever believed that he and the other soldier might have anything in common? The gulf between them was far, far greater than if they belonged to different species. Why had he ever given two thoughts to such a silly, squinty-eyed, bustling little organism? He never would again. It was all very clear.

"We'll get them this time," the other soldier said with conviction. "We've got the stuff now. We'll show the bugs. Come on."

It was wonderful, hysterical, insufferable. Yesterday spiders. Today bugs. Tomorrow worms? The other soldier really believed it was important and noble. Could still pretend there was that kind of meaning and purpose to that sort of slaughter.

"Come on. Get the beta cycling," said the other soldier impatiently, nudging him.

It was all very clear. And he would never lose that clarity. By one action he would cut himself off from the galactic pack and cleave forever to the faces in the sky.

"Come on," ordered the other soldier, jerking at him.

He unsheathed his weapon, touched a button. Silently a dull black spot, not a hole, appeared in the back of the blond soldier's head. He hid the body, walked down the other side of the hill, and attached himself to another unit. By morning they were retreating again, the monster badly hurt and automatically resisting dissolution.

He was an officer now.

"I don't like him," said a soldier. "Of course, they all try to scare you, whether they know it or not. Part of the business. But with him it's different. I know he doesn't talk tough, or threaten or act grim. I know he's pleasant enough when he takes time to notice you. Even sympathetic. But there's something there I can't put my finger on. Something cold-blooded. Like he wasn't even alive—or as if we weren't. Even when he acts especially decent or thoughtful toward me, I know he doesn't give a damn. It's his eyes. I can read meaning in the eyes of a Fomalhautian blind-worm. But I can't read anything in his."

The soaring city seemed alien though it had once been home. He liked it the better for that. Civilian clothes felt strange against his skin.

He whisked briskly along the slidewalk, taking the turns aimlessly when it split at the pedestrian cloverleafs. He looked at the passing faces with frank inquisitiveness, as if he were at a zoo. He just wanted to enjoy the feeling of anonymity for a little while. He knew what he was going to do afterwards. There were his friends, and there were the animals. And the fortunes of his friends were to be advanced.

Beside the next cloverleaf was a speaker, and a little crowd. There had been a good deal of that sort of stuff since the truce. Curiously he listened, recognized the weakness of the words. They were sloshed with ideals, tainted with unprofitable, poorly selected hatreds. The call to action was tinged by an undercurrent of bitterness that argued inaction would be better. They were civilized words and therefore useless to one who wanted to become an animal trainer on a galactic scale. What a zoo he'd have some day—every single beast in it advertised as intelligent!

Other words and phrases began to ooze up into his mind. "Thinkers! Listen to me . . . cheated of what you deserve . . . misled by misled men . . . the galactic runaround . . . this engineered truce . . . the creatures who used the war to consolidate their power . . . The Cosmic Declaration of Servitude . . . life—to lose . . . liberty—to obey . . . and as for the pursuit of happiness—happiness is a light-millennium ahead of all of us . . . our universal rights. . . . We have thirty armored planetoids orbiting uselessly, three hundred starships, three thousand spaceships, and three million space veterans sweating in servile jobs in this system alone! Free Martial Terra for All! Revenge . . ."

These spoken words, he felt, were the harbingers of leadership. Alexander had done it. Hitler had done it. Smith had done it. Hrivlath had done it. The Neuron had done it. The Great Centaur had done it. All murderers—and only murderers won. He saw the brilliant light-years of his future stretch ahead, endlessly. He saw no details, but it was all of the same imperial color. Never again would he hesitate. Each moment would decide something. Each of his future actions would drop like a grain of sand from an ancient hour glass, inevitably.

Profound excitement seized him. The scene around him grew

and grew until he seemed at the center of a vast, ominous spellbound crowd that filled the galaxy. The faces of his friends were close, eager and confident. And from a great distance, as if the stars themselves pricked out its pattern on the dark like a new constellation, he seemed to see his own face staring back at him, pale, skulleyed, and insatiably hungry.

CONQUEROR

Larry Eisenberg

Joe found much of the Sentient city quaint, even charming, but it was not like home. It was an ancient, sophisticated city on an ancient planet, and yet it did not display the material comforts that Terra had attained after a meager fifty thousand years out of the Stone Age.

He walked through the shattered cobbled streets in full gear, outfitted in the smart dark dress blues of the invading forces, looking for women and entertainment. It was not easy to find. Determined to make this a model Occupation, the commanding general had worked out a limited schedule of available services and had set up severe rationing standards. Only three drinks of the potent *ragacsi* were permitted daily. And at most one woman a day. Meals and food packages were also strictly regulated by item and quantity.

Rationing control was handled by the Central Terran Computer. Payment had to be *in advance*. Small input scan devices were located all over the city which only accepted dogtags and recorded serial numbers plus the nature of the transaction. Joe sighed. He had been scouring the shops for souvenirs to send home and he had already used up his quota of drinks for the day. But he still had a woman coming.

The Sentients were behaving with scrupulous propriety. They had been badly beaten, but they hadn't relinquished their basic dignity. As reparations for their prolonged and costly resistance, they had been forced to give up tremendous quantities of treasure and goods. Hence everyone was living on a substandard basis. But there was almost no black marketeering.

There was very little prostitution, too. Traditionally the Sentients used android women for this purpose, amazingly lifelike figures designed for erotic pleasures, good enough to pass muster with the most exacting of men. But most of the Terran soldiers, like Joe, considered this practice emasculating, a sign of the degeneration of the Sentient culture, and avoided the android women like the plague. Only a handful of the men, weak in moral fiber and controls, joking to cover their inner shame, had defiled themselves in this way.

Fortunately there were a few *real* women around, whose circumstances were so straitened that they had gone to the streets to earn Terran credits. But only a few. Joe had waited now for fifty-three days. And the torment was growing stronger with each day.

He stepped into one of the very neat candy-pink social clubs maintained by the Sentients for the Terran soldiers. There were four women seated quietly about the room—all of them android, he was certain. They were uncannily like the Sentient women in appearance. None were pretty by Terran standards. Their noses were too broad, their eyes set very wide apart, the skin an almost alabaster white. But they were extraordinarily sensuous creatures. He stared at each one in turn, tempted but not quite enough. He took great pride in maintaining his own self-respect, in holding on to his masculinity.

He advanced to the bar and asked the Sentient bartender for a *ragacsi*.

"Your dogtag, please," said the bartender.

Joe slipped the metal disk into the scanner and waited stoically for the intermittent red flash to appear. It did and the bartender sighed.

"I'm sorry, sir. You've reached your quota for the day. But I'll be happy to serve you tomorrow."

"The hell with it," snapped Joe. "I didn't want the goddam drink anyway."

He stepped angrily into the street and looked along the narrow lane. There was no one in view. High above, two young Sentient women had been leaning out of an oval picture window but when they caught his glance they both withdrew and closed the outer blinds. He was terribly depressed.

"I'm hungry," he thought, "but it isn't sex alone. I want intimate contact with another human being."

He stopped off at a curio shop and chatted politely with the proprietor. He even priced several expensive items although he knew he didn't have sufficient credits left to pay for them. The Sentient dealer was courteous, but no more. Joe tried to hint obliquely at how lonely he was, but the Sentient didn't seem to grasp his meaning. They parted on correct but distant terms.

And then he saw her. She wasn't even as pretty as the android women he had seen, but she was *alive*. He was certain of that. She had her head averted and was looking wistfully into a shop window. He came up just behind her and looked over her shoulder. She was eyeing a lavishly packaged food assortment.

"It looks mighty tempting, doesn't it?" he said softly.

She turned to look at him, but said nothing.

On sudden impulse, he went into the store and used up his food allowance on the package. When he came out into the street he handed it to the Sentient woman.

"I cannot take this from you," she said.

"No strings," said Joe and when he saw the look of puzzlement on her face, he rephrased his words. "I want nothing in return," he said.

She looked at him warily for a moment and then reached out for the package. He was elated because she had accepted it.

"Where do you live?" he said.

"You wish to come home with me?"

"Only to talk. Nothing more."

She shrugged and took his hand in hers, the warmth of her fingers coming almost as a shock to him. Together they wove through the maze of darkening streets, dimly lit by the orange glow of the setting Star above. There were tangles of debris everywhere since much of the destruction had not yet been cleared away by the Sentient population. He pretended not to see it.

When they arrived outside her home, she asked him to wait while she went within. She returned in a few moments.

"I can't ask you in," she said quietly. "My parents will not permit it. But since I have accepted your gift, I feel I owe you something."

"You don't owe me a thing," he said vigorously.

"No, no," she insisted. "I will go to your home with you, now."

His home? He had no home on this planet. He was quartered with an elderly Sentient couple in a small bedroom with a private side entrance. He told her this, and she shrugged her indifference. But he wanted more than gratitude.

They walked to one of the few parks that had not been shattered by the invasion. It was on a hill of several hundred feet that overlooked a river winding below like a metallic ribbon. He talked hesitantly about his parents, and when she looked at him sympathetically, he fished a frayed picture out of his wallet to show to her. She smiled and remarked about the resemblance.

He asked her about herself, her family, but she wouldn't answer.

"I see only destruction about me," she said, and she pointed a slender finger toward the heaps of rubble that lay at the foot of the hill. Then she leaned toward him, and for the first time that evening, she ran her fingers gently over his cheek. His blood began to race at the implications of her caress.

"Do you like me?" he said earnestly. "*Really* like me?"

"I do," she said seemingly in earnest.

Although it was terribly expensive, he hailed one of the few helibuses that hovered over the ravaged city. He had the pilot place them down a few blocks before his destination so that he might stop to purchase a corsage. He pinned the exotic flowers, despite her mild objections, to the shoulder of her brightly colored blouse.

They entered noiselessly through the side door and quickly undressed. Afterward, he caressed her hair and spoke to her of intimate things, of his home, his loneliness, his contrition for the wanton destruction of her city, of his gratitude to her. She smiled at him as she reached out for her purse. She opened it and took out one of the small scanning devices issued by the Occupying Forces.

He felt icy fingers close about his heart.

"What are you doing?" he cried.

"Reporting the transaction to your Computer," she said, the word *your* heavily accented. "I should have recorded it in advance."

"But this wasn't just a transaction," he said. "It was one human being showing friendship to another."

She laughed outright.

"Me?" she said. "Human?"

He sat bolt upright in the bed. "What do you mean?" he said.

"You even have parents! You said so."

"*Parents* was just a euphemism for my owners," she said. "I always give them Terran food packages."

He went to the closet and gathered up her clothes.

"Get the hell out of here," he said.

She dressed before him with exaggerated slowness, moving her body seductively in a caricature of sensuality. She curtsied grandly before she left, a grotesque mockery, he knew, of his Terran values.

She walked through the streets in a leisurely manner until she reached one of the city's communication centers. There she called her home, collect. Her mother's face came alive on the visiscreen. It was without emotion.

"I did it," she told her mother. "He is humiliated and unnerved. I made him something less than a man."

"It was a courageous and patriotic thing to do," said her mother. "And yet I wish the glory were being garnered by someone else's daughter."

Her mother's face faded from the screen like a wraith of smoke. And then, after straightening the hem of her skirt and discarding the corsage, the girl walked out onto the street looking for another Terran soldier.

WARRIOR

Gordon R. Dickson

The spaceliner coming in from New Earth and Freiland, worlds under the Sirian sun, was delayed in its landing by traffic at the spaceport in Long Island Sound. The two police lieutenants, waiting on the bare concrete beyond the shelter of the Terminal buildings, turned up the collars of their cloaks against the hissing sleet, in this unweatherproofed area. The sleet was turning into tiny hailstones that bit and stung all exposed areas of skin. The gray November sky poured them down without pause or mercy, the vast, reaching surface of concrete seemed to dance with their white multitudes.

"Here it comes now," said Tyburn, the Manhattan Complex police lieutenant, risking a glance up into the hailstorm. "Let me do the talking when we take him in."

"Fine by me," answered Breagan, the spaceport officer, "I'm only here to introduce you—and because it's my bailiwick. You can have Kenebuck, with his hood connections, and his millions. If it were up to me, I'd let the soldier get him."

"It's him," said Tyburn, "who's likely to get the soldier—and that's why I'm here. You ought to know that."

The great mass of the interstellar ship settled like a cautious mountain to the concrete two hundred yards off. It protruded a landing stair near its base like a metal leg, and the passengers began to disembark. The two policemen spotted their man immediately in the crowd.

137

"He's big," said Breagan, with the judicious appraisal of someone safely on the sidelines, as the two of them moved forward.

"They're all big, these professional military men off the Dorsai world," answered Tyburn, a little irritably, shrugging his shoulders against the cold, under his cloak. "They breed themselves that way."

"I know they're big," said Breagan. "This one's bigger."

The first wave of passengers was rolling toward them now, their quarry among the mass. Tyburn and Breagan moved forward to meet him. When they got close they could see, even through the hissing sleet, every line of his dark, unchanging face looming above the lesser heights of the people around him, his military erectness molding the civilian clothes he wore until they might as well have been a uniform. Tyburn found himself staring fixedly at the tall figure as it came toward him. He had met such professional soldiers from the Dorsai before, and the stamp of their breeding had always been plain on them. But this man was somehow moreso, even than the others Tyburn had seen. In some way he seemed to be the spirit of the Dorsai, incarnate.

He was one of twin brothers, Tyburn remembered now from the dossier back at his office. Ian and Kensie were their names, of the Graeme family at Foralie, on the Dorsai. And the report was that Kensie had two men's likability, while his brother Ian, now approaching Tyburn, had a double portion of grim shadow and solitary darkness.

Staring at the man coming toward him, Tyburn could believe the dossier now. For a moment, even, with the sleet and the cold taking possession of him, he found himself believing in the old saying that, if the born soldiers of the Dorsai ever cared to pull back to their own small, rocky world, and challenge the rest of humanity, not all the thirteen other inhabited planets could stand against them. Once, Tyburn had laughed at that idea. Now, watching Ian approach, he could not laugh. A man like this would live for different reasons from those of ordinary men—and die for different reasons.

Tyburn shook off the wild notion. The figure coming toward him, he reminded himself sharply, was a professional military man—nothing more.

Ian was almost to them now. The two policemen moved in through the crowd and intercepted him.

"Commandant Ian Graeme?" said Breagan. "I'm Kaj Breagan of the spaceport police. This is Lieutenant Walter Tyburn of the Manhattan Complex Force. I wonder if you could give us a few minutes of your time?"

Ian Graeme nodded, almost indifferently. He turned and paced

138

along with them, his longer stride making more leisurely work of their brisk walking, as they led him away from the route of the disembarking passengers and in through a blank metal door at one end of the Terminal, marked *Unauthorized Entry Prohibited*. Inside, they took an elevator tube up to the offices on the Terminal's top floor, and ended up in chairs around a desk in one of the offices.

All the way in, Ian had said nothing. He sat in his chair now with the same indifferent patience, gazing at Tyburn, behind the desk, and at Breagan, seated back against the wall at the desk's right side. Tyburn found himself staring back in fascination. Not at the granite face, but at the massive, powerful hands of the man, hanging idly between the chair-arms that supported his forearms. Tyburn, with an effort, wrenched his gaze from those hands.

"Well, Commandant," he said, forcing himself at last to look up into the dark, unchanging features, "you're here on Earth for a visit, we understand."

"To see the next-of-kin of an officer of mine." Ian's voice, when he spoke at last, was almost mild compared to the rest of his appearance. It was a deep, calm voice, but lightless—like a voice that had long forgotten the need to be angry or threatening. Only . . . there was something sad about it, Tyburn thought.

"A James Kenebuck?" said Tyburn.

"That's right," answered the deep voice of Ian. "His younger brother, Brian Kenebuck, was on my staff in the recent campaign on Freiland. He died three months back."

"Do you," said Tyburn, "always visit your deceased officers' next of kin?"

"When possible. Usually, of course, they die in line of duty."

"I see," said Tyburn. The office chair in which he sat seemed hard and uncomfortable underneath him. He shifted slightly. "You don't happen to be armed, do you, Commandant?"

Ian did not even smile.

"No," he said.

"Of course, of course," said Tyburn, uncomfortable. "Not that it makes any difference." He was looking again, in spite of himself, at the two massive, relaxed hands opposite him. "Your . . . extremities by themselves are lethal weapons. We register professional karate and boxing experts here, you know—or did you know?"

Ian nodded.

"Yes," said Tyburn. He wet his lips, and then was furious with himself for doing so. Damn my orders, he thought suddenly and whitely, I don't have to sit here making a fool of myself in front

of this man, no matter how many connections and millions Kenebuck owns.

"All right, look here, Commandant," he said, harshly, leaning
forward. "We've had a communication from the Freiland-North
Police about you. They suggest that you hold Kenebuck—James
Kenebuck—responsible for his brother Brain's death."

Ian sat looking back at him without answering.

"Well," demanded Tyburn, raggedly after a long moment, "do
you?"

"Force-leader Brian Kenebuck," said Ian calmly, "led his
Force, consisting of thirty-six men at the time, against orders
farther than was wise into enemy perimeter. His Force was
surrounded and badly shot up. Only he and four men returned to
the lines. He was brought to trial in the field under the Mercenaries Code for deliberate mishandling of his troops under combat
conditions. The four men who had returned with him testified
against him. He was found guilty and I ordered him shot."

Ian stopped speaking. His voice had been perfectly even, but
there was so much finality about the way he spoke that after he
finished there was a pause in the room while Tyburn and Breagan
stared at him as if they had both been tranced. Then the silence,
echoing in Tyburn's ears, jolted him back to life.

"I don't see what all this has to do with James Kenebuck, then,"
said Tyburn. "Brian committed some . . . military crime, and
was executed for it. You say you gave the order. If anyone's
responsible for Brian Kenebuck's death then, it seems to me it'd
be you. Why connect it with someone who wasn't even there at the
time, someone who was here on Earth all the while, James Kenebuck?"

"Brian," said Ian, "was his brother."

The emotionless statement was calm and coldly reasonable in
the silent, brightly-lit office. Tyburn found his open hands had
shrunk themselves into fists on the desk top. He took a deep breath
and began to speak in a flat, official tone.

"Commandant," he said, "I don't pretend to understand you.
You're a man of the Dorsai, a product of one of the splinter cultures out among the stars. I'm just an old-fashioned Earthborn—
but I'm a policeman in the Manhattan Complex and James
Kenebuck is . . . well, he's a taxpayer in the Manhattan Complex."

He found he was talking without meeting Ian's eyes. He forced
himself to look at them—they were dark unmoving eyes.

"It's my duty to inform you," Tyburn went on, "that we've had
intimations to the effect that you're to bring some retribution to

James Kenebuck, because of Brian Kenebuck's death. These are only intimations, and as long as you don't break any laws here on Earth, you're free to go where you want and see whom you like. But this *is Earth, Commandant*."

He paused, hoping that Ian would make some sound, some movement. But Ian only sat there, waiting.

"We don't have any Mercenaries Code here, Commandant," Tyburn went on harshly. "We haven't any feud-right, no *droit-de-main*. But we do have laws. Those laws say that, though a man may be the worst murderer alive, until he's brought to book in our courts, under our process of laws, no one is allowed to harm a hair of his head. Now, I'm not here to argue whether this is the best way or not; just to tell you that that's the way things are." Tyburn stared fixedly into the dark eyes. "Now," he said, bluntly, "I know that if you're determined to try to kill Kenebuck without counting the cost, I can't prevent it."

He paused and waited again. But Ian still said nothing.

"I know," said Tyburn, "that you can walk up to him like any other citizen, and once you're within reach you can kill him with your bare hands before anyone can stop you. *I* can't stop you in that case. But what I can do is catch you afterwards, if you succeed, and see you convicted and executed for murder. And you *will* be caught and convicted, there's no doubt about it. You can't kill James Kenebuck the way someone like you would kill a man, and get away with it here on Earth—do you understand that, Commandant?"

"Yes," said Ian.

"All right," said Tyburn, letting out a deep breath. "Then you understand. You're a sane man and a Dorsai professional. From what I've been able to learn about the Dorsai, it's one of your military tenets that part of a man's duty to himself is not to throw his life away in a hopeless cause. And this cause of yours to bring Kenebuck to justice for his brother's death, is hopeless."

He stopped. Ian straightened in a movement preliminary to getting up.

"Wait a second," said Tyburn.

He had come to the hard part of the interview. He had prepared his speech for this moment and rehearsed it over and over again—but now he found himself without faith that it would convince Ian.

"One more word," said Tyburn. "You're a man of camps and battlefields, a man of the military; and you must be used to thinking of yourself as a pretty effective individual. But here, on Earth, those special skills of yours are mostly illegal. And without them you're ineffective and helpless. Kenebuck, on the other

141

hand, is just the opposite. He's got money—millions. And he's got connections, some of them nasty. And he was born and raised here in Manhattan Complex." Tyburn stared emphatically at the tall, dark man, willing him to understand. "Do you follow me? If you, for example, should suddenly turn up dead here, we just might not be able to bring Kenebuck to book for it. Where we absolutely could, and would, bring you to book if the situation were reversed. Think about it."

He sat, still staring at Ian. But Ian's face showed no change, or sign that the message had gotten through to him.

"Thank you," Ian said. "If there's nothing more, I'll be going."

"There's nothing more," said Tyburn, defeated. He watched Ian leave. It was only when Ian was gone, and he turned back to Breagan that he recovered a little of his self-respect. For Breagan's face had paled.

Ian went down through the Terminal and took a cab into Manhattan Complex, to the John Adams Hotel. He registered for a room on the fourteenth floor of the transient section of that hotel and inquired about the location of James Kenebuck's suite in the resident section; then sent his card up to Kenebuck with a request to come by to see the millionaire. After that, he went on up to his own room, unpacked his luggage, which had already been delivered from the spaceport, and took out a small, sealed package. Just at that moment there was a soft chiming sound and his card was returned to him from a delivery slot in the room wall. It fell into the salver below the slot and he picked it up, to read what was written on the face of it. The penciled note read:

Come on up—
K.

He tucked the card and the package into a pocket and left his transient room. And Tyburn, who had followed him to the hotel, and who had been observing all of Ian's actions from the second of his arrival, through sensors placed in the walls and ceilings, half rose from his chair in the room of the empty suite directly above Kenebuck's, which had been quietly taken over as a police observation post. Then, helplessly, Tyburn swore and sat down again, to follow Ian's movements in the screen fed by the sensors. So far there was nothing the policeman could do legally—nothing but watch.

So he watched as Ian strode down the softly carpeted hallway to the elevator tube, rose in it to the eightieth floor and stepped out to face the heavy, transparent door sealing off the resident section of the hotel. He held up Kenebuck's card with its message to a concierge screen beside the door, and with a soft sigh of air the door slid back to let him through. He passed on in, found a second elevator tube, and took it up thirteen more stories. Black doors opened before him—and he stepped one step forward into a small foyer to find himself surrounded by three men.

They were big men—one, a lantern-jawed giant, was even bigger than Ian—and they were vicious. Tyburn, watching through the sensor in the foyer ceiling that had been secretly placed there by the police the day before, recognized all of them from his files. They were underworld muscle hired by Kenebuck at word of Ian's coming; all armed, and brutal and hair-trigger—mad dogs of the lower city. After that first step into their midst, Ian stood still. And there followed a strange, unnatural cessation of movement in the room.

The three stood checked. They had been about to put their hands on Ian to search him for something, Tyburn saw, probably to rough him up in the process. But something had stopped them, some abrupt change in the air around them. Tyburn, watching, felt the change as they did; but for a moment he felt it without understanding. Then understanding came to him.

The difference was in Ian, in the way he stood there. He was, saw Tyburn, simply . . . waiting. That same patient indifference Tyburn had seen upon him in the Terminal office was there again. In the split second of his single step into the room he had discovered the men, had measured them, and stopped. Now, he waited, in his turn, for one of them to make a move.

A sort of black lightning had entered the small foyer. It was abruptly obvious to the watching Tyburn, as to the three below, that the first of them to lay hands on Ian would be the first to find the hands of the Dorsai soldier upon him—and those hands were death.

For the first time in his life, Tyburn saw the personal power of the Dorsai fighting man, made plain without words. Ian needed no badge upon him, standing as he stood now, to warn that he was dangerous. The men about him were mad dogs; but, patently, Ian was a wolf. There was a difference with the three, which Tyburn now recognized for the first time. Dogs—even mad dogs—fight, and the losing dog, if he can, runs away. But no wolf runs. For a wolf wins every fight but one, and in that one he dies.

After a moment, when it was clear that none of the three would move, Ian stepped forward. He passed through them without even brushing against one of them, to the inner door opposite, and opened it and went on through.

He stepped into a three-level living room stretching to a large, wide window, its glass rolled up, and black with the sleet-filled night. The living room was as large as a small suite in itself, and filled with people, men and women, richly dressed. They held cocktail glasses in their hands as they stood or sat, and talked. The atmosphere was heavy with the scents of alcohol, and women's perfumes and cigarette smoke. It seemed that they paid no attention to his entrance, but their eyes followed him covertly once he had passed.

He walked forward through the crowd, picking his way to a figure before the dark window, the figure of a man almost as tall as himself, erect, athletic-looking with a handsome, sharp-cut face under whitish-blond hair that stared at Ian with a sort of incredulity as Ian approached.

"Graeme . . . ?" said this man, as Ian stopped before him. His voice in this moment of off-guardedness betrayed its two levels, the semi-hoodlum whine and harshness underneath, the polite accents above. "My boys . . . you didn't—" he stumbled, "leave anything with them when you were coming in?"

"No," said Ian. "You're James Kenebuck, of course. You look like your brother." Kenebuck stared at him.

"Just a minute," he said. He set down his glass, turned and went quickly through the crowd and into the foyer, shutting the door behind him. In the hush of the room, those there heard, first silence than a short, unintelligible burst of sharp voices, then silence again. Kenebuck came back into the room, two spots of angry color high on his cheekbones. He came back to face Ian.

"Yes," he said, halting before Ian. "They were supposed to . . . tell me when you came in." He fell silent, evidently waiting for Ian to speak, but Ian merely stood, examining him, until the spots of color on Kenebuck's cheekbones flared again.

"Well?" he said, abruptly. "Well? You came here to see me about Brian, didn't you? What about Brian?" He added, before Ian could answer, in a tone suddenly brutal, "I know he was shot, so you don't have to break that news to me. I suppose you want to tell me he showed all sorts of noble guts—refused a blindfold and that sort of—"

"No," said Ian. "He didn't die nobly."

Kenebuck's tall, muscled body jerked a little at the words, almost as if the bullets of an invisible firing squad had poured into it.

"Well . . . that's fine!" he laughed angrily. "You come light-years to see me and then you tell me that! I thought you liked him—liked Brian."

"Liked him? No," Ian shook his head. Kenebuck stiffened, his

144

face for a moment caught in a gape of bewilderment. "As a matter of fact," went on Ian, "he was a glory-hunter. That made him a poor soldier and a worse officer. I'd have transferred him out of my command if I'd had time before the campaign on Frieland started. Because of him, we lost the lives of thirty-two men in his Force, that night."

"Oh." Kenebuck pulled himself together, and looked sourly at Ian. "Those thirty-two men. You've got them on your conscience is that it?"

"No," said Ian. There was no emphasis on the word as he said it, but somehow to Tyburn's ears above, the brief short negative dismissed Kenebuck's question with an abruptness like contempt. The spots of color on Kenebuck's cheeks flamed.

"You didn't like Brian and your conscience doesn't bother you—what're you here for, then?" he snapped.

"My duty brings me," said Ian.

"Duty?" Kenebuck's face stilled, and went rigid.

Ian reached slowly into his pocket as if he were surrendering a weapon under the guns of an enemy and did not want his move misinterpreted. He brought out the package from his pocket.

"I brought you Brian's personal effects," he said. He turned and laid the package on a table beside Kenebuck. Kenebuck stared down at the package and the color over his cheekbones faded until his face was nearly as pale as his hair. Then slowly, hesitantly, as if he were approaching a booby-trap, he reached out and gingerly picked it up. He held it and turned to Ian, staring into Ian's eyes, almost demandingly.

"It's in here?" said Kenebuck, in a voice barely above a whisper, and with a strange emphasis.

"Brian's effects," said Ian, watching him.

"Yes . . . sure. All right," said Kenebuck. He was plainly trying to pull himself together, but his voice was still almost whispering. "I guess . . . that settles it."

"That settles it," said Ian. Their eyes held together. "Goodby," said Ian. He turned and walked back through the silent crowd and out of the living room. The three muscle-men were no longer in the foyer. He took the elevator tube down and returned to his own hotel room.

Tyburn, who with a key to the service elevators, had not had to change tubes on the way down as Ian had, was waiting for him when Ian entered. Ian did not seem surprised to see Tyburn there, and only glanced casually at the policeman as he crossed to a decanter of Dorsai whisky that had since been delivered up to the room.

"That's that, then!" burst out Tyburn, in relief. "You got in to see him and he ended up letting you out. You can pack up and go, now. It's over."

"No," said Ian. "Nothing's over yet." He poured a few inches of the pungent, dark whisky into a glass, and moved the decanter over another glass. "Drink?"

"I'm on duty," said Tyburn sharply.

"There'll be a little wait," said Ian, calmly. He poured some whisky into the other glass, took up both glasses, and stepped across the room to hand one to Tyburn. Tyburn found himself holding it. Ian had stepped on to stand before the wall-high window. Outside, night had fallen; but—faintly seen in the lights from the city levels below—the sleet here above the weather shield still beat like small, dark ghosts against the transparency.

"Hang it, man, what more do you want?" burst out Tyburn. "Can't you see it's you I'm trying to protect—as well as Kenebuck? I don't want *anyone* killed! If you stay around here now, you're asking for it. I keep telling you, here in Manhattan Complex you're the helpless one, not Kenebuck. Do you think he hasn't made plans to take care of you?"

"Not until he's sure," said Ian, turning from the ghost-sleet, beating like lost souls against the windowglass, trying to get in.

"Sure about what? Look, Commandant," said Tyburn, trying to speak calmly, "half an hour after we hear from the Freiland-North Police about you, Kenebuck called my office to ask for police protection." He broke off, angrily. "Don't look at me like that! How do I know how he found out you were coming? I tell you he's rich, and he's got connections! But the point is, the police protection he's got is just a screen—an excuse—for whatever he's got planned for you on his own. You saw those hoods in the foyer!"

"Yes," said Ian, unemotionally.

"Well, think about it!" Tyburn glared at him. "Look, I don't hold any brief for James Kenebuck! All right—let me tell you about him! We knew he'd been trying to get rid of his brother since Brian was ten—but blast it, Commandant, Brain was no angel, either—"

"I know," said Ian, seating himself in a chair opposite Tyburn.

"All right, you know! I'll tell you anyway!" said Tyburn. "Their grandfather was a local kingpin—he was in every racket on the eastern seaboard. He was one of the mob, with millions he didn't dare count because of where they'd come from. In their father's time, those millions started to be fed into legitimate businesses. The third generation, James and Brian, didn't inherit anything that wasn't legitimate. Hell, we couldn't even make a jaywalking ticket stick against one of them, if we'd ever wanted

146

to. James was twenty and Brian ten when their father died, and when he died the last bit of tattle-tale gray went out of the family linen. But they kept their hoodlum connections, Commandant!"

Ian sat, glass in hand, watching Tyburn almost curiously.

"Don't you get it?" snapped Tyburn. "I tell you that, on paper, in law, Kenebuck's twenty-four carat gilt-edge. But his family was hoodlum, he was raised like a hoodlum, and he thinks like a hood! He didn't want his young brother Brian around to share the crown prince position with him—so he set out to get rid of him. He couldn't just have him killed, so he set out to cut him down, show him up, break his spirit, until Brian took one chance too many trying to match up to his older brother, and killed himself off."

Ian slowly nodded.

"All right!" said Tyburn. "So Kenebuck finally succeeded. He chased Brian until the kid ran off and became a professional soldier—something Kenebuck wouldn't leave his wine, women and song long enough to shine at. And he can shine at most things he really wants to shine at, Commandant. Under that hood attitude and all those millions, he's got a good mind and a good body that he's made a hobby out of training. But, all right. So now it turns out Brian was still no good, and he took some soldiers along when he finally got around to doing what Kenebuck wanted, and getting himself killed. All right! But what can you do about it? What can anyone do about it, with all the connections, and all the money and all the law on Kenebuck's side of it? And, why should you think about doing something about it, anyway?"

"It's my duty," said Ian. He had swallowed half the whisky in his glass, absently, and now he turned the glass thoughtfully around, watching the brown liquor swirl under the forces of momentum and gravity. He looked up at Tyburn. "You know that, Lieutenant."

"Duty! Is duty that important?" demanded Tyburn. Ian gazed at him, then looked away, at the ghost-sleet beating vainly against the glass of the window that held it back in the outer dark.

"Nothing's more important than duty," said Ian, half to himself, his voice thoughtful and remote. "Mercenary troops have the right to care and protection from their own officers. When they don't get it, they're entitled to justice, so that the same thing is discouraged from happening again. That justice is a duty."

Tyburn blinked, and unexpectedly a wall seemed to go down in his mind.

"Justice for those thirty-two dead soldiers of Brian's!" he said, suddenly understanding. "That's what brought you here!"

147

"Yes." Ian nodded, and lifted his glass almost as if to the sleet-ghosts to drink the rest of his whisky.

"But," said Tyburn, staring at him, "You're trying to bring a civilian to justice. And Kenebuck has you out-gunned and out-maneuvered—"

The chiming of the communicator screen in one corner of the hotel room interrupted him. Ian put down his empty glass, went over to the screen and depressed a stud. His wide shoulders and back hid the screen from Tyburn, but Tyburn heard his voice.

"Yes?"

The voice of James Kenebuck sounded in the hotel room.

"Graeme—listen!"

There was a pause.

"I'm listening," said Ian, calmly.

"I'm alone now," said the voice of Kenebuck. It was tight and harsh. "My guests have gone home. I was just looking through that package of Brian's things . . ." He stopped speaking and the sentence seemed to Tyburn to dangle unfinished in the air of the hotel room. Ian let it dangle for a long moment.

"Yes?" he said, finally.

"Maybe I was a little hasty . . ." said Kenebuck. But the tone of his voice did not match the words. The tone was savage. "Why don't you come up, now that I'm alone, and we'll . . . talk about Brian, after all?"

"I'll be up," said Ian.

He snapped off the screen and turned around.

"Wait!" said Tyburn, starting up out of his chair. "You can't go up there!"

"Can't?" Ian looked at him. "I've been invited, Lieutenant."

The words were like a damp towel slapping Tyburn in the face, waking him up.

"That's right . . ." He stared at Ian. "Why? Why'd he invite you back?"

"He's had time," said Ian, "to be alone. And to look at that package of Brian's."

"But . . ." Tyburn scowled. "There was nothing important in that package. A watch, a wallet, a passport, some other papers . . . Customs gave us a list. There wasn't anything unusual there."

"Yes," said Ian. "And that's why he wants to see me again."

"But what does he want?"

"He wants me," said Ian. He met the puzzlement of Tyburn's gaze. "He was always jealous of Brian," Ian explained, almost gently. "He was afraid Brian would grow up to outdo him in things. That's why he tried to break Brian even to kill him. But now Brian's come back to face him."

"Brian . . . ?"

"In me," said Ian. He turned toward the hotel door.

Tyburn watched him turn, then suddenly—like a man coming out of a daze, he took three hurried strides after him as Ian opened the door.

"Wait!" snapped Tyburn. "He won't be alone up there! He'll have hoods covering you through the walls. He'll definitely have traps set for you . . ."

Easily, Ian lifted the policeman's grip from his arm.

"I know," he said. And went.

Tyburn was left in the open doorway, staring after him. As Ian stepped into the elevator tube, the policeman moved. He ran for the service elevator that would take him back to the police observation post above the sensors in the ceiling of Kenebuck's living room.

When Ian stepped into the foyer the second time, it was empty. He went to the door to the living room of Kenebuck's suite, found it ajar, and stepped through it. Within the room was empty, with glasses and overflowing ashtrays still on the tables; the lights had been lowered. Kenebuck rose from a chair with its back to the far, large window at the end of the room. Ian walked toward him and stopped when they were a little more than an arm's length apart.

Kenebuck stood for a second, staring at him, the skin of his face tight. Then he made a short almost angry gesture with his right hand. The gesture gave away the fact that he had been drinking. "Sit down!" he said. Ian took a comfortable chair and Kenebuck sat down in the one from which he had just risen. "Drink?" said Kenebuck. There was a decanter and glasses on the table beside and between them. Ian shook his head. Kenebuck poured part of a glass for himself.

"That package of Brian's things," he said, abruptly, the whites of his eyes glinting as he glanced up under his lids at Ian, "there was just personal stuff. Nothing else in it!"

"What else did you expect would be in it?" asked Ian, calmly.

Kenebuck's hands clenched suddenly on the glass. He stared at Ian, and then burst out into a laugh that rang a little wildly against the emptiness of the large room.

"No, no . . ." said Kenebuck, loudly. "I'm asking the questions, Graeme. I'll ask them! What made you come all the way here, to see me, anyway?"

"My duty," said Ian.

"Duty? Duty to whom—Brian?" Kenebuck looked as if he would laugh again, then thought better of it. There was the white, wild flash of his eyes again. "What was something like Brian to you? You said you didn't even like him."

"That was beside the point," said Ian, quietly. "He was one of my officers."

"One of your officers! He was my brother! That's more than being one of your officers!"

"Not," answered Ian in the same voice, "where justice is concerned."

"Justice?" Kenebuck laughed. "Justice for Brian? Is that it?"

"And for thirty-two enlisted men."

"Oh—" Kenebuck snorted laughingly. "Thirty-two men . . . those thirty-two men!" He shook his head. "I never knew your thirty-two men, Graeme, so you can't blame me for them. That was Brian's fault; him and his idea—what was the charge they tried him on? Oh, yes, that he and his thirty-two or thirty-six men could raid enemy Headquarters and come back with the enemy Commandant. Come back . . . covered with glory." Kenebuck laughed again. "But it didn't work. Not my fault."

"Brian did it," said Ian, "to show you. You were what made him do it."

"Me? Could I help it if he never could match up to me?" Kenebuck stared down at his glass and took a quick swallow from it then went back to cuddling it in his hands. He smiled a little to himself. "Never could even *catch* up to me." He looked whitely across at Ian. "I'm just a better man, Graeme. You better remember that."

Ian said nothing. Kenebuck continued to stare at him; and slowly Kenebuck's face grew more savage.

"Don't believe me, do you?" said Kenebuck, softly. "You better believe me. I'm not Brian, and I'm not bothered by Dorsais. You're here, and I'm facing you—alone."

"Alone?" said Ian. For the first time Tyburn, above the ceiling over the heads of the two men, listening and watching through hidden sensors, thought he heard a hint of emotion—contempt—in Ian's voice. Or had he imagined it?

"Alone—Well!" James Kenebuck laughed again, but a little cautiously. "I'm a civilized man, not a hick frontiersman. But I don't have to be a fool. Yes, I've got men covering you from behind the walls of the room here. I'd be stupid not to. And I've got this . . ." He whistled, and something about the size of a small dog, but made of smooth, black metal, slipped out from

150

behind a sofa nearby and slid on an aircushion over the carpeting to their feet.

Ian looked down. It was a sort of satchel with an orifice in the top from which two metallic tentacles protruded slightly.

Ian nodded slightly.

"A medical mech," he said.

"Yes," said Kenebuck, "cued to respond to the heartbeats of anyone in the room with it. So you see, it wouldn't do you any good, even if you somehow knew where all my guards were and beat them to the draw. Even if you killed me, this could get to me in time to keep it from being permanent. So, I'm unkillable. Give up!" He laughed and kicked at the mech. "Get back," he said to it. It slid back behind the sofa.

"So you see . . ." he said. "Just sensible precautions. There's no trick to it. You're a military man—and what's that mean? Superior strength. Superior tactics. That's all. So I outpower your strength, outnumber you, make your tactics useless—and what are you? Nothing." He put his glass carefully aside on the table with the decanter. "But I'm not Brian. I'm not afraid of you. I could do without these things if I wanted to."

Ian sat watching him. On the floor above, Tyburn had stiffened.

"Could you?" asked Ian.

Kenebuck stared at him. The white face of the millionaire contorted. Blood surged up into it, darkening it. His eyes flashed whitely.

"What're you trying to do—test me?" he shouted suddenly. He jumped to his feet and stood over Ian, waving his arms furiously. It was, recognized Tyburn overhead, the calculated, self-induced hysterical rage of the hoodlum world. But how would Ian Graeme below know that? Suddenly, Kenebuck was screaming. "You want to try me out? You think I won't face you? You think I'll back down like that brother of mine, that . . . " He broke into a flood of obscenity in which the name of Brian was freely mixed. Abruptly, he whirled about to the walls of the room, yelling at them. "Get out of there! All right, out! Do you hear me? All of you! Out—"

Panels slid back, bookcases swung aside and four men stepped into the room. Three were those who had been in the foyer earlier when Ian had entered for the first time. The other was of the same type.

"Out!" screamed Kenebuck at them. "Everybody out. Outside, and lock the door behind you. I'll show this Dorsai, this . . ." Almost foaming at the mouth, he lapsed into obscenity again.

Overhead, above the ceiling, Tyburn found himself gripping the

151

edge of the table below the observation screen so hard his fingers ached.

"It's a trick!" he muttered between his teeth to the unhearing Ian. "He planned it this way! Can't you see that?"

"Graeme armed?" inquired the police sensor technician at Tyburn's right. Tyburn jerked his head around momentarily to stare at the technician.

"No," said Tyburn. "Why?"

"Kenebuck is." The technician reached over and tapped the screen, just below the left shoulder of Kenebuck's jacket image. "Slugthrower."

Tyburn made a fist of his aching right fingers and softly pounded the table before the screen in frustration.

"All right!" Kenebuck was shouting below, turning back to the still-seated form of Ian, and spreading his arms wide. "Now's your chance. Jump me! The door's locked. You think there's anyone else near to help me? Look!" He turned and took five steps to the wide, knee-high to ceiling window behind him, punched the control button and watched as it swung wide. A few of the whirling sleet-ghosts outside drove from out of ninety stories of vacancy, into the opening—and fell dead in little drops of moisture on the windowsill as the automatic weather shield behind the glass blocked them out.

He stalked back to Ian, who had neither moved nor changed expression through all this. Slowly, Kenebuck sunk back down into his chair, his back to the night, the blocked-out cold and the sleet.

"What's the matter?" he asked, slowly, acidly. "You don't do anything? Maybe *you* don't have the nerve, Graeme?"

"We were talking about Brian," said Ian.

"Yes, Brian . . ." Kenebuck said, quite slowly. "He had a big head. He wanted to be like me, but no matter how he tried—how I tried to help him—he couldn't make it." He stared at Ian. "That's just the way, he never could make it—the way he decided to go into enemy lines when there wasn't a chance in the world. That's the way he was—a loser."

"With help," said Ian.

"What? What's that you're saying?" Kenebuck jerked upright in his chair.

"You helped him lose." Ian 's voice was matter of fact. "From the time he was a young boy, you built him up to want to be like you—to take long chances and win. Only your chances were always safe bets, and his were as unsafe as you could make them."

Kenebuck drew in an audible, hissing breath.

"You've got a big mouth, Graeme!" he said, in a low, slow voice.

"You wanted," said Ian, almost conversationally, "to have him kill himself off. But he never quite did. And each time he came back for more, because he had it stuck into his mind, carved into his mind, that he wanted to impress you—even though by the time he was grown, he saw what you were up to. He knew, but he still wanted to make you admit that he wasn't a loser. You'd twisted him that way while he was growing up, and that was the way he grew."

"Go on," hissed Kenebuck. "Go on, big mouth."

"So, he went off-Earth and became a professional soldier," went on Ian, steadily and calmly. "Not because he was drafted like someone from Newton or a born professional from the Dorsai, or hungry like one of the ex-miners from Coby. But to show you you were wrong about him. He found one place where you couldn't compete with him, and he must have started writing back to you to tell you about it—half rubbing it in, half asking for the pat on the back you never gave him."

Kenebuck sat in the chair and breathed. His eyes were all one glitter.

"But you didn't answer his letters," said Ian. "I suppose you thought that'd make him desperate enough to finally do something fatal. But he didn't. Instead he succeeded. He went up through the ranks. Finally, he got his commission and made Force-Leader, and you began to be worried. It wouldn't be long, if he kept on going up, before he'd be above the field officer grades, and out of most of the actual fighting."

Kenebuck sat perfectly still, a little leaning forward. He looked almost as if he were praying, or putting all the force of his mind to willing that Ian finish what he had started to say.

"And so," said Ian, "on his twenty-third birthday—which was the day before the night on which he led his men against orders into the enemy area—you saw that he got this birthday card . . ." He reached into a side pocket of his civilian jacket and took out a white, folded card that showed signs of having been savagely crumpled but was now smoothed out again. Ian opened it and laid it beside the decanter on the table between their chairs, the sketch and legend facing Kenebuck. Kenebuck's eyes dropped to look at it.

The sketch was a crude outline of a rabbit, with a combat rifle and battle helmet discarded at its feet, engaged in painting a broad yellow stripe down the center of its own back. Underneath this picture was printed in block letters, the question—"WHY FIGHT IT?"

Kenebuck's face slowly rose from the sketch to face Ian, and the millionaire's mouth stretched at the corners, and went on stretching into a ghastly version of a smile.

"Was that all . . . ?" whispered Kenebuck.

"Not all," said Ian. "Along with it, glued to the paper by the rabbit, there was this—"

He reached almost casually into his pocket.

"No, you don't!" screamed Kenebuck triumphantly. Suddenly he was on his feet, jumping behind his chair, backing away toward the darkness of the window behind him. He reached into his jacket and his hand came out holding the slugthrower, which cracked loudly in the room. Ian had not moved, and his body jerked to the heavy impact of the slug.

Suddenly, Ian had come to life. Incredibly, after being hammered by a slug, the shock of which should have immobilized an ordinary man, Ian was out of the chair on his feet and moving forward. Kenebuck screamed again—this time with pure terror—and began to back away, firing as he went.

"Die, you—! Die!" he screamed. But the towering Dorsai figure came on. Twice it was hit and spun clear around by the heavy slugs, but like a football fullback shaking off the assaults of the tacklers, it plunged on, with great strides narrowing the distance between it and the retreating Kenebuck.

Screaming finally, Kenebuck came up with the back of his knees against the low sill of the open window. For a second his face distorted itself out of all human shape in a grimace of its terror. He looked, to right and to left, but there was no place left to run. He had been pulling the trigger of his slugthrower all this time, but now the firing pin clicked at last upon an empty chamber. Gibbering, he threw the weapon at Ian, and it flew wide of the driving figure of the Dorsai, now almost upon him, great hands outstretched.

Kenebuck jerked his head away from what was rushing toward him. Then, with a howl like a beaten dog, he turned and flung himself through the window before those hands could touch him, into ninety-odd stories of unsupported space. And his howl carried away down into silence.

Ian halted. For a second he stood before the window, his right hand still clenched about whatever it was he had pulled from his pocket. Then, like a toppling tree, he fell.

—As Tyburn and the technician with him finished burning through the ceiling above and came dropping through the charred opening into the room, they almost landed on the small object that had come rolling from Ian's now-lax hand. An object that was really two objects glued together. A small paintbrush and a transparent tube of glaringly yellow paint.

"I hope you realize, though," said Tyburn, two weeks later on an icy, bright December day as he and the recovered Ian stood just inside the Terminal waiting for the boarding signal from the spaceliner about to take off for the Sirian worlds, "what a chance you took with Kenebuck. It was just luck it worked out for you the way it did."

"No," said Ian. He was as apparently emotionless as ever; a little more gaunt from his stay in the Manhattan hospital, but he had mended with the swiftness of his Dorsai constitution. "There was no luck. It all happened the way I planned it."

Tyburn gazed in astonishment.

"Why . . ." he said, "if Kenebuck hadn't had to send his hoods out of the room to make it seem necessary for him to shoot you himself when you put your hand into your pocket that second time—or if you hadn't had the card in the first place—" He broke off, suddenly thoughtful. "You mean . . . ?" He stared at Ian. "Having the card, you planned to have Kenebuck get you alone . . . ?"

"It was a form of personal combat," said Ian. "And personal combat is my business. You assumed that Kenebuck was strongly entrenched, facing my attack. But it was the other way around."

"But you had to come to him—"

"I had to appear to come to him," said Ian, almost coldly, "otherwise he wouldn't have believed that he had to kill me— before I killed him. By his decision to kill me, he put himself in the attacking position."

"But he had all the advantages!" said Tyburn, his head whirling. "You had to fight on his ground, here where he was strong . . ."

"No," said Ian. "You're confusing the attack position with the defensive one. By coming here, I put Kenebuck in the position of finding out whether I actually had the birthday card, and the knowledge of why Brian had gone against orders into enemy territory that night. Kenebuck planned to have his men in the foyer shake me down for the card—but they lost their nerve."

"I remember," murmured Tyburn.

"Then, when I handed him the package, he was sure the card was in it. But it wasn't," went on Ian. "He saw his only choice was to give me a situation where I might feel it was safe to admit having the card and the knowledge. He had to know about that, because Brian had called his bluff by going out and risking his neck after getting the card. The fact Brian was tried and executed later made no difference to Kenebuck. That was a matter of law—something apart from hoodlum guts, or lack of guts. If no one knew that Brian was braver than his older brother, that was all right; but if I knew, he could only save face under his own standards by killing me."

"He almost did," said Tyburn. "Any one of those slugs—"

"There was the medical mech," said Ian, calmly. "A man like Kenebuck would be bound to have something like that around to play safe—just as he would be bound to set an amateur's trap." The boarding horn of the spaceliner sounded. Ian picked up his luggage bag. "Good-by," he said, offering his hand to Tyburn.

"Good-by . . ." he muttered. "So you were just going along with Kenebuck's trap, all of it. I can't believe it . . ." He released Ian's hand and watched as the big man swung around and took the first two strides away toward the bulk of the ship shining in the winter sunlight. Then, suddenly, the numbness broke clear from Tyburn's mind. He ran after Ian and caught at his arm. Ian stopped and swung half-around, frowning slightly.

"I can't believe it!" cried Tyburn. "You mean you went up there, *knowing* Kenebuck was going to pump you full of slugs and maybe kill you—all just to square things for thirty-two enlisted soldiers under the command of a man you didn't even like? I don't believe it—you can't be that cold-blooded! I don't care how much of a man of the military you are!"

Ian looked down at him. And it seemed to Tyburn that the Dorsai face had gone away from him, somehow become as remote and stony as a face carved high up on some icy mountain's top.

"But I'm not just a man of the military," Ian said. "That was the mistake Kenebuck made, too. That was why he thought that stripped of military elements, I'd be easy to kill."

Tyburn, looking at him, felt a chill run down his spine as icy as wind off a glacier.

"Then, in heaven's name," cried Tyburn, "what are you?"

Ian looked from his far distance down into Tyburn's eyes and the sadness rang as clear in his voice finally, as iron-shod heels on barren rock.

"I am a man of war," said Ian softly.

With that, he turned and went on; and Tyburn saw him black against the winter-bright sky, looming over all the other departing passengers, on his way to board the spaceship.

MESSAGE
TO AN ALIEN

Keith Laumer

Dalton tossed the scorched, plastic-encased diagram on the Territorial governor's wide, not recently polished, desk. The man seated there prodded the document with a stylus as if to see if there were any life left in it. He was a plump little man with a wide, brown, soft-leather face finely subdivided by a maze of hair-like wrinkles.

"Well, what's this supposed to be?" He had a brisk, no-nonsense voice, a voice that said it had places to go and things to do. He pushed out his lips and blinked up at the tall man leaning on his desk. Dalton swung a chair around and sat down.

"I closed up shop early today, Governor," he said, "and took a little run out past Dropoff and the Washboard. Just taking the air, not headed anywhere. About fifty miles west I picked up a radac pulse, a high one, coming in fast from off-planet."

Governor Marston frowned. "There's been no off-world traffic cleared into the port since the Three-Planet shuttle last Wednesday, Dalton. You must have been mistaken. You—"

"This one didn't bother with a clearance. He was headed for the desert, well away from any of the settlements."

"How do you know?"

"I tracked him. He saw me and tried some evasive maneuvers, too close to the ground. He hit pretty hard."

"Good God, man! How many people were aboard? Were they killed?"

"No people were killed, Governor."

"I understood you to say—"

"Just the pilot," Dalton went on. "It was a Hukk scoutboat."

Several expressions hovered over Governor Marston's very mobile face; he picked amused disbelief.

"I see: you've been drinking. Or possibly this is your idea of hearty frontier humor."

"I took that off him." Dalton nodded at the plastic-covered paper on which a looping pattern of pale blue lines was drawn. "It's a chart of the Island. Being amphibious, the Hukks don't place quite the same importance on the interface between land and water as we do; they trace the contour lines right down past the shore line, map sea bottoms and all. Still, you can pick out the outline easily enough."

"So?"

"The spot marked with the pink circle was what he was interested in. He crumped in about ten miles short of it."

"What the devil would a Hukk be looking for out there?" the governor said in a voice from which all the snap had drained.

"He was making a last-minute confirmation check on a landing site."

"A landing site—for what?"

"Maybe I should have said beachhead."

"What kind of nonsense is this, Dalton? A *beach*head?"

"Nothing elaborate. Just a small Commando-type operation, about a hundred troops, light armor, hand weapons, limited objectives—"

"Dalton, what is this?" the official exploded. "It's been only seven years since we beat the Hukks into the ground! They know better than to start anything now!"

Dalton turned the chart over and pushed it toward the governor. There were complex characters scrawled in columns across it.

"What am I supposed to make of this . . . this Chinese laundry list?" the governor snapped.

"It's a brief of a Hukk Order of Battle. Handwritten notes, probably jotted down by the pilot, against regulations."

"Are you seriously suggesting the Hukks are planning an *invasion*?"

"The advance party is due in about nine hours," Dalton said. "The main force—about five thousand troops, heavy equipment— is standing by off-planet, waiting to see how it goes."

"This is fantastic! Invasions don't happen like this! Just . . . just out of a clear sky!"

"You expect them to wait for a formal invitation?"

"How do you know all this?"

"It's all there. The scout was a fairly high-ranking Intelligence officer. He may even have planned the operation."

The governor gave an indignant grunt, then pursed his lips, pushing his brows together. "See here, if this fellow you intercepted doesn't report back—"

"His report went out right on schedule."

"You said he was killed!"

"I used his comm gear to send the prearranged signal. Just a minimike pulse on the Hukk LOS freke."

"You warned them off?"

Dalton shook his head. "I gave them the all-clear. They're on the way here now, full gate and warheads primed."

The governor grabbed up his stylus and threw it at the desk. It bounced across the floor.

"Get out of here, Dalton! You've had your fun! I could have you thrown into prison for this! If you imagine I have nothing better to do than listen to the psychotic imaginings of a broken-down social misfit—"

"If you'd like to send someone out to check," Dalton cut in, "they'll find the Hukk scoutboat right where I left it."

Governor Marston sat with his mouth open, eyes glued to Dalton.

"You're out of your mind. Even if you did find a wrecked boat—and I'm not conceding you did—how would *you* know how to make sense of their pothooks?"

"I learned quite a bit about the Hukks at the Command and Staff school."

"At the Com—" The governor barked a laugh. "Oh, certainly, the Admiralty opens up the Utter Top Secret C&S school to tourists on alternate Thursdays. You took two weeks off from your junk business to drop over and absorb what it takes a trained expert two years to learn."

"Three years," Dalton said. "And that was before I was in the junk business."

The governor looked Dalton up and down with sudden uncertainty. "Are you hinting that you're a . . . a retired admiral, or something of the sort?"

"Not exactly an admiral," Dalton said. "And not exactly retired."

"Eh?"

"I was invited to resign—during the Hukk treaty debates."

The governor looked blank, then startled.

"You're not . . . *that* Dalton?"

"If I am—you'll concede I might know the Hukk hand-script?"

The governor rammed himself bolt upright.

"Why, I have a good mind to—" he broke off. "Dalton, as soon as word gets around who you are, you're finished here! There's not a man on Grassroots who'd do business with a convicted traitor!"

"The charge was insubordination, Governor."

"I remember the scandal well enough! You fought the treaty, went around making speeches undermining public confidence in the Admiralty that just saved their necks from a Hukk takeover! Oh, I remember you, all right! Hardline Dalton! Going to grind the beaten foe down under a booted heel! One of those ex-soldier-turned-rabble-rousers!"

"Which leaves us with the matter of a Hukk force nine hours out of Grassroots."

"Bah, I . . ." The governor paused, twisting in his chair. "Man, are you sure of this?" He muttered the words from the corner of his mouth, as if trying to avoid hearing them.

Dalton nodded.

"All right," the governor said, reaching for the screen. "Subject to check, of course, I'll accept your story. I'll notify CDT HQ at Croanie. If this is what you say it is, it's a gross breach of the treaty—"

"What can Croanie do? The official Love Thine Enemy line ties their hands. A public acknowledgment of a treaty violation by the Hukks would discredit the whole Softline party—including some of the top Admiralty brass and half the major candidates in the upcoming elections. They won't move—even if they had anything to move with—and if they could get it here in time."

"What are you getting at?"

"It's up to us to stop them, Governor."

"Us—stop an armed force of trained soldiers? That's Admiralty business, Dalton!"

"Maybe—but it's our planet. We have guns and men who know how to use them."

"There are other methods than armed force for handling such matters, Dalton! A few words in the right quarter—"

'The Hukks deal in actions. Seven years ago they tried and missed. Now they're moving a new pawn out onto the board. That makes it our move."

"Well—suppose they do land a small party in the desert, perhaps they're carrying out some sort of scientific mission; perhaps they don't even realize the world is occupied. After all, there are less than half a million colonists here . . ."

Dalton was smiling a little. "Do you believe that, Governor?"

"No, damn it! But it *could* be that way!"

"You're playing with words, Marston. The Hukks aren't wasting time talking."

"And your idea is . . . is to confront them—"

"Confront, Hell," Dalton growled. "I want a hundred militiamen who know how to handle a gun; the blast rifles locked up in the local armory will do. We'll pick our spots and be waiting for them when they land."

"You mean—ambush them?"

"You could call it that," Dalton said indifferently.

"Well . . ." The governor looked grave. "I *could* point out to the council that in view of the nature of their provocative and illegal act on the part of—"

"Sure," Dalton cut off the speech. "I'll supply transport from my yard, there's an old ore tug that will do the job. You can make it legal later. Right now I need an authorization to inspect the armory."

"Well . . ." Frowning, the governor spoke a few words into the dictyper, snatched the slip of paper as it popped from the slot, signed it with a slash of the stylus.

"Have the men alerted to report to the arms depot at twenty-two hundred hours," Dalton said as he tucked the chit away. "In field uniform, ready to move out."

"Don't start getting too big for your breeches yet, Dalton!" the governor barked. "None of this is official, you're still just the local junk man as far as I'm concerned."

"While you're at it, you'd better sign a commission for me as a lieutenant of militia, Governor. We may have a guardhouse lawyer in the bunch."

"Rather a comedown for a former commodore, isn't it?" Marston said with a slight lift of the lip. "I think we'll skip that. You'd better just sit tight until the Council acts."

"Twenty-two hundred, Governor," Dalton said. "That's cutting it fine. And tell them to eat a good dinner. It may be a long wait for breakfast."

II

The Federation Post Office was a blank gray five-story front of local granite, the biggest and ugliest building in the territorial capital. Dalton went in along a well-lit corridor lined with half-glass doors, went through the one lettered TERRAN SPACE ARM, and below, in smaller letters, Sgt. Brunt—Recruiting Officer. Behind the immaculate counter decorated with colorful posters of clear-eyed young models in smart uniforms, a thick-necked man of medium height and age, with a tanned face and close-cropped sandy hair, looked up from the bare desk with an expression of cheerful determination that underwent an invisible change to wary alertness as his eyes flicked over his caller.

"Good morning, Sergeant," Dalton said. "I understand you hold the keys to the weapons storage shack north of town."

Brunt thought that over, nodded once. His khakis were starched and creased to a knife-edge. A Combat Crew badge glinted red and gold over his left shirt pocket.

Dalton handed over the slip of paper the governor had signed. Brunt read it, frowned faintly, read it again, folded it and tapped it on the desk.

"What's it all about, Dalton?" He had a rough-edged voice.

"For now that has to be between the Governor and me, Brunt."

Brunt snapped a finger at the note. "I'd like to oblige the Governor," he said, "but the weapons storage facility is a Security area. No civilians allowed in, Dalton." He tossed the note across the desk.

Dalton nodded. "I should have thought of that," he said. "Excuse the interruption."

"Just a minute," Brunt said sharply as Dalton turned away. "If you'd like to tell me what's behind this . . . ?"

"Then you might stretch a regulation, eh? No thanks, Sergeant. I couldn't ask you to do that."

As Dalton left, Brunt was reaching for his desk screen.

III

Dalton lived a mile from town in a small pre-fab at the side of a twenty-acre tract covered with surplus military equipment, used mining rigs, salvaged transport units from crawlers to pogos. He parked his car behind the house and walked back between the looming hulks of gutted lighters, stripped shuttle craft ten years obsolete, wrecked private haulers, to a big, use-scarred cargo carrier. He started it up, maneuvered it around to the service ramp at the back, spent ten minutes checking it over. In the house, he ate a hasty meal, packed more food in a carton, changed clothes. He strapped on a well-worn service pistol, pulled on a deck jacket.

He cranked up the cargo hauler, steered it out to the highway. It was a ten-minute drive past the two-factory heavy industry belt, past scattered truck gardens, on another three miles into the pink chalk, ravine-sliced countryside. The weapons depot was ribbed-metal Quonsett perched on a rise of ground to the left of the road. Dalton turned off, pulled to a stop and waited for the dust to settle before stepping down from the high cab.

There was a heavy combination lock on the front door. It took Dalton ten minutes with a heavy-duty cutter to open it. Inside the long, narrow building, he switched on an unshielded overhead light. There was a patina of dust over the weapons racked in lock-frames along the walls.

Another three minutes with the cutter had the lock-bars off the racks. The weapons were 2mm Norges, wartime issue, in fair shape. The charge indicators registered *nil*.

There was a charging unit against the end wall, minus the energy coil. Dalton went out to the big vehicle, opened the access hatch, lifted out the heavy power unit, lugged it inside, used cables to jump it to the charger.

It took him an hour and thirty-eight minutes to put a full charge on each of one hundred and two weapons. It was twenty-one thirty when he put through a call on the vehicle's talker to the Office of the Governor. The answering circuit informed him that the office was closed. He tried the gubernatorial residence, was advised that the governor was away on official business. As he switched off, a small blue-painted copter with an Admiralty eagle and the letters FRS on the side settled in beside him. The hatch popped open and Brunt emerged, crisp in his khakis. He stood, fists on hips, looking up at the hauler's cab.

"All right, Dalton," he called. "Game's over. You can haul that clanker back to the yard. Nobody's coming—and you're not going anywhere."

"I take it that's a message from his Excellency the Governor?" Dalton said.

Brunt's eyes strayed past the big vehicle to the shed door, marred by a gaping hole where the lock had been.

"What the—" Brunt's hand went to his hip, came up gripping a palm-gun.

"Drop it," Dalton said.

Brunt froze. "Dalton, you're already in plenty of trouble—"

"The gun, Brunt."

Brunt tossed the small gun to the ground. Dalton climbed down, his pistol in his hand.

"The Council said no, eh?"

"What did you expect, you fool? You want to start a war?"

"No—I want to finish one." Dalton jerked his head. "Inside."

Brunt preceded him into the hut, and, at Dalton's direction, gathered up half a dozen weapons, touching only the short, thick barrels. He carried them out and stowed them in the rear of the hauler.

Dalton ordered Brunt into the cab, climbed up beside him. As he did, Brunt aimed a punch at his head; Dalton blocked it and caught his wrist.

"I've got thirty pounds and the reach on you, Sergeant," he said. "Just sit quietly. Under the circumstances I'm glad you happened along." He punched the door-lock key, started up, lifted onto the aircushion and headed west into the desert.

IV

Dusk was trailing purple veils across the sky when Dalton pulled the carrier in under a wind-carved wing of violet chalk at the base of a jagged rock wall and cut power. Brunt grumbled but complied when Dalton ordered him out of his seat.

"You've got a little scramble ahead, Sergeant." Dalton glanced up the craggy slope looming above.

"You could have picked an easier way to go off your rails," the recruiter said. "Suppose I won't go?"

Dalton smiled faintly, doubled his right fist and rotated it against his left palm. Brunt spat.

"If I hadn't been two years in a lousy desk job, I'd take you, Dalton, reach or no reach."

"Just pick up the guns, Brunt."

It took Dalton most of an hour to place the five extra blast rifles in widely-spaced positions around the crater's half-mile rim, propping them firmly, aimed at the center of the rock-strewn natural arena below. Brunt laughed at him.

"The old Fort Zinderneuf game, eh? But you don't have any corpses to man the ramparts."

"Over there, Brunt—where I can keep an eye on you." Dalton settled himself behind a shielding growth of salt weed, sighting along the barrel of the blast rifle. Brunt watched with a sour smile.

"You really hate these fellows, don't you, Dalton? Your were out to get them with the treaty, and failed, and now you're going to even it all up, single-handed."

"Not quite single-handed. There are two of us."

"You can kidnap me at gun point, Dalton, and you can bring me out here. But you can't make me fight."

"That's right."

Brunt made a disgusted sound. "You crazy fool! You'll get us both killed!"

"I'm glad you concede the possibility that this isn't just a party of picnickers we're here to meet."

"What do you expect, if you open fire on them?"

"I expect them to shoot back."

"Can you blame them?" Brunt retorted.

Dalton shook his head. "That doesn't mean I have to let them get away with it."

"You know, Dalton, at the time of your court, I wondered about a few things. Maybe I even had a few doubts about the treaty myself. But this"—he waved a hand that took in the black desert, the luminous horizon, the sky—"confirms everything they threw at you. You're a paranoiac—"

"But I can still read Hukk cursive," Dalton said. He pointed overhead. A flickering point of pink light was barely visible against the violet sky.

"I think you know a Hukk drive when you see one," Dalton said. "Now let's watch and see whether it's stuffed eggs or blast cannon they brought along."

V

"It doesn't make sense," Brunt growled. "We've shown them we can whip them in war, we gave them generous peace terms, let them keep their space capability almost intact, even offered them economic aid—"

"While we scrapped the fighting ships that we didn't build until ten years of Hukk raids forced us to."

"I know the Hardline, Dalton. O.K., you told 'em so. Maybe there was something in it. But what good is this caper supposed to do? You want to be a martyr, is that it? And I'm a witness—"

"Not quite. The Hukks picked this spot because it's well shielded from casual observation, close enough to Grassport and Bedrock to launch a quick strike, but not so close as to be stumbled over. That's sound, as far as it goes, but as a defensive position, it couldn't be worse. Of course, they didn't expect to have to defend it."

"Look, Dalton, O.K., you were right, the Hukks are making an unauthorized landing on Grassroots soil. Maybe they're even an armed party, as you said. Swell. I came out here with you, I've seen the ship, and I'll so testify. So why louse it up? We'll hand the file to the CDT and let them handle it! It's their baby, not yours! Not mine! We've got no call to get ourselves blasted to kingdom come playing One-Man Task Force!"

"You think Croanie will move in fast and slap 'em down?"

"Well . . . it might take some time—"

"Meanwhile the Hukks will have brought in their heavy stuff. They'll entrench half a mile under the surface and then start spreading out. By the time the Admiralty gets into the act, they'll hold half the planet."

"All right! Is that fatal? We'll negotiate, arrange for the release of Terry nationals, the return of Terry property—"

"Compromise, in other words."

"All right, you give a little, you get a little!"

"And the next time?"

"What next time?"

"The Hukks will take half of Grassroots with no more expense than a little time at a conference table. That will look pretty good to them. A lot better than an all-fronts war. Why gulp, when you can nibble?"

"If they keep pushing, we'd slap them down, you know that."

"Sure we will—in time. Why not do it now?"

"Don't talk like a fool, Dalton! What can one man do?"

The Hukk ship was visibly lower now, drifting down silently on the stuttering column of light that was its lift-beam. It was dull black, bottle-shaped, with a long ogee curve to the truncated prow.

"If I had any heavy stuff up here, I'd go for her landing jacks," Dalton said. "But a 2mm Norge doesn't pack enough wallop to be sure of crippling her. And if I miss her, they're warned: they can lift and cook us with an ion bath. So we'll wait until they're off-loaded, then pour it into the port. That's a weak spot on a Hukk ship. The iris is fragile, and any malfunction there means no seal, ergo no lift. Then we settle down to picking them off, officers first. With fast footwork, we should have them trimmed down to manageable size before they can organize a counter-attack."

"What if I don't go along with this harebrained suicide scheme?"

"Then I'll have to wire your wrists and ankles."

"And if you're killed, where does that leave me?"

"Better make up your mind."

"Suppose I shoot at you instead of them?"

"In that case I'd have to kill you."

"You're pretty sure of yourself, Dalton." When Dalton didn't answer Brunt licked his lips and said: "I'll go this far: I'll help you burn the port, because if you foul it up it's my neck, too. But as for shooting fish in a barrel—negative, Dalton."

"I'll settle for that."

"But afterwards, once she's grounded—all bets are off."

"Tell that to the Hukks," Dalton said.

VI

"Lousy light for this work," Brunt said over his gunsights. Dalton, watching the Hukk ship settle almost soundlessly in a roll of dust, didn't answer. Suddenly, floodlights flared around the base of the ship, bathing it in a reflected violet glow as, with a grating of rock, the Hukk vessel came to rest.

"Looks like a stage all set up for 'Swan Lake,'" Brunt muttered.

For five minutes, nothing happened. Then the circular exit valve dilated, spilling a widening shaft of green light out in a long path across the crater floor, casting black shadows behind the thickly scattered boulders. A tiny silhouette moved in the aperture, jumped down, a long-legged shadow matching its movements as it stepped aside. Another followed, and more, until five Hukks stood outside the ship. They were slope-backed quadrupeds, hunched, neckless, long faced, knob-jointed, pendulous bellied, leathery-hided. A cluster of sheathed digital numbers lay on either side of the slablike cheeks.

"Ugly bastich," Brunt said. "But that's got nothing to do with it, of course."

Now more troops were emerging, falling-in in orderly rows. At a command faintly audible to Dalton as a squeaky bark, the first squad of ten Hukks about-faced and marched fifty feet from the ship, halted, opened ranks.

"Real parade-ground types," Brunt said. "Kit inspection, no less."

"What's the matter, Sergeant? Annoyed they didn't hit the beach with all guns blazing?"

"Dalton, it's not too late to change your mind."

"I'm afraid it is—by about six years."

The disembarkation proceeded with promptness and dispatch. It was less than ten minutes before nine groups of ten Hukks had formed up, each with an officer in charge. At a sharp command, they wheeled smartly, executed a complicated maneuver which produced a single hollow square two Hukks deep around the baggage stacked at the center.

"All right, Brunt, off-loading complete," Dalton said. "Commence firing on the port."

The deep *chuff! chuff!* of the blast rifles echoed back from the far side of the crater as the two guns opened up. Brilliant flashes winked against the ship. The Hukks stood fast, with the exception of two of the officers who whirled and ran for the ship. Dalton switched sights momentarily, dropped the first one, then the second, returned to the primary target.

Now the square broke suddenly, but not in random fashion; each side peeled away as a unit, spread out, hit the dirt, each Hukk scrambling for shelter, while the four remaining officers took up their positions in the centers of their respective companies. In seconds, the dispersed troops were virtually invisible. Here and there the blink and *pop!* of return fire crackled from behind a boulder or a gully.

The port was glowing cherry red; the iris seemed to be jammed half closed. Dalton shifted targets, settled the cross-hairs on an officer, fired, switched to another as the first fell. He killed three before the remaining Hukk brasshat scuttled for the protection of a ridge of rock. Without a pause, Dalton turned his fire on the soldiers scattered across the open ground.

"Stop, you bloodthirsty fool!" Brunt was yelling. "The ship's crippled, the officers are dead! The poor devils are helpless down there—"

There was a violet flash from near the ship, a deep-toned *warhoom!*, a crashing fall of rock twenty feet to their left. A second flash, a second report, more rock exploded, closer.

"Time to go," Dalton snapped, and without waiting to see Brunt's reaction, slid down the backslope, scrambled along it while rock chips burst from the ridge above him amid the smashing impacts of the Hukk power cannon. He surfaced two hundred yards to the left of his original position, found the rifle emplacement. He aimed the weapon, depressed the trigger and set the hold-down for automatic rapid fire, paused long enough to fire half a dozen aimed bolts at the enemy, then moved onto the next gun to repeat the operation.

VII

Twenty minutes later Dalton, halfway around the crater from his original location, paused for a breather, listening to the steady crackle of the Hukk return fire, badly aimed but intense enough to encourage him to keep his head down. As well as he could judge, he had so far accounted for eight Hukks in addition to the five officers. Of the five blast rifles he had left firing on automatic, two had been knocked out or had exhausted their charges. The other three were still firing steadily, kicking pits in the bare rock below.

A few of the ship's ground lights were still on; the rest had been shot out by the Hukk soldiery. By their glow Dalton picked an exposed target near the ship, brought his rifle to bear on him. He was about to pull the trigger when he saw Brunt sliding downslope thirty degrees around the perimeter of the ringwall from him, waving an improvised white flag.

VIII

The words from the Hukk PA system were loud and clear if somewhat echoic, and were delivered in excellent Terran, marred only by the characteristic Hukk difficulty with nasals:

· "Terran warrior," the deep, booming voice rolled across the crater. "Hwe hno hnow that you are alone. You have fought hwell. Hnow you must surrender or be destroyed."

The lone Hukk officer stood in an exposed position near the center of the semicircular dispersement of soldiers, holding the end of the rope which was attached to Brunt's neck.

"Unless you show yourself at once," the amplified voice boomed out, "you hwill be hunted out and killed."

The Hukk officer turned to Brunt. A moment later Brunt's hoarse voice echoed across the crater:

"For God's sake, Dalton, they're giving you a chance! Throw down your gun and surrender!"

Sweat trickled down across Dalton's face. He wiped it away, cupped his hands beside his mouth and shouted in the Hukk language:

"Release the prisoner first."

There was a pause, "You offer an exchange, himself for yourself?"

"That's right."

Another pause. "Very well, I accept," the Hukk called. "Come forward now. I assure you safe-conduct."

Dalton lifted his pistol from it's holster, tucked it inside his belt, under the jacket. He studied the ground below, then worked his way fifty feet to the right before he stood, the blast gun in his hands, and started down the slope along the route he had selected, amid a rattle of dislodged rock fragments.

"Throw down your weapon!" the PA ordered as he reached the crater floor. Dalton hesitated, then tossed the gun aside. Empty-handed, he advanced among the boulders toward the waiting Hukks. The captain—Dalton was close enough to see his rank badge now—had pulled Brunt in front of him. The latter, aware of his role as a human shield, looked pale and damp. His mouth twitched as though there were things it wanted to say, but was having trouble finding words equal to the occasion.

When Dalton was twenty feet from the officer, passing between two six-foot-high splinters of upended rock, he halted abruptly. At once, the captain barked an order. There was a flicker of motion to Dalton's left. He darted a hand under his jacket, came out with the pistol, fired, and was facing the officer again as a yapping wail came from the target.

"Tell your troops to throw down their guns and pull back," Dalton said crisply.

"You call on *me* to surrender?" The officer was carefully keeping his members in Brunt's shadow.

"You've been had, Captain. Only three of your soldiers can bear on me here—and they have to expose themselves to fire. My reaction time is quicker than theirs."

"You bluff—"

"The gun in my hand will penetrate two inches of flint steel," Dalton said. "The man in front of you is a lot softer than armor."

"You would kill the man for whose freedom you offered your life?"

"What do you think?"

"My men surely will kill you!"

"Probably. But you won't be here to transmit the all-clear to the boys standing by off-planet."

"Then what do you hope to gain, Man?"

"Dalton's the name, Captain."

"That name is known to me. I am Ch'oova. I was with the Grand Armada at Van Doom's world."

"The Grand Armada fought well—but not quite well enough."

"True, Commodore. Perhaps our strategy has been a fault." The captain raised his head, barked an order. Hukk soldiers began rising from concealment, gun muzzles pointing at the ground; they cantered away toward the ship by twos and threes, their small hooves raising cottony puffs of dust.

When they were alone, Captain Ch'oova tossed the rope aside.

"I think," he said, with a small formal curtsy, "that we had best negotiate."

"That fellow Ch'oova told me something funny," Brunt said as the cargo carrier ploughed toward the dawn. "Seven years ago, at Van Doom's world, you were left in command of the Fleet after Admiral Hayle was hit. You were the one who brought the Grand Armada to a standstill."

"I took over from Hayle, yes."

"And won the battle. Funny, that part didn't get in the papers. But not so funny, maybe, at that. According to Ch'oova, after the fighting was over, you refused a direct Admiralty order."

"Garbled transmission," Dalton said.

"Tempers run high in wartime," Brunt said. "The Hukks had made a lot of enemies before we finally faced up to going to war. The High Command wanted a permanent solution. They gave you secret orders to accept the Hukks' surrender, and then blow them out of space. You said no."

"Not really; I just didn't get around to carrying out the order."

"And in a few days, cooler heads prevailed. But not before you were relieved and posted to the boondocks, and your part in the victory covered up."

"Just a routine transfer," Dalton said.

"And then, by God, you turned around . . . you, the white-haired boy who'd saved the brass from making a blunder that would have ruined them when it got known—and went after the treaty hammer and tongs, to toughen it up! First you save the Hukks' necks—and then you break yourself trying to tighten the screws on them!"

Dalton shook his head. "Nope; I just didn't want to mislead them."

"You wanted their Armada broken up, occupation of their principal worlds, arms limitations with inspections—"

"Brunt, this night's work cost the lives of fourteen Hukk soldiers, most of them probably ordinary citizens who were drafted and sent out here all full of patriotic fervor. That was a dirty trick."

"What's that got to do—"

"We beat them once. Then we picked 'em up, dusted 'em off, and gave them back their toys. That wasn't fair to a straightforward bunch of opportunists like the Hukks. It was an open invitation to blunder again. And unless they were slapped down quick, they'd keep on blundering in deeper—until they goaded us into building another fleet. And this time, there might not be enough pieces left to pick up."

Brunt sat staring thoughtfully out at the paling sky ahead; he laughed shortly. "When you went steaming out there with fire in your eye, I thought you were out for revenge on the Hukks for losing you your fat career. But you were just delivering a message."

"In terms that they could understand," Dalton said.

"You're a strange man, Commodore. For the second time, singlehanded, you've stopped a war. And because you agreed with Ch'oova to keep the whole thing confidential, no one will ever know. Result: You'll be a laughingstock for your false alarm. And with your identity known, you're washed up in the junk business. Hell, Marston will have the police waiting to pick you up for everything from arms theft to spitting on the sidewalk! And you can't say a word in your own defense."

"It'll blow over."

"I could whisper a word in Marston's ear—"

"No, you won't, Brunt. And if you do, I'll call you a liar. I gave Ch'oova my word; if this caper became public knowledge, it would kick the Hukks out of every Terran market they've built up in the past six years."

"Looks like you've boxed yourself into a corner, Commodore," Brunt said softly.

"That's twice you've called me Commodore—Major."

Brunt made a surprised sound. Dalton gave him a one-sided smile.

"I can spot a hot-shot Intelligence type at half a mile. I used to wonder why they posted you out here."

"To keep an eye on you, Commodore, what else?"

"Me?"

"A man like you is an enigma. You had the brass worried. You didn't hew to any party line. But I think you've gotten the message across now—and not just to the Hukks."

Dalton grunted.

"So I think I can assure that you won't need to look for a new place to start up your junk yard. I think the Navy needs you. It'll take some string pulling, but it can be done. Maybe not as a commodore—not for a while—but at least you'll have a deck under your feet. How does it sound?"

"I'll think about it," Dalton said.

. . . NOT A
PRISON MAKE

Joseph P. Martino

GUERRILLA WARFARE: An obsolete form of warfare practiced intermittently throughout history until the XX Century. It was characterized by conflict between professional soldiers formally organized into regular armies, on the one side, and nonprofessional, informally organized forces on the other side. As such, it could not exist except when warfare was customarily conducted by professional armies. Its most recent appearance was during the XVIIth through the XXth Centuries. Its name, in fact, originated during that period, and means "little war" in the Spanish language—a Latin-based language formerly spoken in southeastern Europe; (see SPAIN).

It was widely practiced during the anti-colonial wars of the middle XXth Century, and received intensive theoretical and practical study by adherents of Communism (which see). This emphasis on guerrilla warfare led to a reaction on the part of the forces against which it was being used, among which were most of the industrially and technologically advanced nations of the world. The apparent paradox of poorly-trained and ill-equipped irregulars being able to defeat well-trained and well-equipped regular troops sparked an intensive program of research among these advanced nations.

The inevitable result was the development of surveillance, mobility and communication techniques which gave the regular soldier of an advanced nation considerable advantage over his guerrilla opponent.

The guerrilla, of course, could not adopt these techniques, since they required an industrial base to supply them, an organized logistics system to maintain them, and highly trained personnel to operate them. The guerrilla could not survive against an opponent who was invulnerable to surprise, and who could move over any terrain faster than the guerrilla could move. Thus after the XXth Century, only a professional army could stand against another one. This in turn led to an accelerated spiral of measure and countermeasure . . . From the *Terran Encyclopedia,* 37th Edition. KREG WAR: One of the interstellar wars fought by the First Terran Confederation during its early period of expansion. It was named for the Kregs, a chlorine-breathing race occupying several solar systems in the vicinity of Polaris. The war climaxed a series of disputes over possession of a number of mineral-rich but airless minor planets in the region between the Terran and Kreg spheres of influence. After a number of raids and counter-raids on mining settlements, a major attack . . . The war was ended by the Treaty of Polaris, which granted to each side those planets already occupied, and provided an arbitration procedure to determine ownership of those unoccupied.

An interesting sidelight of the war was the resulting relationship between Terrans and the Kanthu, a humanoid race of oxygen-breathers. Their home planet, Kanth, occupied a strategic position outflanking several of the Kregs' advanced bases. A Terran task force landed there and set up a base which was intended to serve as a staging point for attacks against the Kregs' inner defenses. The initial policy of noninterference with the Kanthu turned out to be impossible, and . . . From the *Terran Encyclopedia.* 41st Edition.

Private Chalat Wongsuwan was growing bored. The Task Force had hit dirt three weeks ago, and at first there was plenty to keep everyone busy. The first hastily-constructed defenses had been strengthened by round-the-clock work, in anticipation of the expected Kreg counterattack. However, no attack had come. Surely the Kregs knew the Task Force was there. What was delaying them? What were they up to? But after three weeks, even these questions lost their power to keep anyone alert. Private Chalat Wongsuwan, being an experienced combat soldier, recognized the symptoms of boredom, and knew that when on sentry duty was a poor time to get bored. He got up from the rock on which he was sitting, and reviewed his sector.

He was responsible for an area which was a rough square, one kilometer on edge, and the first one hundred meters of airspace above it. This area had been saturated with detectors of all kinds, which noticed anything out of the ordinary going on around them. The first few nights after landing, of course, had been spent finding out what was ordinary. The scents, sounds, electromagnetic radiations, seismic vibrations, and so on associated with the normal physical and animal activity of the area had been cataloged.

Now the ultrasonic pickups no longer reported the cries of an insectivorous batlike creature, but made a report only when the number of cries per minute deviated by more than a calculated percentage from what had been found to be the normal value for the time and place. The scent pickups no longer reported the mating odor of the females of a species of hard-shelled, ten-legged pseudo-beetles. The infra-red pickups no longer reported the intense emission from a small insect which, had its emission been visible, could have been called a firefly. And so on with all the other phenomena of the night in the forest.

The cataloging was not perfect yet, of course. There hadn't been time for that. Even back on Terra the detectors still pulled a few surprises now and then, and they had had centuries of refinement in the Terran environment. So several times during each watch the situation display, which portrayed the reports of all the sensors in the area in multicolored coded lights on the inside of the transparent face shield hanging from Private Chalat Wongsuwan's helmet, signaled a warning which turned out to be a false alarm when investigated.

Private Chalat Wongsuwan's boredom ended when an alarm signal appeared at a point near the center of the eastern edge of his area. He checked first with the sentry in the sector to the east.

"Ruongwit, this is Chalat. I've got a bogey at coordinates X—3917, Y—4231. Have you had anything heading my way?"

"Chalat, this is Ruongwit. Not a thing out of the ordinary in my sector. There hasn't been an alarm over your way all night, although I did have a couple on the other side earlier. When I got there, I couldn't find a thing wrong. The alarms had ceased, and everything was O.K. by then."

"Looks like the technicians are going to have to redefine what's normal for the area again. I'd better have a look anyway. Over and out."

There was still the possibility that something might have dropped out of the sky. He should have been informed by the Sergeant of the Guard if anything had been reported by the aerial patrol, or even the off-planet patrol, but slipups did happen from time to time.

"Sergeant of the Guard, this is Private Chalat."

"Go ahead, Chalat."

"I've got a bogey which just appeared in my sector. It didn't come from the next sector. Any reports of activity upstairs?"

"No reports of anything. What kind of an alarm do you have?"

"It just about covers the spectrum. Scent, infrared indicating a temperature near 40° Centigrade, sounds that could pass for breathing, the whole works. Only no footfalls from the seismic detectors. Wait a minute. The alarm just switched locations. The first spot is back to normal except for a reduced count on bird calls, as though the birds hadn't got over being scared. The alarm is now at a point halfway between me and the first point—exactly the same set of indications. I'd better take a look at both spots."

"Give me a report on anything, especially if it moves again."

"Roger, over and out."

He switched on his personal lifter, and reached treetop level. He drifted in the general direction of the alarm, threading his way through the treetops, getting as much concealment from them as he could without getting too close to them. His face mask display included a purple dot which was supposed to indicate his location, but he really didn't need it. The display also showed the swath of disturbance he was cutting through the night, as the many sensors reported his passage within their detection range. They couldn't be set to consider him as a normal part of the environment, without running the risk of failing to detect other humans who shouldn't be there. He reflected that, if there were any natives around who knew their way in these woods, they would have no trouble detecting him by the change in the behavior of the animal and bird life. The purpose of his multitude of sensors was to give him the equivalent of a lifetime's experience in the environment, without taking a lifetime to acquire it, and to give him more detection range than his organic sensors possessed.

The alarm was coming from a small clearing ahead of him. He hung behind a screen of branches and looked over the clearing. There was what appeared to be a man standing in the middle of it. Just before he could call the Sergeant of the Guard, the man disappeared. Had he really seen anything, or was his gear playing tricks on him? Now there appeared to be two men at opposite edges of the clearing. There was another. No, one of the two had disappeared. He ought to make a report, but what would make sense?

He switched the lifter to a high-speed attack mode, and charged down at one of the figures. The figure disappeared. He halted and altered course toward the other figure, which also disappeared. He turned around. Both were behind him, on the other side of the clearing. He drifted toward the center of the clearing, gaining altitude. A microphone near the two figures picked up the twang of bowstrings, but by the time he could interpret the sound, two crossbow bolts had struck him. As he lost consciousness, the lifter lowered him to the ground to await medical pickup. "Sergeant of the Guard. I've got a 'man down' signal on Chalat. He's badly wounded. No, there's a change. He's dead."

"Where is he?"

"Coordinates X—3820, Y—4417."

"Squad One, head directly for Chalat's position, Squads Two through Five, seal off the borders of his sector. Squads Six and Seven start combing the sector." Then switching channels, "Aerial patrol, give me a tight roof over Sector 82. There's at least one hostile in it."

At this point the Officer of the Guard arrived. "Good response so far, Sergeant, but you'd better call up two or three reserve squads. We don't have enough left on duty to handle a similar attack on another sector. And warn all other sentries about what happened. I wish Chalat had given us more details as he went along."

"Sergeant of the Guard. Call from Ruongwit, in the sector next to Chalat's."

"I'll take it. Put him on."

"Sergeant, this is Ruongwit. I've got a bunch of bogeys just like the ones Chalat described. They keep jumping around. There are about a dozen oaf them, as near as I can tell. They won't hold still long enough to count. Now they seem to be clustering about my position."

"Get some altitude and get out of there. Shoot anything you see. Acknowledge, Ruongwit."

"Sergeant, I can't raise him. Now there's a 'man down' signal on him. He's dead, too."

"Sergeant, double the guard in all sectors. Call up all reserve squads. Call off the search in Sector 82. The next sector that reports some bogeys is to be saturated with all available forces."

"Yes, sir. Shall I sound a General Alert?"

"Better do that. The Kregs've clearly found some counter for our detectors. They may hit the Base next."

The Task Force Commander was distinctly unhappy, as any man who has been awakened at four in the morning to be told he's under attack has a right to be. "Well, Major Sakul, you were Officer of the Guard. Let's hear what happened."

"Yes, sir. Well, the first thing was Private Chalat. He was investigating a bogey that seemed to have jumped from one place to another. When we found him, he had two crossbow bolts in him, and his throat had been cut. In addition, he'd been stripped of all his loose equipment. Fortunately his recorders were still on him, so we could reconstruct what had happened. Forces had just been ordered out to comb his sector when the attackers struck the next sector. Same thing there. Ruongwit was found with three crossbow bolts in him. He must have been dead when he hit the ground, since his throat was still intact. He, too, was stripped of all his loose equipment.

"After that, bedlam broke loose. Every sector reported bogeys all over the place, all the same kind. They jumped from one place to another without seeming to be any place in between. We lost a total of eighteen guards out of the one hundred twenty we had out. In all cases, they were stripped of their equipment. Those that weren't dead when they hit the ground had their throats cut. Next they started appearing inside the Base. They didn't seem to do any attacking there, they would just be reported somewhere, and then vanish. There were a few attempts to shoot at them, but no one hit them.

"I figured that we would do more damage to ourselves firing inside the Base than they seemed to be doing, so I ordered a halt to the firing within the boundary. After about thirty minutes the appearances seemed to peter out. There were a few reports for as long as an hour after the attack on Private Chalat, but I think they were all false alarms. I feel that the attackers first hit our guards, then penetrated the Base for reconnaissance purposes, and withdrew in order after they had what they came for. All in all, it looks like a well-coordinated attack, and if they decide to pull another one, I think they'll get away with it, too."

"Colonel Bunyarit."

The Executive Officer replied, "Yes, sir."

"What have you to report?"

"Well our first reaction, naturally, was that the Kregs had come up with something new. Somehow they had managed to drop landing parties near our Base, without their ships being detected on the way in, and then the landing parties had managed to spoof and jam our detectors so we couldn't keep up with them."

"And it wasn't the Kregs?"

The Executive Officer replied slowly. "No, sir. When Chalat attacked one of the intruders, his action recorder went on. We got a good look at the one he went after. Then we saw the figure of the intruder disappear. The same thing happened to the next one he went after. He turned and spotted some more. However, they were the same two he started after. Despite the fact that both moons were down, there was enough starlight for the image intensifier to give us a good picture. We could identify the marking on the loincloths of the two figures, facial features, scars, and so on well enough to tell that there were only two, and they were jumping around from one spot to another. Then when they got Chalat, the recorder showed them suddenly appearing next to him, cutting his throat, stripping him of his equipment, then disappearing, equipment and all."

"Well, man," the commander burst out, "who were they?"

The Executive Officer was enjoying himself. "The natives of the planet, sir."

"But, according to the Intelligence reports of the pre-landing survey, the natives are very primitive. If I remember correctly, they practice a very destructive form of agriculture, so that they have to shift their villages every few years, and most of their protein comes from hunting. They have no cultures to speak of. How do they get the technological capability to bollix up our surveillance devices? Are the Kregs supporting them?"

"While it is possible they are getting Kreg support, sir, I think it is unlikely. If the Kregs had got another jump on us in the detection field, they would have made the attack themselves, rather than trying to work through primitive allies like the local natives. I believe that the detectors were giving us a true report of exactly what was going on. The attackers were really jumping from one place to the other without being in between. I believe they are natural teleports. And considering the way they coordinated their attack, they are telepaths, too."

"Pardon me, General."

The Task Force Commander turned to his Operations Officer. "Yes, Colonel Arun."

"As you know, sir, before I was recalled to active duty I was Professor of Military History at the University of Callisto. My period of specialization was the XXth Century. One of the more common types of military action during that period was something called 'guerrilla warfare'. It was commonly used by nations under occupation by foreign invaders, colonialists, and so forth. It is particularly adapted for use by weak and poorly organized forces

179

against strong, well-organized forces. It seems to me that's precisely what we're up against here. It even fits the traditional pattern, since the first action of the native guerrillas was arms-gathering. They obviously carried out last night's raid in order to get their hands on some of our weapons."

"Supposing what you say is true, what do you recommend?"

"In the XXth Century, guerrillas weren't defeated until the forces opposing them learned to eliminate the genuine grievances of the people who supported the guerrillas. I recommend we use the same course of action here. We must communicate with the natives, explain our reasons for coming here, and use some of our resources in solving their more serious problems. In that way we can gain their support instead of their enmity."

"Now wait a minute," interjected Colonel Bunyarit. "Let's not go losing our sense of perspective. Our job here is to fight the Kregs, not to wipe the noses of a bunch of natives. With all due respect to Colonel Arun's academic background, I think that's precisely what his recommendations are: academic. We've got a defeatist attitude. Already we seem to think they can come in and repeat their raids as often as they feel like it. Well, last night they hit us without any warning. Next time we'll be ready for them. We ought to get many more of them than they get of us. And the raiding doesn't have to be all one sided. There's nothing to stop us from going out and raiding a few of their villages. After getting their noses bloodied every time they come after us, and losing a few villages too, they'll quit bothering us. That's the way to treat them. Let's not mess around with this do-gooder attitude."

"But Colonel Bunyarit, you're making precisely the same mistake nearly every colonial power made in the XXth Century. They felt that a show of force was all that was required . . ."

"Now you look here. I've been on worlds before where the natives started trouble—caravan raiding, robbery, and so forth. You shoot up their villages a few times, and they learn who's boss. You ought to get out from behind that professor's desk of yours once in a while, and find out how the galaxy works."

"Your attitude, Colonel Bunyarit, is typically military in its obtuseness. Your suggested treatment may be quite satisfactory for handling pirates and bandits, who value their village more than they value the loot they might acquire from another raid. But it won't work against a people who are united in their opposition to the foreign invader. To them, the loss of a village is a small thing. They have their minds focused on the long pull, and are willing to make considerable sacrifices to gain ultimate victory."

"Are you trying to tell me that a bunch of half-naked savages, who haven't progressed beyond the crossbow, are going to chase us off this planet? If it even looks like they might do it, we can wipe them all out with radioactive . . ."

"Stop that task," from the Tank Force Commander. "Don't say it. Don't even think it. If ever the rumor got out that Terra had committed genocide, we'd have every race we know about, and as many we never heard of, down on our necks. If there's anything that unites the races of the galaxy, it's their opposition to genocide. We'll hear no more talk about wiping anyone out. If we can't settle the problem some other way, we'll get off their planet and let them alone. And cut out the bickering. We've all had a hard night; there's no point in taking it out on each other." Then in a calmer voice, "We seem to have two policies proposed. One is to make friends with the natives, the other is to civilize them with a blaster.

"It's clear to me, anyway, that if we try the second policy first, and it fails, we'll never get a chance to try making friends. So we'll try the policy of making friends first.

"Colonel Bunyarit, you seem to think we can defend ourselves against any more raids. Get busy and set up the defenses. I think we're going to need them tonight. Colonel Arun, you will figure out how we're going to go about making friends with people who can vanish from our grasp before we can learn even one word of their language. That's all. Dismissed."

"Colonel Prapat." The Task Force Commander turned to the Provost Marshal.

"Yes General?"

"Come to my office with me. There are a couple of things I want to talk over with you. Have you had breakfast yet?"

"No, sir."

"Neither have I. I'll have some sent in. I don't think any of us are going to have time for regular meals for a while."

"You know, General, there are times when I wonder how much more I can take of Arun and his professional attitude. He seems to think none of us ever read a book. I admit I've never heard the word 'guerrilla' before today, but, if these are guerrillas, their tactics don't seem to be much different from those of a lot of bandits I've fought on a number of worlds."

"Yes, I know Arun gets on a lot of people's nerves. First of all, Reserve officers who are called up at the outbreak of a war often have a low opinion of us Regulars. The fact that we had to call them up seems to be proof that we weren't competent to win the war without them. In addition, college professors seem to have a firmly fixed opinion that a military officer is a wooden-headed dunce. And when you combine both in the same man, as we have with Arun, he sometimes gets hard to live with. However, don't forget he has a good point. Although the tactics may be similar, there is considerable difference between a bandit and a guerrilla.

"The motivation of the guerrilla makes him willing to put up with a lot of punishment. Even a long series of defeats won't dishearten him and severe repression actually provides him with recruits from people who figure they have nothing to lose. As long as things are going to be tough anyway, they might as well be doing some fighting, and getting in a few licks at the people who are making things tough. At the moment I'm more concerned about Bunyarit. If there's anything I've learned in my career, it's that you should never underestimate an opponent. Treating an opponent with anything other than respect is a good way to get whipped in a hurry. If we don't treat them with respect, we'll try to beat them with half-measures, and get bogged down in a messy, indecisive war just like what happened to the XXth Century colonialists."

"That scared me, too, while I was listening to Arun. To a bandit a gun is a means to money. He gets one so he can use it to commit banditry, or to sell it to someone else who will use it to commit banditry. From Arun's description, a guerrilla considers a gun a means to more guns. He uses it to get another gun, to give to a friend, so they can both go out and get more guns, to give to more friends, until they have a big enough force to wipe you out. I don't see how you can beat a thing like that."

"Don't be too shaken by the idea. Despite Arun's air of authority, he's not the only one around here who's read some history. He wasn't quite correct on one point. Historically the guerrilla was whipped when surveillance devices were developed to the point where he couldn't surprise you, when mechanized armies quit being roadbound and learned to move over any territory a man on foot could move over, and do it faster too, and when communications were developed to the point where you could coordinate the actions of a lot of scattered units.

"The trouble with whipping him is that it isn't enough. He won't stay whipped. You can't relax your guard. Even in supposedly pacified towns, troops have to go around in pairs, or they'll end up in an alley with their heads caved in. And you can't bring in civilians as tradesmen, miners, and so on. They'll be murdered as soon as you turn your back. As Arun pointed out, if you want them to stay whipped, you've got to eliminate their legitimate grievances. It's important that you be able to whip them, of course. If you simply do things for them after they attack

182

you, you merely whet their appetite for more. But if you do whip them, you can afford to take the attitude that they have been done an injustice, and deserve better treatment. If you neglect either half of the program, however, you're in for trouble.

"That's the sort of thing we've got to avoid here. In the long run we'll have to come to some agreement with these people or get off their planet. But in the short run, maybe we can hold our own against their banditlike tactics by using the tactics that work against bandits. That's what I want to talk to you about."

"Well, as a Provost Marshal, I've had considerable experience with bandits on various worlds. I've found that by and large bandits have a good sense of economics. If their gain from banditry is less than their loss from your reprisal for the banditry, they soon take up some other line of business, like fleecing tourists legally. But your reprisals, if they are going to be effective, have to be quick and precise. The bandits have to see the justice in your reprisal. If a small gang in a village engages in a raid, and you bomb the whole village, all you've done is get a lot of people mad at you. You've provided the bandit with allies. You have to identify the bandits and conduct your reprisals against them alone."

"That sounds reasonable. Now how do you find out who the bandits are?"

"I think of that part of the work as nothing but conventional police procedures, just patient collection and sifting of facts. To get the facts, you have to know the area and the people. You have to build up nets of informers and agents in the villages. You have to keep watch over roads, and such natural convergence points as bridges, fords and mountain passes. If you suspect anyone, you arrange to have them watched constantly. You offer open rewards for information, and secret bribes and offers of reduced sentences for members of the gang who provide evidence. In extreme cases, you can take a few squads of police or troops and seal off a whole village. Then you arrange to interview each and every person in the village, separately. You arrange so that all the interviews are approximately the same length, so that no one stands out as particularly suspect for having spent a lot of time with you.

"In the meantime, while the others are standing around, you might have a doctor giving shots, passing out pills, giving a health lecture, or something, so you don't antagonize the innocent. Sometimes in these interviews you actually get information; other times you can only recruit agents who will later pay off for you. But that's the sort of thing you have to do. It's just patient, detailed

183

police investigation, putting together small scraps of information, and trying to get more information."

"How would you apply your techniques here?"

"Frankly, I'm baffled. Even if I could get one of them to stand still, I don't know how to talk to them. I don't know what they value, so can't offer rewards. And even if I did know what to use as a reward, they could steal it from me more easily than they could earn it anyway. It seems to be a circular proposition. If we could stop them from attacking us, I could probably build up a net of agents who could tell me who did the attacking. But, then I wouldn't need to, since they wouldn't be attacking any more. And until I can get information out of them, I can't do anything to stop their attacks."

"I can see the vicious circle clearly enough. I had hoped your methods might help us to break out of it. All right, thanks for the information. Now I'd better go see what kind of defenses Colonel Bunyarit is working out."

The Task Force Commander sat at his console in the Battle Control Center. All the other Duty Officers and NCOs were seated at their own consoles, all wearing battle armor. The consoles were tightly packed against one side of the long room, instead of being spread throughout the room, as was usual. A freshly-painted white strip marked off the now-empty remainder of the room from the consoles. Coils of barbed wire hung from the ceiling, festooned the walls, and draped over the sides of the consoles, filling every possible cubic centimeter of the space between the white strip and the wall, leaving the men at the consoles just barely room to move. At the far end of the room, the end wall was covered with a newly-installed bank of electronic apparatus.

The room below, containing the computer complex and auxiliary power supply, was also crammed with barbed wire. The Center itself was, of course, underground, and reasonably safe from any ordinary attack. However, the commander scanned the interior of the room carefully, wondering if any additional improvements would make it better protected against attack by teleports. Then he caught his first glimpse of one of the natives, standing in the cleared portion of the room.

This particular native had spent the day practicing a particular tactic. He would choose a target, and a spot near it, teleport to the desired spot, attempting to arrive facing the target and with his gun pointed at it, fire quickly, and return to his starting point. He had, in fact, become quite proficient at it. Now, moving with the speed of thought, he appeared in the Battle Control Center just behind one of the consoles, corrected his aim on the duty officer slightly, and squeezed the trigger.

Unfortunately for him, the speed of thought can be measured in milliseconds. In the newly-installed bank of equipment at the end of the room an electronic circuit, operating in microseconds, reacted to a sensor which had detected his presence and closed the circuit on a blast rifle which happened to be pointed through the volume of space he was occupying. Long before the nerve impulses arrived at his trigger finger, he was dead and falling to the floor, receiving more blaster bolts as he activated other sensors during his fall. A second native, attempting to retrieve his fallen weapon, was likewise cut down. After that, there were no more attacks on the Battle Control Center.

Sergeant Sawang Nakvirote drifted slowly across the base, at an altitude of slightly less than fifty meters. His squad, in diamond formation, followed him. Just below him stood a row of obviously fresh pyramids of earth. All the hand-weapons of the Base, except those actually issued to someone, were buried under those pyramids. It had been explained that this would keep the natives from raiding the armory. They would have to fight for each weapon they captured. Ahead of him stood the vast parking area of the space field, normally crowded with ships, but now empty. All spaceships had been moved well away from the planet, as a precaution against attack or sabotage.

He was beginning to wonder whether the natives were going to attack this night, or give it up as a bad job, when the crackle of blaster fire reached his ears. Almost simultaneously, a voice from the Battle Control Center blared from his communicator. "Attacking force in Barracks 34-D. Squad 17 counterattack."

Sergeant Sawang led his squad in a high-speed, swooping dive for the front entrance of Barracks 34-D. It was a long, low, one-story structure, with a door in the center of each of the two long sides. Inside were two rows of cots, with a footlocker at the foot of each cot. A separate room at one end contained the precise number and kind of sanitary facilities specified by regulations for thirty-two men. Sergeant Sawang led the front vee of the diamond as it merged into a single line, passed through the door, and spread out again. The rear vee of the diamond swung up over the roof of the barracks, turned, and opened fire on the figures who had suddenly appeared in front of the barracks, firing at the rest of the squad as it entered.

One of the figures dropped, and immediately another one appeared beside it, retrieved its fallen weapon, and disappeared.

The rest of the figures had by this time also disappeared, although not without drawing blood in turn. The last of the squad members entering the barracks stopped short in mid-flight, as he was hit. His personal lifter, instead of lowering him to the ground, took him up to an altitude of a hundred meters, and hovered there. His body could be recovered later for proper burial. In the meantime, his weapons were safe from capture.

Inside the barracks, Sergeant Sawang found considerable damage, and some smoke from several cots which had been set on fire. However, there was no sign of the attackers. Half the men immediately took up positions at the front windows, to cover the entry of the rest of the squad. The others tried to cover the interior of the barracks, but without success. A native suddenly appeared in line with the doorway, fired once, and disappeared. A man just inside the doorway flung his arms out in a spasmodic jerk, then drifted toward the ceiling as his lifter attempted to raise him to the programmed hundred-meter altitude. A native appeared on the floor below him, grasped vainly for his feet, and died on the spot as someone realized what was going on and fired. The dead man was unceremoniously hauled out the door by two of his comrades, and allowed to float upwards out of reach.

At this point Sergeant Sawang's communicator spoke up again. "We're sending Squad 32 to reinforce you. As long as the natives want to fight in Barracks 34-D, we might as well accommodate them. Try to capture a few of their weapons, if you possibly can."

Squad 32 was led by Sergeant Jirote Phranakorn. Switching channels, Sergeant Sawang spoke. "Jirote, this is Sawang. Since your squad's still at full strength, you take the main bay of the barracks, I'll take the 'fresher."

The reply came back. "Fine by me, Sawang. Cover me as I come in the door, then I'm going to have my squad sweep up and down the length of the barracks, in line abreast, so we'll provide poorer targets."

Sergeant Sawang hovered in the doorway of the 'fresher, and watched Jirote's squad sweep through the barracks in precise formation, half the men facing ahead, half to the rear. Again with a suddenness which defied belief, a group of natives appeared. Sawang noted that these seemed to have different markings on their loincloths than the two he had seen earlier. There were eight of the natives, one for each member of Jirote's squad, and each native seemed to have placed himself directly in the path of one of the squad members. In a time-span so short that Sawang still hadn't reacted, there was the crackle of blasters, and the natives were gone again. Six of the squad members drifted toward the ceiling. The remaining two stopped, confused and uncertain. Their uncertainty was brought to an end as four more natives appeared at the far end of the barracks and sent their blaster bolts into the two remaining soldiers.

Sawang flung himself out of the doorway just in time, as more attackers appeared and fired at him. At the end of the crackling barrage of blaster bolts, he swung past the doorway again, glancing into the main bay as he passed. It seemed to be full of natives, all attempting to form gymnastic pyramids in order to reach the men floating against the ceiling.

Sawang zipped past the door again, flinging a grenade into the main bay as he went by. He led his squad into the main bay immediately after the blast, to find nearly a dozen of the natives crumpled on the floor, and several patches of blood evidently left by others who had escaped. He put his men to work immediately, getting Jirote's men and their weapons out of the barracks. No sooner was the task completed when he heard another voice from his communicator. This one was flat and metallic, and he knew he was being addressed directly by the Battle Computer, not by any of the humans at the Battle Control Center.

"Switch your lifter to Remote Control." Sawang did so. "Your direction of motion and velocity will be altered at random intervals, to make your motion as unpredictable as possible. From time to time you will be ordered to look and point your weapons in a specific direction. Fire immediately if you see an attacker, and fire anyway if ordered to do so."

Sawang watched his men move around the interior of the barracks in a mysterious, seemingly pointless dance. They moved up, down, right, left, forward, backward, without apparent reason. Suddenly he heard a blaster bolt crackle past him, just after he had felt a sudden change in motion. He glanced briefly in the direction from which the shot had come, to see no one, then returned his gaze to his assigned direction. He spotted one of the natives, fired quickly, and missed. The attacker disappeared before he had another chance to fire.

The next few minutes were a confused, whirling nightmare. Sawang's men danced around inside the barracks at what would have been an insanely dangerous speed, if they had had to depend on human reaction times to keep them from colliding with the barracks walls and each other. Attackers appeared, fired, disappeared. Sawang's men returned the fire as best they could. Neither side seemed to be able to draw blood.

Then Sawang noticed a subtle change in the pattern of the

187

dance. All the changes in direction seemed to be nearly at right angles now, and they came at greater intervals. Furthermore, the direction he was ordered to look no longer coincided with his direction of motion. The flat voice of the computer came to him again.

"Look thirty-seven degrees." He did so, the direction being slightly to the left of his course. "Fire, and keep firing." He fired once, at nothing. He fired again, and just as he squeezed the trigger, a native appeared in the path of his aim. He was so surprised he hesitated before firing the third shot, which turned out to be unnecessary, as it passed over the dead native.

The next few minutes were another confused whirl. "Look forty-five degrees. Fire and keep firing." And another native down. "Look ten degrees. Fire. Look ninety degrees. Fire. Look. Fire. Look. Fire. Look. Fire." It was clear what had happened. The computer had deduced the habits of this particular group of natives, and their reaction times. It kept each human on a single course long enough for a native to track him and decide to attack. It then predicted where the native would appear, and had someone else fire at the predicted point of arrival. That way the native was never alerted by a hostile move on the part of the human he was tracking.

Finally the crackle of blasters ceased. There was another human floating near the ceiling, and another dozen natives dead on the floor. The important fact was that this time all the dead natives were armed, except two who had died in the act of trying to retrieve weapons from their fallen comrades. The computer had caught on to that practice, too.

Before anything else could happen, Sergeant Sawang ordered his men to recover all the loose weapons, and then go back on remote control. However, apparently someone had decided that the Battle of Barracks 34-D was over. Another voice, this time a human one, came from his communicator.

"Squad 17, proceed to the Electronics Repair Shop. It is under attack."

The Electronics Repair Shop was a single-story structure consisting of a long, narrow central building with a number of shorter but equally narrow wings branching out on either side. Both the central building and the wings consisted of a hallway lined on both sides with small cubicles, each closed off by a door. The building was entirely windowless, but there were doors at the end of each of the wings.

As Sergeant Sawang's squad circled around the Electronics

Repair Shop, in a now somewhat ragged diamond formation, another message reached them.

"Sawang, this is Major Prasert." That would be Major Prasert Tanwong, Sawang's Battalion Commander. "The attackers are apparently trying to draw us into a fight. They've been appearing in the test cubicles, smashing some equipment, and leaving. By the time we get there, they're somewhere else causing more trouble. In order to keep them from wrecking everything, I'm going to have to put a man in every cubicle, with more men patrolling the halls as a backup. I've already got all the rooms in the northernmost wing manned. I want your squad to patrol the hall in that wing. As I get more men, I'll extend our control into the other wings."

Sawang decided that on the face of it the plan sounded good, but the natives might have some other surprises they hadn't revealed yet. Before he committed the remainder of his squad to a particular tactic, he wanted to reconnoiter the territory he was going to have to fight in. He left the squad to circle the building, and dove through the doorway at the end of the hall he was going to patrol. He came to the door of a cubicle, knocked, and opened the door. The soldier guarding the room was floating back and forth across one end of the room, with his back to the end wall and his head brushing the ceiling. His gun was pointed toward the center of the room, ready to fire. While the man's course was fairly predictable, he still presented a moving target instead of a sitting one. Sawang nodded his head in satisfaction, waved at the man, and left the room.

He then studied the hallway thoughtfully. After his experience in the barracks, he didn't like the idea of his men moving up and down the length of the hallway, where they could be picked off easily by enfilade fire. Nor was he happy about the hallway down the central portion of the building. It was uncontrolled, and his men would be subject to flank attacks as they crossed the entrance to the hallway, at the center of the wing. He decided the alternatives regarding the central hallway were to attempt to control it, or to abandon it to the attackers and accept that his squad would be split into two halves, on either end of the wing.

The first alternative would be difficult to achieve, but the second went against all his training and experience. He decided to station himself at the juncture of the central hallway and his wing, keeping near the ceiling and partially protected by a corner, so that he could watch the hallway and fire if anyone appeared. He could then put two men in each wing, and his central position would give him better control over the action as it developed.

He called the squad in and told off two men for each end of the wing. They were to stay abreast of each other, and face in opposite directions. They would move in a corkscrew spiral along the length of the hallway, reversing direction as they reached the end, or middle, of the wing. He then took up his position at the middle of the wing.

Hardly had Sergeant Sawang gotten into position when a series of explosions rocked the building. He glanced around, and saw the door of one of the cubicles sag open, and smoke drift out. He called to his squad to maintain the patrol, and swooped for the nearest cubicle. He yanked the door open and swept inside, to find a native standing on a test bench and removing a blaster from the unresisting hand of the soldier now floating lifelessly against the ceiling of the cubicle. Before Sawang could fire, the native was gone, gun and all. He ordered his squad to stop patrolling and check the cubicles. He then tried the next door, to find it bolted from the inside. He blasted the lock and hurtled inside, to find the room empty and its guard dead and stripped of weapons. In the next room the guard still alive, and the badly mangled body of a native lay on the floor.

"He appeared right in front of me, Sergeant, and dropped a grenade on the floor. My gun was pointed at him, and I must have fired by reflex. He fell over the grenade and soaked up the force of the burst."

"Reflex or not, that's nice shooting. Keep up the good work."

Sawang returned to the hallway, to find it filling up with guards from the rooms which had not been attacked. He was in the process of sorting his squad out from the strays when a volley of blaster fire erupted from the central hallway. He turned to see a group of natives standing in the middle of the wing, having a field day firing at the troops in both ends of the wing. In the confusion, no one seemed to be able to organize any counter-fire.

Someone yelled "Out the doors! Let's get out of here," and a rush started for the doorway at the end of the wing. This escape route was closed by more blaster fire from natives stationed outside the doorway. An incredible jam formed at the door as men milled about, fired on from front and rear. Sawang and the other NCO's started herding the men out of the hallway into the cubicles, where they started returning the fire of the natives, who were now rapidly shifting their positions along the length of the hallway.

Suddenly a voice roared over the emergency communicator channel. "All troops in the Electronics Repair Shop. Take cover. Get under something quickly."

Sawang and his men had just ducked under a workbench in one of the cubicles when a shattering explosion sounded in the hall outside, followed by the earsplitting shriek of a one-man scout fighter as it whipped over the building at low altitude and high speed, then headed back for the stratosphere. There was now a gaping hole in the roof over the hallway, through which an orderly flow of men was escaping, while others still in the cubicles provided covering fire for them. Sawang led his men out in their turn, then circled back over the building. When all the men appeared to be out, he received permission to lead his squad back to look for wounded and retrieve weapons.

The fire from the scout had been aimed with precision, and had taken out the roof right over the hallway. This, of course, meant that the beams supporting the roof had been cut through at the center, allowing a portion of the roof to collapse into the hallway. They found a number of bodies, both human and native, under the wreckage. They dragged the humans free and let their lifters carry them out through the roof. The natives, they simply disarmed. As Sawang pulled a blaster away from one of the figures on the floor, he saw it stir slightly. He took a step away, then the significance of the event struck him.

"Battle Control Center, this is Sergeant Sawang, Squad 17. We've got a prisoner. He's been knocked out, temporarily anyway. What do we do with him?"

"Good work, Sawang. Hoist him up to a hundred meters and hold him there so his friends don't try to rescue him, while we figure out what to do with him."

"Sorry I'm late for the meeting, General. I had an experiment in progress, and I wanted to be able to include the results in my report."

"That's all right, Doctor, we were just getting started. Sit down and catch you breath, and we'll hear from you in a few minutes. Now, Colonel Bunyarit, will you give your report?"

"Yes, General. First I'd like to describe some of the thinking that went into the defense planning for last night, then describe how it worked out. To begin with, we had to accept that the natives were teleports. It became clear that the ability to teleport also implied some sort of clairvoyance. If a person is going to teleport himself to some distant point, he has to be sure that there are no objects in the way where he wants to go. Simply remembering the place is not enough. Someone could easily have moved an obstacle into a place remembered as being clear of obstructions. Thus the question became one of how good their clairvoyance was. Did it, in effect, make them omniscient about all events anywhere? If so, we had no hope of defeating them.

"On the other hand, they all have eyes, and on the first night they attacked, it's worth noting that all their victims were shot while silhouetted against a fairly bright starry background. Thus they still depend heavily on their eyes, despite the existence of clairvoyance.

"So I decided to assume that their clairvoyance was not much better than the minimum required for successful teleportation; that they could observe only a small area at a time, as through a peephole, but that they could scan the 'peephole' around to investigate a large area or track a specific target of interest. I assumed also that their ability to inspect some complex object would not necessarily tell them how it worked or what it did, if it depended on principles beyond their level of technological development.

"On the basis of these assumptions, I planned the defense. First, there were certain areas like the Battle Control Center, the Power Plant, and so forth, which had to be made into traps which even teleports could not invade successfully. Limits on time and equipment, of course, meant that the rest of the Base could not be so protected. So all weapons not being carried by someone were buried. All spaceships and other vehicles were moved out of the way to prevent attack or sabotage. Since any soldier standing in a fixed position could be attacked and disarmed before he could react, fixed guard posts had to be abandoned. The simplest solution was to put all the troops up in the air and keep them moving.

"The obvious counter to this was to attack our unprotected installations, forcing us to move troops into them. However, I felt safe in assuming that the natives would be fairly unsophisticated. If they found a tactic that worked, they'd keep trying it. Nor would they be organized to detect our responses to their tactics, and change them as necessary. So I felt that the Battle Computer, with its ability to handle large amounts of data and deduce patterns from it, would give us an edge which might make up for the enemy's ability to teleport, if our troops were drawn into a battle.

"I feel that the defense was quite successful. Certain points were defended with complete success. In those places where our men had room to maneuver, we put up a good defense, inflicting more losses than we took. In other areas, the battle was more nearly even. However, overall we lost forty-two men, while they lost one hundred eighty. I could say that is a very favorable ratio. I expect that we can make further improvements in the defenses before tonight, and if they attack again, we should be able to force an even more favorable exchange ratio."

"Thank you, Colonel Bunyarit. Now Colonel Arun, you look like you want to say something."

"Yes, sir. I beg to differ with the optimistic conclusions just voiced. First of all, the actions of guerrillas tend to be limited by the number of weapons available, not their manpower. And their chief source of weapons is capture from their opponents. Thus in combating guerrillas the measure of success is not the casualty ratio of the forces, but the ratio of weapons lost by each side. The attackers started the battle last night with what weapons they had seized the previous night, namely eighteen blasters, eighteen blast rifles, and fifty-four grenades. Last night they expended twenty grenades, and we recaptured twenty-five other weapons. However, they captured twenty-two blasters, twenty blast rifles, and sixty grenades. In last night's attack, then, they essentially doubled their supply of weapons.

"Furthermore, much of last night's defense was based on the assumption that they cannot teleport themselves into a position in space, say a hundred meters off the ground. It may be that they had never had to do it, but that is no reason to assume they can't learn to do it.

"In short, I consider last night a defeat for us. Without any change in tactics, they can come back and double their weapons supply again. And they may be able to change their tactics in such a way as to nullify most of our defenses."

"Thank you, Colonel. You have some good points. However, things are not all black. We did manage to get a prisoner, so the night wasn't a total loss. Doctor, may we have your report now?"

The Staff Surgeon slid his chair back and stood up. "The most important news, of course, is the prisoner. When he was delivered to us last night, he was still unconscious from having a roof fall on him. Our first check, naturally, was to see if he had suffered any serious injury. A hasty examination showed that there were no bones broken, or anything like that. Next we made some rapid checks to see if any anesthetics we had would be safe and effective on him. We had to keep him unconscious, or he would have simply left us.

"It turned out that one of our standard anesthetics would work on him, and as far as we could tell it would be safe. Naturally we started with light doses, and monitored his heart and lung action. However, we, of course, had no idea what his normal pulse and respiration rate should be. The anesthetic seemed to do the trick, so we started sampling everything we could without doing him any permanent damage, as well as taking electrocardiograms, encephalograms, and so on.

"After about an hour, we observed that his pulse and respiration seemed to be weakening, so we cut down on the dose of anesthetic. This helped, but after a while he started to get worse again, so we cut out the anesthetic entirely. In short order he returned to consciousness, and did the expected thing. He vanished right off the table. It was quite a surprise, even after having been told it could happen.

"In all, we spent about two hours examining the prisoner. We have a great deal of useful data, although most of it is still in raw form, and can't be used for anything yet. It must be remembered that we never examined him under normal conditions. He was knocked out when we got him, and was anesthetized in addition. So we are still not completely satisfied with our data. And in any case, we would like to have a lot more. We are performing autopsies on the attacker corpses. These, in conjunction with the data from the prisoner, are telling us quite a bit about their nature."

"If we managed to get another prisoner, could you do better with a new anesthetic?"

"Yes, General, we now know enough about them to be able to synthesize an anesthetic which would be both safe and effective."

"Do you have enough information to design a knockout gas sufficiently effective to have military utility, and with no serious side effects?"

"Oh, yes. That would present no serious problem. We could even design one which would be absorbed rapidly through the skin, so they couldn't avoid it by holding their breath. We could even design it to have no effect on humans. I would say we could have a sample synthesized by noon. Any larger quantities, of course, would have to come from the Materiel Officer."

"All right, Doctor, you get your staff busy on the synthesis. Have them work closely with the Materiel and Armament Officers. I want a reasonable quantity of gas bombs available by no later than midafternoon. In the meantime, Colonel Bunyarit, get some high altitude patrols out, and locate a few villages. Then get a strike force organized. As soon as the gas bombs are ready, we're going to get us a few prisoners."

"But General, there's not much more I can learn from an anesthetized prisoner. What good will capturing a few more do?"

"I've got an idea about how to hang onto an unanesthetized prisoner. Now let's get busy. Meeting's dismissed.

"Another drink, Commissioner?"

"Thank you, General, I will. It's not the sort of luxury one normally expects at a forward base like this."

"I believe in being comfortable, Commissioner. Any fool can be uncomfortable. And besides, one doesn't normally expect to find a Commissioner for Native Affairs at a forward base, either. You realize, I hope, that we've already had one Kreg attack, and there may be more."

"Yes, but I've been under fire before. The Kregs can't possibly be any worse than some of the natives I've had responsibility for. But tell me, how did you manage to work out an agreement with the natives? I've read your report, of course, but it's so blasted brief. I mean, how did you learn their language, how did you analyze their culture, how did you learn what would induce them to behave? And for that matter, how did you manage to get them to hold still for you?"

"Commissioner, as you are aware, the basic problem was holding one, voluntarily or involuntarily, and getting the information out of him. By a stroke of good luck, we acquired a prisoner. Naturally we couldn't hold him permanently, but from a study of him we learned enough to enable us to capture some more. It turned out that the ones we worked with had no inhibitions about telling us what we wanted to know, after we learned a bit of the language. After all, learning an alien language is a pretty well-developed technique, nowadays, and these people don't have a very complicated one.

"We confirmed earlier reports that they move around a lot. They farm by burning off a stretch of forest, thus fertilizing the soil. They farm it for a few years, by which time it's worn out, and they move on. Naturally they can't come back to the same site until the forest is regrown. This means that each tribe has to have a pretty large area it can call its own. Naturally there's a lot of jockeying between tribes for particularly choice areas, such as those with good rivers, and so on. The social structure, as between tribes, approaches anarchy. Their Golden Rule is 'Do unto others before they have a chance to do unto you.'

"We learned that about fifty years ago a spaceship crashed on this continent, and one tribe managed to get some modern weapons from it. They cut quite a swath for a while, until they ran out of power packs. None of the tribes, however, forgot what energy weapons were, or how they could be used. When we landed, a few of the nearby tribes viewed us as their golden opportunity. They gave each other the bare minimum of co-operation which would enable each to get some weapons. They then were each going to grab themselves some more territory. Eventually, I suppose, they would have fought each other for the best land, but it never came to that stage.

"Once we understood the situation, we simply flew over their villages and broadcast to them that if they didn't let us alone, we'd supply weapons and instructors to their most deadly enemies. That was the stick. For the carrot, we recognized that in their chaotic situation, they would be willing to follow anyone who could offer them protection from each other. We offered them that protection, if they would help us in enforcing it. That's where you come in. They quickly saw the good sense of our offer, and came to terms. The only problem was to prevent ourselves from being robbed blind by teleporting thieves, and we solved that by sealing all the buildings, putting on double-door air locks, and flooding them with anesthetic."

"But blast it, General, you still haven't told me . . ."

"How we managed to hold a conscious prisoner? That turned out to be fairly simple. We realized that their teleporting range had to be limited, since it was we who found them, not vice versa. So we loaded our unconscious captives into a scout cruiser, and took them several planetary diameters off-world. It turned out we guessed right the first time, and we had them far enough out they couldn't teleport back. When they realized they weren't going anywhere, we had no further trouble with them. They were model prisoners."

THE HERO

George R. R. Martin

The city was dead and the flames of its passing spread a red stain across the green-gray sky.

It had been a long time dying. Resistance had lasted almost a week and the fighting had been bitter for a while. But in the end the invaders had broken the defenders, as they had broken so many others in the past. The alien sky with its double sun did not bother them. They had fought and won under skies of azure blue and speckled gold and inky black.

The Weather Control boys had hit first, while the main force was still hundreds of miles to the east. Storm after storm had flailed at the streets of the city, to slow defensive preparations and smash the spirit of resistance.

When they were closer the invaders had sent up howlers. Unending high-pitched shrieks had echoed back and forth both day and night and before long most of the populace had fled in demoralized panic. By then the attackers' main force was in range and launched plague bombs on a steady westward wind.

Even then the natives had tried to fight back. From their defensive emplacements ringing the city the survivors had sent up a hail of atomics, managing to vaporize one whole company whose defensive screens were overloaded by the sudden assault. But the gesture was a feeble one at best. By that time incendiary bombs were raining down steadily upon the city and great clouds of acid gas were blowing across the plains.

And behind the gas, the dreaded assault squads of the Terran Expeditionary Force moved on the last defenses.

Kagen scowled at the dented plastoid helmet at his feet and cursed his luck. A routine mopping-up detail, he thought. A perfectly routine operation—and some damned automatic interceptor emplacement somewhere had lobbed a low-grade atomic at him.

It had been only a near miss but the shock waves had damaged his hip rockets and knocked him out of the sky, landing him in this godforsaken little ravine east of the city. His light plastoid battle armor had protected him from the impact but his helmet had taken a good whack.

Kagen squatted and picked up the dented helmet to examine it. His long-range com and all of his sensory equipment were out. With his rockets gone, too, he was crippled, deaf, dumb and half-blind. He swore.

A flicker of movement along the top of the shallow ravine caught his attention. Five natives came suddenly into view, each carrying a hair-trigger submachine gun. They carried them at the ready, trained on Kagen. They were fanned out in line, covering him from both right and left. One began to speak.

He never finished. One instant, Kagen's screech gun lay on the rocks at his feet. Quite suddenly it was in his hand.

Five men will hesitate where one alone will not. During the brief flickering instant before the natives' fingers began to tighten on their triggers. Kagen did not pause, Kagen did not hesitate, Kagen did not think.

Kagen killed.

The screech gun emitted a loud, ear-piercing shriek. The enemy squad leader shuddered as the invisible beam of concentrated high-frequency sound ripped into him. Then his flesh began to liquefy. By then Kagen's gun had found two more targets.

The guns of the two remaining natives finally began to chatter. A rain of bullets enveloped Kagen as he whirled to his right and he grunted under the impact as the shots caromed off his battle armor. His screech gun leveled—and a random shot sent it spinning from his grasp.

Kagen did not hesitate or pause as the gun was wrenched from his grip. He bounded to the top of the shallow ravine with one leap, directly toward one of the soldiers.

The man wavered briefly and brought up his gun. The instant was all Kagen needed. With all the momentum of his leap behind it, his right hand smashed the gun butt into the enemy's face and his left, backed by fifteen hundred pounds of force, hammered into the native's body right under the breastbone.

Kagen seized the corpse and heaved it toward the second native, who had ceased fire briefly as his comrade came between himself and Kagen. Now his bullets tore into the airborne body. He took a quick step back, his gun level and firing.

And then Kagen was on him. Kagen knew a searing flash of pain as a shot bruised his temple. He ignored it, drove the edge of his hand into the native's throat. The man toppled, lay still.

Kagen spun, still reacting, searching for the next foe.

He was alone.

Kagen bent and wiped the blood from his hand with a piece of the native's uniform. He frowned in disgust. It was going to be a long trek back to camp, he thought, tossing the blood-soaked rag casually to the ground.

Today was definitely not his lucky day.

He grunted dismally, then scrambled back down into the ravine to recover his screech gun and helmet for the hike.

On the horizon, the city was still burning.

Ragelli's voice was loud and cheerful as it came crackling over the short-range communicator nestled in Kagen's fist.

"So it's you, Kagen," he said laughing. "You signaled just in time. My sensors were starting to pick up something. Little closer and I would've screeched you down."

"My helmet's busted and the sensors are out," Kagen replied. "Damn hard to judge distance. Long-range com is busted, too."

"The brass was wondering what happened to you," Ragelli cut in. "Made 'em sweat a little. But I figured you'd turn up sooner or later."

"Right," Kagen said. "One of these mudworms zapped the hell out of my rockets and it took me a while to get back. But I'm coming in now."

He emerged slowly from the crater he had crouched in, coming in sight of the guard in the distance. He took it slow and easy.

Outlined against the outpost barrier, Ragelli lifted a ponderous silver-gray arm in greeting. He was armored completely in a full duralloy battlesuit that made Kagen's plastoid armor look like tissue paper, and sat in the trigger-seat of a swiveling screech-gun battery. A bubble of defensive screens enveloped him, turning his massive figure into an indistinct blur.

Kagen waved back and began to eat up the distance between them with long, loping strides. He stopped just in front of the barrier, at the foot of Ragelli's emplacement.

"You look damned battered," said Ragelli, appraising him from behind a plastoid visor, aided by his sensory devices. "That light

199

armor doesn't buy you a nickel's worth of protection. Any farm boy with a pea shooter can plug you."

Kagen laughed. "At least I can move. You may be able to stand off an Assault Squad in that duralloy monkey suit, but I'd like to see you do anything on offense, chum. And defense doesn't win wars."

"Your pot," Ragelli said. "This sentry duty is boring as hell." He flicked a switch on his control panel and a section of the barrier winked out. Kagen was through it at once. A split second later it came back on again.

Kagen strode quickly to his squad barracks. The door slid open automatically as he approached it and he stepped inside gratefully. It felt good to be home again and back at his normal weight. These light-gravity mudholes made him queasy after awhile. The barracks were artificially maintained at Wellington-normal gravity, twice Earth-normal. It was expensive but the brass kept saying that nothing was too good for the comfort of our fighting men.

Kagen stripped off his plastoid armor in the squad ready room and tossed it into the replacement bin. He headed straight for his cubicle and sprawled across the bed.

Reaching over to the plain metal table alongside his bed, he yanked open a drawer and took out a fat greenish capsule. He swallowed it hastily, and lay back to relax as it took hold throughout his system. The regulations prohibited taking synthastim between meals, he knew, but the rule was never enforced. Like most troopers, Kagen took it almost continuously to maintain his speed and endurance at maximum.

He was dozing comfortably a few minutes later when the com box mounted on the wall above his bed came to sudden life.

"Kagen."

Kagen sat up instantly, wide awake.

"Acknowledged," he said.

"Report to Major Grady at once."

Kagen grinned broadly. His request was being acted on quickly, he thought. And by a high officer, no less. Dressing quickly in loose-fitting brown fatigues, he set off across the base.

The high officers' quarters were at the center of the outpost. They consisted of a brightly lit, three-story building, blanketed overhead by defensive screens and ringed by guardsmen in light battle armor. One of the guards recognized Kagen and he was admitted on orders.

Immediately beyond the door he halted briefly as a bank of sensors scanned him for weapons. Troopers, of course, were not allowed to bear arms in the presence of high officers. Had he been carrying a screech gun alarms would have gone off all over the building while the tractor beams hidden in the walls and ceilings immobilized him completely.

But he passed the inspection and continued down the long corridor toward Major Grady's office. A third of the way down, the first set of tractor beams locked firmly onto his wrists. He struggled the instant he felt the invisible touch against his skin—but the tractors held him steady. Others, triggered automatically by his passing, came on as he continued down the corridor.

Kagen cursed under his breath and fought with his impulse to resist. He hated being pinned by tractor beams, but those were the rules if you wanted to see a high officer.

The door opened before him and he stepped through. A full bank of tractor beams seized him instantly and immobilized him. A few adjusted slightly and he was snapped to rigid attention, although his muscles screamed resistance.

Major Carl Grady was working at a cluttered wooden desk a few feet away, scribbling something on a sheet of paper. A large stack of papers rested at his elbow, an old-fashioned laser pistol sitting on top of them as a paperweight.

Kagen recognized the laser. It was some sort of heirloom, passed down in Grady's family for generations. The story was that some ancestor of his had used it back on Earth, in the Fire Wars of the early twenty-first century. Despite its age, the thing was still supposed to be in working order.

After several minutes of silence Grady finally set down his pen and looked up at Kagen. He was unusually young for a high officer but his unruly gray hair made him look older than he was. Like all high officers, he was Earth-born; frail and slow before the assault squad troopers from the dense, heavy-gravity War Worlds of Wellington and Rommel.

"Report your presence," Grady said curtly. As always, his lean, pale face mirrored immense boredom.

"Field Officer John Kagen, assault squads, Terran Expeditionary Force."

Grady nodded, not really listening. He opened one of his desk drawers and extracted a sheet of paper.

"Kagen," he said, fiddling with the paper, "I think you know why you're here." He tapped the paper with his finger. "What's the meaning of this?"

"Just what it says, Major," Kagen replied. He tried to shift his weight but the tractor beam held him rigid.

Grady noticed and gestured impatiently. "At rest," he said. Most of the tractor beams snapped off, leaving Kagen free to move, if only at half his normal speed. He flexed in relief and grinned.

"My term of enlistment is up within two weeks. So I've requested transportation to Earth. That's all there is to it."

Grady's eyebrows arched a fraction of an inch but the dark eyes beneath them remained bored.

"Really?" he asked. "You've been a soldier for almost twenty years now, Kagen. Why retire? I'm afraid I don't understand."

Kagen shrugged. "I don't know. I'm getting old. Maybe I'm just getting tired of camp life. It's all starting to get boring, taking one damn mudhole after another. I want something different. Some excitement."

Grady nodded. "I see. But I don't think I agree with you, Kagen." His voice was soft and persuasive. "I think you're underselling the T.E.F. There is excitement ahead, if you'll only give us a chance." He leaned back in his chair, toying with a pencil he had picked up. "I'll tell you something, Kagen. You know, we've been at war with the Hrangan Empire for nearly three decades now. Direct clashes between us and the enemy have been few and far between up to now. Do you know why?"

"Sure," Kagen said.

Grady ignored him. "I'll tell you why," he continued. "So far each of us has been struggling to consolidate his position by grabbing these little worlds in the border regions. These mudholes, as you call them. But they're very important mudholes. We need them for bases, for their raw materials, for their industrial capacity and for the conscript labor they provide. "That's why we try to minimize damage in our campaigns. And that's why we use psychwar tactics like the howlers. To frighten away as many natives as possible before each attack. To preserve labor."

"I know all that," Kagen interrupted with typical Wellington bluntness. "What of it? I didn't come here for a lecture."

Grady looked up from the pencil. "No," he said. "No, you didn't. So I'll tell you, Kagen. The prelims are over. It's time for the main event. There are only a handful of unclaimed worlds left. Soon now, we'll be coming into direct conflict with the Hrangan Conquest Corps. Within a year we'll be attacking their bases."

The major stared at Kagen expectantly, waiting for a reply. When none came, a puzzled look flickered across his face. He leaned forward again.

"Don't you understand, Kagen?" he asked. "What more excitement could you want? No more fighting these piddling civilians in uniform, with their dirty little atomics and their primitive projectile guns. The Hrangans are a real enemy. Like us, they've had a professional army for generations upon generations.

They're soldiers, born and bred. Good ones, too. They've got screens and modern weapons. They'll be foes to give our assault squads a real test."

"Maybe," Kagen said doubtfully. "But that kind of excitement isn't what I had in mind. I'm getting old. I've noticed that I'm definitely slower lately—even Synthastim isn't keeping up my speed."

Grady shook his head. "You've got one of the best records in the whole T.E.F., Kagen. You've received the Stellar Cross twice and the World Congress Decoration three times. Every com station on Earth carried the story when you saved the landing party on Torego. Why should you doubt your effectiveness now? We're going to need men like you against the Hrangans. Re-enlist."

"No," said Kagen emphatically. "The regs say you're entitled to your pension after twenty years and those medals have earned me a nice bunch of retirement bonuses. Now I want to enjoy them." He grinned broadly. "As you say, everyone on Earth must know me. I'm a hero. With that reputation, I figure I can have a real screechout."

Grady frowned and drummed on the desk impatiently. "I know what the regulations say, Kagen. But no one ever really retires—you must know that. Most troopers prefer to stay with the front. That's their job. That's what the War Worlds are all about."

"I don't really care, Major," Kagen replied. "I know the regs and I know I have a right to retire on full pension. You can't stop me."

Grady considered the statement calmly, his eyes dark with thought.

"All right," he said after a long pause. "Let's be reasonable about this. You'll retire with full pension and bonuses. We'll set you down on Wellington in a place of your own. Or Rommel if you like. We'll make you a youth barracks director—any age group you like. Or a training camp director. With your record you can start right at the top."

"Uh-uh," Kagen said firmly. "Not Wellington. Not Rommel. Earth."

"But why? You were born and raised on Wellington—in one of the hill barracks, I believe. You've never seen Earth."

"True," said Kagen. "But I've seen it in camp telecasts and flicks. I like what I've seen. I've been reading about Earth a lot lately, too. So now I want to see what it's like." He paused, then grinned again. "Let's just say I want to see what I've been fighting for."

Grady's frown reflected his displeasure. "I'm from Earth,

Kagen," he said. "I tell you, you won't like it. You won't fit in. The gravity is too low—and there are no artificial heavy gravity barracks to take shelter in. Synthastim is illegal, strictly prohibited. But War Wonders need it, so you'll have to pay exorbitant prices to get the stuff. Earthers aren't reaction trained, either. They're a different kind of people. Go back to Wellington. You'll be among your own kind."

"Maybe that's one of the reasons I want Earth," Kagen said stubbornly. "On Wellington I'm just one of hundreds of old vets. Hell, every one of the troopers who *does* retire heads back to his old barracks. But on Earth I'll be a celebrity. Why, I'll be the fastest, strongest guy on the whole damn planet. That's got to have some advantages."

Grady was starting to look agitated. "What about the gravity?" he demanded. "The Synthastim?"

"I'll get used to light gravity after a while, that's no problem. And I won't be needing that much speed and endurance, so I figure I can kick the Synthastim habit."

Grady ran his fingers through his unkempt hair and shook his head doubtfully. There was a long, awkward silence. He leaned across the desk.

And, suddenly, his hand darted towards the laser pistol.

Kagen reacted. He dove forward, delayed only slightly by the few tractor beams that still held him. His hand flashed toward Grady's wrist in a crippling arc.

And suddenly wrenched to a halt as the tractor beams seized Kagen roughly, held him rigid and then smashed him to the floor.

Grady, his hand frozen halfway to the pistol, leaned back in the chair. His face was white and shaken. He raised his hand and the tractor beams let up a bit. Kagen climbed slowly to his feet.

"You see, Kagen," said Grady. "That little test proves you're as fit as ever. You'd have gotten me if I hadn't kept a few tractors on you to slow you down. I tell you, we need men with your training and experience. We need you against the Hrangans. Re-enlist."

Kagen's cold blue eyes still seethed with anger. "Damn the Hrangans," he said. "I'm not re-enlisting and no goddamn little tricks of yours are going to make me change my mind. I'm going to Earth. You can't stop me."

Grady buried his face in his hands and sighed.

"All right, Kagen," he said at last. "You win. I'll put through your request."

He looked up one more time, and his dark eyes looked strangely troubled.

"You've been a great soldier, Kagen. We'll miss you. I tell you that you'll regret this decision. Are you sure you won't reconsider?"

"Absolutely sure," Kagen snapped.

The strange look suddenly vanished from Grady's eyes. His face once more took on the mask of bored indifference.

"Very well," he said curtly. "You are dismissed."

The tractors stayed on Kagen as he turned. They guided him—very firmly—from the building.

"You ready, Kagen?" Ragelli asked, leaning casually against the door of the cubicle.

Kagen picked up his small travel bag and threw one last glance around to make sure he hadn't forgotten anything. He hadn't. The room was quite bare.

"Guess so," he said, stepping through the door.

Ragelli slipped on the plastoid helmet that had been cradled under his arm and hurried to catch up as Kagen strode down the corridor.

"I guess this is it," he said as he matched strides.

"Yeah," Kagen replied. "A week from now I'll be taking it easy back on Earth while you're getting blisters on your tail sitting around in that damned duralloy tuxedo of yours."

Ragelli laughed. "Maybe," he said. "But I still say you're nuts to go to Earth of all places, when you could command a whole damned training camp on Wellington. Assuming you wanted to quit at all, which is also crazy—"

The barracks door slid open before them and they stepped through, Ragelli still talking. A second guard flanked Kagen on the other side. Like Ragelli, he was wearing light battle armor.

Kagen himself was in full dress whites, trimmed with gold braid. A ceremonial laser, deactivated, was slung in a black leather holster at his side. Matching leather boots and a polished steel helmet set off the uniform. Azure blue bars on his shoulder signified field officer rank. His medals jangled against his chest as he walked.

Kagen's entire third assault squad was drawn up at attention on the spacefield behind the barracks in honor of his retirement. Alongside the ramp to the shuttlecraft, a group of high officers stood by, cordoned off by defensive screens. Major Grady was in the front row, his bored expression blurred somewhat by the screens.

Flanked by the two guards, Kagen walked across the concrete slowly, grinning under his helmet. Piped music welled out over

205

the field, and Kagen recognized the T.E.F. battle hymn and the Wellington anthem.

At the foot of the ramp he turned and looked back. The company spread out before him saluted in unison on a command from the high officers and held the position until Kagen returned the salute. Then one of the squad's other field officers stepped forward, and presented him with his discharge papers.

Jamming them into his belt, Kagen threw a quick, casual wave to Ragelli, then hurried up the ramp. It lifted slowly behind him.

Inside the ship, a crewman greeted him with a curt nod. "Got special quarters prepared for you," he said. "Follow me. Trip should only take about fifteen minutes. Then we'll transfer you to a starship for the Earth trip."

Kagen nodded and followed the man to his quarters. They turned out to be a plain, empty room, reinforced with duralloy plates. A viewscreen covered one wall. An acceleration couch faced it.

Alone, Kagen sprawled out on the acceleration couch, clipping his helmet to a holder on the side. Tractor beams pressed down gently, holding him firmly in place for the liftoff.

A few minutes later a dull roar came from deep within the ship and Kagen felt several gravities press down upon him as the shuttlecraft took off. The viewscreen, suddenly coming to life, showed the planet dwindling below.

The viewer blinked off when they reached orbit. Kagen started to sit up but found he still could not move. The tractor beams held him pinned to the couch.

He frowned. There was no need for him to stay in the couch once the craft was in orbit. Some idiot had forgotten to release him.

"Hey," he shouted, figuring there would be a com box somewhere in the room. "These tractors are still on. Loosen the damned things so I can move a little."

No one answered.

He strained against the beams. Their pressure seemed to increase. The blasted things were starting to pinch a little, he thought. Now those morons were turning the knob the wrong way.

He cursed under his breath. "No," he shouted. "Now the tractors are getting heavier. You're adjusting them the wrong way."

But the pressure continued to climb and he felt more beams locking on him, until they covered his body like an invisible blanket. The damn things were really starting to hurt now.

"You idiots," he yelled. "You morons. Cut it out, you bastards." With a surge of anger he strained against the beams, cursing. But even Wellington-bred muscle was no match for tractors. He was held tightly on the couch.

One of the beams was trained on his chest pocket. Its pressure was driving his Stellar Cross painfully into his skin. The sharp edge of the polished medal had already sliced through the uniform and he could see a red stain spreading slowly through the white.

The pressure continued to mount and Kagen writhed in pain, squirming against his invisible shackles. It did no good. The pressure still went higher and more and more beams came on.

"Cut it out!" he screeched. "You bastards, I'll rip you apart when I get out of here. You're killing me, dammit!"

He heard the sharp snap of a bone suddenly breaking under the strain. Kagen felt a stab of intense pain in his right wrist. An instant later there was another snap.

"Cut it out!" he cried, his voice shrill with pain. "You're killing me. Damn you, you're killing me!"

And suddenly he realized he was right.

Grady looked up with a scowl at the aide who entered the office.

"Yes, What is it?"

The aide, a young Earther in training for high officer rank, saluted briskly. "We just got the report from the shuttlecraft, sir. It's all over. They want to know what to do with the body."

"Space it," Grady replied. "Good as anything." A thin smile flickered across his face and he shook his head. "Too bad. Kagen was a good man in combat but his pysch training must have slipped somewhere. We should send a strong note back to his barracks conditioner. Though it's funny it didn't show up until now."

He shook his head again. "Earth," he said. "For a moment he even had me wondering if it was possible. But when I tested him with my laser, I knew. No way, no way." He shuddered a little. "As if we'd ever let a War Worlder loose on Earth." Then he turned back to his paperwork.

As the aide turned to leave, Grady looked up again.

"One other thing," he said. "Don't forget to send that PR release back to Earth. Make it War-Hero-Dies-When-Hrangans-Blast-Ship. Jazz it up good. Some of the big com networks should pick it up and it'll make good publicity. And forward his medals to Wellington. They'll want them for his barracks museum."

The aide nodded and Grady returned to his work. He still looked quite bored.

END GAME

Joe W. Haldeman

Sometime in the Twenty-third Century they started calling it "the Forever War." Before that, it had just been the war, the only war.

And we had never met the enemy. The Taurans started the war at the end of the Twentieth Century, attacking our first starships with no provocation. We had never exchanged a word with the enemy; had never captured one alive.

I was drafted in 1997, and in 2458 still had three years to serve. I'd gone all the way from private to major in less than half a millennium. Without actually living all those years, of course; time dilation between collapsar jumps accounted for all but five of them.

Most of those five years I had been reasonably content, since the usual disadvantages of military service were offset by the fact that I was allowed to endure them in the company of the woman I loved. The three battles we had been in, we'd been in together: we'd shared a furlough on Earth, and even had the luck to be wounded at the same time, winning a year-long vacation on the hospital planet Heaven. After that, everything fell apart.

We had known for some time that neither of us would live through the war. Not only because the fighting was fierce—you had about one chance in three of surviving a battle—but also, the government couldn't afford to release us from the army: our back pay, compounded quarterly over the centuries, would cost them as much as a starship! But we did have each other, and there was always the possibility that the war might end.

But at Heaven, they separated us. On the basis of tests (and our embarrassing seniority) Marygay was made a lieutenant and I became a major. She was assigned to a Strike Force leaving from Heaven, though, and I was to go back to Stargate for combat officer training, eventually to command my own Strike Force.

I literally tried to move Heaven and Earth to get Marygay assigned to me; it didn't seem unreasonable for a commander to have a hand in the selection of his executive officer. But I found out later that the Army had good reason not to allow us together in the same company: heterosexuality was obsolete, a rare dysfunction, and we were too old to be "cured." The Army needed our experience, but the rule was one pervert per company; no exceptions.

We weren't simply lovers. Marygay and I were each other's only link to the real world, the 1990s. Everyone else came from a nightmare world that seemed to get worse as time went on. And neither was it simply separation: even if we were both to survive the battles in our future—not likely—time dilation would put us centuries out of phase with one another. There was no solution. One of us would die and the other would be alone.

My officer's training consisted of being immersed in a tank of oxygenated fluorocarbon with 239 electrodes attached to my brain and body. It was called ALSC, Accelerated Life Situation Computer, and it made my life accelerated and miserable for three weeks.

Want to know who Scipio Aemilianus was? Bright light of the Third Punic War. How to counter a knife-thrust to the abdomen? Crossed-wrists block, twist right, left side-kick to the exposed kidney.

What good all this was going to be, fighting perambulating mushrooms, was a mystery to me. But I was that machine's slave for three weeks, learning the best way to use every weapon from the sharp stick to the nova bomb, and absorbing two millennia's worth of military observation, theory, and prejudice. It was supposed to make me a major. Kind of like making a duck by teaching a chicken how to swim.

My separation from Marygay seemed, if possible, even more final when I read my combat orders: Sade-138, in the Greater Magellanic Cloud, four collapsar jumps and 150,000 light-years away. But I had already learned to live with the fact that I'd never see her again.

I had access to all of my new company's personnel records, including my own. The Army's psychologist had said that I "thought" I was tolerant toward homosexuality—which was wounding, because I'd learned at my mother's knee that what a person does with his plumbing is his own business and nobody else's. Which is all very fine when you're in the majority, I found out. When you're the one being tolerated, it can be difficult. Behind my back, most of them called me "the Old Queer," even though no one in the company was more than nine years younger than me. I accepted the inaccuracy along with the irony; a commander always gets names. I should have seen, though, that this was more than the obligatory token disrespect that soldiers accord their officers. The name symbolized an attitude of contempt and estrangement more profound than any I had experienced during my years as a private and noncommissioned officer.

Language, for one thing, was no small problem. English had evolved considerably in 450 years; soldiers had to learn Twenty-first Century English as a sort of lingua franca with which to communicate with their officers, some of whom might be "old" enough to be their nine-times-great-grandparents. Of course, they only used this language when talking to their officers, or mocking them, so they got out of practice with it.

At Stargate, maybe they should have spared some ALSC time to teach me the language of my troops. I had an "open door" policy, where twice weekly any soldier could come talk to me without going up through the chain of command, everything off the record. It never worked out well, and after a couple of months they stopped coming altogether.

There were only three of us who were born before the Twenty-fifth Century—the only three who had been *born* at all, since they didn't make people the sloppy old-fashioned way any more. Each embryo was engineered for a specific purpose . . . and the ones that wound up being soldiers, although intelligent and physically perfect, seemed deficient in some qualities that I considered to be virtues. Attila would have loved them, though; Napoleon would have hired them on the spot.

The other two people "of woman born" were my executive officer, Captain Charlie Moore, and the senior medic, Lieutenant Diana Alsever. They were both homosexual, having been born in the Twenty-second Century, but we still had much in common, and they were the only people in the company whom I considered friends. In retrospect I can see that we insulated one another from

210

the rest of the company, which might have been comfortable for them—but it was disastrous for me.

The rest of the officers, especially Lieutenant Hilleboe, my Field First, seemed only to tell me what they thought I wanted to hear. They didn't tell me that most of the troops thought I was inexperienced, cowardly, and had only been made their commander by virtue of seniority. All of which was more or less true—after all, I hadn't volunteered for the position—but maybe I could have done something about it if my officers had been frank with me.

Our assignment was to build a base on Sade-138's largest planet, and defend it against Tauran attack. Tauran expansion was very predictable, and we knew that they would show up there sooner or later. My company, Strike Force Gamma, would defend the place for two years, after which a garrison force would relieve us. And I would theoretically resign my commission and become a civilian again—unless there happened to be a new regulation forbidding it. Or an old one that they had neglected to tell me about.

The garrison force would automatically leave Stargate two years after we had, with no idea what would be waiting for them at Sade-138. There was no way we could get word back to them, since the trip took 340 years of "objective" time, though ship-time was only seven months, thanks to time dilation.

Seven months was long enough, trapped in the narrow corridors and tiny rooms of *Masaryk II*. It was a relief to leave the ship in orbit even though planetside meant four weeks of unrelenting hard labor under hazardous, uncomfortable conditions. Two shifts of 38.5 hours each, alternating shipboard rest and planetside work.

The planet was an almost featureless rock, an off-white billiard ball with a thin atmosphere of hydrogen and helium. The temperature at the equator varied from 25° Kelvin to 17° on a 38.5-hour cycle, daytime heat being provided by the bright blue spark of S Doradus. When it was coldest, just before dawn, hydrogen would condense out of the air in a fine mist, making everything so slippery that you had to just sit down and wait it out. At dawn a faint pastel rainbow provided the only relief from the black-and-white monotony of the landscape.

The ground was treacherous, covered with little granular chunks of frozen gas that shifted slowly, incessantly in the anemic breeze. You had to walk in a slow waddle to stay on your feet; of the four people who died during the construction of the base, three were the victims of simple falls.

From the sky down, we had three echelons of defense. First was the *Masaryk II*, with its six tachyon-drive fighters and fifty robot drones equipped with nova bombs. Commodore Antopol would take off after the Tauran ship when it flashed out of Sade-138's collapsar field. If she nailed it, we'd be home free.

If the enemy got through Antopol's swarm of fighters and drones, they would still have some difficulty attacking us. Atop our underground base was a circle of twenty-five self-aiming bevawatt lasers, with reaction times on the order of a fraction of a microsecond. And just beyond the laser's effective horizon was a broad ring with thousands of nuclear land mines that would detonate with any small distortion of the local gravitational field: a Tauran walking over one or a ship passing overhead.

If we actually had to go up and fight, which might happen if they reduced all our automatic defenses and wanted to take the base intact, each soldier was armed with a megawatt laser finger, and every squad had a tachyon rocket launcher and two repeating grenade launchers. And as a last resort, there was the stasis field.

I couldn't begin to understand the principles behind the stasis field; the gap between present-day physics and my master's degree in the same subject was as long as the time that separated Galileo and Einstein. But I knew the effects.

Nothing could move at a speed greater than 16.3 meters per second inside the field, which was a hemispherical (in space, spherical) volume about fifty meters in radius. Inside, there was no such thing as electromagnetic radiation; no electricity, no magnetism, no light. From inside your suit, you could see your surroundings in ghostly monochrome—which phenomenon was glibly explained to me as being due to "phase transference of quasi-energy leaking through from an adjacent tachyon reality," which was so much phlogiston to me.

But inside the field, all modern weapons of warfare were useless. Even a nova bomb was just an inert lump. And any creature, Terran or Tauran, caught inside without proper insulation would die in a fraction of a second.

Inside the field we had an assortment of old-fashioned weapons and one fighter, for last-ditch aerial support. I made people practice with the swords and bows and arrows and such, but they weren't enthusiastic. The consensus of opinion was that we would be doomed if the fighting degenerated to where we were forced into the stasis field. I couldn't say that I disagreed.

For five months we waited around in an atmosphere of comfortably boring routine.

The base quickly settled into a routine of training and waiting. I was almost impatient for the Taurans to show up, just to get it over with one way or the other.

The troops had adjusted to the situation much better than I had, for obvious reasons. They had specific duties to perform and ample free time for the usual soldierly anodynes to boredom. My duties were more varied but offered little satisfaction, since the problems that percolated up to me were of the "buck stops here" type: the ones with pleasing, unambiguous solutions were taken care of in the lower echelons.

I'd never cared much for sports or games, but found myself turning to them more and more as a kind of safety valve. For the first time in my life, in these tense, claustrophobic surroundings, I couldn't escape into reading or study. So I fenced, quarterstaff and saber, with the other officers; worked myself to exhaustion on the exercise machines and even kept a jump rope in my office. Most of the other officers played chess, but they could usually beat me—whenever I won it gave me the feeling I was being humored. And word games were difficult because my language was an archaic dialect that they had trouble manipulating. And I lacked the time and talent to master "modern" English.

For a while I let Diana feed me mood-altering drugs, but the cumulative effect of them was frightening—I was getting addicted in a way that was at first too subtle to bother me—so I stopped short. Then I tried some systematic psychoanalysis with Lieutenant Wilber. It was impossible. Although he knew all about my problems in an academic kind of way, we didn't speak the same cultural language; his counseling me about love and sex was like me telling a Fourteenth Century serf how best to get along with his priest and landlord.

And that, after all, was the root of my problem. I was sure I could have handled the pressures and frustrations of command, of being cooped up in a cave with these people who at times seemed scarcely less alien than the enemy; even the near-certainty that it could only lead to painful death in a worthless cause—if only I could have had Marygay with me. And the feeling got more intense as the months crept by.

He got very stern with me at this point and accused me of romanticizing my position. He knew what love was, he said; he had been in love himself. And the sexual polarity of the couple made no difference—all right, I could accept that; that idea had been a cliché in my parents' generation (though it had run into some predictable resistance in my own). But love, he said, love

213

was a fragile blossom; love was a delicate crystal; love was an unstable reaction with a half-life of about eight months. Crap, I said, and accused him of wearing cultural blinders; thirty centuries of pre-war society taught that love was one thing that could last to the grave and even beyond *and if he had been born instead of hatched he would know that without being told!* Whereupon he would assume a wry, tolerant expression and reiterate that I was merely a victim of self-imposed sexual frustration and romantic delusion.

In retrospect, I guess we had a good time arguing with each other. Cure me, he didn't.

2.

It was exactly 400 days since the day we had begun construction. I was sitting at my desk not checking out Hilleboe's new duty roster. Charlie was stretched out in a chair reading something on the viewer. The phone buzzed and it was a voice from on high, the Commodore.

"They're here."

"What?"

"I said they're here. A Tauran ship just exited the collapsar field. Velocity .8 c. Deceleration thirty G's. Give or take."

Charlie was leaning over my desk. "What?"

"How long before you can pursue?" I asked.

"Soon as you get off the phone." I switched off and went over to the logistic computer, which was a twin to the one on *Masaryk II*, and had a direct data link to it. While I tried to get numbers out of the thing, Charlie fiddled with the visual display.

The display was a hologram about a meter square by half a meter thick and was programmed to show the positions of Sade-138, our planet, and a few other chunks of rock in the system. There were green and red dots to show the positions of our vessels and the Taurans'.

The computer said that the minimum time it could take the Taurans to decelerate and get back to this planet would be a little over eleven days. Of course, that would be straight maximum acceleration and deceleration all the way; Commodore Antopol could pick them off like flies on a wall. So, like us, they'd mix up their direction of flight and degree of acceleration in a random way. Based on several hundred past records of enemy behavior, the computer was able to give us a probability table:

DAYS TO CONTACT	PROBABILITY
11	.000001
15	.001514
20	.032164
25	.103287
30	.676324
35	.820584
40	.982685
45	.993576
50	.999369
MEDIAN	
28.9554	.500000

Unless, of course, Antopol and her gang of merry pirates managed to make a kill. The chances for that, I had learned in the can, were slightly less than fifty-fifty.

But whether it took 28.9554 days or two weeks, those of us on the ground had to just sit on our hands and watch. If Antopol was successful, then we wouldn't have to fight until the regular garrison troops replaced us here, and we moved on to the next collapsar.

"Haven't left yet." Charlie had the display cranked down to minimum scale; the planet was a white ball the size of a large melon and *Masaryk II* was a green dot off to the right some eight melons away; you couldn't get both on the screen at the same time.

While we were watching, a small green dot popped out of the ship's dot and drifted away from it. A ghostly number "2" drifted beside it, and a key projected on the display's lower left-hand corner identified it as 2-PURSUIT DRONE. Other numbers in the key identified the *Masaryk II*, a planetary defense fighter, and fourteen planetary defense drones. Those sixteen ships were not yet far enough away from one another to have separate dots.

"Tell Hilleboe to call a general assembly. Might as well break it to everyone at once."

The men and women didn't take it very well, and I couldn't really blame them. We had all expected the Taurans to attack much sooner—and when they persisted in not coming, the feeling grew that Strike Force Command had made a mistake, and they'd never show up at all.

I wanted them to start weapons training in earnest; they hadn't used any high-powered weapons in almost two years. So I activated their laser-fingers and passed out the grenade and rocket launchers. We couldn't practice inside the base, for fear of damaging the external sensors and defensive laser ring. So we turned off half the circle of bevawatt lasers and went out about a klick beyond the perimeter; one platoon at a time, accompanied by either me or Charlie. Rusk kept a close watch on the early-warning screens. If anything approached, she would send up a flare, and the platoon would have to get back inside the ring before the unknown came over the horizon, at which time the defensive lasers would come on automatically. Besides knocking out the unknown, they would fry the platoon in less than .02 second.

We couldn't spare anything from the base to use as a target; but that turned out to be no problem. The first tachyon rocket we fired scooped out a hole twenty meters long by ten wide by five deep; the rubble gave us a multitude of targets from twice-man-sized on down.

They were good, a lot better than they had been with the primitive weapons in the stasis field. The best laser practice turned out to be rather like skeet shooting: pair up the people and have one stand behind the other, throwing rocks at random intervals. The one who was shooting had to gauge the rock's trajectory and zap it before it hit the ground. Their eye-hand coordination was impressive (maybe the Eugenics Council had done something right). Shooting at rocks down to pebble-size, most of them could do better than nine out of ten. Old nonbioengineered me could hit maybe seven out of ten, and I'd had a good deal more practice than they'd had.

They were equally facile at estimating trajectories with the grenade launcher, which was a more versatile weapon than it had been in the past. Instead of just shooting one-microton bombs with a standard propulsive charge, it had four different charges and a choice of one-, two-, three-, or four-microton bombs. For really close-in fighting, where it was dangerous to use the lasers, the barrel of the launcher would unsnap, and you could load it with a magazine of "shotgun" rounds. Each shot would send out an expanding cloud of a thousand tiny flechettes, that were instant death out to five meters and turned to harmless vapor at six.

The tachyon rocket launcher required no skill whatsoever. All you had to do was be careful no one was standing behind you when you fired it; the backwash from the rocket was dangerous for several meters behind the launching tube. Otherwise, you just lined your target up in the crosshairs and pushed the button. You didn't have to worry about trajectory; the rocket just traveled in a straight line for all practical purposes. It reached escape velocity in less than a second.

It improved the troops' morale to get out and chew up the landscape with their new toys. But the landscape wasn't fighting back. No matter how physically impressive the weapons were, their effectiveness would depend on what the Taurans could throw back. A Greek phalanx must have looked pretty impressive, but it wouldn't do too well against a single man with a flamethrower.

And as with any engagement, because of time dilation, there was no way to tell what sort of weaponry they would have. It depended on what the Tauran level of technology had been when their mission had begun; they could be a couple of centuries ahead of us or behind us. They might never have heard of the stasis field. Or they might be able to say a magic word and make us disappear.

I was out with the fourth platoon burning rocks, when Charlie called and asked me to come back in, urgent. I left Heimoff in charge.

"Another one?" The scale of the holograph display was such that our planet was pea-sized, about five centimeters from the X that marked the position of Sade-138. There were forty-one red and green dots scattered around the field; the key identified number forty-one as TAURAN CRUISER (2).

"That's right." Charlie was grim. "Appeared a few minutes ago. When I called. It has the same characteristics as the other one: 30 G's, .8 c."

"You called Antopol?"

"Yeah." He anticipated the next question. "It'll take almost a day for the signal to get there and back."

"It's never happened before." But of course Charlie knew that.

"Maybe this collapsar is especially important to them."

"Likely." So it was almost certain we'd be fighting on the ground. Even if Antopol managed to get the first cruiser, she wouldn't have a fifty-fifty chance on the second one. Low on drones and fighters. "I wouldn't like to be Antopol now."

"She'll just get it earlier."

"I don't know. We're in pretty good shape."

"Save it for the troops, William." He turned down the display's scale to where it showed only two objects: Sade-138 and the new red dot, slowly moving.

We spent the next two weeks watching dots blink out. And if you knew when and where to look, you could go outside and see the real thing happening, a hard bright speck of white light that faded in about a second.

In that second, a nova bomb had put out over a million times the

217

power of a bevawatt laser. It made a miniature star half a klick in diameter and as hot as the interior of the Sun. Anything it touched it would consume. The radiation from a near miss could botch up a ship's electronics beyond repair—two fighters, one of ours and one of theirs, had evidently suffered that fate; silently drifting out of the system at a constant velocity, without power.

We had used more powerful nova bombs earlier in the war, but the degenerate matter used to fuel them was unstable in large quantities. The bombs had a tendency to explode while they were still inside the ship. Evidently the Taurans had the same problem—or they had copied the process from us in the first place—because they had also scaled down to nova bombs that used less than a hundred kilograms of degenerate matter. And they deployed them much the same way we did, the warhead separating into dozens of pieces as it approached the target, only one of which was the nova bomb.

They would probably have a few bombs left over after they finished off *Masaryk II* and her retinue of fighters and drones. So it was likely that we were just wasting time and energy in weapons practice.

The thought did slip by my conscience, that I could gather up eleven people and board the fighter we had hidden safe behind the stasis field. It was preprogrammed to take us back to Stargate.

I even went to the extreme of making a mental list of the eleven, trying to think of that many people who meant more to me than the rest. Turned out I'd be picking six at random.

I put the thought away, though. We did have a chance, maybe a damned good one, even against a fully armed cruiser. It wouldn't be easy to get a nova bomb close enough to include us inside its kill-radius.

Besides, they'd just space me for desertion. So why bother.

Spirits rose when one of Antopol's drones knocked out the first Tauran cruiser. Not counting the ships left behind for planetary defense, she still had eighteen drones and two fighters. They wheeled around to intercept the second cruiser, by then a few light-hours away, still being harassed by fifteen enemy drones.

One of the drones got her. Her ancillary craft continued the attack, but it was a rout. One fighter and three drones fled the battle at maximum acceleration, looping up over the plane of the ecliptic, and were not pursued. We watched them with morbid interest while the enemy cruiser inched back to do battle with us. The fighter was headed back for Sade-138, to escape. Nobody blamed them. In fact, we sent them a farewell solidus good-luck message; they didn't respond, naturally, being zipped up in the acceleration tanks. But it would be recorded.

It took the enemy five days to get back to the planet and be comfortably ensconced in a stationary orbit on the other side. We settled in for the inevitable first phase of the attack, which would be aerial and totally automated: their drones against our lasers. I put a force of fifty men and women inside the stasis field, in case one of the drones got through. An empty gesture, really; the enemy could just stand by and wait for them to turn off the field; fry them the second it flickered out.

Charlie had a weird idea that I almost went for.

"We could boobytrap the place."

"What do you mean?" I said. "This place is boobytrapped, out to twenty-five klicks."

"No, not the mines and such. I mean the base itself, here, underground."

"Go on."

"There are two nova bombs in that fighter." He pointed at the stasis field through a couple of hundred meters of rock. "We can roll them down here, boobytrap them, then hide everybody in the stasis field and wait."

In a way it was tempting. It would relieve me from any responsibility for decision making; leave everything up to chance. "I don't think it would work, Charlie."

He seemed hurt. "Sure it would."

"No, look. For it to work, you have to get every single Tauran inside the kill-radius before it goes off—but they wouldn't all come charging in here once they breached our defenses. Least of all if the place seemed deserted. They'd suspect something, send in an advance party. And after the advance party set off the bombs—"

"We'd be back where we started, yeah. Minus the base. Sorry."

I shrugged. "It was an idea. Keep thinking, Charlie." I turned my attention back to the display, where the lopsided space war was in progress. Logically enough, the enemy wanted to knock out that one fighter overhead before he started to work on us. About all we could do was watch the red dots crawl around the planet and try to score. So far the pilot had managed to knock out all of the drones; the enemy hadn't sent any fighters after him yet.

I'd given the pilot control over five of the lasers in our defensive ring. They couldn't do much good, though. A bevawatt laser pumps out a billion kilowatts per second at a range of a hundred meters. A thousand klicks up, though, the beam was attenuated to ten kilowatts. Might do some damage if it hit an optical sensor. At least confuse things.

"We could use another fighter. Or six."

"Use up the drones," I said. We did have a fighter, of course, and a swabbie attached to us who could pilot it. But it might turn out to be our only hope, if they got us cornered in the stasis field.

"How far away is the other guy?" Charlie asked, meaning the fighter pilot who had turned tail. I cranked down the scale and the green dot appeared at the right of the display. "About six light-hours." He had two drones left, too near to him to show as separate dots, having expended one in covering his getaway. "He's not accelerating any more, but he's doing $.9\ c$."

"Couldn't do us any good if he wanted to." Need almost a month to slow down.

At that low point, the light that stood for our own defensive fighter faded out. "Crap."

"Now the fun starts. Should I tell the troops to get ready, stand by to go topside?"

"No . . . have them suit up, in case we lose air. But I expect it'll be a little while before we have a ground attack." I turned the scale up again. Four red spots were already creeping around the globe toward us.

I got suited up and came back to Administration to watch the fireworks on the monitors.

The lasers worked perfectly. All four drones converged on us simultaneously; were targeted and destroyed. All but one of the nova bombs went off below our horizon (the visual horizon was about ten kilometers away, but the lasers were mounted high and could target something at twice that distance). The bomb that detonated on our horizon had melted out a semicircular chunk that glowed brilliantly white for several minutes. An hour later, it was still glowing dull orange, and the ground temperature outside had risen to 50° Absolute, melting most of our snow, exposing an irregular dark gray surface.

The next attack was also over in a fraction of a second, but this time there had been eight drones, and four of them got within ten klicks. Radiation from the glowing craters raised the temperature to nearly 300°. That was above the melting point of water, and I was starting to get worried. The fighting suits were good to over 1000°, but the automatic lasers depended on low-temperature superconductors for their speed.

I asked the computer what the lasers' temperature limit was, and it printed out TR 398–734–009–265, "Some Aspects Concerning the Adaptability of Cryogenic Ordnance to Use in Relatively High-Temperature Environments," which had lots of handy advice about how we could insulate the weapons if we had access to a fully equipped armorer's shop. It did note that the response time of automatic-aiming devices increased as the temperature increased, and that above some "critical temperature," the weapons would not aim at all. But there was no way to predict any individual weapon's behavior, other than to note that the highest critical temperature recorded was 790° and the lowest was 420°.

Charlie was watching the display. His voice was flat over the suit's radio: "Sixteen this time."

"Surprised?" One of the few things we knew about Tauran psychology was a certain compulsiveness about numbers, especially primes and powers of two.

"Let's just hope they don't have thirty-two left." I queried the computer on this; all it could say was that the cruiser had thus far launched a total of forty-four drones, and some cruisers had been known to carry as many as 128.

We had more than a half-hour before the drones would strike. I could evacuate everybody to the stasis field, and they would be temporarily safe if one of the nova bombs got through. Safe, but trapped. How long would it take the crater to cool down, if three or four—let alone sixteen—of the bombs made it through? You couldn't live forever in a fighting suit, even though it recycled everything with remorseless efficiency. One week was enough to make you thoroughly miserable. Two weeks, suicidal. Nobody had ever gone three weeks, under field conditions.

Besides, as a defensive position, the stasis field could be a deathtrap. The enemy has all the options, since the dome is opaque; the only way you can find out what they're up to is to stick your head out. They didn't have to wade in with primitive weapons unless they were impatient. They could just keep the dome saturated with laser fire and wait for you to turn off the generator. Meanwhile harassing you by throwing spears, rocks, arrows into the dome—you could return fire, but it was pretty futile.

Of course, if one man stayed inside the base, the others could wait out the next half-hour in the stasis field. If he didn't come get them, they'd know the outside was hot. I chinned the combination that would give me a frequency available to everybody Echelon 5 and above.

"This is Major Mandella." That still sounded like a bad joke. I outlined the situation to them and asked them to tell their troops that everyone in the company was free to move into the stasis field. I would stay behind and come retrieve them if things went well—not out of nobility, of course; I preferred taking the chance of being vaporized in a nanosecond, rather than almost certain slow death under the gray dome.

I chinned Charlie's frequency. "You can go, too. I'll take care of things here."

"No, thanks," he said slowly. "I'd just as soon . . . hey, look at this."

The cruiser had launched another red dot, a couple of minutes behind the others. The display's key identified it as being another drone. "That's curious."

"Superstitious bastards," he said without feeling.

It turned out that only eleven people chose to join the fifty who had been ordered into the dome. That shouldn't have surprised me, but it did.

As the drones approached, Charlie and I stared at the monitors, carefully not looking at the holograph display, tacitly agreeing that it would be better not to know when they were one minute away, thirty seconds . . . and then, like the other times, it was over before we knew it had started. The screens glared white and there was a yowl of static, and we were still alive.

But this time there were fifteen new holes on the horizon—or closer!—and the temperature was rising so fast that the last digit in the readout was an amorphous blur. The number peaked in the high 800s and began to slide down.

We had never seen any of the drones, not during that tiny fraction of a second it took the lasers to aim and fire. But then the seventeenth one flashed over the horizon, zig-zagging crazily, and stopped directly overhead. For an instant it seemed to hover, and then it began to fall. Half the lasers had detected it, and they were firing steadily, but none of them could aim; they were all stuck in their last firing position.

It glittered as it dropped, the mirror polish of its sleek hull reflecting the white glow from the craters and the eerie flickering of the constant, impotent laser fire. I heard Charlie take one deep breath and the drone fell so close you could see spidery Tauran numerals etched on the hull, and a transparent porthole near the tip—then its engine flared and it was suddenly gone.

"What the hell?" Charlie said, quietly.

The porthole. "Maybe reconnaissance."

"I guess. So we can't touch them, and they know it."

"Unless the lasers recover." Didn't seem likely. "We better get everybody under the dome. Us; too."

He said a word whose vowel had changed over the centuries, but whose meaning was clear. "No hurry. Let's see what they do."

We waited for several hours. The temperature outside stabilized at 690°—just under the melting point of zinc, I remembered to no purpose—and I tried the manual controls for the lasers, but they were still frozen.

"Here they come," Charlie said. "Eight again."

I started for the display. "Guess we'll—"

"Wait! They aren't drones." The key identified all eight with the legend TROOP CARRIER.

"Guess they want to take the base," he said. "Intact."

That, and maybe try out new weapons and techniques. "It's not much of a risk for them. They can always retreat and drop a nova bomb in our laps."

I called Brill and had her go get everybody who was in the stasis field; set them up with the remainder of her platoon as a defensive line circling around the northeast and northwest quadrants.

"I wonder," Charlie said. "Maybe we shouldn't put everyone topside at once. Until we know how many Taurans there are."

That was a point. Keep a reserve, let the enemy underestimate our strength. "It's an idea . . . there might be just 64 of them in eight carriers." Or 128 or 256. I wished our spy satellites had a finer sense of discrimination. But you can only cram so much into a machine the size of a grape.

I decided to let Brill's seventy people be our first line of defense, and ordered them into a ring in the ditches we had made outside the base's perimeter. Everybody else would stay downstairs until needed.

If it turned out that the Taurans, either through numbers or new technology, could field an unstoppable force, I'd order everyone into the stasis field. There was a tunnel from the living quarters to the dome, so the people underground could go straight there in safety. The ones in the ditches would have to fall back under fire. If any of them were still alive when I gave the order.

I called in Hilleboe and had her and Charlie keep watch over the lasers. If they came unstuck, I'd call Brill and her people back. Turn on the automatic aiming system again, then just sit back and watch the show. But even stuck, the lasers could be useful. Charlie marked the monitors to show where the rays would go; he and Hilleboe could fire them manually whenever something moved into a weapon's line-of-sight.

We had about twenty minutes. Brill was walking around the perimeter with her men and women, ordering them into the ditches a squad at a time, setting up overlapping fields of fire. I broke in and asked her to set up the heavy weapons so that they could be used to channel the enemy's advance into the path of the lasers.

There wasn't much else to do but wait. I asked Charlie to measure the enemy's progress and try to give us an accurate countdown, then sat at my desk and pulled out a pad, to diagram Brill's arrangement and see whether I could improve on it.

The first line that I drew ripped through four sheets of paper. It had been some time since I'd done any delicate work in a suit. I remembered how, in training, they'd made us practice controlling the strength-amplification circuits by passing eggs from person to person, messy business. I wondered if they still had eggs on Earth.

The diagram completed, I couldn't see any way to add to it. All those reams of theory crammed in my brain; there was plenty of tactical advice about envelopment and encirclement, but from the wrong point of view. If you were the one who was being encircled, you didn't have many options. Just sit tight and fight. Respond quickly to enemy concentrations of force, but stay flexible so the enemy can't employ a diversionary force to divert strength from some predictable section of your perimeter. *Make full use of air and space support*, always good advice. Keep your head down and your chin up and pray for the cavalry. Hold your position and don't contemplate Dien Bien Phu, the Alamo, the Battle of Hastings.

"Eight more carriers out," Charlie said. "Five minutes. Until the first eight get here."

So they were going to attack in two waves. At least two. What would I do, in the Tauran commander's position? That wasn't too far-fetched; the Taurans lacked imagination in tactics and tended to copy human patterns.

The first wave could be a throwaway, a kamikaze attack to soften us up and evaluate our defenses. Then the second would come in more methodically and finish the job. Or vice versa; the first group would have twenty minutes to get entrenched, then the second could skip over their heads and hit us hard at one spot—breach the perimeter and overrun the base.

Or maybe they sent out two forces simply because two was a magic number. Or they could only launch eight troop carriers at a time (that would be bad, implying that the carriers were large; in different situations they had used carriers holding as few as 4 troops or as many as 128).

"Three minutes." I stared at the cluster of monitors that showed various sectors of the mine field. If we were lucky, they'd land out there, out of caution. Or maybe pass over it low enough to detonate mines.

I was feeling vaguely guilty. I was safe in my hole, doodling, ready to start calling out orders. How did those seventy sacrificial lambs feel about their absentee commander?

Then I remembered how I had felt about Captain Stott, that first mission, when he'd elected to stay safely in orbit while we fought on the ground. The rush of remembered hate was so strong I had to bite back nausea.

"Hilleboe, can you handle the lasers by yourself?"

"I don't see why not, sir."

I tossed down the pen and stood up. "Charlie, you take over the unit coordination; you can do it as well as I could. I'm going topside."

"I wouldn't advise that, sir."

"Hell no, William. Don't be an idiot."

"I'm not taking orders, I'm giv—"

"You wouldn't last ten seconds up there," Charlie said.

"I'll take the same chance as everybody else."

"Don't you hear what I'm saying? *They'll* kill you!"

"The troops? Nonsense. I know they don't like me especially, but—"

"You haven't listened in on the squad frequencies?" No, they didn't speak my brand of English when they talked among themselves. "They think you put them out on the line for punishment, for cowardice. After you'd told them anyone was free to go into the dome."

"Didn't you, sir?" Hilleboe said.

"To punish them? No, of course not." Not consciously. "They were just up there when I needed . . . hasn't Lieutenant Brill said anything to them?"

"Not that I've heard," Charlie said. "Maybe she's been too busy to tune in."

Or she agreed with them. "I'd better get—"

"There!" Hilleboe shouted. The first enemy ship was visible in one of the mine field monitors; the others appeared in the next second. They came in from random directions and weren't evenly distributed around the base. Five in the northeast quadrant and only one in the southwest. I relayed the information to Brill.

But we had predicted their logic pretty well; all of them were coming down in the ring of mines. One came close enough to one of the tachyon devices to set it off. The blast caught the rear end of the oddly streamlined craft, causing it to make a complete flip and crash nose-first. Side ports opened up and Taurans came crawling out. Twelve of them; probably four left inside. If all the others had sixteen as well, there were only slightly more of them than of us.

In the first wave.

The other seven had landed without incident, and yes, there were sixteen each. Brill shuffled a couple of squads to conform to the enemy's troop concentration, and we waited.

They moved fast across the mine field, striding in unison like bow-legged, top-heavy robots, not even breaking stride when one of them was blown to bits by a mine, which happened eleven times.

When they came over the horizon, the reason for their apparently random distribution was obvious: they had analyzed beforehand which approaches would give them the most natural cover, from the rubble that the drones had kicked up. They would be able to get within a couple of kilometers of the base before we got any clear line of sight on them. And their suits had augmentation circuits similar to ours, so they could cover a kilometer in less than a minute.

Brill had her troops open fire immediately, probably more for morale than out of any hope of actually hitting the enemy. They probably were getting a few, though it was hard to tell. At least the tachyon rockets did an impressive job of turning boulders into gravel.

The Taurans returned fire with some weapon similar to the tachyon rocket, maybe exactly the same. They rarely found a mark, though; our people were at and below ground level, and if the rocket didn't hit something it would keep on going forever, amen. They did score a hit on one of the bevawatt lasers, though, and the concussion that filtered down to us was strong enough to make me wish we had burrowed a little deeper than twenty meters.

The bevawatts weren't doing us any good. The Taurans must have figured out the lines of sight ahead of time, and gave them wide berth. That turned out to be fortunate, because it caused Charlie to let his attention wander from the laser monitors for a moment.

"What the hell?"

"What's that, Charlie?" I didn't take my eyes off the monitors. Waiting for something to happen.

"The ship, the cruiser—it's gone." I looked at the holograph display. He was right, the only red lights were those that stood for the troop carriers.

"Where did it go?" I asked inanely.

"Let's play it back." He programmed the display to go back a couple of minutes and cranked out the scale to where both planet and collapsar showed on the cube. The cruiser showed up, and with it, three green dots. Our "coward," attacking the cruiser with only two drones.

But he had a little help from the laws of physics.

Instead of going into collapsar insertion, he had skimmed *around* the collapsar field in a slingshot orbit. He had come out going .9 *c;* the drones were going .99 *c,* headed straight for the enemy cruiser. Our planet was about a thousand light-seconds from the collapsar, so the Tauran ship had only ten seconds to detect and stop both drones. And at that speed, it didn't matter whether you'd been hit by a nova bomb or a spitball.

The first drone disintegrated the cruiser and the other one, .01 second behind, glided on down to impact on the planet. The fighter missed the planet by a couple of hundred kilometers and hurtled on into space, decelerating with the maximum twenty-five G's. He'd be back in a couple of months.

But the Taurans weren't going to wait. They were getting close enough to our lines for both sides to start using lasers, but they were also within easy grenade range. A good-sized rock could shield them from laser fire, but the grenades and rockets were slaughtering them.

At first, Brill's troops had the overwhelming advantage: fighting from ditches, they could only be harmed by an occasional lucky shot or an extremely well-aimed grenade (which the Taurans threw by hand, with a range of several hundred meters). Brill had lost four, but it looked as if the Tauran force was down to less than half its original size.

Eventually, the landscape had been torn up enough so that the bulk of the Tauran force was also able to fight from holes in the ground. The fighting slowed down to individual laser duels, punctuated occasionally by heavier weapons. But it wasn't smart to use up a tachyon rocket against a single Tauran, not with another force of unknown size only a few minutes away.

Something had been bothering me about that holographic replay. Now, with the battle's lull, I knew what it was.

When that second drone crashed at near-light-speed, how much damage had it done to the planet? I stepped over to the computer and punched it up; found out how much energy had been released in the collision, and then compared it with geological information in the computer's memory.

Twenty times as much energy as the most powerful earthquake ever recorded. On a planet three-quarters the size of Earth.

On the general frequency: "Everybody—topside! Right now!" I palmed the button that would cycle and open the airlock and tunnel that led from Administration to the surface.

"What the hell, Will—"

"Earthquake!" How long? "Move!"

Hilleboe and Charlie were right behind me.

"Safer in the ditches?" Charlie said.

"I don't know," I said. "Never been in an earthquake." Maybe the walls of the ditch would close up and crush you.

I was surprised at how dark it was on the surface. S Doradus had almost set; the monitors had compensated for the low light level.

An enemy laser raked across the clearing to our left, making a quick shower of sparks when it flicked by a bevawatt mounting. We hadn't been seen yet. We all decided yes, it would be safer in the ditches, and made it to the nearest one in three strides.

There were four men and women in the ditch, one of them badly wounded or dead. We scrambled down the ledge and I turned up my image amplifier to log two, to inspect our ditchmates. We were lucky; one was a grenadier and they also had a rocket launcher. I could just make out the names on their helmets. We were in Brill's ditch, but she hadn't noticed us yet. She was at the opposite end, cautiously peering over the edge, directing two squads in a flanking movement. When they were safely in position, she ducked back down. "Is that you, Major?"

"That's right," I said cautiously. I wondered whether any of the people in the ditch were among the ones after my scalp.

"What's this about an earthquake?"

She had been told about the cruiser being destroyed, but not about the other drone. I explained in as few words as possible.

"Nobody's come out of the airlock," she said. "Not yet. I guess they all went into the stasis field."

"Yeah, they were just as close to one as the other." Maybe some of them were still down below, hadn't taken my warning seriously. I chinned the general frequency to check, and then all hell broke loose.

The ground dropped away and then flexed back up; slammed us so hard that we were airborne, tumbling out of the ditch. We flew several meters, going high enough to see the pattern of bright orange and yellow ovals, the craters where nova bombs had been stopped. I landed on my feet but the ground was shifting and slithering so much that it was impossible to stay upright.

With a basso grinding I could feel through my suit, the cleared area above our base crumbled and fell in. Part of the stasis field's underside was exposed when the ground subsided; it settled to its new level with aloof grace.

I hoped everybody had had time and sense enough to get under the dome.

A figure came staggering out of the ditch nearest to me and I realized with a start that it wasn't human. At this range, my laser burned a hole straight through his helmet; he took two steps and fell over backward. Another helmet peered over the edge of the ditch. I sheared the top of it off before he could raise his weapon.

I couldn't get my bearings. The only thing that hadn't changed

228

was the stasis dome, and it looked the same from any angle. The bevawatt lasers were all buried, but one of them had switched on, a brilliant flickering searchlight that illuminated a swirling cloud of vaporized rock.

Obviously, though, I was in enemy territory. I started across the trembling ground toward the dome.

I couldn't raise any platoon leaders. All of them but Brill were probably inside the dome. I did get Hilleboe and Charlie; told Hilleboe to go inside the dome and roust everybody out. If the next wave also had 128, we were going to need everybody.

The tremors died down and I found my way into a "friendly" ditch—the cooks' ditch, in fact, since the only people there were Orban and Rudkoski.

I got a beep from Hilleboe and chinned her on. "Sir . . . there were only ten people there. The rest didn't make it."

"They stayed behind?" Seemed like they'd had plenty of time.

"I don't know, sir."

"Never mind. Get me a count, how many people we have, all totaled." I tried the platoon leaders' frequency again and it was still silent.

The three of us watched for enemy laser fire, for a couple of minutes, but there was none. Probably waiting for reinforcements.

Hilleboe called back. "I only get fifty-three, sir. Some others may be unconscious."

"All right. Have them sit tight until—" Then the second wave showed up, the troop carriers roaring over the horizon with their jets pointed our way, decelerating. *"Get some rockets on those bastards!"* Hilleboe yelled to everyone in particular. But nobody had managed to stay attached to a rocket launcher while he was being tossed around. No grenade launchers, either, and the range was too far for the hand lasers to do any damage.

These carriers were four or five times the size of the ones in the first wave. One of them grounded about a kilometer in front of us, barely stopping long enough to disgorge its troops. Of which there were over fifty, probably sixty-four times eight made 512. No way we could hold them back.

"Everybody listen, this is Major Mandella." I tried to keep my voice even and quiet. "We're going to retreat back into the dome, quickly but in an orderly way. I know we're scattered all over hell. If you belong to the second or fourth platoon, stay put for a minute and give covering fire while the first and third platoons, and support, fall back.

"First and third and support, fall back to about half your present distance from the dome, then take cover and defend the second and fourth as they come back. They'll go to the edge of the dome and cover you while you come back the rest of the way." I shouldn't have said "retreat"; that word wasn't in the book. Retrograde action.

There was a lot more retrograde than action. Eight or nine people were firing, and all the rest were in full flight. Rudkoski and Orban had vanished. I took a few carefully aimed shots, to no great effect, then ran down to the other end of the ditch, climbed out and headed for the dome.

The Taurans started firing rockets, but most of them seemed to be going too high. I saw two of us get blown away before I got to my half-way point; found a nice big rock and hid behind it. I peeked out and decided that only two or three of the Taurans were close enough to be even remotely possible laser targets, and the better part of valor would be in not drawing unnecessary attention to myself. I ran the rest of the way to the edge of the field and stopped to return fire. After a couple of shots, I realized that I was just making myself a target; as far as I could see there was only one other person who was still running toward the dome.

A rocket zipped by, so close I could have touched it. I flexed my knees and kicked, and entered the dome in a rather undignified posture.

3.

Inside, I could see the rocket that had missed me drifting lazily through the gloom, rising slightly as it passed through to the other side of the dome. It would vaporize the instant it came out the other side, since all of the kinetic energy it had lost in abruptly slowing down to 16.3 meters per second would come back in the form of heat.

Nine people were lying dead, face-down just inside of the field's edge. It wasn't unexpected, though it wasn't the sort of thing you were supposed to tell the troops.

Their fighting suits were intact—otherwise they wouldn't have made it this far—but sometime during the past few minutes rough-and-tumble, they had damaged the coating of special insulation that protected them from the stasis field. So as soon as they entered the field, all electrical activity in their bodies ceased, which killed them instantly. Also, since no molecule in their bodies could move faster than 16.3 miles per second, they instantly froze solid, their body temperatures stabilized at a cool 0.426° Absolute.

I decided not to turn any of them over to find out their names, not yet. We had to get some sort of defensive position worked out, before the Taurans came through the dome. If they decided to slug it out rather than wait.

With elaborate gestures, I managed to get everybody collected in the center of the field, under the fighter's tail, where the weapons were racked.

There were plenty of weapons, since we had been prepared to outfit three times this number of people. After giving each person a shield and short-sword, I traced a question in the snow: GOOD ARCHERS? RAISE HANDS. I got five volunteers, then picked out three more so that all the bows would be in use. Twenty arrows per bow. They were the most effective long-range weapon we had; the arrows were almost invisible in their slow flight, heavily weighted and tipped with a deadly sliver of diamond-hard crystal.

I arranged the archers in a circle around the fighter (its landing fins would give them partial protection from missiles coming in from behind) and between each pair of archers put four other people: two spear-throwers, one quarterstaff, and a person armed with battleax and a dozen chakram throwing knives. This arrangement would theoretically take care of the enemy at any range from the edge of the field to hand-to-hand combat.

Actually, at some 600-to-42 odds, they could probably walk in with a rock in each hand, no shields or special weapons, and still beat the crap out of us.

Assuming they knew what the stasis field was. Their technology seemed up to date in all other respects.

For several hours nothing happened. We got about as bored as anyone could, waiting to die. No one to talk to, nothing to see but the unchanging gray dome, gray snow, gray space-ship, and a few identically gray soldiers. Nothing to hear, taste, or smell but yourself.

Those of us who still had any interest in the battle were keeping watch on the bottom edge of the dome, waiting for the first Taurans to come through. So it took us a second to realize what was going on when the attack did start. It came from above, a cloud of catapulted darts swarming in through the dome some thirty meters above the ground, headed straight for the center of the hemisphere.

The shields were big enough that you could hide most of your body behind them by crouching slightly; the people who saw the darts coming could protect themselves easily. The ones who had their backs to the action, or were just asleep at the switch, had to rely on dumb luck for survival; there was no way to shout a warning, and it only took three seconds for a missile to get from the edge of the dome to its center.

We were lucky, losing only five. One of them was an archer, Shubik. I took over her bow and we waited, expecting a ground attack immediately.

It didn't come. After a half-hour, I went around the circle and explained with gestures that the first thing you were supposed to do, if anything happened, was to touch the person on your right. He'd do the same, and so on down the line.

That might have saved my life. The second dart attack, a couple of hours later, came from behind me. I felt the nudge, slapped the person on my right, turned around and saw the cloud descending. I got the shield over my head and they hit a split-second later.

I set down my bow to pluck three darts from the shield and the ground attack started.

It was a weird, impressive sight. Some 300 of them stepped into the field simultaneously, almost shoulder-to-shoulder around the perimeter of the dome. They advanced in step, each one holding a round shield barely large enough to hide his massive chest. They were throwing darts similar to the ones we had been barraged with.

I set the shield up in front of me—it had little extensions on the bottom to keep it upright—and with the first arrow I shot, I knew we had a chance. It struck one of them in the center of his shield, went straight through, and penetrated his suit.

It was a one-sided massacre. The darts weren't very effective without the element of surprise—but when one came sailing over my head from behind, it did give me a crawly feeling between the shoulderblades.

With twenty arrows I got twenty Taurans. They closed ranks every time one dropped; you didn't even have to aim. After running out of arrows, I tried throwing their darts back at them. But their light shields were quite adequate against the small missiles.

We'd killed more than half of them with arrows and spears, long before they got into range of the hand-to-hand weapons. I drew my sword and waited. They still outnumbered us by better than three to one.

When they got within ten meters, the people with the chakram throwing knives had their own field day. Although the spinning disc was easy enough to see, and it took more than a half-second to get from thrower to target, most of the Taurans reacted the same ineffective way, raising up the shield to ward it off. The razor-sharp, tempered heavy blade cut through the light shield like a buzz-saw through cardboard.

The first hand-to-hand contact was with the quarterstaffs, which were metal rods two meters long, that tapered at the ends to a double-edged, serrated knife blade. The Taurans had a cold-blooded—or valiant, if your mind works that way—method for dealing with them. They would simply grab the blade and die. While the human was trying to extricate his weapon from the frozen death-grip, a Tauran swordsman, with a scimitar over a meter long, would step in and kill him.

Besides the swords, they had a bolo-like thing that was a length of elastic cord that ended with about ten centimeters of something like barbed wire, and a small weight to propel it. It was a dangerous weapon for all concerned; if they missed their target it would come snapping back unpredictably. But they hit their target pretty often, going under the shields and wrapping the thorny wire around ankles.

I stood back-to-back with Private Erikson and with our swords we managed to stay alive for the next few minutes. When the Taurans were down to a couple of dozen survivors, they just turned around and started marching out. We threw some darts after them, getting three, but we didn't want to chase after them. They might turn around and start hacking again.

There were only twenty-eight of us left standing. Nearly ten times that number of dead Taurans littered the ground, but there was no satisfaction in it.

They could do the whole thing over, with a fresh 300. And this time it would work.

We moved from body to body, pulling out arrows and spears, then took up places around the fighter again. Nobody bothered to retrieve the quarterstaffs. I counted noses: Charlie and Diana were still alive (Hilleboe had been one of the quarterstaff victims) as well as two supporting officers, Wilber and Szydlowska. Rudkoski was still alive but Orban had taken a dart.

After a day of waiting, it looked as if the enemy had decided on a war of attrition, rather than repeating the ground attack. Darts came in constantly, not in swarms anymore, but in twos and threes and tens. And from all different angles. You couldn't stay alert forever; they'd get somebody every three or four hours.

We took turns sleeping, two at a time, on top of the stasis field generator. Sitting directly under the bulk of the fighter, it was the safest place in the dome.

Every now and then, a Tauran would appear at the edge of the field, evidently to see whether any of us were left. Sometimes we'd shoot an arrow at him, for practice.

The darts stopped falling after a couple of days. I supposed it was possible that they'd simply run out of them. Or maybe they'd decided to stop when we were down to twenty survivors.

There was a more likely possibility. I took one of the quarter-staffs down to the edge of the field and poked it through, a centimeter or so. When I drew it back, the point was melted off. When I showed it to Charlie, he just rocked back and forth (the only way you can nod in a suit); this sort of thing had happened before, one of the first times the stasis field hadn't worked. They simply saturated it with laser fire and waited for us to go stir-crazy and turn off the generator. They were probably sitting in their ships playing the Tauran equivalent of pinochle.

I tried to think. It was hard to keep your mind on something for any length of time in the hostile environment, sense-deprived, looking over your shoulder every few seconds. Something Charlie had said. Only yesterday, I couldn't track it down. It wouldn't have worked then; that was all I could remember. Then finally it came to me.

I called everyone over and wrote in the snow:

GET NOVA BOMBS FROM SHIP.

CARRY TO EDGE OF FIELD.

MOVE FIELD.

Szydlowska knew where the proper tools would be, aboard ship. Luckily, we had left all of the entrances open before turning on the stasis field: they were electronic and would have been frozen shut. We got an assortment of wrenches from the engine room and climbed up to the cockpit. He knew how to remove the access plate that exposed a crawl space into the bomb-bay. I followed him in through the meter-wide tube.

Normally, I supposed, it would have been pitch-black. But the stasis field illuminated the bomb-bay with the same dim, shadowless light that prevailed outside. The bomb-bay was too small for both of us, so I stayed at the end of the crawl space and watched.

The bomb-bay doors had a "manual override" so they were easy; Szydlowska just turned a hand-crank and we were in business. Freeing the two nova bombs from their cradles was another thing. Finally, he went back down to the engine room and brought back a crowbar. He pried one loose and I got the other, and we rolled them out the bomb-bay.

Sergeant Anghelov was already working on them by the time we climbed back down. All you had to do to arm the bomb was to unscrew the fuse on the nose of it and poke something around in the fuse socket to wreck the delay mechanism and safety restraints.

We carried them quickly to the edge, six people per bomb, and set them down next to each other. Then we waved to the four people who were standing by at the field generator's handles. They picked it up and walked ten paces in the opposite direction. The bombs disappeared as the edge of the field slid over them.

There was no doubt that the bombs had gone off. For a couple of seconds it was hot as the interior of a star outside, and even the stasis field took notice of the fact: about a third of the dome glowed a dull pink for a moment, then was gray again. There was a slight acceleration, like you would feel in a slow elevator. That meant we were drifting down to the bottom of the crater. Would there be a solid bottom? Or would we sink down through molten rock to be trapped like a fly in amber—didn't pay to even think about that. Perhaps if it happened, we could blast our way out with the fighter's bevawatt laser.

Twelve of us, anyhow.

HOW LONG? Charlie scraped in the snow at my feet.

That was a damned good question. About all I knew was the amount of energy two nova bombs released. I didn't know how big a fireball they would make, which would determine the temperature at detonation and the size of the crater. I didn't know the heat capacity of the surrounding rock, or its boiling point. I wrote ONE WEEK, SHRUG? HAVE TO THINK.

The ship's computer could have told me in a thousandth of a second, but it wasn't talking. I started writing equations in the snow, trying to get a maximum and minimum figure for the length of time it would take for the outside to cool down to 500°. Anghelov, whose physics was much more up-to-date, did his own calculations on the other side of the ship.

My answer said anywhere from six hours to six days (although for six hours, the surrounding rock would have to conduct heat like pure copper), and Anghelov got five hours to four and a half days. I voted for six and nobody else got a vote.

We slept a lot. Charlie and Diana played chess by scraping symbols in the snow; I was never able to hold the shifting positions of the pieces in my mind. I checked my figures several times and kept coming up with six days. I checked Anghelov's computations, too, and they seemed all right, but I stuck to my guns. It wouldn't hurt us to stay in the suits an extra day and a half. We argued good-naturedly in terse shorthand.

There had been nineteen of us left the day we tossed the bombs outside. There were still nineteen six days later, when I paused with my hand over the generator's cutoff switch. What was waiting for us out there? Surely we had killed all the Taurans within several klicks of the explosion. But there might have been a reserve force farther away, now waiting patiently on the crater's lip. At least you could push a quarterstaff through the field and have it come back whole.

I dispersed the people evenly around the area, so they might not get us with a single shot. Then, ready to turn it back on immediately if anything went wrong, I pushed.

4.

My radio was still tuned to the general frequency; after more than a week of silence my ears were suddenly assaulted with loud, happy babbling.

We stood in the center of a crater almost a kilometer wide and deep. Its sides were a shinny black crust shot through with red cracks, hot but no longer dangerous. The hemisphere of earth that we rested on had sunk a good forty meters into the floor of the crater, while it had still been molten, so now we stood on a kind of pedestal.

Not a Tauran in sight.

We rushed to the ship, sealed it and filled it with cold air and popped our suits. I didn't press seniority for the one shower; just sat back in an acceleration couch and took deep breaths of air that didn't smell like recycled Mandella.

The ship was designed for a maximum crew of twelve, so we stayed outside in shifts of seven to keep from straining the life-support systems. I sent a repeating message to the other fighter, which was still over six weeks away, that we were in good shape and waiting to be picked up. I was reasonably certain he would have seven free berths, since the normal crew for a combat mission was only three.

It was good to walk around and talk again. I officially suspended all things military for the duration of our stay on the planet. Some of the people were survivors of Brill's mutinous bunch, but they didn't show any hostility toward me.

We played a kind of nostalgia game, comparing the various eras we'd experienced on Earth, wondering what it would be like in the 700-years-future we were going back to. Nobody mentioned the fact that we would at best go back to a few months' furlough, and then be assigned to another Strike Force, another turn of the wheel.

Wheels. One day Charlie asked me from what country my name originated; it sounded weird to him. I told him it originated from the lack of a dictionary and that if it were spelled right, it would look even weirder.

I got to kill a good half-hour explaining all the peripheral details to that. Basically, though, my parents were "hippies" (a kind of subculture in late Twentieth Century America, that rejected materialism and embraced a broad spectrum of odd ideas) who lived with a group of other hippies in a small agricultural community. When my mother got pregnant, they wouldn't be so conventional as to get married: this entailed the woman taking the man's name, and implied that she was his property. But they got all intoxicated and sentimental and decided they would both change their names to be the same. They rode into the nearest town, arguing all the way as to what name would be the best symbol for the love-bond between them—I narrowly missed having a much shorter name—and they settled on Mandala.

A mandala is a wheel-like design the hippies had borrowed from a foreign religion, that symbolized the cosmos, the cosmic mind, God, or whatever needed a symbol. Neither my mother nor my father really knew how to spell the word, and the magistrate in town just wrote it down the way it sounded to him. And they named me William in honor of a wealthy uncle, who unfortunately died penniless.

The six weeks passed rather pleasantly: talking, reading, resting. The other ship landed next to ours and did have nine free berths. We shuffled crews so that each ship had someone who could get it out of trouble if the preprogrammed jump sequence malfunctioned. I assigned myself to the other ship, hoping it would have some new books. It didn't.

We zipped up in the tanks and took off simultaneously.

We wound up spending a lot of time in the tanks, just to keep from looking at the same faces all day long in the crowded ship. The added periods of acceleration got us back to Stargate in ten months, subjective. Of course it was still 340 years (minus seven months) to the hypothetical objective observer.

There were hundreds of cruisers in orbit around Stargate. Bad news: with that kind of backlog we probably wouldn't get any furlough at all.

I supposed I was more likely to get a court martial than a furlough, anyhow. Losing eighty-eight percent of my company, many of them because they didn't have enough confidence in me to obey that direct earthquake order. And we were back where we'd started on Sade-138; no Taurans there but no base, either.

We got landing instructions and went straight down, no shuttle. There was another surprise waiting at the spaceport. More dozens of cruisers were standing around on the ground—they'd never done that before for fear that Stargate would be hit—and two captured Tauran cruisers as well. We'd never managed to get one intact.

Seven centuries could have brought us a decisive advantage, of course. Maybe we were winning.

We went through an airlock under a "returnees" sign. After the air cycled and we'd popped our suits, a beautiful young woman came in with a cartload of tunics and told us, in perfectly accented English, to get dressed and go to the lecture hall at the end of the corridor to our left.

The tunic felt odd, light yet warm. It was the first thing I'd worn besides a fighting suit or bare skin in almost a year.

The lecture hall was about a hundred times too big for the twenty-two of us. The same girl was there, and asked us to move down to the front. That was unsettling; I could have sworn she had gone down the corridor the other way—I *knew* she had; I'd been captivated by the sight of her clothed behind.

Hell, maybe they had matter transmitters. Or teleportation. Wanted to save herself a few steps.

We sat for a minute and a man, clothed in the same kind of unadorned tunic we and the girl were wearing, walked across the stage with a stack of thick notebooks under each arm.

The same girl followed him on, also carrying notebooks.

I looked behind me and she was still standing in the aisle. To make things even more odd, the man was virtually a twin to both of the women.

The man riffled through one of the notebooks and cleared his throat. "These books are for your convenience," he said, also with perfect accent, "and you don't have to read them if you don't want to. You don't have to do anything you don't want to do, because . . . you're free men and women. The war is over."

Disbelieving silence.

"As you will read in this book, the war ended 221 years ago. Accordingly, this is the year 220. Old style, of course, it is 3138 A.D.

"You are the last group of soldiers to return. When you leave here, I will leave as well. And destroy Stargate. It exists only as a rendezvous point for returnees, and as a monument to human tupidity. And shame. As you will read. Destroying it will be a leansing."

He stopped speaking and the woman started without a pause.

"I am sorry for what you've been through and wish I could say hat it was for good cause, but as you will read, it was not.

"Even the wealth you have accumulated, back salary and ompound interest, is worthless, as I no longer use money or redit. Nor is there such a thing as an economy, in which to use hese . . . things."

"As you must have guessed by now," the man took over, "I am, ve are, clones of a single individual. Some 250 years ago, my aame was Kahn. Now it is Man.

"I had a direct ancestor in your company, a Corporal Larry Kahn. It saddens me that he didn't come back."

"I am over ten billion individuals but only one consciousness," he said. "After you read, I will try to clarify this. I know that it vill be difficult to understand.

"No other humans are quickened, since I am the perfect pattern. ndividuals who die are replaced. There are planets, however, on vhich humans are born in the normal, mammalian way. If my ociety is too alien for you, you may go to one of these planets. f you wish to take part in procreation, we will not discourage it. Many veterans ask us to change their polarity to heterosexual so hat they can more easily fit into these other societies. This I can lo very easily."

Don't worry about that, Man, just make out my ticket.

"You will be my guest here at Stargate for ten days, after which jou will be taken wherever you want to go," he said. "Please read his book in the meantime. Feel free to ask any questions, or equest any service." They both stood and walked off the stage.

Charlie was sitting next to me. "Incredible," he said. "They et . . . they encourage . . . men and women to do *that* again? Together?"

The female aisle Man was sitting behind us, and she answered Defore I could frame a reasonably sympathetic, hypocritical reply. 'It isn't a judgment on your society," she said, probably not eeing that he took it a little more personally than that. "I only eel that it's necessary as a eugenic safety device. I have no evidence that there is anything wrong with cloning only one ideal ndividual, but if it turns out to have been a mistake, there will be a large genetic pool with which to start again."

She patted him on the shoulder. "Of course, you don't have to zo to these breeder planets. You can stay on one of my planets. I nake no distinction between heterosexual play and homosexual."

She went up on the stage to give a long spiel about where we were going to stay and eat and so forth while we were on Stargate.

"Never been seduced by a computer before," Charlie muttered.

The 1,143-year-long war had been begun on false pretenses and only continued because the two races were unable to communicate.

Once they could talk, the first question was "Why did you start this thing?" and the answer was "Me?"

The Taurans hadn't known war for millennia, and toward the beginning of the Twenty-first Century it looked as if mankind was ready to outgrow the institution as well. But the old soldiers were still around, and many of them were in positions of power. They virtually ran the United Nations Exploratory and Colonization Group, that was taking advantage of the newly discovered collapsar jump to explore interstellar space.

Many of the early ships met with accidents and disappeared. The ex-military men were suspicious. They armed the colonizing vessels and the first time they met a Tauran ship, they blasted it.

They dusted off their medals and the rest was going to be history.

You couldn't blame it all on the military, though. The evidence they presented for the Taurans' having been responsible for the earlier casualties was laughably thin. The few people who pointed this out were ignored.

The fact was, Earth's economy needed a war, and this one was ideal. It gave a nice hole to throw buckets of money into, but would unify humanity rather than divide it.

The Taurans relearned war, after a fashion. They never got really good at it, and would eventually have lost.

The Taurans, the book explained, couldn't communicate with humans because they had no concept of the individual; they had been natural clones for millions of years. Eventually, Earth's cruisers were manned by Man, Kahn-clones, and they were for the first time able to get through to each other.

The book stated this as a bald fact. I asked a Man to explain what it meant, what was special about clone-to-clone communication, and he said that I a priori couldn't understand it. There were no words for it, and my brain wouldn't be able to accommodate the concepts even if there were words.

All right. It sounded a little fishy, but I was willing to accept it. I'd accept that up was down if it meant the war was over.

I'd just finished dressing after my first good night's sleep in years, when someone tapped lightly on my door. I opened it and it was a female Man, standing there with an odd expression on her face. Almost a leer; was she trying to look seductive?

"Major Mandella," she said, "may I come in?" I motioned her to a chair but she went straight to the bed and sat daintily on the rumpled covers.

"I have a proposition for you, Major." I wondered whether she knew the word's archaic second meaning. "Come sit beside me, please."

Lacking Charlie's reservations about being seduced by a computer, I sat. "What do you propose?" I touched her warm thigh and found it disappointingly easy to control myself. Can reflexes get out of practice?

"I need permission to clone you, and a few grams of flesh. In return, I offer you immortality."

Not the proposition I'd expected. "Why me? I thought you were already the perfect pattern."

"For my own purposes, and within my powers to judge, I am. But I need you for a function . . . contrary to my own nature. And contrary to my Tauran brother's nature."

"A nasty job." Spend all eternity cleaning out the sewers; immortality of a sort.

"You might not find it so." She shifted restlessly and I removed my hand. "Thank you. You have read the first part of the book?"

"Scanned it."

"Then you know that both Man and Tauran are gentle beings. We do not fight among ourselves or with each other, because physical aggressiveness has been bred out of our sensibilities. Engineered out."

"A laudable accomplishment." I saw where this was leading and the answer was going to be no.

"But it was just this lack of aggressiveness that allowed Earth, in your time, to successfully wage war against a culture uncountable millennia older. I am afraid it could happen again."

"This time to Man."

"Man and Tauran; philosophically there is little difference."

"What you want, then, is for me to provide you with an army. A band of barbarians to guard your frontiers."

"That's an unpleasant way of—"

"It's not a pleasant idea." My idea of hell. "No. I can't do it."

"Your only chance to live forever."

"Absolutely not." I stared at the floor. "Your aggressiveness was bred out of you. Mine was knocked out of me."

She stood up and smoothed the tunic over her perfect hips. "I cannot use guile. I will not withhold this body from you, if you desire it."

I considered that but didn't say anything.

"Besides immortality, all I can offer you is the abstract satisfaction of service. Protecting humanity against unknown perils."

I'd put in my thousand-odd years of service, and hadn't got any great satisfaction. "No. Even if I thought of you as humanity, the answer would still be no."

She nodded and went to the door.

"Don't worry," I said. "You can get one of the others."

She opened the door and addressed the corridor outside. "No, the others have already declined. You were the least likely, and the last one I approached."

Man was pretty considerate, especially so in light of our refusal to cooperate. Just for us twenty-two throwbacks, he went to the trouble of rejuvenating a little restaurant/tavern and staffing it at all hours (I never saw a Man eat or drink—guess they'd discovered a way around it). I was sitting in there one evening, drinking beer and reading their book, when Charlie came in and sat down.

Without preamble, he said, "I'm going to give it a try."

"Give what a try?"

"Women. Hetero." He shuddered. "No offense . . . it's not really very appealing." He patted my hand, looking distracted. "But the alternative . . . have you tried it?"

"Well . . . no, I haven't." Female Man was a visual treat, but only in the same sense as a painting or a piece of sculpture. I just couldn't see them as human beings.

"Don't." He didn't elaborate. "Besides, they say—he says, she says, it says—that they can change me back just as easily. If I don't like it."

"You'll like it, Charlie."

"Sure, that's what *they* say." He ordered a stiff drink. "Just seems unnatural. Anyway, since, uh, I'm going to make the switch, do you mind if . . . why don't we plan on going to the same planet?"

"Sure, Charlie, that'd be great." I meant it. "You know where you're going?"

"Hell, I don't care. Just away from here."

"I wonder if Heaven's still as nice—"

"No." Charlie jerked a thumb at the bartender. *"He* lives there."

"I don't know. I guess there's a list."

A Man came into the tavern, pushing a car piled high with folders. "Major Mandella? Captain Moore?"

"That's us," Charlie said.

"These are your military records. I hope you find them of interest. They were transferred to paper when your Strike Force was the only one outstanding, because it would have been impractical to keep the normal data retrieval networks running to preserve so few data."

They always anticipated your questions, even when you didn't have any.

My folder was easily five times as thick as Charlie's. Probably thicker than any other, since I seemed to be the only trooper who'd made it through the whole duration. Poor Marygay. "Wonder what kind of report old Stott filed about me." I flipped to the front of the folder.

Stapled to the front page was a small square of paper. All the other pages were pristine white, but this one was tan with age and crumbling around the edges.

The handwriting was familiar, too familiar even after so long. The date was over 250 years old.

I winced and was blinded by sudden tears. I'd had no reason to suspect that she might be alive. But I hadn't really known she was dead, not until I saw that date.

"William? What's—"

"Leave me be, Charlie. Just for a minute." I wiped my eyes and closed the folder. I shouldn't even read the damned note. Going to a new life, I should leave old ghosts behind.

But even a message from the grave was contact of a sort. I opened the folder again.

11 Oct 2878

William—

All this is in your personnel file. But knowing you, you might just chuck it. So I made sure you'd get this note.

Obviously, I lived. Maybe you will, too. Join me.

I know from the records that you're out at Sade-138 and won't be back for a couple of centuries. No problem.

I'm going to a planet they call Middle Finger, the fifth planet out from Mizar. It's two collapsar jumps, ten months subjective. Middle Finger is a kind of Coventry for heterosexuals. They call it a "eugenic control baseline."

No matter. It took all of my money, and all the money of

five other old-timers, but we bought a cruiser from UNEF. And we're using it as a time machine.

So I'm on a relativistic shuttle, waiting for you. All it does is go out five light-years and come back to Middle Finger, very fast. Every ten years I age about a month. So if you're on schedule and still alive, I'll only be twenty-eight when you get here. Hurry!

I never found anybody else and I don't want anybody else. I don't care whether you're ninety years old or thirty. If I can't be your lover, I'll be your nurse.

—Marygay

"Say, bartender."

"Yes, Major?"

"Do you know of a place called Middle Finger? Is it still there?"

"Of course it is. Where would it be?" Reasonable question. "A very nice place. Garden planet. Some people don't think it's exciting enough."

"What's this all about?" Charlie said.

I handed the bartender my empty glass. "I just found out where we're going."

5. Epilog

From *The New Voice*,
Paxton, Middle Finger 24-6
14/2/3143
OLD-TIMER HAS FIRST BOY

Marygay Potter-Mandella (24 Post Road, Paxton) gave birth Friday last to a fine baby boy, 3.1 kilos.

Marygay lays claim to being the second-"oldest" resident of Middle Finger, having been born in 1977. She fought through most of the Forever War and then waited for her mate on the time shuttle, 261 years. Her mate, William Mandella-Potter, is two years older.

The baby, not yet named, was delivered at home with the help of a friend of the family, Dr. Diana Alsever-Moore.